LEGACIES

LEGACIES

F. PAUL WILSON

A TOM DOHERTY ASSOCIATES BOOK • NEW YORK

LEGACIES

Copyright © 1998 by F. Paul Wilson

This book is printed on acid-free paper.

Edited by David G. Hartwell

A Forge Book
Published by Tom Doherty Associates, Inc.
175 Fifth Avenue
New York, NY 10010

Forge® is a registered trademark of Tom Doherty Associates, Inc.

Design by Patrice Sheridan

LIBRARY OF CONGRESS CATALOGING-IN-PUBLICATION DATA

Wilson, F. Paul (Francis Paul)
    Legacies / F. Paul Wilson. —1st. ed.
      p.   cm.
    "A Tom Doherty Associates book."
    ISBN 0–312–86414–0 (alk. paper)
    I. Title.
    PS3573.I45695L44   1998
    813'.54—dc21   98–14322

First Edition: August 1998

Printed in the United States of America

0 9 8 7 6 5 4 3 2 1

ACKNOWLEDGMENTS

For technical advice, many thanks to Simson Garfinkel, writer, commentator on the wired life, and honest-to-God, real-life building hacker (retired). Jack uses a variation on the Garfinkel Method of elevator surfing.

To my wife and first reader, Mary.

To Joe Bogdan, MD, and Daphne Keshishian, MD, for sharing their experiences with pediatric AIDS.

To the WB store managers of District 1: remember September 26, 1996, in Albany? Pages 68–80 are for you.

And for their generous and expert editorial help: Elizabeth Monteleone's sharp eye for character detail, Steven Spruill's psychological insights, Deidre Lonza's copyediting skills and candy savvy, and Al Zuckerman, the maestro.

AUTHOR'S NOTE

Jack is back.

Of all my seventeen novels, none has generated more mail than *The Tomb*. It's been in print since 1984, and I still get a steady stream of letters asking the same question: When are you bringing back Repairman Jack?

The truth is, I've brought him back half a dozen times in short stories and novelettes, and as a supporting character in *Nightworld*. But never in another novel of his own.

Why no Repairman Jack novel since *The Tomb*? Lots of reasons. Prime among them is that Jack is very special to me. I didn't want to abuse him, so I held him back, letting him loose for a quick hit, then tucking him away again, waiting for the right set of circumstances where he could range free for an entire novel.

Legacies is that novel.

And the nicest thing is, I found I still like working with Jack. We're going to do this again sometime. But I promise not to wait another decade and a half before I get down to it. (Neither of us is getting any younger, you know.)

NB: There is no Center for Children with AIDS on Seventh Avenue near St. Vincent's. I made it up. Tragically, I did not have to make up the kids who need such a facility.

LEGACIES

FRIDAY

1

"It's okay!" Alicia shouted as the cab jerked to the left to swing around a NYNEX truck plodding up Madison Avenue. "I'm not in a rush!"

The driver—curly dark hair, a Saddam Hussein mustache, and swarthy skin—didn't seem to hear. He jogged his machine two lanes left, then three lanes right, hitting the brakes and gunning the engine, hitting and gunning, jerking Alicia back and forth, left and right in the rear seat, then swerving to avoid another yellow maniacmobile trying a similar move through the morning traffic.

Her cab's net gain: one car length. Maybe.

Alicia rapped on the smudged, scratched surface of the plastic divider. "Slow down, dammit! I want to arrive in one piece."

But the driver ignored her. If anything, he upped his speed. He seemed to be engaged in a private war against every other car in Manhattan. And God help you if you were a pedestrian.

Alicia should have been used to this. She'd grown up in Manhattan. She hadn't been here for a while, though. She'd moved away at eighteen for college and had stayed away for medical school and her residencies in pediatrics and infectious diseases. She hadn't wanted to come back—what with that man and her half brother Thomas still living here—but St. Vincent's had made her the proverbial offer she couldn't refuse.

So now, after a little over a year, she was still getting used to the city's changes. Who'd have believed they'd be able to scour off the grim sleaziness that she'd assumed to be permanently etched on Times Square?

Cabbies too. What had happened to them? They'd always been pushy, brazen drivers—you had to be to get around in this city—but this new crop were maniacs.

Finally they hit the Forties.

Almost there, Alicia thought. Maybe I'll live to see another sunset after all.

But as they neared Forty-eighth she noticed her cab was still in the center lane, accelerating. At first she thought he was going to miss her turn off, then she saw the opening: two lanes to the right, behind a graffiti-coated delivery truck and just ahead of a bus pulling away from the curb.

"You're not!" Alicia cried. "Please tell me you're not going to try to—"

He did. And he made it—just barely—but not without forcing the bus to slam on its brakes and give him a deafening blast from its horn.

The cabbie floored it along the open stretch of Forty-eighth, then swerved violently rightward toward the curb. The cab jerked to a halt at the address Alicia had given him when she'd slid into its rear seat down in Greenwich Village.

"Six-seventy-five," he said.

Alicia sat there fuming, wishing she were strong enough to break through the partition and throttle him. She wasn't. But she could give him a taste of his own medicine—in reverse.

Slowly, she inched toward the curbside door, opened it with the greatest of care, and edged herself out. Then she took out her wallet and began to count her change . . . carefully. She had about two dollars' worth. She picked out a dollar-seventy-five in dimes and nickels.

"Come on, lady," the cabbie said, leaning over the passenger seat and looking up at her through the window. "I haven't got all day."

Alicia made no sign she'd heard him as she slowly pulled five singles from her wallet, one . . . at . . . a . . . time. Finally, when she had exactly six-seventy-five in her hand, she handed it through the window.

And waited.

It didn't take long—three seconds, tops—before the driver popped out his door and glared at her over the roof of his cab.

"Ay! Where is tip?" He pronounced it *teep*.

"Pardon me?" Alicia said sweetly. "I can't hear you."

"My tip, lady! Where is it?"

"I'm sorry," she said, holding a hand to her ear. "Your lips appear to be moving, but I can't hear a word you're saying. Something about my slip?"

"My tip, goddammit! *My tip! My tip! My fucking tip!*"

"Did I enjoy my trip?" she said, then let her voice go icy. "On a scale of one to ten, I enjoyed it zero . . . exactly the amount of your tip."

He made a move to come around the cab, probably figuring he could intimidate this slight, pale woman with the fine features and the glossy black hair, but Alicia held her ground. He gave her a venomous look and slipped back into his seat.

As she turned away, she heard the cabbie shout an inarticulate curse, slam his door, and burn rubber as he tore off.

We're even, she thought, her anger fading. But what an awful way to start a beautiful fall day.

She put it behind her. She'd been looking forward to this meeting with Leo Weinstein, and she wasn't going to let some crazy cabbie upset her.

At last she'd found an attorney who wasn't afraid to tackle a big law firm. All of the others she'd tried—those in her limited price range— had reacted with a little too much awe when they'd heard the name Hinchberger, Rainey & Guran. Not Weinstein. Hadn't fazed him in the least. He'd read through the will and within a day came up with half a dozen suggestions he seemed to believe would put the big boys on the defensive.

"Your father left you that house," he'd said. "No way they can keep it from you. Just leave it to me."

And so she'd done just that. Now she was going to see what he'd accomplished with the blizzard of paper he'd fired at Hinchberger, Rainey & Guran.

She heard a honk behind her and stiffened. If it was that cab . . .

She turned and relaxed as she saw Leo Weinstein waving through the open window of a silver Lexus. He was saying something she couldn't catch. She stepped closer.

"Good morning," she said.

"Sorry I'm late," he said. "The LIE was jammed. Just let me pull into the garage down there and I'll be right with you."

"No problem."

She was almost to the front door of the building where Cutter and Weinstein had their offices when she was staggered by a thunderous noise. The shock wave slammed against her back like a giant hand and almost knocked her off her feet.

Turning she saw a ball of flame racing skyward from the middle of the block, and flaming pieces of metal crashing to the ground all about her. Cars were screeching to a halt as pedestrians dove for the pavement amid glittering shards of glass tumbling from windows up and down the block. Alicia jumped back as a blackened, smoking chunk of a car trunk lid landed in front of her and rolled to her feet.

An icy coil of horror tightened around her throat as she recognized the Lexus insignia.

She craned her neck to look for Leo's car, but it was . . . gone.

"Oh, no!" she cried. "Oh, my God, *no!*"

She hurried forward a few steps on wobbly knees to see if there was anything she could do, but . . . the car . . . nothing was left where it had been . . . just burning asphalt.

"Oh, God, Leo!" she gasped. "Oh, I'm so sorry!"

She couldn't breathe. What had happened to all the air? She had to get away from here.

She forced her stricken body to turn and blunder back up the sidewalk, away from the smoke, the flames, the wreckage. She stopped when she reached Madison Avenue. She leaned against a traffic light post and gulped air. When she'd caught her breath, she looked back.

Already the vultures were gathering, streaming toward the flames, wondering what happened. And not too far away, sirens.

She couldn't stay here. She couldn't help Weinstein and she didn't want to be listed as a witness. The police might get it into their heads that she was hiding something, and they might start looking into her background, her family. She couldn't allow that. Couldn't stand it.

Alicia didn't look for a taxi—the thought of being confined was unbearable. She needed space, light, air. She turned downtown.

Poor Leo!

She sobbed as she started walking, moving as fast as her low-heeled shoes would allow. But even if she'd worn her sneakers she would not have been able to outrun the guilt, the terrible suspicion that she was somehow responsible for Leo Weinstein's death.

2

"Thank God you're here!" Raymond said as Alicia walked though the Center's employee entrance. "I've been beeping you since eight o'clock. Why didn't . . . ?" His voice trailed off as he looked at her. "Christ, Alicia, you look like absolute shit."

Actually, that was a generous assessment of how she felt, but she didn't want to talk about it.

"Thank you, Raymond. You don't know the half of it."

She didn't head for her office, but toward the front reception area instead. Raymond paced her.

"Where are you going?"

"Just give me a minute, will you, Raymond?" she snapped. "I'll be right back."

She regretted being so short with him, but she felt stretched to the breaking point. One more tug in the wrong direction . . .

She was vaguely aware of Tiffany saying hello as she hurried past the reception desk on her way to the front door. Stepping aside to allow a middle-aged woman and her two grandchildren to enter, Alicia peered through the glass at the street outside, looking for the gray car.

She was sure it had followed her back from Forty-eighth Street. At least she thought it had. A gray car—what would you call it? A sedan? She didn't know a damn thing about cars. Couldn't tell a Ford from a Chevy. But whatever it was, she'd kept catching sight of this gray car passing her as she walked. It would turn a block or two ahead of her, and disappear for a few minutes, then cruise by again. Never too close. Never too slow. Never a definite sign of interest in her. But it was always *there*.

She scanned Seventh Avenue outside, half expecting to see it roll by. Across the street and slightly downtown, she checked the curb in front of her least favorite part of the St. Vincent's complex. The O'Toole Building squatted at the corner of Twelfth. Its white-tiled, windowless, monolithic facade did not fit here in the Village. It looked as if a clumsy giant had accidentally dropped the modernistic monstrosity on his way to someplace like Minneapolis.

No gray car, though. But with all the gray cars in Manhattan, how could she be sure?

Her nerves were getting to her. She was becoming paranoid.

But who could blame her after this morning?

She headed back to her office. Raymond picked her up in the hall.

"*Now* can we talk?"

"Sorry I snapped at you."

"Don't be silly, honey. Nobody snaps at me. Nobody *dares*."

Alicia managed a smile.

Raymond—never "Ray," always "Raymond"—Denson, NP had been one of the original caregivers at the Center for Children with AIDS. The Center had MDs who were called "director" and "assistant director," but it was this particular nurse practitioner who ran the place. Alicia doubted the Center would survive if he left. Raymond knew all the ins and outs of the day-to-day functions, all the soft touches for requisitions, knew where all the bodies were buried, so to speak. He clocked in at around fifty, she was sure—God help you if you asked his age—but he kept himself young-looking: close cropped air, neat mustache, trim, athletic body.

"And about my beeper," she said, "I turned it off. Dr. Collings was covering for me. You knew that."

He paced her down the narrow hallway to her office. All the walls in the Center had been hurriedly erected and the haste showed. Slap-dash taping and spackling, and a quick coat of bright yellow paint that was already wearing through in places. Well, the decor was the least important thing here.

"I know," he said, "but this wasn't medical. This wasn't even administrative. This was fucking criminal."

Something in Raymond's voice . . . his eyes. He was furious. But not at her. But then, what?

A premonition chilled her. Were her personal troubles going to spill over into the Center now?

As she continued walking she noted knots of staff—nurses, secretaries, volunteers—all with their heads together, all talking animatedly.

All furious.

An icy gale blew through her.

"All right, Raymond. Lay it on me."

"The toys," he said. "Some rat bastard motherfucker stole the toys."

Astonished, disbelieving, Alicia stopped and stared at him. No way.

This had to be some cruel, nasty joke. But Raymond was anything but cruel.

And were those tears in the corners of his eyes?

"The donations? Don't tell me—"

But he was nodding and biting his upper lip.

"Aw, no."

"Every last one."

Alicia felt her throat tighten. Strangely enough—and she damned herself for it—this was hitting her harder than Leo Weinstein's death.

A man she knew, a man with a wife and family was dead, and yet . . . and yet . . . this felt so much worse.

She'd met Weinstein only a couple of times. But these toys . . . she and Raymond—especially Raymond—had been collecting them for months, sending staff and volunteers to forage all through the city for donors—companies, stores, individuals, anybody. The response had been slow at first—who was thinking about Christmas gifts in October? But once Thanksgiving was past, the giving had picked up. Last night they'd had a storeroom full of dolls, trucks, rockets, coloring books, action figures . . . the works.

This morning . . .

"How?"

"Pried open the outer door and took them away through the alley. Must have had some sort of panel truck to hold everything."

The ground floor of this building had been a business supply store before being converted to the Center for Children with AIDS. The former owners probably had loaded their delivery trucks the same way the thieves had stolen the gifts.

"Isn't that door alarmed? Aren't *all* the doors alarmed?"

Raymond nodded. "Supposed to be. But the alarm didn't go off."

Poor Raymond. He'd put his whole heart into this effort.

Alicia reached her office, tossed her bag onto her desk, and dropped into her chair. She was still shaken. And her feet were killing her. She closed her eyes. Only halfway through the morning and she felt exhausted.

"Did anything like this ever happen to Dr. Landis?"

Raymond shook his head. "Never."

"Great. They wait until she's gone, *then* they strike."

"I think that's all for the best, don't you think? I mean, considering her condition."

Alicia had to agree. "Yeah, I guess you're right."

Dr. Rebecca Landis was the director of the Center—at least she had the title. But she was in her third trimester and developing preeclamptic symptoms. Her OB had ordered her to stay home in bed.

This only a week after the assistant director had left to take a position at Beth Israel, leaving the place to be "directed" by Alicia and the other pediatric infectious disease specialist, Ted Collings. Ted had begged off any directing duties, claiming a wife and a new baby. And so the burden of administrative duties had fallen on the Center's newbie: Alicia Clayton, MD.

"Any chance it was an inside job?"

"The police are looking into it," Raymond said.

"The police?"

"Yes. Been here and gone. I made out the report."

"Thank you, Raymond." Good old Raymond. She couldn't imagine how he could be more efficient. "What do they think about our chances of getting those toys back?"

"They're going to 'work on it.' But just to make sure they do, I want to call the papers. That okay with you?"

"Yeah, good idea. Make this a high-profile crime. Maybe that'll put extra pressure on the cops."

"Great. I've already spoken to the *Post*. The *News* and the *Times* will have people here later this morning."

"Oh. Well . . . good. You'll see them, okay?"

"If you wish."

"I wish. Tell them it's not just stealing, and it's not just stealing from little kids—it's stealing from kids who've already got less than nothing, who're carrying a death sentence in their bloodstreams and may not even *be* here next Christmas."

"That's beautiful. Maybe you should—"

"No, please, Raymond. I can't."

Feeling utterly miserable, she tuned out for a moment.

"What else can happen today?" she muttered. Bad news always comes in threes, doesn't it?

Raymond still hovered beyond her desk. "Something with that 'family matter' you've been dealing with?" he said, then added—pointedly: "All by yourself?"

He knew she'd been seeing lawyers and had been preoccupied lately, and he seemed to take it personally that she wouldn't discuss it with him. She felt sorry for him. He freely discussed his personal life with her—she knew more about it than she really cared to—but she couldn't reciprocate. Her own personal life was pretty much a void, and the toxic disaster area that posed as her family was not something Alicia wanted to share, even with someone as sympathetic and nonjudgmental as Raymond.

"Yes," she said. "That 'family matter.' But that's not as important as getting those toys back. We had a super Christmas set up for those kids, and I don't want it going down the tubes. I want those toys back, Raymond, and dammit—get me the police commissioner's number. I'm going to call him myself. I'm going to call him every day until those toys are back."

"I'll look it up right now," he said, and was gone, closing the door behind him.

Alicia folded her arms on the scarred top of her beat-up old desk and dropped her forehead onto them. Everything seemed to be spinning out of control. She felt so helpless, so damn *impotent*. Systems . . . always these huge, complex, lumbering systems to deal with.

The Center's toys were gone. She'd have to depend on the police to get them back. But they had their own agenda, their own higher priorities, and so she'd have to wait until they got around to hers, if they ever did. She could call the commissioner until she wore out the buttons on her phone, but he'd probably never take the call.

And the will had said the house was hers, but Thomas was using the system's labyrinth to keep it from her. On her own, Alicia would have been swallowed up by his legal pit bulls, so she'd been forced to hire someone to fend them off.

Leo . . . oh, God, poor Leo. She could still hear the blast, see the flames. Nothing had been left of him after that explosion.

A cold sick dread seeped through her. When's my turn? If I keep pushing Thomas and whoever's backing him, will I be next?

She pounded her fist on the desk. *Damn them!*

She wanted one of those big samurai blades—a dai-katana—to cut right to the heart of—

"Excuse me."

Alicia looked up. One of the volunteers, a pretty blonde in her early thirties, stood halfway through the doorway, looking at her.

"I knocked but I guess you didn't hear me."

Alicia straightened and shook back her hair. She put on her professional face.

"Sorry. I was a million miles away, dreaming about chasing down the rats who stole those presents."

The woman slipped her svelte body the rest of the way through and shut the door behind her. Alicia wished she had a body like that.

She'd seen her around a lot. Sometimes she brought her daughter with her—cute little girl, maybe seven or eight. What were their names?

"You won't have to go a million miles to find them," the woman said. "One or two should cover it."

"You're probably right," Alicia said.

Her name . . . her name . . . what was her name?

Got it. "Gia, isn't it?"

She smiled. "Gia DiLauro."

A dazzling smile. Alicia wished she had a smile like that. And *Gia* . . . what a great name. Alicia wished—

Enough.

"Yes, you and your daughter . . ."

"Vicky."

"Right. Vicky. You donate a lot of time here."

Gia shrugged. "Can't think of a place that needs it more."

"You've got that right."

The Center was a black hole of need.

"Can I talk to you a minute?"

She looked at Gia more closely and saw that her eyes were red. Had she been crying?

"Sure." She had no time, but this woman donated so much of hers to the Center, the least Alicia could do was give her a few minutes. "Sit down. Are you okay?"

"No," she said, gliding into the chair. Her eyes got redder. "I'm so angry I could . . . I don't like thinking about what I'd like to do to the scum that stole those toys."

"It's okay," Alicia said. "The police are working on it."

"But you're not holding your breath, right?"

Alicia shrugged and sighed. "No. I guess not. But they're all we've got."

"Not necessarily," Gia said.

"What do you mean?"

She leaned forward and lowered her voice. "I know someone . . ."

3

Jack kept an eye out for Dwight Frye on the TV screen as he scrolled through the messages left on the Repairman Jack Web site.

He was celebrating his discovery of the 1931 version of the *Maltese Falcon* with a Dwight Frye film festival. He had the *Maltese Falcon* running in the front room of his apartment. Frye played the role of Wilmer Cook in this one, and for Jack's money, he out-psychoed Elisha Cook's portrayal in the later John Huston version. But Ricardo Cortez was on the screen now, and he wasn't such a hot Sam Spade.

Back to the World Wide Web.

Most of the questions on Jack's home page were about refrigerators and microwaves, which he didn't mind. Web wanderers who stumbled onto his page thought he was some sort of appliance answer man. Fine. After no replies to their questions, they'd delete his URL from their bookmarks.

But this one . . . from a guy named "Jorge."

I BEEN RIPPED OFF. CAN'T GET MONEY OWED TO ME FOR WORK I DO. CAN'T GO ANYWHERE ELSE. CAN YOU FIX?

Yeah. That sounded like business.

Jack typed in a reply to Jorge's E-mail address:

SEND ME YOUR PHONE #. I'LL BE IN TOUCH.

RJ

He'd call the guy and see what this was about. If he was having trouble with his bookie, tough. But he'd said it was money he'd "earned." So maybe Jorge was a potential customer.

The phone rang but Jack let the machine pick up. He heard his outgoing message . . . *"Pinocchio Productions—I'm out at the moment. Leave a message after the beep"* . . . then:

"Jack, this is Dad. Are you there?" A pause as he waited for Jack to pick up. Jack closed his eyes and didn't move. He felt bad about leaving his father hanging, but he wasn't up to another conversation with him right now. *"All right . . . when you get in, give me a call. I came across another great opportunity for you down here."*

Jack exhaled when he heard the click of the connection breaking.

"Dad," he said softly, "you're making me crazy."

His father had moved down to Florida a few months ago and Jack had thought it was a good idea at the time. Better to be a retired widower down there than in Burlington County, New Jersey.

But as soon as Dad had settled in, he began seeing all sorts of opportunities for Jack. His older brother and sister were both professionals, pillars of their respective communities. They were set. But Jack . . . Dad still saw his younger son as unfinished business.

His brother and sister had given up on him long ago. The annual Christmas card was the extent of their contact. But not Dad. He never gave up. He didn't want to go to his grave thinking his prodigal dropout son was living hand to mouth in New York as an appliance repairman.

I've probably got more socked away than you do, Dad.

He winced as he remembered their last conversation.

You've got to see this place, Jack. It's growing like crazy—a gold mine for someone like you. You establish yourself here as a reliable repair service, and in no time you'll have a fleet of trucks all over the county . . .

Be still my heart, he thought. A fleet of trucks, and maybe, if I play my cards right, the cover of *Entrepreneur* magazine.

Jack had been begging off, hoping Dad would get the message, but obviously he hadn't. When Jack called back, he was going to have to tell his father point-blank: No way was he leaving New York. The Jets would be wearing new Super Bowl rings before he moved to Florida.

Then again, if things didn't pick up, maybe he'd have to rethink that.

He'd just checked the answering machine in the drop on Tenth Avenue. Nothing there. Business had been kind of slow lately. He was getting bored.

And when he got bored, he bought things. He'd picked up his latest treasure from the post office just this morning.

He rose and rubbed his eyes. The computer screen tended to bother them. He stood about five-eleven, maybe six foot if he stretched. He had a tight wiry build, dark brown hair, lips on the thin side, and mild brown eyes. Jack worked very hard at looking average.

He removed the clock from its packing to admire it again.

A genuine Shmoo pendulette alarm clock. In beautiful condition. He ran his fingers over its smooth, white, unmarred ceramic surface, touching the eyes and whiskers on the creature's smiling face. It had come in its original box and looked brand-new.

Now was as good a time as any to hang it on the wall. But where? His walls were already crowded with framed official membership certificates in the Shadow and Doc Savage fan clubs, Captain America's Sentinels of Liberty, the Junior Justice Society of America, the David Harding CounterSpy Junior Agents Club, and the Don Winslow Creed.

What can I say? he thought. I'm a joiner.

His apartment was crowded with wavy-grained Victorian golden oak furniture. The wall shelves sagged under the weight of the neat stuff he'd accumulated over the years, and every horizontal surface on the hutch, the secretary, the claw-and-ball-footed end tables were cluttered as well.

And then he saw where the clock could go: right above the pink Shmoo planter . . . which still didn't have anything planted in it.

He was just about to look for his hammer when the phone rang again. Dad, give me a break, will you?

But it wasn't his father.

"Jack? It's Gia. You there?"

Something in her voice . . . Jack snatched up the handset.

"Always here for you. What's up?"

"I'm waiting for a cab. Just wanted to make sure you were in."

"Something wrong?"

"I'll tell you when I get there."

And then a click.

Slowly, Jack replaced the handset. Definitely upset. He wondered what was wrong. Nothing with Vicky, he hoped. But she would have told him that.

Well, he'd find out soon enough. The West Village to the Upper West Side wasn't too bad a trip this time of day. No matter what the circumstance, an unexpected visit from Gia was a treat.

He thought back on their stormy, off-again, on-again relationship. He'd been crushed and thought it was off forever when she'd found out how he earned his living—or thought she had. She'd concluded that he was some sort of hit man, which was as wrong as could be, but even after she'd learned what he really did, even after he'd used those skills to save her daughter Vicky's life, she still didn't approve.

But at least she'd come back to him. Jack didn't know where he'd be without Gia and Vicky.

A short while later, he heard her footsteps on the stairs leading to his third-floor apartment. Jack turned the knob that retracted the four-way bolt system, and opened the door.

The sight of Gia standing on the landing started that warm funny twitch he got deep inside every time he saw her. Her short blond hair, her perfect skin, her blue eyes—Jack felt he could stand and stare at her face for hours.

But right now her features were strained, her usual tight composure seemed to be slipping, her normally flawless complexion looked blotchy.

"Gia," Jack said, wincing at the pain in her eyes as he pulled her inside. "What is it?"

And then she was clinging to him, loosing a torrent about Christmas toys being stolen from the AIDS kids. She was sobbing by the time she finished.

"Hey, hey," Jack said, tightening his arms around her. "It'll be all right."

He knew Gia wasn't much for emotional displays. Yeah, she was Italian, but northern Italian—the blood running in her veins was probably more Swiss than anything else. For her to be sobbing like this . . . she had to be hurting something fierce.

"It's just the *heartlessness* of it," she said, sniffing. "How could somebody *do* such a thing? And how can you be so damn *calm* about it!"

Uh-oh.

"I hear anger looking for a target. I know this has really cut you deep, Gia, but I'm not the bad guy here."

"Oh, I know, I know. It's just—you've never been down there. Never seen these kids. Never held them. Jack, they've got nothing. Not even a parent who cares, let alone a future. We were collecting those toys so they'd have a nice Christmas, a *great* Christmas—the last Christmas for a lot of them. And now—"

Another sob.

Jeez, this was awful. He had to say something, do something, anything so she wouldn't feel like this.

"Do you know what the presents were? I mean, do you have some sort of a list. Because if you do, just give it to me and I'll replace—"

She pushed back and stared at him. "They were donations, Jack. Most of them all wrapped up and ready for giving. Replacing them's not important. Getting them *back* is. Understand?"

"Yes . . . and no."

"Somebody's got to find these guys—the ones who did this—and teach them a lesson . . . make an example of them . . . a very public example. Know what I mean?"

Jack fought to suppress a grin. "I think so. You mean, make it so that the next creep who gets the same idea will think twice, maybe three times before he decides to go through with it."

"Exactly. *Exactly*."

With exaggerated innocence—and still fighting a smile—he said, "And, um, just who could we be thinking of to make such an example?"

"You know damn well who," she said, fixing him with those eyes.

"Moi?" And now he had to grin. "But I thought you didn't approve of that sort of thing."

"I don't. And I never will. But just this once . . ."

". . . you could live with it."

"Yes." She turned away and folded her arms across her chest. "But just this once."

She began wandering around his living room, aimlessly tracing her fingers across the golden oak hutch, the rolltop desk where he kept his computer . . .

"But, Gia—"

"Please," she said, raising her hand. "I know what you're going to say. *Please* don't start pressing me for some sort of moral and philosophical consistency between not marrying you because of what you do and then coming to you when there's a problem that looks like it can only be solved by your kind of tactics. I've been battling that all morning—I mean, trying to decide whether I should even *mention* it to you. Even in the cab, I was ready to tell him to turn onto Fifty-ninth and forget the whole thing—"

"Oh, great," he said, stung. "That really hurts. Since when is it that you can't come to me for *anything?*"

She stopped and looked at him. "You know what I mean. How many times have I mouthed off about this 'Repairman Jack' thing?"

"About a million." More like three million, he thought, but what's a couple of million between friends?

"Right. And about how it's stupid and dangerous and violent and dangerous and how if you don't end up dead you're going to wind up in jail for the rest of your life. And I haven't changed my opinion one bit. So you can imagine how this thing must have got to me if I'm asking you to fix it."

"All right," he said. "I won't say another word about it."

"Maybe not now, but I know you will later."

Jack raised two fingers. "I won't. Scout's honor."

"I think that takes three fingers, Jack."

"Whatever. I promise I won't." He reached for her hand. "Come on over here."

She took his hand and he pulled her onto his lap. She settled on his thighs, light as a feather, and they kissed—not a long one, but long enough to warm him up.

"There. That's better. Now . . . let's get down to practicalities. Who's hiring me?"

"I spoke to Dr. Clayton—she's the acting director."

Jack felt his insides tighten. "You told her you know me?"

He'd warned Gia about that. *Never let on you know me—to anyone. Even your best friend.* He'd made too many enemies over the years. And if one of them thought he could get back at him through Gia . . . or Vicky . . .

He shuddered.

"No," Gia said. "I said I knew *of* someone who might be able to help get the toys back. Didn't mention any names. Just said I'd try to contact him and see if he was available."

Jack relaxed. "I guess that's okay."

Still, if he got involved in this, it would leave a link—at least in this Dr. Clayton's mind—between Gia and a guy named Jack who "fixed" something. Probably be okay, but he didn't like it.

"Well?" she said.

"Well what?"

"Are you available?"

"I don't know."

"How can you not know?"

"Well, there's a problem. I mean, the Center can't hire me, because I can't work for a legit business. They've got to account for their expenses, and I don't exactly take checks."

He didn't even have a social security number.

"Don't worry about it. I'll pay you."

"Oh, right. Like I'll take money from you."

"No, I mean it, Jack. This is my idea. I want this. What's your usual and customary fee?"

"Forget it."

"No, I'm serious. Tell me."

"You don't want to know."

"*Please?*"

"Oh, all right." He told her.

She gaped at him. "You charge *that* much?"

"Well, as you said, 'it's stupid and dangerous and violent and dangerous' and if I don't end up dead I'm going to wind up in jail for the rest of my life. So yeah, that's what I charge." He kissed her. "And I'm worth every penny."

"I'm sure you are. Okay. It's a deal."

"No, it's not. Told you: I'm not taking money from you."

"But you've told me you never do freebies. It's against your religion or something."

"It's just a policy. But let's forget about money for now. Let's first see if this is something I can deliver on."

"Fair enough." She was staring at the TV screen. "Why do I know that actor?"

"He's Dwight Frye. You've seen him before."

"Didn't he play that guy in *Dracula* who was always eating flies?"

"Until he graduated to 'big, juicy spiders.' Yeah. He played Renfield."

Gia buried her face in his shoulder. "I can't believe I know that. I've been hanging around you much too long."

"And getting educated in the process. Now . . . where can I meet this Dr. Clayton?"

"In her office."

"When?"

"This afternoon at four."

"How do you know she'll be there?"

She smiled that smile. "Because you have an appointment with her then."

Jack laughed. "You were that sure?"

"Of course. And I'll be there with Vicky to introduce you."

He frowned. "Do you think that's wise?"

"Introducing you?"

"No. Taking Vicky down there."

"Are you kidding? She loves helping with those kids."

"Yeah, but they've got . . . AIDS."

"No, they've got HIV. There's a big difference. And you can't catch HIV by holding a baby in your arms. How many times have I told you that?"

"Lots. But I still . . ."

"When you see, you'll understand. And you'll see at four o'clock, right?"

"Right."

They kissed, but Jack felt a chill. His list of things that scared him was a short one, but the HIV virus was top on the list.

4

Jack took a walk over to Amsterdam Avenue.

After slowing temporarily in the late '80s and early '90s, gentrification was back in full swing on the Upper West Side. New brownstone renovations, new condos, and of course, new eateries. In a few hours the streets and the host of new restaurants, trattorias, and bistros would be crowded with yuppies and dinks out for their Friday night fling to initiate the weekend's respite from buying and selling.

As individuals, Jack didn't have anything against them. Sure they could be empty-headed when it came to one-upsmanship in the conspicuous consumption arena and the endless panting after trends, and as a group they tended to suck the color out of the neighborhoods they invaded. But they weren't evil. At least most of them weren't.

Jack checked his watch. Getting near three. Abe would be ready for a mid-afternoon snack just about now. He stopped in at Nick's Nook, a mom-and-pop grocery—a vanishing breed in these parts—and picked up a little treat.

Next stop was the Isher Sports Shop. The iron grate was pulled back, exposing the blurry windows. Beyond them, an array of faded cardboard placards, dusty footballs, tennis balls, racquets, basketball hoops, backboards, Rollerblades, and other good-time sundries basked in the sunny display space.

Inside was not much better organized. Bikes hanging from the ceiling, weight benches over here, SCUBA gear over there, narrow aisles winding past sagging shelves. ESPN meets *Twister*.

As Jack entered, Abe Grossman was just finishing with a customer—or rather, a customer was finishing with him.

Abe's age was on the far side of fifty and his weight was in calling distance of an eighth of a ton, which wouldn't have been bad if he were on the right side of five-eight. He was dressed in his uniform—black pants and a white half-sleeved shirt. A frown marred his usually jovial

30

round face, a face made all the rounder by the relentless retreat of his gray hair toward the top of his head.

"Hooks?" Abe was saying. "Why should you want hooks? Can you imagine how that must hurt a fish when it bites into it? And those barbs. Oy! You've got to rip them out! Such damage to the tender mouth tissues. Stick a fish hook in your own tongue sometime and see how you like it."

The customer, a sandy-haired thirtysomething in a faded Izod stared at Abe in wonder. He made one false start at a reply, then tried again.

"You're kidding, right?"

Abe leaned over the counter—at least as far as his considerable gut would allow—and spoke in a fatherly fashion.

"It's an ethical position. Baiting a hook, or using those flashing little spinners to catch fish, it's deceitful. Think about it. You're dressing up a nasty little hook to look like food, like sustenance. A fish comes along, thinks it's found lunch and *wham!* It's hooked and pulled out of the water. Is that fair? You're proud of such a thing?" He straightened and fixed the guy with his dark brown eyes. "I should be a party to such a so-called sport based on treachery and deceit? No. I cannot."

"You're serious!" the guy said, backing away. "You're really serious!"

"I should be a comedian?" Abe said. "This place looks look like the Improv to you maybe? No. I sell sporting goods. *Sporting*. That means something to me. A net is sporting. You wait for the fish to come along and then scoop it up with a net. The fastest one wins. *That's* a sport. A net, I'll sell you. But hooks? Uh-Uh. You'll get no hooks from me."

The guy turned away and headed for the door. "Get out while you can," he said as he hurried past Jack. "This fucker is nuts!"

"Really?" Jack said. "What makes you think so?"

As the door slammed, Jack stepped up to the counter. Abe had positioned himself, sitting like a toad on the high stool that was his perch for most of his workday. He sat with his hands on his spread thighs, a middle-aged Humpty-Dumpty.

Jack placed his offering on the counter.

"Entenmann's brownies?" Abe said, hopping off the stool. "Jack, you shouldn't have."

"I figured your stomach would be rumbling about now."

"No, but really you shouldn't have. My diet, you know."

"Yeah, but they're fat free."

Abe touched the yellow sticker that said just that. "So they are." He grinned. "Well, in that case, maybe just a smidge."

His short chubby fingers were surprisingly nimble as they zipped open the box. A knife appeared and carved out a huge section which went directly into Abe's mouth.

"Mmmm," he said, closing his eyes and swallowing. "Who could believe this is fat free? Too bad it's not calorie free." He pointed the knife at Jack. "You're having?"

"Nah. Had a late lunch."

"You should try. All this food you bring me and I never see you eat."

"That is because I bring it for you. Enjoy."

Abe promptly did just that with another piece.

"Where's Parabellum?" Jack asked.

Abe spoke around a mouthful. "Sleeping."

For some reason Jack could not fathom, Abe had bought a little blue parakeet and become paternally attached to it.

"He doesn't like chocolate anyway," he said, wiping his hands on his shirt. Brown smears joined similar yellow smudges that looked like mustard. "Hey. You want to see willpower? Watch."

He closed the top and pushed the box to the side.

"I'm impressed," Jack said. "First time I ever saw you do that."

"I'll be thin as you before you know it." He found a crumb on the counter and popped it into his mouth, then looked longingly at the brownie box. "Yessir. Before you know it."

In what Jack knew was an prodigious act of will, Abe pushed away from the counter and shrugged. "Nu?"

"Need a few things."

"Let's go."

Abe locked the front door, turned a CLOSED FOR LUNCH sign toward the street and, navigating aisles just wide enough to allow his bulk to pass, led the way toward the back. He followed Abe into the rear closet and down to the cellar. The neon sign that overhung the stone steps flickered but never quite came to life.

"Got a sick sign there, Abe."

"I know, but it's too much trouble to get fixed."

He hit the switch that illuminated the cellar's miniature armory. Abe moved among his stock, adjusting the pistols and rifles in their racks, straightening the boxes of ammo on their shelves. Everything neatly arranged down here, in sharp contrast to the floor just above them.

"Restocking or something new?"

"New," Jack said. "Need a pair of weighted gloves."

"You lost the last pair you bought?"

"No, but I need a white pair."

Abe's eyebrows lifted. "White? I never heard of such a thing. Black, of course. Brown, maybe. But white?"

"See if you can find me any."

"I should go asking for white leather gloves with half a pound of fine steel shot packed into the knuckles? You want this in a lady's size perhaps?"

"No, it's for me. To go with formal wear."

Abe sighed. "And I should have it for you when?"

"Tonight if you can, but by early tomorrow at the latest. And listen for any noise about someone with a whole bunch of kids' Christmas gifts to sell . . . cheap . . . already wrapped, most likely. I told Julio to put his ears on too. You hear about someone like that, get word to the guy that you know a buyer. Someone who'll take his whole stock."

Abe's curiosity got the best of him. "Just what is it you're getting into this time, Jack?"

"Something I probably shouldn't be involved with. But to do it right, it looks like I'm going to have to do something stupid."

Abe stared and Jack knew he wanted to know just how stupid. But Abe wouldn't ask, knowing Jack would tell him about it afterward.

Jack looked around and spotted something hanging on a rack in the corner. And that gave him an idea.

"You know what? Maybe I could use one more thing . . ."

5

Jack took the A train downtown and emerged into the bustling Third World bazaar that was Fourteenth Street. He threaded his way among dreadlocked Dominicans, turbaned Sikhs, saried Indians, suited Koreans, Pakistanis, Puerto Ricans, Jamaicans, and an occasional European mixing in the chill air on sidewalks flanked with signs in half a dozen languages.

He arrived early at the Seventh Avenue address Gia had given him. A little placard on the door was the only indication that this nondescript storefront had anything to do with AIDS.

He probably could have started hunting the stolen Christmas gifts without coming down here, but he figured a quick look at the scene wouldn't hurt. Might even give him a handle on the thieves.

"I have a four o'clock with Dr. Clayton, I believe?" he told the slim, attractive black woman at the reception desk. The nameplate read simply, *Tiffany*.

"Name, sir?"

"Jack."

"Jack what?"

He wanted to tell her, *Just Jack*, but that inevitably led to more questions, and further refusal tended to brand his identity in a person's mind. He preferred to slide off the memory without a trace.

He smiled and fished for a name beginning with "N." He'd used Meyers last time he'd been asked, and since he liked to proceed in alphabetical order . . .

"Niedermeyer. Jack Niedermeyer."

"Fine, Mr. Niedermeyer. Dr. Clayton is still in another meeting right now. A reporter. We had a robbery here last night, you know."

"Really? What did they take?"

"All the donated Christmas toys."

"Get out!"

"It's true. The police are on it right now. I think they should—oh, there's Dr. Clayton now. Looks like she's finishing up."

Jack saw a slim brunette in a white coat walking his way with a guy who looked more like a deliveryman than a reporter. She escorted him to the door, then scanned the street outside as if looking for something. Whatever it was, when she turned back Jack's way, she didn't look as if she'd found it. Or maybe she had. Either way, she didn't seem happy.

"Dr. Clayton, this is your four o'clock: Mr. Niedermeyer."

Dr. Alicia Clayton was better-looking close up, but still kind of . . . plain. She had fine, angular features—a thin, sharp nose, sharply etched lips—neither too fine nor too full—and blue-gray eyes. Her hair was fine too, bobbed to chin length, and a deep, deep black—not black-dye black like the Goth kids did their hair, but a genuine, rich, glossy black.

And no makeup. Someone who took such good care of their hair, you'd think they'd want to enhance their other assets. But not, apparently, Dr. Clayton.

Well, if nothing else, the lack of makeup gave her a clean, scrubbed look, which Jack supposed was a good thing for a doctor.

But her eyes . . . something hiding there. Fear? Anger? A little of both, maybe?

She thrust out her hand. "Welcome, Mr. Niedermeyer."

She had a good grip.

"Just call me Jack."

"You'll want to see the scene of the crime, I imagine."

"I was going to suggest that."

No wasting time. All business. Jack liked that.

The Center wasn't at all what he'd expected. The halls were bright, painted cheery shades of yellow and orange.

"You're a pediatrician?" he said as they walked along.

She nodded. "Subspecialty in infectious diseases."

"My sister's a pediatrician."

"Really? Where's she practice."

Jack mentally kicked himself. Why the hell had he said that? He never thought about his sister the doctor. Or his brother the judge. Must be those calls from Dad.

"I'm really not sure," he said. "We don't keep in touch."

Dr. Clayton gave him a strange look.

Yeah, he thought. Sounds pretty lame, I know, but my sister's far better off not being linked to me.

As they passed open doorways he peeked through and saw rooms filled with toddlers laughing and playing and running around. They didn't look sick.

"That's the day-care area," Dr. Clayton said. "Where HIV-positive kids can play with other HIV-positive kids, and no one has to worry about passing on the infection."

A little boy ran out of one of the rooms and skidded to a stop before them.

"Dr. Alith!" he cried. "Look at my hair! I got a buth cut!"

"Very nice, Hector. But you know you're supposed to stay in the playroom."

Hector was all of four years old and maybe thirty pounds. His ultra short light brown hair was about the same shade as his skin. He looked pale under his pigment, but his grin was a winner.

"Feel my head!" he said. "It'th a buth cut."

A heavyset woman in a flowered smock appeared at the door of the playroom, filling it. "C'mon back, Hector," she said. "It's you're turn at the light box."

"No. I want Dr. Alith to feel my buth cut!"

The woman said, "He just got that haircut and he's been driving us all nuts about it."

Dr. Clayton smiled and brushed her hand over Hector's stubbled head. "Okay, Hector, I'll check out your buzz cut, but then—"

Her smile faded and she pressed her hand to his forehead. "I think you feel a little warm."

"He's been running around like a little madman—'Feel my buzz cut! Feel my buzz cut!' I'm sure he's just overheated."

"Could be, Gladys, but bring him by my office before he goes home, okay?"

Hector jumped in front of Jack and angled the top of his head toward him. "Feel my buth cut, mithter!"

Jack hesitated. Hector was a cute little guy, but he was a cute little guy with HIV.

"C'mon, mithter!"

Jack gave the bristly top of Hector's head a quick rub. He didn't like himself for how quickly he pulled his hand away.

"Ithn't it mad?" Hector said.

"The maddest," Jack told him.

Gladys scooted Hector back to his playroom and they moved on to the next area, which wasn't so pleasant. Jack peeked through a window in a door and saw a room full of kids hooked up to IV's.

"This is the clinic area. Kids come in here for outpatient therapy— we infuse them, monitor their progress, then send them home."

And then they came to a huge plate-glass window that stretched from waist level to the ceiling.

"We board the homeless or abandoned infants in there," Alicia said. "We have volunteers to hold them and comfort them. The crack babies need a *lot* of comforting."

Jack spotted Gia cradling a baby in her arms on the far side of the glass, but he didn't pause. He didn't want her to see him.

"You do a lot here," he said as they moved on.

"Yeah, we've had to become a clinic, a nursery, a day-care center, and a foster home."

"And all because of a single virus."

"But we have to deal with more than the virus," Alicia said. "So many of these kids aren't born merely HIV positive—as if 'merely' can some- how be used with 'HIV'—but addicted to crack or heroin as well. They hit the world screaming like any other baby at the insult of being ejected from that warm cozy womb, but then they keep on screaming as the agonies of cold-turkey withdrawal set in."

"A double whammy," Jack said. Poor kids.

"Yes. Some parents leave their kinds an inheritance, some leave hidden scars; these kids were left a virtual death sentence."

Jack sensed something very personal in that last sentence but couldn't latch onto what it might have been.

"Perhaps 'death sentence' is overstating it. We can do a lot for these kids now. The survival rate is way up, but still . . . once they get through withdrawal, they still have the aftereffects of addiction. Crack and heroin burn out parts of the nervous system. I won't bore you with a lecture about dopamine receptors, but the result is fried circuits in the pleasure centers. Which leaves our little crack babies edgy and irritable, unable to take solace in the simple things that comfort normal infants. So they cry. Endlessly. Until the strung-out junkie mothers who made them this way beat them to shut them up."

Jack realized she probably gave this spiel to all the visitors, but he wished she'd stop. He was getting the urge to go hurt somebody.

"The lucky ones"—she cleared her throat harshly—"try to imagine a lucky HIV-positive crack baby—wind up here."

She stopped before a windowless door.

"Here's the storeroom where the toys were kept."

She showed him the room, empty but for some Scotch tape and wrapping paper.

"The toys will be wrapped in this paper?" he said, memorizing the pattern.

"Most, but not all."

He pulled open the door to the alley, and checked the alley itself. Easy to see how it had been done. The outer door frame and the surface around the latch were deeply gouged and warped. Looked like the work of a long pry bar in the hands of someone with the finesse of an orangutan.

He saw Dr. Clayton shiver in the cold wash from the open door. She rubbed the sleeves of her white coat. She was very thin—no insulation.

"How are you going to handle this?" she said as Jack closed the door.

Jack said, "Not here. Can we talk in your office?"

"Follow me."

On the way to her office, Dr. Clayton stopped at the front door and peered out at the street. He saw her stiffen, as if she'd seen something that frightened her.

6

Sam Baker had been sitting here in the car, taking his turn on surveillance for a good hour now, testing his memory, and checking out his hair in the rearview mirror.

And he hated looking in that mirror. People would think he was some sort of fag or something, primping and prissing. But damn, his once thick-and-wavy sandy hair was getting thinner and grayer every goddam day. He was only forty-six and he could see his scalp. If this kept up, he'd be bald before he hit fifty.

Baker glanced up and saw someone staring his way through the front door of the AIDS center. He looked closer and resisted the impulse to duck down when he saw that it was the Clayton broad. Not to worry. She could see the car, but not who was in it.

At least this confirmed that she was still there.

Not that he gave a rat's ass where this crazy broad went. But the towel head who was paying him did, and that was what counted. He—

The cell phone rang. Baker grabbed it and hit the SEND button.

"Yeah?"

"It is I."

Shit. Baker had thought it was one of his men. But it was Ahab the Ay-rab himself: Kemel Muhallal.

"Yes sir."

"I wish to inquire about the status of the object of our mutual interest."

"Say what?"

"The woman. Where is she?"

"Still where she works." Baker didn't want to be more specific than that. Not on a cell phone.

"She has not sought out another lawyer?"

"Nope."

"If she does, I do not want a repeat of what happened to her last attorney."

"All right," Baker said. "We've been over that already. And I told you. Everything will work out fine. Trust me."

He'd been in deep shit since this morning. Christ, he'd thought he'd get high-fived for taking out her lawyer, but no. Kemel the towel head got pissed instead. *Really* pissed. Said it would draw attention to the case and wanted to know why Baker had done it without authorization.

Hey, why not? he thought. When you hire an ex-Special Forces demolition expert, you get a take-charge kinda guy. You already had me plant one bomb—a *big* one—so when you tell me this Weinstein jerk's making too many waves, I figure you're saying you've got a problem you want solved. So I solve it. Permanently, just like the other one. That's the way we handled it when I was with SOG in 'Nam. That's the way I've handled all my assignments since I started going out for hire. No complaints so far.

And not to worry. The coke I planted in the car will have everybody looking in the wrong direction.

But still Kemel was pissed. And that wasn't good. Kemel had deep pockets, and Sam Baker wanted to stay on his good side. In fact, he wanted to attach himself to Kemel and ride him back to Saudi Arabia. Because damn, those Saudis needed all the Sam Bakers they could buy.

Sam figured he'd be square with Kemel if the Clayton bitch didn't go out and hire another lawyer and gave up on this house that everyone was so damn interested in. Then he could step up to him and say, See? Blowing up her lawyer in front of her scared her off. Y'gotta believe, man. I *know* what I'm doing.

"I trust you only when you are doing what you are authorized to do. Watch her and do nothing else."

"Aye-aye, Cap'n. Ten-four, Roger Wilco, over and out." He hit the END button. "Asshole."

Baker ground his teeth. He was pissed, and suddenly realized this was a good time to check his short-term memory. See if talking to that towel head had screwed it up. He closed his eyes and recited the phone number from the sign of the deli across the street. When he checked he saw that he'd got it right.

Good. Sharp as ever. A long time before he wound up like his mother.

He glanced at the AIDS center doorway and caught the Clayton broad slipping back inside.

If Muhallal would let him in on what was going on, he could do a better job. He knew there were two sides here: Alicia Clayton on one side, and her brother Thomas Clayton—one *seriously* creepy dude—on the other. And their father's will between them. How Kemel Muhallal got involved, Baker had no idea. But it had to do with the house. The brother wanted the house, and Kemel was ready to spend big bucks to see to it that he got it.

They'd hired him to help out. They wanted the house guarded. No one allowed in unless authorized by Muhallal or the brother. They also wanted to keep close tabs on the sister, but under absolutely no circumstance—and this had been repeated and repeated until he was sick of hearing it—was he to harm her, or even allow her to be harmed by someone else.

Which was hard to figure. If the sister was dead, wouldn't the house go to the brother?

But the Arab and the brother were keeping all their reasons to themselves. Baker figured they had to be after something in that house. And whatever it was, it had to be pretty damn valuable, because they wanted it pretty damn fucking bad. As to what it was, Baker didn't have a clue. Another one of their secrets.

That was okay for now. He had a *big* payoff coming when the house finally belonged to the Arab. He'd have to share some of it with the crew he'd hired, but there'd still be plenty left over to solve his current financial woes, and even add a little padding to the pitifully thin cushion of his retirement fund.

But before all this was over, Baker was going to know *all* their secrets. And you could take that to the bank.

7

A chill rippled over Alicia's skin and collected at the base of her spine as she watched a gray car double-parked across the street. It idled there, slightly uptown from her vantage point, its motor running.

The same car as this morning? She couldn't be sure. Was it watching the door of the Center or waiting for someone in one of those stores? How could she know? Hell, between the sun glare and the tinted windows, she couldn't even tell how many people were in it.

Damn, this was scary. What were they waiting for? An explosion?

She shuddered. She'd told Tiffany to let her see all the mail, all the UPS deliveries before they were opened. But what would she do if she came across a package with no return address? Call the bomb squad? Luckily she hadn't had to face that choice—all today's deliveries were from the Center's usual suppliers.

She forced herself to turn away.

This was her fifth—or was it her sixth?—trip to the front since her arrival this morning. Tiffany was beginning to give her strange looks.

She lead Jack Niedermeyer back to her office. Maybe it was just her imagination. Why would anybody follow her? What was the point? She did the same thing every day: from her apartment in the Village to the Center, from the Center to her apartment. A model of predictability.

Relax, she told herself. You're making yourself crazy. Stay calm and figure out where you go from here on the will mess.

"Have a seat," she said as they entered her office.

Raymond stopped by to drop off some papers. She introduced them but said nothing about why Mr. Niedermeyer was here.

When Raymond was gone and they were seated, facing each other, she took a good look at this very average-looking brown-haired, mid-thirtyish man in jeans and a reddish flannel shirt.

This is the guy who's going to get the toys back? Alicia thought as she indicated a chair. Oh, I doubt that. I doubt that very much.

"Now, Mr. Niedermeyer—"

"Just call me Jack."

"Okay, Just Jack." *And you can call me Dr. Clayton.* No, she wouldn't say that. "Ms. DiLauro told me you might be able to help. Are you a friend of hers?"

"Not really. I did some work for her once. Got her out of a jam."

"What sort of a jam?"

He leaned forward. "I believe the subject is missing toys?"

A tiny flash of intensity there. Well hidden, but Alicia had spotted it. Something personal between these two? Or simply none of my business?

When he'd leaned forward, he'd put his hands on her desk. Alicia was struck by the length of his thumbnails. His hands were clean, his nails well trimmed . . . all except for the thumbs. Their nails jutted a good quarter inch or more beyond the flesh. She wanted to ask him about them but didn't see how she could do so with any grace.

"I wasn't prying," she said. "I'm simply curious as to how one man could possibly find those toys ahead of the whole New York City Police Department."

Jack shrugged. "First off, it won't be the 'whole' department. Maybe one or two robbery detectives—if you're lucky."

Alicia nodded. He was right.

"Second," he said, "I think it's a safe bet that the guys who ripped you off aren't family men stocking up for their own kids' Christmases. And from the look of that door, they weren't pros. I smell a quickie, spur-of-the-moment heist. I'll bet they don't have a fence in place to dump their loot, which means they'll be looking for one. I know people . . ."

He left that hanging. What people? she wondered. People who buy stolen Christmas gifts? Was he some sort of criminal himself?

She looked at him and realized that his mild brown eyes revealed nothing . . . absolutely nothing.

"So . . . you 'know people' . . . people, I assume, who might lead you to the thieves. And then what?"

"And then I will prevail upon them to return the gifts."

"And if you can't 'prevail?' What then? Call in the police?"

He shook his head. "No. That's one of the conditions of my involvement: no contact with officialdom. If the police recover the gifts, fine. All's well that ends well. If *I* return them, it's a wonderful occurrence, a Christmas miracle. You don't know who's responsible, but God bless 'em. You've never seen me, never even heard of me. As far as you know, I don't exist."

Alicia tensed. Was this some sort of scam? Rob the gifts, then charge a fee to "find" them. Maybe even collect a reward?

But no. Gia DiLauro would never have anything to do with something like that. Her anger this morning had been too real.

But this man, this "Just Jack" . . . he might have involved Gia without her knowledge.

"I see," she said. "And what would you charge for—?"

"It's taken care of."

"I don't understand. Did Gia—?"

"Don't worry about it. All taken care of."

"There'll be a reward."

She'd had calls—businesses and individuals offering to contribute to a reward fund for the arrest of the perpetrators. The total was mounting.

"Keep it. Spend it on the kids."

Alicia relaxed. All right. So it wasn't a scam.

"What I need is some information about the gifts—anything distinctive that'll help me make sure I'm on the right track."

"Well, for one thing, they were all wrapped. We only accepted new toys or clothing—all of it *un*wrapped—and then we wrapped them ourselves as they came in. You saw the kind of paper we used. Other than that, what can I say? It was a real hodgepodge of gifts, a beautiful, generous assortment. . . ."

Alicia felt her throat begin to lock with rage.

And they're all gone!

The man rose and extended his hand across her desk. "I'll see what I can do."

Alicia gripped his hand and held it. Should she tell him about Thomas and the will and the house, about the bomb that obliterated Leo Weinstein, that perhaps the theft of the toys was connected? No, she didn't want to get into that with this man. And besides, the toy theft *felt* different.

"What are our chances?" she said. "The truth. Don't think you have to make me feel good."

"The truth?" he said. "Chances for recovery are zip if they've already fenced the toys. Slim if they haven't. If they're not recovered, say, by Sunday, I'd say they're gone for good."

"I'm sorry I asked." She sighed. "But that's the way it goes around here, I guess. These kids are born under a dark cloud. I don't know why I should expect they'll get a break this time."

He gave her hand a little extra squeeze, then released her.

"You never know, Dr. Clayton." He gave her a crooked smile. "Even the worst losers get lucky once in a while."

Maybe it was the smile that did it. It dropped his shields. Alicia saw into this Jack for an instant—a nanosecond, really—and suddenly she had hope. If it was at all possible to find and return those gifts, this man believed he could pull it off.

And now Alicia was beginning to believe it too.

8

Instead of heading for the front after leaving the doctor's office, Jack ducked to the left and returned to the infant area. He stepped back into the relative shadow of a doorway across from the big plate-glass window and watched.

Gia sat half facing him, but all her attention was on the blanket-wrapped bundle in her arms. She rocked, smiled, cooed, and looked down at that bundle as if it were the most precious child in the world. Someone else's baby, but no one looking at Gia now would know it. Her eyes were aglow with a light Jack had never seen before. And her expression . . . beatific was the only word for it.

And then Vicky hopped into the picture, an eight-year-old slip of a thing; her dark brown braids bouncing as she hurried a bottle of formula to her mother. Jack smiled. He had to smile every time he saw Vicky. She was a doll and he loved her like a daughter.

He'd never met Vicky's father and, from what he'd heard about the late, not-so-great Richard Westphalen, he was glad. Jack had it on excellent authority that the Brit bastard was dead—he knew the where, when, and how of his death—but the remains would never be found. So it would be years before Richard Westphalen was declared legally dead. Gia had taken back her maiden name after the divorce, although Vicky remained a Westphalen—the last of the line.

Vicky didn't seem to miss him. Why should she? She'd hardly known him when he was alive, and now Jack had more than taken his place. Or at least he hoped so.

He watched a few minutes longer, unable to take his eyes off the two most important people in his life. And it worried him no end that they were both in an enclosed room with HIV-positive infants.

Right, right, right. He knew all the facts and figures about how safe they were, and all that. And that was all fine and good for other people. But this was Gia and Vicky. And the threat was a virus, something you couldn't see, and not just any virus. This was HIV.

HIV had always given Jack the creeps. He wasn't generally given to looking for or finding conspiracies, but HIV was so damned *efficient*. An infection that attacks the very weapons the body uses against infections . . . the concept had such an *engineered* feel about it.

Jack felt he could protect those two people in there against just about anything. But not a virus. And they were putting themselves right in its way.

If either one of them should catch it . . . he didn't know what he'd do.

HIV was something he could not fix.

Jack pulled himself away and walked back the way he had come.

He saw the heavyset Gladys leading a line of preschoolers down the hall. She smiled and nodded as she passed, a huge goose with her goslings. He spotted Hector bringing up the rear.

"Hey," he said, pointing. "Who's that kid with the mad buzz cut?"

Jack had expected another offer to "feel my buth cut," or a smile at least. But Hector's eyes were dull when he looked up at Jack. And then he staggered against the wall and dropped to his knees. Before Jack could react, Hector vomited.

"Whoa!" Jack yelled. "Trouble here!"

Gladys was there in a second. "Stay back," she told Jack as she pulled on latex gloves that seemed to appear from nowhere.

She picked up a hall phone, spoke a few words, then knelt beside Hector. Jack couldn't hear what she said, but he saw Hector shake his head.

And then Raymond appeared—he too was wearing latex gloves. He gathered Hector up in his arms and carried him back down the hall. As Gladys directed the other children back into their playroom, a janitor appeared and began mopping up the mess with a solution that reeked of antiseptic.

Jack moved on. He'd been a frozen observer, not knowing what to do. The staff here had its own set of rules and protocols that Jack was not privy to. He felt like a stranger in a foreign country, with no knowledge of the language or the culture.

He quickened his pace. Hector had been smiling and bubbling less than an hour ago, and just now he'd looked like a little rag doll with all its stuffing vacuumed out.

The happy sounds of the children in the day-care rooms attacked Jack as he moved. Each shout felt like a shot, each laugh a knife thrust. Death hovered over every one of them, a fatal infection lurked around every corner, but they didn't know about that. And just as well. They were kids, and they should be happy while they could.

Especially the crack babies. Their short lives had been full of pain from day one, while a virus chewed away at their immune systems.

And now someone had stolen their toys.

Jack felt his jaw muscles bunch. Don't worry, kids . . . Uncle Jack may not know what to do when you're sick, but he's not quite as useless as he looked a few minutes ago. He's going to get your toys back. And in the process he sincerely intends to have a heart-to-heart chat with the oxygen waster who took them.

Life really sucked sometimes.

But it didn't have to suck *all* the time. Sometimes things could be fixed.

SATURDAY

The Nail sat behind the wheel of his truck and rubbed his hands together for warmth. Cold as shit out tonight, man. Cold as *shit!*

But not for long. An hour from now, maybe less if the buyer didn't try to jew him down too much, he'd be flush and warm in his crib, sucking on some rock instead of this piss poor excuse for a joint.

The Nail took a deep toke and held it. He wiped the condensation off his windshield and wished the heater in this damn truck worked. He flicked his Bic to check his watch. The buyer had said like eleven-thirty. Just about that now.

He'd floated the word that if anyone wanted a deep discount on a bunch of new Xmas toys, wrapped and ready to go, The Nail was the man. Word had floated back that a fence who was a friend of a friend of a friend wanted the whole truckload. Yes!

He exhaled and peered down the alley, looking for headlights. Lots of wheels rolling by out there, heading for the nearby Manhattan Bridge. He wished the right set would roll in here so he could get this deal done.

His contact hadn't said so, but The Nail figured the fence was bringing his own truck. Had to be. How else was he going to cart the stuff out of here?

Better not have any ideas about taking *this* truck, man. He patted the little .32 automatic in his belt. Better not be thinking of anything beyond passing the cash and off-loading the stash.

Hey, that rhymes.

Passin' the green and splittin' the scene.

The Nail smiled and took another toke. Too bad he wasn't with the band anymore. Maybe him and the drummer could've like worked that up into a song or something. That'd be cool.

He missed Polio. Best damn punk thrasher band in the world, man, and he'd played bass for them. Well, for a few months, anyway. Until they kicked him out for not showing up.

But it'd been a good few months. That was when he'd picked up the name The Nail. Well, not picked up, actually. That was when he'd started calling himself The Nail. You needed a name like The Nail if you was playing for Polio. Like who'd want a bass player named Joey DeCiglia?

And The Nail was *such* a cool name, having like a double meaning and all.

But even with a handle like The Nail and having gigged with Polio, there wasn't no work out there. Least not for him. Shit, yeah, he got auditions just by name-dropping Polio, and everybody was real interested in hearing him . . . until they heard him.

Then it was like, don't call us, man . . .

Yeah, well, fuck you too.

He sucked the joint down to his fingertips and tossed the roach out the window. Not worth saving, man.

After a bunch of wasted auditions, The Nail said good-bye to the music scene. He had his pride, man. As a lark, he started boosting stuff and selling it off. Wound up making more that way than any of the nowhere, no-name thrasher bands who never called him were gonna pay him.

But then Tina goes and gets herself knocked up and tries to tell him the kid's his. Sure. Right. Like with the way she jumps on anything upright and hard, he's gonna believe that shit? No fucking way.

Then she gets all fucked up in the head and won't have an abortion. Nah. She's gonna have the kid and be a mommy.

Right. Mommy Tina. Sure.

But surprise, surprise. She's goes through with it. And of course the kid's born like totally wasted. And then the word comes down that it's got fucking AIDS, man. *AIDS!*

That meant Tina had the bug, and *that* blew The Nail's mind. Fuck, he could have it too, what with screwing Tina all the time and sharing needles. He should've gotten tested right then, but he was too scared, man. Like he didn't want to *know*.

But for Tina, it was like she wasn't even sick and like the kid wasn't sick either. Her head was royally fucked. So she was all broke up when they took the baby away from her.

And she kept telling him it was *his* kid. Kept saying how it looked just like him. So one day last week she finally hounded him into going over to this place where they keep the kid and look after it. The Nail didn't know what had gotten into him—maybe that Ceylonese brown they'd been using had got him over-mellowed—but he was glad he'd given in. Because as he was hanging around the place, he saw people carrying a bunch of Christmas gifts through this doorway. He took a peek, figuring he might be able to make off with something small, but he saw a whole room *filled* with toys. Whoa.

Merry Christmas to me.

He did the place two nights later.

And the coolest part of the whole thing was the news coverage. Shit, man, last night you couldn't turn a radio or TV without hearing about "the AIDS baby Christmas toy theft." He'd spent hours hopping from channel to channel, one news show after the other, grinning like a total asshole.

That was him they were talking about. The Nail.

The only bad thing was, he couldn't tell anyone. At least not until he'd sold off the stuff. After that he could talk all he wanted because the toys would be gone and no one could prove nothing.

The only thing he didn't get was how pissed off and disgusted all the news geeks acted. Like it really mattered to them. Bull*shit*. Everybody knew how stupid it was to waste presents on those AIDS kids. Really, how long were they going to live anyway? Weren't going to be around long enough to appreciate them. Total waste, man.

Leave it to The Nail to put the stuff to good use.

And it'd been so fucking simple. All he'd had to do was—

The Nail jumped as he heard a *skree-eek* behind him. He twisted around in his seat. That sounded like—

It was! Shit, some asshole had opened one of the truck's back doors. And now he was flashing a light inside.

His first thought was cops, but he hadn't seen a fuzzmobile pull up. And The Nail knew cops had to follow certain rules about searches.

The buyer? Maybe, but he didn't think so. More likely some strung-out junkie trying to boost *his* stuff.

The Nail pulled out the automatic and chambered a round. He'd put an end to that shit *real* quick.

He jumped out and ran around to the back of the truck.

"Hey, man. What the fuck you think—?"

Nobody there. And both rear doors closed. The Nail scanned the alley up and down: not a fucking soul in sight.

He couldn't have imagined it. The weed hadn't been *that* strong. And he'd heard the noise. He'd *seen* the light.

Better check to see if anything was missing.

But as The Nail reached for the handle, the right door sprang open and slammed into him, knocking him flat. He landed on his back, rolled, and popped to his feet, the gun stuck out ahead of him. He saw the open door of the truck, but no one there.

And then he heard a deep voice.

"Ho-ho-ho!"

The Nail looked up and saw this fat guy with a white beard in a red suit standing on top of the truck.

The guy did his ho-ho-ho thing again, then shouted, "So *you're* the one who stole the toys I was putting aside for the AIDS babies! No one steals Santa's toys and gets away with it!"

Aw, man. This asshole thinks he's Santa Claus!

The Nail raised the pistol and plugged a round into his heart.

Santa fucking Claus flew backward off the top of the truck like someone had yanked a leash wrapped around his neck.

No one steals Santa's toys and gets away with it?

Shit, yeah. *I* steal *anybody's* fucking toys and do what I damn well fucking please, asshole!

The Nail hurried around the side of the truck. Time to put another slug in Santa Hole . . .

But he wasn't there.

"What the fuck?" The Nail said aloud.

And then something red and white popped up from the shadows behind a garbage can and slammed a white-gloved fist into his face.

The Nail had heard about seeing stars, but he'd never believed it. Now he did. He heard his nose go *crunch* as his face erupted in a star-studded explosion of pain. He staggered back, caught the heel of his shoe on some alley shit, and felt himself falling backward.

He windmilled his arms, trying to keep his balance, but he was out of control. He went down hard.

And when he looked up, Santa was leaning over him.

"You think you can stop Santa Claus with a bullet? A mere *bullet*? Think again, sonny!"

The voice wasn't quite as deep and strong as it had been a moment ago, but the guy was still standing. And there, not two feet from The Nail's face, was a bullet hole in the red fabric of his suit. Right over his heart.

Shit! What was going down here? The fucker should be dead, man.

Unless of course he really *was* Santa Claus.

But that was crazy.

But so was the guy in the red suit! The Nail saw his eyes gleaming between his white beard and the furry brim of his hat. Whoever he was— hell, maybe he really was Santa Claus—he was pissed. *Royally* pissed.

The Nail started to raise the pistol for another shot, but Santa stomped a foot down on his arm.

"Don't bother trying again, sonny! You can't kill Santa Claus!"

The Nail levered himself up and reached across, trying to grab the gun with his free hand, but Santa clocked him again with a brain-jarring right, rocking his head back against the pavement.

Santa had a punch like a fucking mule kick.

The Nail felt the gun ripped from his hand, heard it skitter across the asphalt. After that, things got fuzzy.

And painful.

The Nail remembered getting flipped over onto his belly, grabbed by his collar and his waistband, and hauled off the ground.

"I checked my list," Santa said. "Checked it twice, in fact. It says you've been naughty, sonny. *Very* naughty!"

Then Santa started using him like a battering ram.

Slam! Headfirst against the bumper of the truck.

"Know what happens when you steal from Santa Claus? *This!*"

Slam! Headfirst into a bunch of trash cans lining the alley.

"If I decide to let you live, spread the word: Don't mess with Santa Claus!"

The Nail was spun around and flung face-first against one of the alley's brick walls.

He let out a puny groan of agony as he slid down the wall, feeling like a splattered egg oozing toward the ground.

But it wasn't over. Not by a long shot. The Nail felt his consciousness fading over the next ten minutes as Santa used him like some sort of rag to wipe up the alley.

Finally Santa released him. The Nail dropped to the ground, a puddle of agony on the broken pavement. He felt his breath bubbling through his bloody mouth. He was sure his jaw was broken. And his ribs—every breath was a dozen stab wounds. Was it over? He hoped so. He *prayed* it was over.

Just leave me be, he thought. Just take the toys, take the whole damn truck and go. Hitch your fucking reindeer to the bumper and you and

Rudolph take off. Just don't mess me up anymore. Please.

But just as he finished the thought, he felt hands go under his armpits and lift him.

"No," he managed to groan past his shattered teeth. "Please . . . no more."

"Should have thought of that before, sonny. Stealing from defenseless little sick kids puts you on Santa's ultra-naughty list."

"I'm sorry." It came out a faint whine. Totally wimpy.

"Well, good. I'm glad to hear it. And I'll take that into consideration next Christmas. But you complicated things by trying to kill Santa. That's *very* naughty. Santa doesn't like to be shot. It makes him cranky. *Very* cranky."

"Oh, no . . ."

Something rough and long slithered past The Nail's cheek, and true panic set in. *Rope!* Oh, fuck no. Santa was going to string him up!

But then he felt the rope snake under his arms instead of around his neck. That was a relief. Of sorts. It still hurt like all hell when the rope tightened around his shattered ribs. He was lifted and seated on the truck's rickety bumper, then tied there.

"Wha—?"

"Quiet, sonny," Santa said in a low voice that had lost all its heartiness. "*Don't* say another word."

The Nail looked up. Everything—Santa, the alley, the whole fucking *world*—was mostly a blur . . . except for Santa's eyes. He'd always thought Santa had blue eyes, but these were brown, and The Nail shriveled up inside when he saw the rage bubbling behind them.

Santa wasn't just pissed. Santa was bugfuck nuts.

The Nail closed his eyes while Santa taped something to his head. By the time it squeezed through to his battered brain that he shouldn't let Santa—even this homicidal psycho Santa—tie him to the front of a truck, it was too late. He tried to wriggle free but the rope that lashed him to the grille crisscrossed his body around the shoulders and between the legs. His legs and his arms were free, but all the knots were somewhere behind him.

With a cold sick certainty, The Nail realized he wasn't going nowhere. Not under his own steam, anyway.

He stiffened as he heard the old engine rumble and shudder to life against his back. He began to blubber as the truck lurched into motion.

Santa was going to run him into the wall!

But no. The truck bounced out of the alley onto the street. After that it was a nightmare ride through the Lower East Side with people staring, pointing, some even laughing, then crosstown on Fourteenth with the truck swerving from lane to lane, running lights, screeching to a halt, inches—*inches!*—from rear bumpers and fenders, then roaring into motion again.

All that was bad enough, man, but when the westbound lanes weren't moving fast enough, the truck swerved into the oncoming traffic and played chicken with a banged-up yellow cab. The Nail knew fuck sure ol' Santa wasn't going to back down, and for the few screaming, terror-filled heartbeats that it looked like the cab wasn't going to either, The Nail lost it. Literally. Warm liquid spilled down his left leg.

But the cab lunged out of the way at the last second and the truck got back on the right side of the street and began accelerating.

A cop! The Nail had never dreamed he'd be in any circumstance when he'd want to see a cop on his tail, but here it was. And where were they? Why wasn't there ever a fucking cop around when you needed one?

The truck fishtailed into a wide, screeching turn onto what The Nail thought might be Seventh Avenue, but he couldn't be sure because he closed his eyes as they scooted within a hair of a horn-blaring bus. Then the truck jumped the curb and scattered terrified pedestrians before skidding to a halt on the sidewalk.

As the engine cut out, The Nail whimpered and waited in terror to see what Santa had planned for him next. But Santa said nothing, did nothing. The Nail twisted around and looked through the windshield. Santa was gone.

But The Nail wasn't alone. A crowd of gawkers was gathering, forming a semicircle around him and the truck, staring, pointing at his bloody face, his pee-stained pants, and whatever it was Santa had taped to his head. Someone laughed. Others joined in.

The Nail wanted to die.

And then he heard the sirens.

SUNDAY

1

"How's it going, Hector?"

Little Hector Lopez looked up at Alicia from his hospital bed but didn't smile.

" 'Kay," he said.

She'd admitted him to the pediatric service on Friday due to intractable vomiting, but he'd been holding down fluids since yesterday afternoon. He looked better. Still had a fever, though. His spinal tap had looked negative, but the culture was still pending. So were blood and urine cultures. She hoped this turned out to be a simple gastrointestinal virus, but his practically nonexistent CD-4 count deeply worried her. Just to be safe, she'd shot him up with some IV gamma globulin.

"How're you feeling?"

"Thith hurtth," he said, pointing to his splinted left arm where the IV tube drained into an antecubital vein.

"We'll take that out as soon as you're better."

"Today?" he said, brightening.

"Maybe. Your fever's got to come down first."

"Oh."

Alicia turned to Jeanne Sorenson, the nurse who was accompanying her on rounds today. The big blonde was barely twenty-five but already a grizzled veteran of the AIDS war.

"Who's been in to see him?" she said in a low voice.

Sorenson shrugged. "No one that I know of. His foster mother called—once."

"All right, then," Alicia said. "Who's Hector's buddy on this shift?"

"We haven't assigned one yet."

Alicia suppressed an angry snap. "I thought we agreed that all my kids would have one buddy per shift," she said evenly.

"We haven't had time, Dr. Clayton," Sorenson said, looking flustered. "It's been hectic here, and we figured he'd be out in a couple of days, so—"

"Even if it's *one* day, I want them assigned a buddy. We've been over this, Sorenson."

"I know that," the nurse said, looking sheepish.

"But apparently it didn't sink in. You know how scary a hospital is for an adult, so imagine yourself a child confined to bed in a place where a bunch of strangers have taken your clothes and sneakers and started sticking needles in you and telling you what you can eat and when you can go to the bathroom. But at least most kids can count on a mother or father or *someone* familiar showing up and lending a little reassurance. Not my kids. They've got nobody to fall back on. Their support system is a black hole. Can you imagine what that's like?"

Sorenson shook her head. "I've tried, but . . ."

"Right. You can't. But trust me, it's terrible."

Alicia knew. She'd been hospitalized a few weeks into her first year at college—for dehydration secondary to a viral gastroenteritis very similar to what had brought Hector here. She was in only two days, but it had been an awful experience. No boyfriend and no close friends, no one to visit her or even ask after her, and damned if she was going to call home. She'd never forgotten that feeling of utter helplessness and isolation.

"So that's why they need someone on every shift who'll come in and talk to them and smile and hold their hand every hour or so, someone they can count on, just so they don't feel so damn *alone*. It's almost as important as the medicine we pump into them."

"I'll get on it right away," Sorenson said.

"Good. But don't do it for me. Do it for him." She turned and rubbed Hector's bristly head. "Hey, guy. That buzz cut looks as mad as ever."

Now she got a smile. "Yeth. It'th—" He coughed. He tried again but interrupted himself with more coughing.

"Easy, Hector," Alicia said.

She sat him up and parted the back flaps of his hospital gown. Pressing the head of her stethoscope against his ribs, she listened for the soft cellophane crinkle that would herald pneumonia. She heard nothing but an isolated wheeze.

Alicia checked Hector's chart. The admitting chest X ray had been negative. She ordered a repeat, plus a sputum culture and gram stain.

She stared down at his bony little body. She didn't like that cough one bit.

2

"Oh, no," Alicia said as she rounded the corner and saw the police cars in front of the Center. "What now?"

She had her donut and coffee from the hospital caf in one hand, the fat Sunday *Times* in the other. She usually spent the rest of Sunday morning at the Center. They still had kids coming in for their treatments, just like every other day, but it was a lot less intense than the rest of the week—nowhere near as many phone calls, for one thing—so she used it to catch up on her paperwork.

She had also planned to devote some of today to figuring out her next step in the saga of the will and the house that supposedly belonged to her but no one wanted to let her have.

But now . . .

Just inside the front door she nearly collided with two cops, one white, one black, talking to Raymond. *Raymond.* He was devoted to the Center, but he rarely if ever showed up on Sunday.

"Oh, Alicia!" he said. "There you are! Isn't it wonderful?"

"Isn't what wonderful?"

"Didn't anyone tell you? The toys! The *toys* are back!"

Suddenly Alicia wanted to cry. She turned to the pair of policemen. Raymond introduced her. She wanted to hug them.

"You found them? Already? That's . . . that's wonderful!" Better than wonderful—fantastic was the word.

"I guess you could say we found them," the black cop said, scratching his buzz-cut head. His name tag read POMUS. "If you can call opening up a truck parked on the sidewalk by your front door really 'finding' them."

"Wait a minute," Alicia said. "Back up just a bit. What truck?"

"A panel truck, Alicia," Raymond said. "Filled with the toys. The police think it was the same one used to haul them away. Someone drove it up on the sidewalk last night and left it there."

"Any idea who it was?" she asked, although she had a pretty good idea of the answer.

The white cop—SCHWARTZ on his tag—grinned. "According to the guy tied to the bumper, it was Santa Claus himself."

"Guy tied to *what?*"

They went on to explain about the man they'd found lashed to the front of the toy-filled truck. Someone had "knocked the crap out of him," as Officer Pomus put it, and taped some rubber antlers to his head. The battered man admitted to the theft and swore that his assailant had been Santa Claus—even admitted to shooting Santa, rambling on about shooting him in the heart without killing him.

"But of course, you can't kill Santa," Officer Schwartz said, grinning.

"He's obviously a user and he sounds like an EDP, so we don't know what to believe," Officer Pomus added. "We've got him up on Bellevue's flight deck now, under observation."

"Flight deck?"

"You know—the psych ward. Sooner or later, we'll get the straight story out of him."

"And throw the book at him, I hope."

"Oh, yeah," Pomus said. "No question about that. But he's already had worse than a book thrown at him." He grinned. "A *lot* worse."

"Yeah," Officer Schwartz said. "Someone worked him over *real* good before dropping him here. The creep seemed almost glad to be arrested."

After they were gone, Alicia and Raymond went to the storeroom and inspected the gifts. Except for a little wrinkling of the paper and an occasional bumped corner, most were in the same condition as before the theft. She told Raymond to get hold of a locksmith—she didn't care that it was Sunday—and have him secure that door, even if it meant putting a bar across it.

Then she went to her office and sipped her coffee, lukewarm by now, and thought about that nothing-special-looking man named Jack—"Just Jack" Niedermeyer.

On Friday afternoon he'd said he'd see what he could do. Thirty-six hours later, the gifts were back and the thief in custody.

A man who could do that just might be able to solve her other problem.

Alicia looked up a number in her computer's directory and began dialing.

3

Jack winced as he reached for the phone. He could think of only one person who'd be calling him this morning, so he picked up before the answering machine.

"Jack, you're wonderful!" Gia said. "Just wonderful!"

"I think you're pretty swell too, Gia."

"No, I'm being serious here. I just got a call from Dr. Clayton, and she told me the toys are back."

"Is that so? Gotta hand it to New York's finest. When they get on the job—"

"Right," she said, and damned if he couldn't *hear* her smile. "You had nothing to do with it."

"Not a thing. You said you didn't approve, so I gave it up."

"Okay. Be that way. But Dr. Clayton said as far as she can tell, every single gift is back, and the guy who stole them is locked up. I don't know how you managed it, but—"

"I simply E-mailed Santa and he did the rest."

"Well, Santa may have to do some more. Dr. Clayton asked me for your number."

Jack stiffened. "You didn't give it to her."

"No. I didn't give her any number. I told her I didn't know it by heart, and I'd have to look it up and get back to her."

Jack relaxed. "You done good, Gia. The perfect answer. Any idea what she wants?"

"Something about a personal matter. She didn't offer any details, and I didn't ask."

"Okay. Write this down." Jack rattled off the number at the Tenth Avenue drop. "Tell her to leave a message on the answering machine. Tell her that's how you get hold of me."

"Will do. Are we still on for this afternoon?"

"Sure are. Westchester, right?"

"No," she said, drawing out the word. "FAO Schwartz."

"We'll discuss that later. See you at noon."

4

"Oh, my God!" Gia said. "What's that?"

"Just a little bruise."

Jack looked down at the large purple area on his left chest wall. Damn. He'd hoped she wouldn't notice, but here in the warm afterglow of their lovemaking, he'd forgot all about it.

They'd dropped Vicky off at her art class after lunch. She spent most of every Sunday afternoon learning the basics of drawing, painting, and sculpture. Her teacher said she showed a real flair for drawing. Jack figured it had to be genetic, what with her mother an artist and all. Vicky loved the classes, and Jack loved the chance to be alone with Gia on Sunday afternoons.

Their routine was to dash here to Jack's apartment immediately after dropping Vicky off. Often they didn't travel ten feet inside the door before they were tearing at each other's clothes. From there they usually wound up on the nearest horizontal surface. Today, however, they'd made it all the way to the bed.

Jack pulled the sheet up to his neck, but she pushed it down.

"I'd hardly call that 'little.' " He watched Gia's fingers trace over it. "Does it hurt?"

"Nah."

She pressed and he winced.

"Right," she said. "Doesn't hurt a bit. How long have you had it?"

"Since last night." Since a little before midnight, to be exact.

He told her about the creep taking a shot at him, and how the Kevlar vest had saved him.

"Thank God you were wearing it!" she said. She couldn't seem to take her eyes off it or stop touching it. "But if the vest is bulletproof, how come you're hurt?"

"Well, it did keep the bullet from going through me, but the slug's still got all that velocity behind it. Something had to absorb it, and that something was me."

Jack still wasn't sure why he'd given in to the impulse to wear the Santa suit. Usually if he dressed up it was either as a lure or to allay suspicion. Last night's flamboyant performance with the ho-ho-ho's and the beard and red suit were not his style.

But somehow . . . this time, this job . . . he'd felt compelled to make a point.

And he'd known that was stupid. Experience had taught him, when you try to make a point instead of simply getting the job done, you up the chances of things going wrong, which ups your chances of getting hurt.

So Jack had taken precautions. He never wore body armor, but had made an exception last night. Normally he would have opened a can of mace and lobbed it into the truck, then taken down the guy or guys with a sap when they tumbled out the door. But doing the Santa thing required more exposure, and he knew sure as hell someone would have a gun.

He'd been right. The guy got off a lucky shot that felt like a four-by-four slamming end-on into Jack's chest. Knocked him off the truck and the wind out of his lungs, but the ten-ply vest had stopped the slug.

Good thing he'd had those weighted gloves. Abe hadn't been able to find white ones, but he'd provided Jack a pair of white cotton gloves to wear over the more traditional black leather. The lead inserts doubled the impact of every punch and allowed him to make short work of the creep.

And then Jack had lost it. Maybe it was the pain, maybe it was thinking how he'd be dead if he hadn't worn the vest, and maybe it was remembering the victims of the slimeball's rip-off. Whatever, the darkness within slipped out of its hole and took over for a little while.

Gia slipped an arm around him and pulled him closer. One of her breasts rested on the bruise. She nuzzled against his neck.

"When are you going to quit this?" she said.

Jack took a deep breath and felt a sharp stab of pain. He figured the bullet impact had caused a minor separation in his rib cartilage. Not the first time for him, probably not the last.

"Oh, we're not going to get into that now, are we?" he said softly, smoothing her soft blond hair.

"It's just that I get so scared when I think about people shooting at you."

"It's not an everyday occurrence. Most of my fix-ups are strictly hands-off affairs."

"But there's always the potential for things to go wrong. I mean, you're not exactly dealing with upstanding citizens in your line of work."

"You've got a point there."

Maybe if he kept agreeing, she'd let it drop.

"I know I owe Repairman Jack, but—"

"You don't owe him anything."

"Yes, I do. Vicky is alive because of him. That crazy Indian killed Grace and Nellie, and if you had been anybody else, he would have fed Vicky to those *things* . . ."

She shuddered and pressed against him.

Jack closed his eyes and remembered the nightmare . . . Kusum Bahkti had traveled from Bengal to honor a vow of vengeance against the Westphalen family stemming from an atrocity during the Raj. With her aunts Grace and Nellie gone, Vicky was the last of the Westphalen line.

Kusum had come *this* close to fulfilling his vow.

"I think ol' RP owes Gia an equal debt. If you hadn't come back here that night . . ."

Jack had been cut up pretty bad saving Vicky. He'd lost a lot of blood, and was too weak to cross the room to the phone. If Gia hadn't come looking for him and taken him over to Doc Hargus . . .

"I'd say we're even," he said.

He felt Gia shake her head against his shoulder.

"No. Anybody off the street could have found you and got you to a hospital. But saving Vicky . . . if you had been a carpenter or a copywriter, or even a cop, anyone but who you are . . . she'd be gone. And that's why I feel like such a hypocrite when I tell you to hang up your Repairman Jack suit—"

"Hey, now. You make me sound like Batman."

"Okay, you're not into spandex, but deep down inside, that's who you are, aren't you?"

"A crime fighter? Gia, you're one of the few people I know who's *not* some sort of criminal. I run a business, Gia. A *business*. I charge for my services."

"You didn't charge for last night."

"And see what I get for it! One freebie, and suddenly I'm Batman. Or that do-gooder who used to be on TV—"The Equalizer." That's why I never do freebies. Once the word got out, *everybody* would expect me to put my butt on the line simply because they need me."

Gia raised her head and grinned at him. "Oh, yeah. You're so tough."

Jack shrugged. "Money talks, bullshit walks."

"And you're only in it for the money."

"If they've got the dime, I've got the time."

Her grin broadened. "And you don't get emotionally involved."

Jack fought a responding smile. "If you don't stay cool, you act like a fool."

Gia placed her palm over the bruise on his chest. "One more rhyme and I push the purple button—hard."

He tried to roll away but she had him. "Okay. If you stop, I'll stop."

"Deal. But admit it: You do get emotionally involved."

"I try not to. It's dangerous."

"That's my point. You identify with everybody you take on as a client."

" 'Customer,' please. Lawyers and accountants have clients. I have customers."

"All right. Customers. My point is, you don't hire out to just anyone who happens to have the necessary cash."

"I go case by case." Jack was growing uncomfortable. He wanted off the subject. "I mean, I've got to feel I can do the job, otherwise we're both wasting time. I'm just a small businessman, Gia."

She groaned and flopped onto her back. "A small businessman who has no social security number, dozens of last names, and never pays taxes."

"I pay sales tax . . . sometimes."

"Face it, Jack, this Repairman Jack stuff gives you a rush, and you're hooked on it."

Jack didn't like to think of himself as hooked on adrenaline, but maybe it was true. He had to admit he'd had a bodacious buzz after leaving the creep and the stolen toys in front of the Center last night. He'd been completely unaware of how much he was hurting until he got home.

"Maybe I am, and maybe I'm not. But let's just say I retire—hang up the 'Repairman Jack suit,' as you so eloquently put it—what then?"

"Then we begin a real life together."

Jack sighed. A life together with Gia and Vicky . . . now *that* was tempting.

And so damn strange. Back in his twenties he'd never imagined himself married or living in any traditional arrangement. And being a father? Him? No way.

But becoming involved with Gia and falling for Vicky had changed all that. He wanted them around, and wanted to be around *them*, all the time.

If only it were that simple.

"You mean, get married?"

"Yes, I mean get married. Is that so awful?"

"Not the ceremony. And certainly not the commitment. But going to a municipal building and registering my name somewhere . . ." He faked a minor seizure. "Aaaaargh!"

"You'll use one of your fake identities—we'll pick one with a name that sounds nice following Gia and Vicky—and that'll be it. Easy."

"Couldn't we just live together?" Jack said, though he already knew the answer. But at least they were off the subject of his work.

"Sure. Soon as Vicky's grown up and moved out and married and on her own. Until then, Vicky's mom doesn't shack up with anyone—not even that man Jack who Vicky and her mom love so much."

Gia had been a Manhattanite and an artist for many years now, and seemed every bit as urbane as the next, but every so often the Iowa farm girl nestling deep within her surfaced to call the shots.

Which was okay with Jack. That Iowa farm girl was part of her appeal, part of what made her Gia.

But marriage wasn't the problem. Repairman Jack was the real barrier to going public with the relationship. For as soon as Jack moved in with Gia and Vicky—or vice versa—he became vulnerable. He tended to make enemies in his line of work. He tried to keep his face out of his fixes, but a certain amount of exposure was unavoidable. A fair number of people with a grudge knew what he looked like. Every so often one of them found out where he lived. What followed was usually unpleasant. But because Jack lived alone, because he was very circumspect about appearing in public with anyone he cared about, the grudge guys had to deal directly with him. Fine. He could handle that. And he did. Most of them were never seen again.

But if Gia and Vicky were linked to him, they'd become targets.

And Jack had no idea how he'd handle that.

If one of them ever suffered because of him . . .

"Okay," he said. "I retire and we get married. Then what?"

"Life."

"Easy for you to say. You go on designing book covers and doing your paintings, but what about me? What do I do in the straight world? I don't know anything else."

Gia rose up on one elbow and gave him one of her intent looks.

"That's because you've never tried anything else. Jack, you're a bright, inventive, intelligent man with an agile body. You can do anything you want."

But I want to do what I'm doing now, he thought.

"But what about the toy theft?" he said. "If I were retired and we were married, what would you have done?" He poked her playfully. "Huh? Huh? What would you have done?"

"I'd have asked you to go get them back."

He stared at her. Not a hint of guile, no sign that she was joking. She meant it.

"Am I the only one in this room who detects just a tiny bit of inconsistency here?"

"Nope," she said. "I'm a hypocrite and I freely admit it. The only time I want you to be Repairman Jack is for me."

Jack was speechless. What did he say to that?

During the silence, a low, guttural laugh filtered in from the front room. Jack felt the gooseflesh rise on Gia's arm.

"My, God, Jack. Did you hear that?"

"Just the TV. That's our old friend Dwight."

Dracula was running in the ongoing Dwight Frye Festival. Jack could picture the scene playing now, one of his all-time favorites: The ship transporting the count to England has washed ashore, and the only man alive is Renfield, looking up from the bottom of the hold, his eyes alive with madness, his insane laugh echoing through the ship.

"It's creepy."

"You got that right. Ol' Dwight did such a great job as Renfield that he was typecast for the rest of his career. Whenever they needed a character whose belt didn't go through all the loops they called Dwight Frye."

Gia glanced at the clock. "God, look at the time. I want to get some Christmas shopping in before we have to pick up Vicky."

"I don't think we have time to go to Westchester," he said.

"Very true. So we're going to FAO Schwartz."

Jack groaned.

"Stop complaining." She kissed him, then rolled out of bed and headed toward the bathroom. "I'm going to take a quick shower, then we're off."

He watched her walk across the room. He loved the sight of her naked—her small, firm breasts, her long legs, the pale pubic patch that proved she was a natural blonde.

Jack wondered what she'd look like pregnant. Probably fabulous.

Strangely enough, he'd been thinking about babies lately. Ever since he'd seen Gia holding that AIDS infant at the Center on Friday. The light in her eyes . . . that nurturing look. Gia was a natural nurturer. Jack knew that from seeing her with Vicky. Physically, Gia was a single parent, but she gave more to Vicky than any half dozen other parents put together.

He heard the bathroom door close and listened to the *shoosh* of the water in the pipes as she turned on the shower.

He closed his eyes and pictured Gia holding another child . . . *their* child. He thought of growing old with Gia and Vicky and a new little person, the fusion of Gia and himself, and the vision lit a little sun inside him.

But to get to that place he'd have to change his life.

Jack got out of bed and went to the bottom drawer of the old oak dresser. He dug through the various wigs, mustaches, eyeglasses, nostril dilators, and other paraphernalia until he found the full beard. He pulled it from its Ziploc and checked it out. Getting kind of ratty-looking. He'd have to get another soon.

He held it up to his face and looked in the mirror.

Not great, but along with a change in the way he combed his hair—moving the part more to the center—it gave his normally rectangular face an oval shape, and hid enough of his features so that no one would recognize him.

Look at you, he thought. You have to wear a beard to go Christmas shopping in midtown. Always looking over your shoulder. What kind of life is that?

If he retired, he could grow his own beard and go wherever he wanted—Gia on one arm and Vicky on the other—and not give a damn who saw them.

Retire . . .

Well, why not? Maybe it was time. He'd had enough close calls for a dozen lifetimes, but never anything permanently damaging. He liked to credit that to his attention to detail, but maybe it was just luck. What was he going to do—wait until he wound up dead or crippled? What was the point of pushing the odds?

Don't be a jerk, a voice said. Quit while you're ahead.

As usual, the voice was right.

As usual, Jack wasn't going to take its advice.

Not yet, anyway.

MONDAY

1

Alicia stood uncertainly outside the bar, squinting in the late-morning glare as she peered through the streaked front window to see what it was like inside.

Was this it? Jack had told her the place was called "Julio's," and that was what the sign over the door said, but it looked so seedy. She'd expected some trendy Upper West Side watering hole, but the grubby-looking men pushing in and out of the door most definitely were *not* yuppies.

Alicia had wanted Jack to drop by her office as he had before, but he'd told her this time she'd have to come to *his* office. Okay. Fair enough. But who had an office in a workingman's bar?

And couldn't the owner maybe clean the front window once in a while? It was so smeared she could barely see through it. And what little she saw of the dark interior wasn't encouraging.

Mostly she saw plants—spider plants, asparagus ferns, wandering Jews—but they were all dead. Worse than dead. Way beyond dead. What few leaves still adhered to the stems were brown and curled and covered with a thick layer of dust. What was this—a mummy's idea of a fern bar?

All was dark as interstellar space beyond the desiccated plants. Not even stars glowing.

But this was the address he'd given her, and it *was* called Julio's . . .

Alicia stepped back and scanned the street. She'd taken a cab up so she hadn't had much opportunity to see if that gray sedan was following her again. She didn't see it on the street now. Maybe it was all in her mind.

And maybe she shouldn't even bother with this Jack. She didn't want to go through another explanation of the whole situation, tiptoeing among the details she could reveal and the ones she couldn't. And then face the questions . . . the inevitable questions.

Because to someone who didn't know what she knew, her actions appeared completely irrational. Thomas was the only other living person who had all the facts, and even he thought she was crazy.

She couldn't answer those questions. And so she had to settle for people thinking she was nuts.

Did she want to add Just Jack to that list?

Not really. But she had nowhere else to turn right now, and she had a feeling Just Jack was the sort who struck straight to the heart of a problem. She'd obtained a medical report on the thief who'd stolen the toys. The cops hadn't been exaggerating. He'd been *thoroughly* worked over . . . numerous fractures, countless contusions. Which told her that Just Jack was not adverse to the judicious application of force.

And after seeing what had happened to Leo Weinstein, that might be just what she needed.

But the possibility that she might be setting him up to end like poor Leo made her hesitate.

She'd looked for other options, but Just Jack seemed the best right now. She was sick to death of anything related to the will and the house, and yesterday she'd flashed on a way to clean up the whole mess. But it was not something a lawyer could handle. She was pretty sure it might be in Jack's line of work.

But did she have the guts to ask him?

Taking a deep breath, Alicia settled her nerves, pulled on the door handle, and stepped inside.

As she waited for her eyes to adjust, she heard the buzz of conversation wither and die . . . just like the plants in the window.

Slowly, the room came into focus. First, the TV screen, playing what looked like ESPN or one of its clones, then the neon beer signs—Bud, Rolling Rock, and Miller only, no Bass Ale or Zima here—glowing behind the bar, reflecting off the bottles lined up like wishes on the mirrored shelves. A sign over the bar, dark letters carved into light wood . . . FREE BEER TOMORROW . . .

And then the patrons, half a dozen grizzled men leaning against the bar, beers and boilermakers before them, all turned her way, staring.

What was this? A gay bar? Never seen a woman in here before?

"You here to see Jack, right?"

Alicia looked down at the short, heavily muscled Hispanic who'd materialized out of the dark. He had a pencil-line mustache and black, wavy, slicked-back hair. His voice was low, his dark eyes bright and active.

"Um, yes. He'd said he was going to be—"

"He's in the back. I'm Julio. Follow me."

Relieved, she followed the swaggering Julio past the bar and into the deeper shadows beyond. Conversation began to flow again as soon as she moved away. Once among the rear tables, she made out a form seated against the far wall. As the figure rose, she recognized Jack.

He extended his hand. "Good to see you again, Doctor."

Alicia's throat tightened as she thought of seeing that toy room full again yesterday. She clasped his hand between both of hers and held it.

"I don't know how to thank you," she said. "How to even *begin* to thank you for returning those gifts."

"No thanks necessary. I was hired to do a job, and I did it."

Somehow Alicia doubted that. No matter how offhanded his tone, she'd seen his eyes on Friday, and she knew what he'd done to that thief. Did a man simply "hired to do a job" wreak that kind of havoc?

He offered her coffee, which she refused. Julio refilled Jack's chipped white mug, then left them alone.

"Was everything there?" Jack said, sipping his black coffee.

Again, she noticed his long thumbnails. Maybe she'd ask him later why he didn't trim them short like the rest.

"As far as we can tell, yes. The staff is simply delirious with joy. They're calling it a Christmas miracle. So are the papers."

"I've seen them. Good. Then we can consider that matter closed. How's that little guy with the new haircut, by the way? The one who got sick right after I saw you?"

"Hector?" she said, surprised he remembered. "Hector's not doing too great."

"Aw, no. You're not going to tell me something awful, are you?"

He cares, she thought in wonder. He genuinely cares.

"His latest chest X ray shows pneumonia."

The lung infiltrates had formed a typical Pneumocystis pattern, and the gram stain had confirmed that as the infecting organism. No big surprise. *Pneumocystis carinii* loved AIDS patients.

Alicia had started him on IV Bactrim. He was supposed to have been on a prophylactic oral dose, but not all the foster parents were that religious about giving daily medication to seemingly well kids.

"He's going to be all right?"

"The medication he's on usually does the trick."

Usually.

"Anything I can do for him? Send him some balloons or a teddy bear or something?"

How about a mother or a father, or better yet, a new immune system? Alicia thought, but said, "That'd be great. He's got nothing. I'm sure he'll love anything."

"He's got nothing," Jack said, shaking his head and looking glum as he stared at his coffee.

When he looked up at her, Alicia knew he was struggling to find words to express the bleakness of the life he was trying to imagine.

Don't try to express it, she thought. You can't.

"I know," she told him.

He nodded. Then he sighed. "Your message said you had a personal matter you wanted to discuss."

Yes, she thought. Let's move on to something you *can* do something about.

"First, call me Alicia. And before we get down to business, I want to know about those dead plants in the window. What's the idea?"

Jack glanced over to the window. The dead stuff had been there so long he hardly noticed it anymore.

"Julio uses them as totems. To ward off evil spirits."

"You're kidding. What evil spirits?"

"The kind that order Chardonnay."

Her smile was crooked. "Oh, I get it. A macho bar . . . testosterone thick in the air."

Jack shrugged. "I can't speak for Julio. He likes a certain type of customer and tries to discourage others. But sometimes it backfires. Sometimes those plants actually attract the wrong type because they think the place is so 'authentic' . . . whatever that means. But let's get back to you."

She sighed, feeling the tension mount. *Here we go.*

"It's a long, complicated story, and I won't bother you with all the details. In a nutshell: A man named Ronald Clayton died in a plane crash two months ago and left every damn thing he owned to me."

"Who was he?"

"He fathered me."

"Your father? I'm sorry to hear—"

"Don't be. We shared some genes, and that was the extent of it. Any-way, when I got the call from the lawyer who's the executor of the estate,

I told him I wasn't interested in that man's belongings or anything connected to him. Then he told me that I was sole heir.

Across the table, Jack raised his eyebrows. "Not your mother?"

"She died twenty-some years ago—and *that* you can be sorry about, if you wish."

Alicia barely remembered her mother. If only she hadn't died . . . things would have been *so* different . . .

"Well, anyway, I was shocked. I hadn't spoken to him in a dozen years. Hadn't even thought about him." *Wouldn't allow myself.* "I told the executor I wanted nothing to do with the damn house and hung up on him."

Jack remained silent. Still waiting for the "problem" part, Alicia figured.

Don't worry, she thought. It's coming.

"Next thing I know, my half brother Thomas is on the phone, and he's—"

"Wait," said Jack. "*Half* brother?"

"Right. Older by four years."

"Which half—the mother or the father?"

"Ronald Clayton is his father."

Jack cocked his head. "And he was left out in the cold."

"Right. Not a dime."

"Any other halves floating around the Clayton family?"

"No. Just Thomas. He's enough, thanks. So Thomas is on the phone saying that if I don't want the house, can he have it. I tell him no. I say I've changed my mind. I *do* want it. I tell him I'm going to donate it to the AIDS Center for use as a satellite facility. So forget about it."

"Got along with your brother about as well as your father, I take it?"

"Worse, if that's possible. The next day Thomas is back on the phone offering me two million for the house."

Jack's eyebrow's jumped. "Where is this place?"

"Murray Hill."

He smiled. "No kidding. That might be cheap for Murray Hill."

"It's a three-story brownstone. Worth every penny."

"So far, I don't see why you think you need me. Take the money and run."

Now came the touchy part. Now he'd start wondering why. But Alicia had evaded the hard questions—the *impossible* questions—with poor Leo Weinstein, and she could evade them with Jack.

"But I didn't. I turned him down."

"You knew the price would go up."

"No way. But it did. Thomas came back and offered me four million. And I gave him the same answer. And then he told me he was tired of bidding against himself and that I should 'name a fucking price'—his words—and I hung up on him."

"Turned him down again . . . sort of like winning the lottery and not cashing in your ticket, isn't it?"

"Not exactly. You see, Thomas hardly has a dime to his name."

Jack leaned forward and stared at her. *Now* he looked interested.

"You know that for sure?"

"I suspected it. I mean, he's been in a low-level research job at ATT since he graduated college. Where would he get approval for a mortgage that size? So I checked him out: His credit rating is the pits, and he quit his job about the time he started calling me."

"So . . . a guy with no money and no job offers you four mil. I don't blame you for hanging up on him."

"No," Alicia said, "you don't understand. I think he does have the money—in cash."

"In *cash?*"

"That's what he offered me—said I can take it or he can donate it all to the charity of my choice. How do you explain that?"

"Either he's crazy or somebody's backing him."

"Exactly, but who? And why not approach me directly? Why go through Thomas?"

"Does it matter?" Jack said, leaning back again. "A valuable piece of real estate lands in your lap. You can either live in it or sell it. You don't need me, you need a tax attorney."

Alicia sensed him withdrawing, losing interest. She rushed forward with the rest of her story.

"But I *can't* live in it, and I can't sell it. When I turned him down, Thomas hired some high-priced attorneys to challenge the will. I can't take possession until this is resolved. They even got a court order to board up the place, so I can't even take a look around inside." *Not that I'd ever want to.*

"Why board it up?"

"Apparently it's been broken into since it's been empty. Thomas says he wants to protect what he expects to be *his* property once his challenge to the will is upheld. He's even hired a security firm to guard the property."

Jack smiled. "All this from a guy with no income. Your half brother is very resourceful."

"That's not the word I'd use for Thomas."

"Still, you don't need me—you need a lawyer."

Alicia bit her lip. No, she needed Jack for what she wanted. But how would he react when she asked?

Sometimes it's good to deviate from routine, Jack thought, trying to look interested. And sometimes it isn't.

This meeting never would have happened if he'd followed his usual MO. He always talked to prospective customers before setting up a face-to-face. That way he avoided the Dr. Claytons of the city—people with problems that could be remedied by more orthodox methods.

But because he'd already met Alicia, he'd set up the meeting without the usual preliminaries.

Not a complete waste of time, he thought, but pretty damn close. The only thing that saved it was the good doctor herself.

Something about Alicia Clayton intrigued him. He met lots of people with secrets. Virtually all of his customers were hiding something. He was used to not hearing the whole story on the first pass. And he'd become adept at spotting the holes. He couldn't tell what they'd skipped, but he knew when they were holding back.

Alicia Clayton was different. He couldn't get a read on her. Either she was hiding nothing, or she was so good at hiding that she could hide everything, even the fact that she was hiding something.

Jack chose the latter. Because looking at her sitting here across the table from him, he sensed that she had a good figure under that coat and bulky cable-knit sweater, but she was hiding it. In fact, she could have been a striking woman with those fine features and dark, dark hair. Attractive in a steely way. But she chose not to be. She chose to downplay her looks. Hide them.

Well, how she looked was her call. And she wasn't exactly in the glamour business.

Didn't pay to read too much into these things, he supposed.

But she was so utterly composed. Too composed. Almost . . . wooden.

What else was she hiding? This woman wasn't just locked down tight, she was hermetically sealed. And that took practice. Many years of practice.

All of which intrigued him. Who was this woman who seemed to want to hide *everything*?

But he knew he was unlikely to pop any of her seals this morning. So he was looking for a way to bring this little tête-à-tête to a close when she leaned forward.

"I *had* a lawyer," Alicia said. "Until Friday when he was murdered."

Jack smiled. Lawyers who did wills and such didn't get murdered. "You mean 'killed,' don't you?"

"No. I mean *murdered*. Can you think of a circumstance when a car bomb is anything *but* murder?"

Jack straightened in his seat. The story had been all over the radio and TV.

"That car explosion in Midtown?" he said. "He was *your* lawyer?"

Alicia nodded. "We were supposed to meet that morning. I guess someone didn't want him to make it."

Uh-oh. Did he detect a little paranoia here?

"What makes you think you're the reason he was killed? I read they found some cocaine in what was left of his glove compartment."

"I see lots of coke users," she said. Her face remained a mask, but Jack noticed her right hand clenching into a fist. "Most of the parents of my babies are drug abusers. Drugs are how they got the virus that they passed on to their kids. I didn't see any signs of that in Leo Weinstein."

She leaned back and seemed to relax—with an effort, Jack thought.

"Of, course, I could be wrong. But Leo's isn't the first violent death connected with this will."

Jack found himself leaning forward. "Another lawyer?"

Alicia shook her head. "No. When I came to the obvious conclusion that someone was bankrolling Thomas, I wanted to find out who. I hired a private investigator—you know, to follow him, find out who he meets with, the TV detective kind of stuff. I didn't know what I was going to do with the information, but all this mystery and subterfuge was bugging me. I mean, if someone wants that man's house so badly, why not approach me directly? Why go through Thomas?"

"And what did you learn?"

"Nothing." Her steel-gray eyes bore into him. "One night, about two weeks after I hired him, the investigator was killed while crossing East Seventy-fifth Street. Hit-and-run."

Jack drummed his fingers on the table's ringed surface. Okay, so maybe she's not paranoid. Could be coincidence, but if you hire two people to look into a problem and both of them wind up dead, who can blame you if you suspect a connection?

Obviously someone who wished to be anonymous wanted the Clayton house. Wanted it bad. They'd made a "name-your-price" offer, and when that was turned down, they went to court.

But it was one hell of a leap from there to say that they were killing anyone who stood in their way. Besides . . .

"Okay. Two people you hired to help you are dead. Maybe there's a connection. But think about it: If someone is eliminating people who get between them and this house, why haven't they removed the biggest stumbling block—you?"

"Don't think that hasn't kept me up nights since Friday. I don't know anything about the will. I didn't attend the reading. And when I hired Leo—the attorney who was murdered—I simply had a copy sent from the executor's office to his. So I've never seen the damn thing. But that's going to change. I'm going to get a copy for myself and see what the terms are. I do remember Leo saying something about the will being 'rather unusual.' "

A question hit him. "Did you ever live there? In the house?"

She didn't move, but Jack had a feeling that Alicia had receded to the other side of Julio's.

"Till I was eighteen. Why?"

He shrugged. "Just curious. I still don't know what you want me to do. I don't do bodyguard work, so—"

"I want you to burn the place down."

Jack stared at her, trying to hide his shock. Not at the request itself— lots of people had come to him over the years looking for a torch job— but at the unexpectedness of it. He hadn't seen this one coming.

He made a show of cleaning out one of his ears. "I'm sorry. I thought you just said you wanted to burn down a house for which you've already been offered four million dollars."

"I did."

"Can I ask you why?"

"No."

"You're going to have to give me some kind of explanation."

Alicia shifted in her seat. "Why should you care?"

"It's the way I work."

She sighed. "All right. Maybe I'm just tired. I may be a doctor, but I don't make a lot of money. I could be making more in private practice, but the Center is what I want to do. Whatever I've managed to save after living expenses and paying back my education loans—and believe me, I've got six figures worth of those—went to retainers for the investigator and the lawyer. I'm just about tapped out, Jack. I don't want to start all over again with a new lawyer. And frankly, I'm a little scared. I just want this over with."

Scared? Jack had a hard time buying this woman as scared. He had a feeling she didn't run from anything.

"But the solution to all your financial problems can be solved by a simple telephone call to your brother."

"*Half* brother. But I don't want to sell to Thomas. And he's preventing me from selling to anyone else."

Jack was baffled. "But if, as you say, you don't want the house and don't care about it, why not sell it to him?"

Alicia's eyes were suddenly ablaze as she spoke through her teeth.

"Because . . . *he* . . . wants it!"

And just as suddenly the fire was gone.

"And you don't get any explanation for that," she said evenly.

Jack leaned back and studied her. Where did he go from here? His instincts told him that here was a lady with a few buttons missing from her remote control, that he should make a beeline for the door and not look back.

Good advice. She'd already told him she was almost tapped out, so no way she could pay his fee. That meant there was nothing in this for him but trouble.

Easy to get out of it. Just tell her arson wasn't his thing—the truth— and that would be that.

So why wasn't he saying it? Why hadn't he said it when she'd first mentioned torching her dead father's house?

Because . . .

Truth was, he didn't have a good *because*, other than the fact that he was intrigued by Alicia and fascinated with the scenario she'd laid out. This lady was turning down a fortune to keep a house that had belonged to a man she wouldn't call "father" out of the hands of a half brother she hated. What was it with the place? Had something happened to her there?

Things were slow and Jack's curiosity was piqued.

"Okay. Here's what I can do. I can't promise you anything now. The best I can do is tell you I'll think about it. I'll have to check out a few things before I decide."

"What's to decide?" she said, a note of irritation creeping into her voice. Either you will or you won't. You didn't have to check out anything with the toys."

"That was a different story. Getting something back is a little bit different from burning something to the ground, don't you think? You're talking about a major fire in midtown Manhattan."

Jack watched her face as she paused. Obviously she thought he'd simply negotiate a fee and go do the job. But her face gave nothing away . . . until she sort of smiled. *Sort of* because it didn't quite make it to her eyes.

"Oh, I get it," she said finally. "You need to check *me* out."

"That's part of it. My gut says to believe you, but I've had some truly excellent storytellers try to hire me from time to time in the past."

She nodded. "For all you know, the house belongs to an ex-lover who'd two-timed me and I'm looking to get even."

"Wouldn't be the first time."

She gathered up her bag and rose. "Well, I can tell you this, Mr. Just Jack," she said coolly, "I don't have a lover. And I don't lie. You do what 'research' you feel you must and get back to me if and when you're satisfied. In the meantime, I'll be researching other options." Another sort of smile as she turned. "Thanks for meeting with me."

Jack whistled softly through his teeth as he watched her go. That lady was all steel inside.

2

Alicia walked toward Columbus Avenue, hunting a cab. Rush hour was over, lunchtime was still an hour or so off, and if Upper West Side traffic had a lull, this was it. A few shoppers were out, but they were walking. Not much business for cabs here right now.

She saw one speed by, but it was occupied. She jumped as it screeched to a halt behind a white car that had stopped in the middle of the street. The cabbie sat on his horn until the white car pulled away.

She smiled: the music of the city . . .

But the smile faded as she thought about what Jack had said.

I'll have to check out a few things before I decide. . . .

She had a bad feeling Jack had already made up his mind, and he wasn't interested.

Damn. She'd been counting on him.

She'd have to look elsewhere for an arsonist. The Yellow Pages wouldn't do. Maybe she could get a line on one through the progenitors of her little charges at the Center—not exactly paragons of society—but she would have preferred Jack. He'd proved that he could deliver. And even if he was stringing her along a little now so he could let her down easy later, she trusted him.

She scanned the streets. No gray sedan. Good. As she reached Columbus Avenue, she saw a taxi round the next corner and start toward her. She raised her hand to flag it, then noticed its OFF DUTY sign was lit.

Come on! She wanted to make a quick stop at the hospital and take another look at Hector before she became mired in the Center.

She pulled her coat closer around her against the chill. Maybe she should try calling for a cab. She opened her shoulder bag and hunted through its jumbled contents. Half her life seemed to be in here. Not much money, but her stethoscope, diagnostic kit, beeper, keys, and somewhere among the old charge card receipts in the bottom, her cell phone.

As she rummaged, she glanced back the way she had come—still looking for that damn gray sedan—and noticed three men huddled around the door of a shiny red sports car parked on Julio's block about fifty feet from where she stood. A motley crew—a pierced-up white guy, a black, and a Hispanic—the two darker ones were shielding the white from view as he shoved a thin flat piece of metal into the car's window slot and worked it up and down.

Alicia didn't know much about cars but had no doubt these three were up to no good: looking to steal either the radio or the air bag, or maybe the whole car. She glanced around to see if anyone was coming, but at the moment the sidewalk was deserted.

Maybe it would be safer to wait for a cab farther down the street. She'd call 911 on her cell phone once she was safely on her way.

But as she turned to slip away, she spotted Jack leaving Julio's. He was ambling in her direction, but if he'd noticed her, he gave no sign. His eyes were fixed on the men trying to break into the car. Alicia noticed a change in his gait as he approached them . . . he was moving like a cat now.

He's not really going to get involved in this, is he? she thought. *He's smarter than that, I hope.*

But sure enough, Jack sidled up to the three men and stood before the two shielders, hands in his pockets, rocking on his heels as if watching them change a tire.

She thought she heard him say, "Hey, guys, whatcha doin'?"

Curiosity got the better of Alicia's common sense. Fascinated, she edged closer for a better look.

The black guy—he had a fade haircut and looked like he worked out a lot—looked at Jack as if he couldn't believe somebody was stupid enough to ask him that.

"What's it look like we're doin'?" He pointed to the white guy. "Our friend here locked himself out of his car and we're helpin' him out, okay? That all right wichoo?"

"Can I watch?" Jack said. His posture was loose and slouched; his voice sounded high and nerdy.

"No. Move on."

"Why not?"

"Because like I'm gettin' my period and I'm real cranky, and you hangin' aroun' is disturbin' our concentration. So just haul your nosy white ass on outta here."

"But I've never seen anybody use a Slim Jim before," Jack said. "I mean, it's really convenient that one of you happened to have one. You know, so you could help him out and all. I didn't think they were legal."

Christ, Alicia thought as she saw the three car thieves freeze. Is he out of his mind?

"Hey, yo," said the white guy, straightening and taking a step toward Jack. He wore a studded black leather jacket and ultra-short blond hair. He sported rings in both ears, his upper lip, and his right eyebrow. "You some sorta fuckin' cop or somethin'?"

"Who me?" Jack said, smiling timidly. "Oh, no. Not me. I'm no cop. But that just happens to be my friend Julio's car. And none of you guys is Julio. So why don't you find yourselves another car to boost."

Now it was the Hispanic's turn. He whipped the Slim Jim out of the window well and waved it in Jack's face.

"Ay, you crazy, meng? This is my man's car, and we're helping him. Now you get outta here 'fore I shove this down your t'roat and pull your asshole outta your mouth!"

They all seemed to think that was pretty funny. As they laughed and low-fived each other, Alicia noticed Jack's left hand ease from his pocket.

Don't do it, she wanted to shout. It's three against one. You haven't got a chance.

But as she watched Jack, she wondered about that. She sensed something primal and electric radiating from him. He'd been so laid back, so low-key in her office and back at the bar a moment ago, but now . . . now he was a different man. He seemed to vibrate with intensity, with fire, as if his daily existence was merely a series of interludes he had to endure until he was allowed a moment like this.

"And after he's finished," the white guy said, taking the metal piece from the Hispanic and holding it under Jack's nose, "*I'm* gonna come in the back door and yank out your tonsils!"

Tension coiled through the air, tightening. Alicia had heard that peo-

ple who survived lightning strikes spoke of a strange, hair-raising—
literally—sensation just before the strike. Alicia felt that now, as if the
air molecules were ionizing and polarizing in anticipation . . .

"You have such nice blue eyes," Jack said over the new burst of
laughter. "Can I have one?"

Before anyone could react or reply, Jack's hand darted up to the
white's face. The move was so fast, so unexpected, that Alicia couldn't
follow it. All she knew was that one second Jack's hand was darting
through the air, and an instant later the white guy was staggering back,
screaming. He dropped the Slim Jim and clawed at his face, almost
knocking over his black buddy as he turned in a wild circle.

Alicia gasped and backed away as she caught a glimpse of bright
crimson flowing down his left cheek before his hands covered it.

Christ in heaven, what did he do?

"What the fuck—?" said the black guy, his head pivoting between
Jack and his buddy who had dropped to his knees now and was pawing
at his eye with bright red fingers and screaming, screaming.

The Hispanic crouched to look at his buddy. "Joey! What he do?"

"My eye! Oh, shit, my *eye!*"

"I like eyes," Jack said in a strange, garbled tone. His own eyes had
a strange, unfocused look, and Alicia noticed with a start that his mouth
was smeared with red. "Blue eyes are especially delicious."

And then he opened his mouth to reveal a bloody eye clenched between his front teeth.

Alicia's stomach lurched. She'd seen traumatic horrors beyond most
people's wildest nightmares on her ER moonlighting stints during her
residencies, but never anything like this. She was sure the gaping shock
on the faces of the black and the Hispanic mirrored her own. She wanted
to turn away but couldn't. She had to keep watching.

As a child, she'd once had the misfortune of being in a pet shop when
it was feeding time for the snakes. She'd been passing the cage of a large
garter snake swallowing a frog headfirst. She'd been repulsed, especially
since the frog's legs were still kicking, but she'd stood rooted to the spot
until the poor frog was gone from view.

That was how she felt now. Only this time the frog was eating the
snakes.

No . . . not eating.

Jack spit out the eyeball. Alicia felt her gorge rise as it splatted against
the side window of the car. The bloody, gelatinous mass stuck there for
a heartbeat or two, then began a slow slide down the glass, leaving a
glistening red trail.

Joey's screams devolved to moans as his two buddies watched the misshapen eye come to rest at the bottom of the window.

"But brown eyes are tasty too," Jack said with a bloody grin as he took a step toward them.

Both men jumped back, the Hispanic almost knocking over the black in his haste to get out of Jack's reach.

"I'm outta here, meng!" he said as he backed away.

"Yo, Ric! What about Joey!"

"Fuck him!"

The black tried to grab him, but Ric slipped from reach and back-pedaled down the sidewalk.

"That guy's fuckin' *crazy*!"

Jack took another step toward the black. "You have such *big* brown eyes."

That did it. The black guy turned and hurried to catch up with Ric.

"Yo, Joey," he said to his fallen buddy. "Catch you later."

But Joey didn't seem to hear. He was bent far over, his head almost on the pavement, wiping at his face.

Jack watched them go, then pumped his fist toward the car.

"*Yes!*"

As Jack spat red into the gutter and wiped his mouth on his sleeve, Alicia began backing away. Slowly. She didn't want to attract Jack's attention. What had she got herself into? She was glad she hadn't hired him to burn the house. She didn't care if he'd found the stolen toys, she wanted nothing more to do with this maniac.

But then Jack turned and spotted her.

"Did you see that?" he said with a bloody grin. "It worked! Worked like a charm!"

And then his grin faded. Maybe he'd seen her expression. Alicia was trying to hide the fear and revulsion roiling within, but she doubted she was doing very well.

"Hey, wait!" he said. "You don't really think—"

He started toward her. Alicia turned to run but felt a hand close about her upper arm after two steps.

"No, please," she said as he pulled her to a stop. "Let me go! Let me go or I'll scream!"

"Just give me a second," he said. "I just want you to look at something, then you can go. Okay?"

He sounded so reasonable, so . . . sane. The nerdy voice was gone. She glanced over her shoulder at him. That vacant look from a moment ago was gone too.

But his mouth was still smeared with red.

"Look," he said, and extended his free hand toward her.

Hesitantly, Alicia glanced down.

Eyes . . . two eyes . . . one brown, one blue . . . soft, glistening, sticky looking, . . . rested in his palm.

She recoiled at first, ready to scream, then noticed the lack of blood. A closer look and she realized . . .

"They're fake."

"Of course they are," Jack said. "You can buy them in any of the funkier novelty shops in the Village."

Alicia glanced over Jack's shoulder at Joey who was sitting up now, but still hunched over, cupping a hand over his eye.

"But what did you do to *him*?"

Jack showed her a little plastic squeeze bottle filled with red liquid. "Just a little squirt with this. It's Hollywood blood mixed with ten percent capsicum—you know, that pepper extract they use in those defense sprays? I fill the eyeballs with non-spicy fake blood so when I bite down on them I get red in my mouth. Excuse me." He turned away and spat more red into the gutter. "Looks real and tastes awful."

"Looks real is right. I could have sworn—"

Jack's eyes were bright as he looked at her. "Really? You bought it too? A doctor and all? That's great! I can't tell you how long I've been waiting for a chance to try this out."

"For a minute I thought you were going to start a fight with them."

"One against three?" He shook his head. "That's movie stuff. You might get away with it if you take them by surprise and you've got a weapon of some sort. But most times, you try something like that in real life, you get your face rearranged. I'm not into pain. And this is *so* much neater."

He stepped over to the car and retrieved the faux-bloody faux eye from the window.

"It worked," he said, more to himself than to her. "It was perfect."

He's like a little boy, she thought. A little boy who made something—a wood block car, or a slingshot, maybe—and is delighted to find that it really works.

She watched him grab the ring in Joey's eyebrow and haul him to his feet.

"Come on, Joey," he said, turning him toward Alicia. "I don't think the lady really believes me. Show her your eye."

"I believe you," she said.

But Jack didn't seem to be listening. "Come on, Joey. Open up and show her both baby blues."

Joey's red-smeared left eyelids parted to reveal a teary, very irritated but intact eye.

"Good boy," Jack said, then turned Joey and pushed him off in the direction his friends had taken. "Go find your buddies."

Jack watched Joey for a moment as he stumbled away, then he turned to Alicia.

"I'll be in touch."

He waved, then turned and walked off.

Alicia stared after him. She hoped he decided to help her out. This was someone she wanted in her corner.

3

"*There* you are!"

Sam Baker spoke aloud in the otherwise empty car as he caught sight of the Clayton babe. For a few bad moments there he'd thought he'd lost her.

He settled back in the driver seat and loosened his grip on the wheel. His shoulders ached. He hadn't realized how tense he'd been since that cop had told him to move his car.

Relax, he told himself. We're back on track now.

He'd followed her to the Upper West Side from the AIDS center, and had watched her go into that dive called Julio's. He'd found a spot with a good view of the door and had settled in to watch.

Well, he'd been sitting there only a few minutes, just starting to memorize the license plates around him, when this cop came along. Seemed Baker's vantage point came with a fire hydrant attached to it. And though Baker had tried to explain that he was just waiting for someone and would keep the motor running, the cop didn't care.

"Drive it away or it gets towed away."

Not much of a choice.

So he'd pulled out and rolled down the street, looking for an empty legal spot. Fat chance. He would have loved to step into that bar and have a quick beer while he checked out who she was meeting, but he couldn't risk getting towed. So he'd kept moving, kept circling the block, waiting for her to come out.

But then when he finally did spot her coming though the door, he was already past the bar. And when he stopped and blocked the street, some bastard cab started honking like he was coming from a wedding. Baker had been driving this rented white Plymouth for two days now. After he'd seen the Clayton babe staring his way on Friday, he figured she might have made the gray Buick. He didn't want to draw any attention to this one, so he'd raced into another circle of the block, which turned into an agonizing crawl.

But now everything was cool. He didn't know what she'd been doing since he'd scooted out of sight, but who cared? She was just about where he'd left her.

The cell phone rang. Baker could guess who that was—the Arab had been on his case something fierce since the girl's lawyer exploded.

"Yeah?"

"You are with the woman?"

"Like stink on shit."

"Pardon?"

"She's uptown. Flagging down a cab as we speak."

"Where has she been? Meeting another lawyer?"

"She was in a bar."

"In a bar? Does she appear inebriated?"

"You mean drunk?" Really weird the way this guy talked. Arab to the bone but he spoke English like a Brit. "No. Tell you the truth, I don't think it has anything to do with what we're interested in. Probably meeting a boyfriend or something."

"She does not *have* a boyfriend."

Baker watched the Clayton babe's loose skirt tighten across her butt as she bent to get into the cab. Nice ass.

Hard to believe she was completely unattached. She wasn't bad-looking. At least what he'd been able to see of her. A little makeup, a tight skirt, she could be a real looker. Instead . . .

Maybe she was a lez. Nothing wrong with that. He could get off on a lez. He figured their only problem was they hadn't met the right man yet.

"If you say so," Baker said.

"And you have no idea who she was meeting."

"Didn't get a chance to find out. But I don't think she met a lawyer in that dump." Baker almost added, *But you never know*, but decided against it.

He hoped to hell she hadn't.

"You are not paid to think. I do not like what happens when you try to think."

Here we go, he thought. But the Arab didn't push it.

"Where is she headed?" Muhallal said.

"On her way back downtown. I'm right behind her."

"Good. Follow her and do nothing else."

Baker cut the connection and slammed his hand against the steering wheel. He thought about the wad of cash waiting in escrow for him, and he kept it in mind as he drove. A big fucking payoff, and he deserved every fucking penny of it for all the shit he was taking.

4

Yoshio Takita finished off the second burrito as he followed Sam Baker's car. He'd picked them up earlier from someplace called Burritoville. He'd never heard of the chain, but was glad he'd tried it. He smacked his lips. These had been called "Phoenix Rising" burritos. He *loved* them. In fact, he'd yet to meet an American fast food he didn't like. And it was all so cheap over here. Back home in Tokyo it cost a small fortune to eat at one of the American chains that dotted the city.

He worried about getting fat, but his metabolism seemed to chew up the calories as fast as he shoved them in. That was good. It wouldn't do to develop a potbelly in his line of work, not at age thirty.

He wiped his hands and his mouth with the napkin, then settled both hands on the wheel. Had to be watchful here. Not for Baker—the man was a soldier for hire, not an operative; his tailing skills were crude at best, and he hadn't the slightest idea he himself was being followed. No, the problem was getting left behind at a light. If Yoshio were tailing only one of them, the task would be fairly easy. But tailing Baker as he tailed the woman, that tended to stretch the chain too far for comfort.

But what Baker lacked in grace and style, he more than made up for in ruthlessness. Yoshio had learned that last week when he followed him out to that attorney's house on Long Island. He'd seen Baker tampering with the man's car, but had assumed he was installing either a tracer or a bug. If he'd realized that Baker was planting a bomb, he'd have called the attorney to warn him.

Enough people had died already.

According to Yoshio's employer, Kaze Group in Tokyo, 247 people were already dead because of something Ronald Clayton knew or had discovered. Yoshio had witnessed the death of one other a few weeks ago. And last Friday, the death of Leo Weinstein raised the grand total to 249.

Apparently the board of Kaze Group knew no more than Yoshio. Or at least they pretended not to. They told him they did not know why Ronald Clayton and his house were so important to this Arab Kemel Muhallal; but if it was worth the lives of so many innocent people, then certainly it was worth their effort to look into it.

They knew more than that, he was sure. Although nominally just a simple holding company, Kaze Group was more powerful than the largest *keiretsu*. It had global reach. But obviously they didn't know all they wished to know.

And so the board had called upon Yoshio, as they tended to do when they had a problem that needed to be handled with discretion, and sent him to America to learn more for them. It helped that English was one of the four languages he spoke fluently. His assignment was to be their eyes and ears here. They had secured a set of diplomatic license plates to afford him more latitude with the city's traffic and parking regulations. He was to watch, to listen, and to report back to them.

They had sent him alone. He had no backup here now, but should the need arise, help could arrive within hours.

So far he had learned nothing knew. But Kaze Group was patient. Always it took the long view. He would stay here as long as they wished him to.

Gladly. The food was wonderful. He glanced at his dashboard clock. Soon it would be lunchtime. He could hardly wait.

5

Jack sat in the front window on the second floor of Pinky's Drive-in and watched Seventh Avenue directly below. "Jingle Bell Rock" wafted from the speakers set among the hubcaps on the wall as he sipped a Snapple peach iced tea from the bottle and scanned the mob below.

And a mob it was. Christmas shoppers, school trips, parents with their bundled-up kids waddling behind them like chubby ducklings, all streaming onto the already congested streets from Penn Station, heading for Macy's, FAO Schwartz, the Warner and Disney stores, the Christmas show at Radio City Music Hall. And this was only a Monday. Wait till Wednesday—matinee day.

The crowds brought out the flyer guys in force, standing like starter jacket-wrapped stones in the flow, handing out party-colored sheets offering everything from a dollar off a fried chicken special, to a Special Overstock Sale, to Live Girls—Nude! Nude! Nude!

Catty-corner across the intersection Jack could see workmen inflating a huge snowman above the Madison Square Garden marquee.

Christmastime in the Big Apple . . .

And then he spotted a guy with a pink carnation sticking out of his jacket. He watched closely to see if anyone appeared to be with him.

Nope. Looked like Jorge had arrived alone, as instructed.

Jack went over to the stairs and scanned the first floor. The lunch crowd hadn't hit yet. Jack didn't see anyone who looked like he might be with Jorge—no rules against your backup preceding you to a meet—so he leaned over the stair rail and signaled to him.

"Jorge!" he called. "With the carnation. Buy something and then—" He jerked his thumb back up the stairs.

Jorge nodded.

A few minutes later he came up the stairs, spotted Jack, came over. He extended his hand.

"Mr. Jack?" he said in thickly accented English. He wore a heavy shirt that mixed black, yellow, and orange in an odd pattern; a chrome chain stretched fore and aft from a loop of his black denims to his wallet and heavy key ring. His nose and lips were thick, his cheeks deeply and extensively pocked. He looked like an overweight Noriega, but without the sinister smugness. "Thank you for meeting me."

"Welcome to my office," Jack said, shaking hands.

Used to be, Jack met all his potential customers at Julio's. It was still his favorite place for a first meet. Julio was an excellent screener—had a sixth sense about people, and he could pat someone down without their having an inkling they'd been searched. But then Jack began to worry that he was getting too closely connected with the place—and that could be bad for him *and* Julio.

So he'd started varying the location of his "office." Pinky's Drive-in was a new one. He kind of liked the idea of a place with no parking and no drive-through that had the guts to call itself a drive-in. He liked the tacky retro ambiance of the turquoise-and-white tile and pink neon in the service area below, and the hubcaps—not shiny new hubcaps, but old banged-up veterans of the road—nailed to the wall up here in the second-floor seating area. Liked this high perch over the street, liked the emergency exit door at his back that opened onto a stairway to the first floor.

Plus it was easy enough to find: Go to Seventh and Thirty-third and look for a place with a big neon Cadillac above the door.

Jorge deposited a quarter-pound Pinky Burger and a Budweiser on the table as he seated himself.

"So let's talk," Jack said. "I know the basics, but I want to get more details to see if this is workable."

According to Jorge, he was an Ecuadorean who ran a small office-maintenance business. Nothing big, just a couple of crews of three—he worked on one of the crews himself—who cleaned offices by night. Hard work, long hours, but it was a living. He was able to pay his bills and his workers. But he had a problem: a deadbeat client named Ramirez.

"And what really pisses me off," Jorge said, "is he's a brother."

"Your *brother?*"

"No way, man. I mean a brother of Ecuador. He tol' me he was giving me the work because we come from the same country. He say he is a peasant who come here and make good, and he want to help me, a brother peasant, become rich like him." He swigged his Bud and slammed it on the table. "All bullshit! The real reason he hire me and my guys is he know he can rip us off."

"You said he owes you six thousand."

"Right. And I never would have let the bastard get so far behind. But he keep telling me that business is slow, that his own customers are not paying him, but a big contract is due at the end of the year and he will settle up everything then with interest. And because he is a fellow Ecuadorian, a brother *peasant*"—he spat the word—"I believe him and keep coming back with my crew, night after night, week after week." Another sip, another slam on the table. "More bullshit! He never intend to pay me. Never!"

"Here's where I start to lose you," Jack said. "You must have some sort of contract with him."

Jorge nodded. "Of course. I always get one."

"But you tell me you've tried every legal means of getting the money back. Seems to me if you have a contract—"

"Can't," Jorge said, shaking his head.

"Why not?"

"My crew. Two of them are cousins of my wife." His gaze shifted away. "They are not, um, legal."

"And this Ramirez guy knows that?"

"He know it from the start."

"Ah-ha." Jack leaned back and took a sip from his Snapple. "The plot sickens."

"Eh?"

"Nothing. So how do things stand between you two now?"

"I finally tol' him I can't go on working for him without *some* payment. He give me that same dance about the contract coming in, and when I tol' him it was supposed to be in by now, he get mad. We go roun' and roun' about the same old stuff, but I do not back down this time. I was not going away empty-handed as I had every time before."

"So what did he do?"

"He fire me."

Jack had to smile. "*He* fired *you*? That took balls."

Jorge bared his teeth. "It is worse. He tell me I do inferior work. Me! Let me tell you, Mr. Jack, my work is *de primera!*"

Jack believed him. He could see the fierce pride in his eyes. This was a man trying to build something; more than a business—a reputation . . . a life. Jack sensed his anger, and something else: hurt. He'd been betrayed by someone he'd trusted.

"Jorge," he said. "I think you're right. I think our friend Ramirez was planning to rip you off from the start. And I'll bet that even as we speak, he's hunting up a new office cleaning service."

"Yes. I will not be surprised. He would steal from a dying man. But what do I do now?"

"Well," Jack said, "you and your cousins can go break his legs."

Jorge smiled. "Yes. I have thought of that. We have even talked of killing him, but we are not that sort of people."

"The other thing is to do about $6,000 worth of damage to his property."

"Yes, but I would rather have the money. The sweet taste of revenge will not pay my bills. And I am trying to *avoid* trouble with the police. The truth is, Mr. Jack, I need money more than I need revenge. I just want what is mine. Will you help me?"

Jack leaned back, thinking. Jorge was the type of customer that kept Jack in the business. A guy with a genuine beef and nowhere else to turn. But right now, Jack had no idea what he could do for him.

"I will if I can. But I need to know more about Ramirez. Tell me all you know about him. Everything you've learned during all these months of working for him."

Slowly, as Jorge spoke, a plan took shape . . .

6

Alicia wasn't hungry, so she put off lunch. She liked this quiet time when no IV-therapy sessions were scheduled for the clinic and the day-care kids were having lunch; the staff and volunteers who weren't with the kids were out grabbing a quick bite. Usually she stayed in her office and caught up on her paperwork. But today she was restless.

And she didn't know why. It wasn't because of Hector—the little guy with the "mad buth cut" seemed to be responding to the antibiotic. She simply had to move.

She left her cluttered desk and took a stroll through the empty halls, lost in thought, wondering what to do next. Wait for Jack, or make another contact? She'd scraped up the name of someone else. Should she—?

She stopped. She'd heard a sound . . . almost like a whimper. She stood frozen, her body tingling as she listened.

And then she heard it again, fainter. And then a low voice, whispering . . . from somewhere around the corner . . .

Moving on tiptoe, and glad she was wearing sneakers, Alicia peeked around the corner and saw . . .

An empty hall.

She was beginning to think she'd imagined the noises when she heard the whisper again . . . coming from a hall closet just a few feet away. The door was cracked open, and the voice was definitely male . . .

"See? Didn't I tell you it wouldn't hurt? There now . . . doesn't that feel nice?"

Biting back a surge of bile that almost choked her, Alicia reached for the door. She watched her hand tremble like a leaf in a gale as it neared the knob. She forced it to grip it and pull.

And then she saw them, like a flash picture: a middle-aged white man—a volunteer she'd seen around recently but didn't know by name yet—blinking in the sudden light, his hand down the pants of a little black girl, no more than four years old—Kanessa Jackson.

And then the light exploded around her, as if her world suddenly became an overexposed video in which she heard her voice shouting, screaming, with glaring light everywhere as she spun into a wild 180-degree pan, stopping at a fire hose and chemical extinguisher recessed in the wall. Her hands pulling open the glass door, grabbing the canister and turning, swinging it at the man, watching him duck but not soon enough, catching him on the side of his head, watching him try to stumble in one direction as Kanessa ran in the other, following him, beating him on his head, his back, beating him down, and then bludgeoning him until—

"Alicia! Alicia, my God, you'll kill him!"

She felt hands grabbing her arms, restraining her, but she didn't want to stop. She wanted to kill him. She wanted him dead.

"Alicia, *please!*"

Raymond's voice. She stopped struggling. She looked down at the bloody man, cowering and whimpering beneath her. And suddenly she wanted to be sick. She stumbled back but did not release her grip on the fire extinguisher.

"Call 911!" she gasped.

"Why?" Raymond said. "What happened?"

She glanced at Raymond and saw the shock and concern in his eyes. He'd never seen her like this. Of course not. No one had. She'd never *been* like this. And it wasn't over. Blood lust still pounded in her ears like a war drum. Alicia didn't know who was more afraid—the creep on the floor, Raymond, or herself.

"Get the cops!" she said. "I want this perv out of here and locked up! Now!"

"Okay!" Raymond said, backing away, "but just be cool, okay, Alicia? Just be cool."

"And find Kanessa Jackson. Have one of the nurses check her over. Make sure she's all right."

As Raymond moved off, she turned back to the creep. The sick feeling waned as rage flared again.

"And you," she said through her teeth. It took all her restraint to keep from taking a few more swings at him. "You stay right where you are, or so help me God, I'll kill you."

7

After leaving Jorge—they'd come to an agreement on how they'd approach Ramirez and on Jack's split of the proceeds—Jack walked east, crossing Fifth Avenue into Murray Hill.

The area reminded him a little of his own neighborhood, with its brownstones and occasional trees. But Murray Hill was a lot older. Robert Murray's farm used to sit here back in revolutionary times. And when Jack's neighborhood was still "the country," this area here between Park and Fifth had been home to the highest of New York's high society.

Murray Hill seemed to be changing. Jack noticed a fair number of the stately old brownstones sporting discreet plaques engraved with Whatever, Inc. Through the windows he could see bustling offices belonging to architects, designers, and boutique ad agencies.

He found the address Alicia had given him and checked it out from the other side of the street. A three-story brick front nestled in with others of its type on Thirty-eighth Street, but even without the unsightly plywood sheets bolted over the windows, this building stood out. It had a yard.

Well, not a real yard, not even close to the small front yard of Jack's tiny family home back in Jersey. But the Clayton house *was* set back a couple of dozen extra feet from the sidewalk, and a few blades of pale grass sprouted in the hard-packed dirt behind the low wrought-iron fence.

He spotted an occupied gray Buick with a faded CLINTON / GORE IN '96 bumper sticker parked at the curb before it. Two shadowy forms slouched in the front seat. Must have been there awhile: The street outside the driver's window was littered with butts.

Jack kept moving, ambling to the corner, then crossing over and returning along the near side.

On this pass he spotted a walkway around the east side of the house, passing under a trellis that once might have sported roses; now only a gnarled tangle of dead brown branches remained.

He sneaked a glance inside the Buick as he passed. A pair of tough-looking slabs of beef, one bearded, one mustached, sat hunched in the front seat. The "private security" Alicia had mentioned, no doubt.

Jack finished his circuit of the street and stood at the west end of the block, looking back. He imagined the Clayton house in flames, saw those flames spreading, jumping from building to building . . .

He wondered if Alicia had thought about that. She might be crazy enough to try to destroy the place, but he didn't think she wanted to raze the entire block.

Maybe he ought to mention that possibility to her. He found a pay phone on the next corner and called the Center. He recognized Tiffany's voice, but she told him things were "a bit confused" there at the moment. Could Dr. Clayton call him back?

He wondered about that and asked to speak to Ms. DiLauro, if she was there. She was.

"I didn't see it happen," Gia told him, "but I saw the guy as the EMTs took him out. He was a mess."

"A fire extinguisher, ay?" Jack said, smiling. "I like it. Sounds like the guy deserved every bit of it."

"What's wrong with people, Jack?" Gia said, and he heard a note of despair in her voice. "Are there any limits to the depths people will sink? Isn't there a floor where you say, I won't go below that?"

"If there is, I don't think it's been found yet." He shook his head, reluctantly remembering some of the slimeballs that had slithered through his life over the years. "Every time you think you've found that floor, Gia, I'm afraid you're going to learn it's some guy's ceiling."

Silence on the other end. Finally Jack said, "How's Alicia doing? She okay?"

"A little shaken up. I guess I would be too. Funny thing is, she's the last one I'd expect to do something like that—I mean, take on someone herself . . . beat them with a fire extinguisher. She always seems so laid back and in control."

Get her talking about her family sometime, Jack thought, but said nothing. He considered Julio's a secular confessional. Whatever was said there, stayed there.

But he'd sensed the pressure building inside Alicia. Sitting across from her in Julio's had been like chatting with a lump of C-4. She'd had disgruntled post office employee written all over her. But maybe this incident had been a good thing. Maybe she'd released enough steam so he could talk her out of torching her father's old house.

"Yeah," he said as noncommittally as he could. "I was thinking of stopping down there and having a word with her."

"Is this about that 'personal matter' she wanted to discuss with you?"

"Could be," he teased. He knew Gia was dying to know what her Dr. Clayton could want with Repairman Jack, but would never ask.

"Sure," Gia said. "Come on down. I mean, there's a police detective here right now, taking her statement. But I'm sure when he's through—"

"That's okay," Jack said quickly. "Maybe some other time."

She laughed. "I thought you'd say that."

Jack had to smile. "Very funny. Catch you later."

He hung up and walked back to the corner of Thirty-eighth for another look at the Clayton house and its cozy neighbors.

Nope. A fire here would definitely not be a good thing.

8

Kemel Muhallal rose from his evening prayers, carefully rolled up his prayer rug, and returned it to the closet. As he moved toward the front of the living room, his gaze was drawn to the catalog lying facedown on the coffee table. He averted his eyes. Not now. Not so soon after prayer.

Kemel stepped to the front window and stretched as he looked down on West Seventy-seventh Street, five stories below. It was always good to shed those restrictive Western clothes and get into a comfortable *thobe*.

He shifted the narrow shoulders of his lean frame within the flowing white floor-length garment as he watched the traffic crawl along the street. Everything in this city seemed always to be in high gear—the way its people walked and talked, the frantic pace of its business, the headlong rush of its daily life . . . and yet its traffic progressed by inches.

He turned away from the window, and immediately his eyes, his shameless, rebellious eyes, fixed on the catalog. They drew him forward. He felt as if he were on a wire, being reeled toward the coffee table. Slowly, he lowered himself to the sofa and stared at the glossy back cover. It was addressed to this apartment, but not to him. As the landlord had explained, the previous tenant had left a forwarding address for first-class mail only. The rest of it continued to be delivered here.

"You don't want it," the man had told him, "just chuck it out."

Of course. How simple. But in order to "chuck it out," Kemel first had to sift through it, to make sure nothing was intended for him. So many catalogs in the course of a week. Did Americans buy everything by mail? Often he would flip through them, marvel at the variety of merchandise available via a simple phone call, then drop them in the trash.

Except this one. This catalog entranced him. He could not bring himself to "chuck it out" with the rest. He was weak, he knew, and he hated himself for that weakness. He cursed his hand for reaching out and flipping it over. He cursed his eyes for staring at the cover.

Victoria's Secret.

"Forgive my sin," he whispered as he opened it.

He felt a warm tingle in his groin as the now-familiar images swam before him. Such perfect female flesh, and so much of it exposed. He'd been told that America was a devil country, decadent beyond redemption, and surely this proved it.

Back home in Saudi Arabia there were no theaters or clubs. How could there be? Public entertainment is a sin. But this city especially abounded in public places of entertainment, much of it sex drenched. Pornography seemed to be for sale everywhere. The sidewalks were dotted with dens where one could buy pictures and films of people of any mix of genders having sex and engaging in nameless perversions. No act was off-limits. But those places were easy to avoid. They openly advertised their wares, and one did not cross their thresholds without knowing what lurked within.

But the magazines for sale on the newsstands and in the convenience stores were little better. Wholesome-looking publications offered cookie recipes along with twenty ways to a better sex life. And in the back racks lurked covers strewn with naked women in provocative poses, promising greater exposure within. But those too were easily avoided. One simply kept moving.

But this . . . this *Victoria's Secret* . . . it came free, delivered to one's door by the U.S. government.

Surely this was a nation on the brink of doom.

Gazing at the pages, Kemel had to wonder: Is this the way all American women dress under their street clothes? Is this the way their husbands see them?

He thought of his own wife, his Nahela, imagining her wearing such skimpy, frilly things under her *abaaya* . . . in his mind's eye he saw her lifting the hem of the billowing black cloak . . . and beneath she was clad only in these . . .

He glanced again at the catalog. Unfortunately, Nahela would not look as enticing as these women. She had been sixteen when they married, he eighteen. Now, after eight children—five glorious sons—and twenty years of sitting around the *hareem* and eating imported chocolates, she had grown large and saggy.

How he'd love to take *Victoria's Secret* with him when he returned . . . make it *his* secret. But did he dare try to smuggle it past customs?

His homeland, as custodian of Mecca and Medina, had a sacred duty to scrutinize and filter all items crossing its borders. And it took that duty seriously. It had to. The whole Moslem world was watching. Perhaps a member of the royal family, if he was discreet, might be able to slip *aurat* photos past the guards, but anyone else—never.

The list of *aurat*—forbidden items—included pork and alcohol, of course, but any depiction of a bare female arm or leg, or even a woman's hair, was forbidden as well. Which meant that Saudi customs officers confiscated virtually every Western magazine at the airports; for even magazines that might be devoted to cooking or housekeeping would carry advertisements that exhibited too much bare flesh. Kemel knew this *Victoria's Secret* would be considered outright pornography.

He jumped at the sound of the doorknob rattling. He heard a key in the lock. That could only be Nazer. Panic engulfed him for an instant. No one—most of all Khalid Nazer—must see this catalog. *Victoria's Secret* must remain just that—a secret.

He jammed it under the sofa and made a quick, frantic survey of the room as he hurried to the door. Was everything in order? He double-checked to assure himself that no trace of *Victoria's Secret* was visible.

The door opened, but the safety chain caught it.

"One moment," Kemel said, leaping to the door.

And a curse on Nazer for not having the courtesy to knock. Yes, Iswid Nahr, the organization that employed them, owned this apartment, but Kemel had been living here for months. Just because Nazer had a key didn't mean he should enter without knocking.

He pushed the door closed—wishing he could catch Nazer's fingers—and released the chain. Then he put on a pleasant face.

Be calm, he told himself. And above all, be confident.

After all, Khalid Nazer was his superior here. As long as Kemel remained in America, he would answer directly to Nazer. And Nazer liked to receive his progress reports in person.

Nazer waited on the threshold. He was as fat as Kemel was lean; where Kemel's beard was ragged and untrimmed—as it should be, according to the Prophet—Nazer's was neatly edged and clipped to a uniform length. Nazer's excuse was that an unkempt beard was a hindrance to his work here as a trade envoy attached to the U.N. Kemel suspected that Nazer simply wanted to appear more attractive to the infidel women he consorted with in the weeks and months he spent away from his wife.

Kemel did not like this man. His antipathy began with the man's lax attitude toward the faith, but from there his reasons were strictly personal. He would dislike Nazer's superior air even if he were a righteous believer.

As he pulled the door open, Kemel smiled and said, "Welcome."

He stood aside and allowed Nazer to huff his considerable bulk through the door, then followed him into the apartment.

"Well, Kemel," he said as soon as the door was closed. "I go away for a weekend recess, and when I return, I learn that the Clayton woman's lawyer is dead—murdered. How does such a thing happen?"

Kemel was taken aback by Nazer's abruptness. Usually they went through the routine of Kemel offering coffee and sweet cakes and Nazer refusing, as if such things could not possibly interest him.

And he resented the fat one's tone. Yes, Nazer was his superior, but only in his position in Iswid Nahr. In every other way, Kemel exceeded him. In brains, in courage, in lineage. His grandfather was a bedouin from the desert Nejd region, who fought side by side with Abdel Aziz al-Saud in the wars to unite the country now called Saudi Arabia. And Kemel had been with Iswid Nahr for almost twenty years. He was well-known and respected in Riyadh. His duties had brought him into contact with members of the royal family many times. Yes, America was Nazer's domain, but he had no right to treat Kemel as if he were a mere hireling, recruited like Baker. Who was this overstuffed toad to speak to him so?

"It happens because I am forced to work with fools," he said, venting only a small portion of the heat he felt. "This mercenary you assigned to me is like a mad scorpion, stinging everything he nears."

Nazer blinked at Kemel's reply, then shrugged. "We had to move quickly. We had a record of this man Baker offering his demolition services for hire to the government during the Gulf War. We contacted him. And he has proved most useful so far."

"But we don't need him anymore. We should be rid of him and simply hire a commercial security company to watch over the property."

"Get rid of Baker?" Nazer said, shaking his head. "No, I'm afraid that even if we had the time to make other arrangements, we are, in a sense, married to this man. And as you well know, time is in short supply. This has dragged on far too long already."

Kemel knew . . . knew all too well. He wanted this matter settled, not simply because the fate of his homeland and the entire Arab world depended on it, but because he was not cut out for this sort of . . . intrigue.

Yes, the blood of bedouin warriors ran in his veins, but he was a businessman, a negotiator, a—what was the American term? A lobbyist. When he succeeded in his mission, he expected to be well rewarded, *enormously* rewarded, and would spend the rest of his days in wealth and leisure, adding a second and perhaps a third wife, both in their teens, of course, to his *hareem*.

And yet he would give up the chance at that dream life in a heartbeat if someone showed up and offered to remove the burden of this terrible responsibility from his shoulders. He would give it up gladly, and then flee this devil country back to his home and his sons in Riyadh.

But that was a fantasy. No one was waiting to take over. Only a few in Iswid Nahr knew of Ronald Clayton's secret, and Kemel was one of them. To reveal it to even one more person was unthinkable.

And so he had to remain here, taking orders from Khalid Nazer, consorting with the likes of Sam Baker, and doing whatever was necessary to succeed.

"Baker is dangerous. This is a delicate matter—"

"Perhaps it is less delicate than you think," Nazer said. "Perhaps witnessing the sudden, violent death of her lawyer will finally convince the Clayton woman that selling the house is the wiser—and safer—course."

"Perhaps," Kemel said slowly. "But I would not count on it. She has not acted rationally since this began. I see no reason why we should expect her to start now."

Nazer sighed. "This is what happens when women are let out of the *hareem* and permitted to act as equals. The Prophet said it best: 'Men have authority over women because Allah has made one superior to the other.' "

Not to be outdone, Kemel could not resist adding, "He also said, 'Do not give to the feebleminded the property with which Allah has entrusted you.' "

They stood in silence a moment, then Nazer said, "Is it still working?"

Kemel nodded, hiding his annoyance. "Yes, of course. I would call you immediately if it stopped."

"I know you would, but I wish to see it."

Kemel could not blame the man. He saw it every day and was still awestruck by the wonder of it.

"Come."

And he led Nazer to the rear of the apartment.

9

Yoshio Takita heard the voices fade from the living room pickup, so he switched to the one in the second bedroom. If Kemel Muhallal and Khalid Nazer followed their usual routine, that was where they'd be headed. He put down the stick of Little Caesar's Crazy Bread, wiped his fingers on a kitchen towel, and raised his binoculars. He focused on the lighted window.

Sure enough, through the slightly open slits of the other apartment's Venetian blinds, he saw the two bearded Arabs enter the room and go directly to the lamp. And as usual, they stood over it, staring down at something.

But a *what?*

Yoshio had been recording every conversation and every phone call in and out of that apartment, and he still didn't have a clue as to what they found so fascinating in that room.

Whatever it was, it must need light, because Kemel Muhallal left it burning day and night. Yoshio figured they had to be growing something—a fungus, a plant, an algae—something that needed light.

Again—*what?*

Yoshio hadn't been aware of anything special going on in the second bedroom when he'd planted the bugs. They must have brought it in after.

He might have to return for a second look, but only if absolutely necessary. So far, the Arabs had no inkling they were being watched. Or listened to. Yoshio knew only a smattering of Arabic, so he sent the tapes downtown to an office in the financial district leased by Kaze Group. There they were translated and then transcribed; one set of the encrypted text files was immediately expressed to Tokyo; another was returned to him on disk the following day. Yoshio pored over each transcript but could not find a clue in anything that was said.

The two Arabs were saying nothing now.

Speak! he urged, wishing he were telepathic. Say *something* about what you are staring at!

But they did not heed him. Yoshio watched them hover around the lamp in silence, seemingly in awe.

And then the fat one left, leaving Muhallal alone. Muhallal retired soon after, turning off all the lights but one. He left the lamp in the second bedroom lit, just as he had every other night.

Why?

Yoshio doubted the Arab was afraid of the dark . . .

TUESDAY

1

Alicia jumped at the sound of the chime.

After the robbery on Friday, the return of the toys over the weekend, and the molestation incident yesterday, she needed a day off. She'd made her rounds this morning, discharging a two-year-old girl who'd bounced back from a Pneumocystis pneumonia, and hoped to be doing the same with Hector soon. His fever was down, and his latest chest X ray showed partial resolution of his pneumonia. He was on his way.

She would stay in contact with the Center via Raymond throughout the day, and could rush in on a moment's notice if something arose that Collins couldn't handle, but she simply couldn't bring herself to go in today.

She wondered at the ferocity of her reaction yesterday. She'd been out of control—totally out of control—and that frightened her. And worse, the incident had left her physically and emotionally drained.

She needed some time alone, with no phone, no crises. Just her, in her apartment, tending to her plants and trees. They needed her too. She'd been neglecting them lately. Small wonder with the little time she was able to spend here.

She loved her top-floor apartment. Originally it had been designed as an artist's loft, with half a dozen skylights offering light from both north and south, so it perfectly suited the needs of her plants. And its West

Village location on Charles Street—a street with *trees*—was convenient
to the Center.

As the bell sounded again, she looked up from the pear sapling she'd
been about to cut. Someone in the foyer downstairs, ringing the button
to her apartment. She'd figured the first one to be an accident, but this
sounded like someone here to see her.

Who on earth . . . ?

She hardly ever had company. Couldn't remember the last time someone had been here.

Alicia rose and stepped over to the door and studied the intercom
panel on the wall to the right. How did this thing work again . . . ? Two
buttons—one labeled SPEAKER, the other labeled BUZZER. She pressed
the one under SPEAKER.

"Yes?"

"Miss Clayton?" said a male voice. "This is Will Matthews, the police
detective from yesterday. Can I speak to you for a few minutes?"

Detective Matthews, she thought with a start. What does he want?

He was the one who'd taken her statement. Youngish, about her age,
maybe a little older, he'd been kind and sympathetic yesterday, waiting
patiently while she got over the shakes and adrenaline letdown that followed the incident.

But why was he *here?* And why now?

Irrationally, she feared he might have learned of her plans to burn
down the house. She couldn't see how, but maybe they'd traced her
movements, connected her to Jack or to the people she'd asked about
contacting an arsonist. If—

"Miss Clayton?" he said. "Are you there?"

"Yes," she said. "Yes, I'm here. You just took me by surprise, is all.
I didn't expect you. What's this about?"

"Can we speak upstairs . . . in your place?"

"Of course," she said. "Sorry."

She pressed the BUZZER button and held it for a few seconds, then
stood back and began to pace.

Be calm, she told herself. It's just about that creep yesterday. Has to
be. This detective couldn't possibly know anything else.

She glanced down at her legs and gasped when she realized she was
wearing only panties from the waist down. She rushed into the bedroom
and grabbed the bottom half of her sweatsuit. She caught sight of herself
in the mirror over the dresser.

You're a mess, she thought. Look at that *hair.*

She grabbed a brush and tried to straighten out the sleep tangles. Not that she wanted to impress New York City Police Detective Third Grade William Matthews with her looks—far from it—but she at least wanted to look presentable.

Another glance in the mirror, then a shrug—What are you going to do? You can only work with what you've got.

She went back to the apartment door and opened it. She could hear the detective's footsteps on the stairs as he worked his way up. Finally his head appeared above the landing. His face was red, and his overcoat was draped over his shoulder. He stopped and stared at her.

"How many times a day do you do this?" he said, puffing.

"At least four."

He climbed the final steps and shuffled toward her.

"You must be in great shape."

Alicia smiled. "My personal stair master."

Living in a fourth-floor walk-up had its drawbacks—moving in had been utterly exhausting, and it was a pain when she had packages, but she wouldn't trade the studio area and its skylights for anything.

The detective stopped at her threshold. "May I?"

"Of course," she said, stepping back.

As he passed, Alicia saw how his blond hair was receding above the temples on both sides. She hadn't noticed that yesterday. Probably because he kept it cut so short. Even so, he still had a boyish look, especially when he smiled. Tall, good build, clear skin with ruddy cheeks and bright blue eyes. Most women probably found him irresistible.

Not Alicia.

"What can I do for you, Detective?" she said as she closed the door and turned to face him. "Something wrong?"

Look casual, she told herself. Caaaasual . . . relaaaaxed.

"Yes, and no." He looked around, as if searching for a place to put his coat. Alicia said nothing. Don't ask him in. She didn't want him getting too comfortable.

"About yesterday?"

"Right. Floyd Stevens, the man you charged with molesting that child, he's making threatening noises."

"From jail?"

"Oh, he's not in jail. His lawyer got bail set, and he was home in time for dinner."

Damn! She'd hoped he'd have to spend at least one night in a cell with other lowlifes like himself. She'd heard jailbirds tended to get a little rough with child molesters.

"Great," she said. "So he's out on the street where he can make threats and hunt other little kids. What a system."

"Actually, he's not making threats—his lawyer is."

Alicia stiffened. "About what? About finding his pervo client with his hand down a little girl's pants? Fondling a four-year-old's genitals?"

"Well, of course, he says his client did no such thing, that you were completely mistaken and physically assaulted poor Mr. Stevens without the slightest provocation."

"Just what you'd expect a lawyer to say."

"Yeah, but . . ."

"Yeah, but *what?*" Alicia swallowed. Her tongue felt like crepe paper. "You're not buying that, are you?"

"No. But I gotta tell you, Kanessa Jackson is *no* help. That little girl is a ball of confusion."

"Well, what do you expect? She's only four, and she was scared out of her mind."

"And she's . . . not exactly . . ."

He seemed to be having trouble settling on the next word, so Alicia helped him out.

" 'With it'? Is that what you want to say?"

"I wanted to say retarded, but I'm told no one uses that anymore."

"You were told right. 'Mentally challenged' is currently in vogue, but Kanessa's challenges go far beyond mental. She's not only HIV positive, she was also a crack baby. She got *zero* prenatal care. Before she was born she lived inside a woman named Anita Jackson who was stoned out of her mind most of the time; and when Anita wasn't high, she was having sex any which way you can imagine to get the cash for her next vial of rock. Finally, after seven months of abuse, her uterus spit Kanessa out into the world in an alley. We're not sure when—either during or shortly after she was born—Kanessa's brain didn't get quite all the oxygen it needed, leaving her in a state of bemused confusion most of the time."

She watched Matthews squeeze his eyes shut.

"Christ," he muttered. "Talk about child abuse."

Damn if he didn't seem genuinely moved. Alicia appreciated that.

"Physical *and* emotional," Alicia said. She could feel her anger rising; it sprang to life every time she thought about Kanessa's mother. "Anita Jackson hasn't bothered to stop by and see her once. She's had eight children. God knows where half of them are."

"Eight," Matthews said. "Christ."

"And she's pregnant again."

"Aw, no."

"Yep. You know, if you'd asked me about mandatory sterilization when I was a student, or even a resident, I probably would have taken your head off. But now . . . now . . ."

She let the thought trail off. She didn't like to go where it led. She'd followed it once into a realm of fantasies where the Anita Jacksons of the city were kidnapped, anesthetized, had their tubes tied, then returned to the streets, leaving them free to do whatever they wanted to themselves, but unable to harm any more unborn children.

"Yeah, well," he sighed. "Then, I guess you know Kanessa's not going to be able to back you up. It's going to come down to your word against Floyd Stevens's."

"Fine."

He stared at her, and it made Alicia uncomfortable. Almost as if he was studying her.

"You're a tough one."

"Where those kids are concerned? You betcha."

"Well, you'd better be. Stevens's lawyer—a guy named Barry Fineman, who you'll be hearing from soon, I'm sure—was mouthing off after the bail hearing. I heard him telling his client how he's going to demand criminal charges of assault and battery against you, then bring a civil suit for pain and suffering from the injuries you inflicted. He was also talking about going to the hospital board and having you removed from your position because—and these are his words—'her violent and unstable personality is a danger to everyone around her.' "

Alicia felt her gut tighten as she sagged back against the door. "Oh, great."

Just what she needed—more legal expenses. And a threat to her job as well. This was scary. What was happening to her life?

"But he said he'd offer to drop everything if you withdraw your child molestation charges against Stevens."

Alicia stiffened as anger shot through her spine. "Never. I want this creep on record as a pedophile so he'll never be allowed near kids again."

Matthews smile was tight and grim, but his approving nod bolstered her.

"Good for you. But I hope you know you've got a bumpy road ahead of you on this."

Alicia knew. And she wondered if she'd make it to the end.

"Can I ask you something?" she said. "What's your interest in this?"

"Oh, a couple of things," he said, and she noticed that his cheeks reddened as he answered. "I worked Vice for a while, and these kiddie hawks were always the toughest to nail. They tend to have money and can afford good lawyers, their victims make poor witnesses, and they seem to be upright citizens, which makes it—"

"I know all that," Alicia said quickly, swallowing back the queasy feeling in her gut. "But why this particular case?"

His cheeks reddened further. "Because I like the work you're doing with those kids at the Center." A smile, almost embarrassed. "And I like the way you took after Stevens. That took guts."

Not guts, Alicia thought. I was more nutsy than gutsy.

"And finally," he continued, "I wanted to give you a heads-up on what to expect from Stevens's lawyer. So you'd be ready for him."

"Thanks," she said. "I appreciate that." And she meant it.

"And I want to let you know that you're not alone in this. The system chews up the wrong people sometimes. Even when you're right, the Barry Finemans of the world can use the courts to punish you instead of their clients. But you've got an ally. I'm going to do a little research on Floyd Stevens and see what I can come up with."

"Will that help?"

He shrugged. "You never know. Sometimes—"

The phone rang. Probably the Center.

"Excuse me," she said, and stepped past Matthews into the main room. But it wasn't Raymond's voice she heard when she lifted the handset.

"Alicia? Jack. We've got to talk."

Jack! She glanced guiltily at the detective cooling his heels in the foyer. She couldn't exactly discuss arson now.

She lowered her voice. "Um, I can't talk right now."

"Well, I wouldn't want to discuss this on the phone anyway."

"I'm not going back to that horrible Julio's again."

"I was thinking your place."

Two visitors in one day? That might be a record. She found Jack a little frightening. Would it be reckless to be alone with him here?

"Gee, I don't know."

"You going to be around?"

"Yes, but—"

"Good. Your place, then."

She gave in. "Okay, but how about . . . later?"

"Sure. After lunch. What's your address?"

She gave it to him, hoping she hadn't made a big mistake, then hung up and returned to the foyer.

"I've got some appointments to keep," she said, thrusting out her hand. "But I do want to thank you again, Detective Matthews. This is all very kind of you."

"Call me Will," he said, taking her hand and holding it.

Alicia pulled away and opened the door. "Okay . . . Will."

She felt terribly awkward, shooing him out like this, but she had a sudden, overwhelming urge to be alone.

"You'll be hearing from me," he said as he stepped outside.

"With good news, I hope."

She made a stab at a smile as she closed the door. Then let it fade as she pressed her forehead against its rough surface. Suddenly she felt exhausted.

Criminal charges . . . a civil suit . . . complaint to the hospital board. What else could go wrong?

And this visit from a police detective—what was *that* all about? He could have called and told her all this. Why go to all the trouble to come over and tell her in person?

Alicia groaned. "I hope he's not interested in me."

But the more she thought about it, the more she was sure that was it. Detective Matthews's personal interest in this case was just that . . . personal.

"Forget about it, Will," she muttered. "You don't know what you're getting into."

2

Jack bounded up the stairs and knocked on the sturdy oak door—or more precisely, on the countless coats of paint that blunted the details of the door's carved surface.

Four A was spelled out in brass at eye level, and he wondered why the "A?" This was the only apartment on the floor.

He'd pushed to meet her here because he wanted to get more of a handle on the enigmatic Dr. Alicia Clayton—treater of children with AIDS, buster of child-molester skulls, and would-be burner of ancestral homes.

The door swung in and Alicia stood there, staring at him—a little tentatively, he thought—with those steely eyes. Her black hair was pulled back into a short ponytail, giving her an almost girlish look. She was wearing dirty gardener's gloves.

"You're not breathing hard," she said.

"Well, I admit you're attractive, but I don't think—"

She smiled. "No-no. I mean, the walk up the steps. Most people are winded by the time they get here."

Winded? Why?

"Oh, yeah," he said. "Me too. Really winded. Can I come in and rest?"

She hesitated.

"I won't bite," he said. "Promise."

"Sorry," she said, and stepped aside to let him in. "It's just that you can't be too careful, you know?"

As she closed the door behind them, Jack popped the Semmerling out of his sleeve and held it out to her. She gasped when she saw the tiny pistol.

"Take it," he said. "It's loaded. The world's smallest four-shot .45. Keep it handy while I'm here."

She stared at it as if it were alive and going to bite her. "That's okay. Really."

"Sure?"

When she nodded, he tucked it into a pocket. He didn't know who was more relieved right then: Alicia, because he'd offered her the weapon, or himself, because she hadn't taken it. He didn't feature anyone else messing with his Semmerling.

She led him out of the foyer. "Come on. We can talk in here."

Jack followed her as far as the threshold, then stopped, staring.

A jungle. A high-ceilinged room, almost a loft, with big skylights, and green everywhere. Not houseplants. Trees. Little trees, yes, but trees. Some with their tops wrapped in clear plastic, like oxygen tents, and others with bandages around their trunks.

"What is this?" he said. "A tree hospital?"

She laughed, and Jack realized this was the first time he'd heard that sound from her.

"You ought to do that more often," he told her.

"What?"

"Laugh."

Her smile faded. "I might do just that . . . once the house is gone." Before Jack could say anything, she turned and waved a gloved hand at the room. "Anyway, this is my hobby: plant grafting."

"No kidding?" he said, stepping into the room and looking about. "That's a hobby?"

"It is for me. Or maybe it's therapy of sorts. Whatever it is, it gives me . . . pleasure."

For an instant there he'd had the strangest feeling she was going to say "peace."

"How'd you get into something like this?"

"I don't know, exactly. It started in college. There was this sickly tree right outside my dorm window. All the other trees around it were doing fine, but this one was stunted, had fewer leaves, and those it did have were shriveled and smaller than its neighbors'. I took it upon myself to save it. It became my mission. So I watered it, fertilized it, but no good. It just got worse. So I asked one of the groundskeepers what he thought, and he said, 'Bad roots. Nothing you can do about bad roots.' They were going to rip it up and plant a replacement there."

"Don't tell me," Jack said. "You started a save-the-tree movement."

"Yeah, right . . . 'Woodsman, woodsman, spare that tree.' " She shook her head. "Believe me, between my pre-med courses and my waitressing job, I barely had time to sleep, let alone become some sort of tree-hugging activist. No, I simply read up on grafting, took a couple of cuttings— they're called 'scions'—from the sick tree, and cleft-grafted them onto a branch of a healthy one, then I sealed the union with grafting wax. Shortly after that, they cut down the sick tree and replaced it. But it wasn't really dead, you see. Part of it was alive and well on its neighbor. By the time I graduated, the grafted limb was growing like crazy—easily the leafiest branch on the tree."

Her blue-gray eyes beamed at the memory.

"Congratulations," Jack said.

"Thank you. After that, I sort of got the bug. I go to a nursery— the plant kind—and pick out the sickliest-looking sapling. I buy it for a song, along with another healthier-looking tree of the same or similar species, bring them home, and graft the runt onto the healthy one."

"Does that make you the tree world's Florence Nightingale, or its Frankenstein?"

"Florence, I hope. The graft union is actually stronger than the rest of the tree, and the scion usually grows faster and lusher than the understock's own branches. But maybe there's a little Frankenstein in me too. I've got what you might call a 'lymon' tree over there: I grafted a branch from a sickly lime tree onto a healthy lemon tree. In a few years it'll yield lemons *and* limes."

"Sure," Jack said. "And what are you asking for that nice bridge to Brooklyn?"

"No, it's true. You can cross-graft the same species, but you can't cross genera."

"You're losing me."

"Lemons, limes, grapefruit are all in the citrus group—one will usually accept another of the same species. But that lime scion wouldn't have taken if I'd grafted it to, say, apple or pear understock."

Jack walked around the room, checking out the recovering plants.

"So . . . you take two trees and make them into one."

"It's a strange sort of math," Alicia said. "As one of my grafting books put it: One plus one equals one. And the nice thing is, there's no loser. The understock's roots are getting fed by the scion's leaves."

"I bet you wish you could do that with people."

When Alicia didn't answer, Jack turned and found her standing rigid in the center of the room, staring at him. Her face was pale, and her voice sounded strained when she finally spoke.

"What did you say?"

"I said it would be great if it were that easy with people. You know, cut them loose from their crummy roots and let them grow free and uncontaminated by their past."

She seemed even paler.

"Is something wrong?"

"No," she said, but Jack couldn't believe it. "I just want to know why you said that."

"Well, I was thinking of your AIDS kids. I mean, they inherited their sickness from their roots . . . too bad you can't find a way to graft them onto healthy stock that'll allow them to grow up disease free."

"Oh." She visibly relaxed. "You know, I never thought of that. But it's a wonderful thought, isn't it."

She still seemed troubled, though, as if she'd taken a step back into another dimension, and only appeared to be in the room. Jack wondered what nerve he'd touched, what region of her psyche it sprang from, and where it led.

"If only it were possible," she said softly from that other place.

"Speaking of those kids," Jack said, "how's my man, Hector?"

And then abruptly, she was back. "Coming along," she said. "The antibiotic seems to be doing the trick." She clapped her hands once. "Now . . . I guess we have business to discuss."

"Uh, yes . . . and no," Jack said.

"Oh, I don't think I like the sound of that."

Might as well get it out on the table: "I checked out your father's house yesterday, and I think if you really want to get rid of it, you've got to find some way other than fire."

"No," she said stonily. "It's got to be fire."

"But the rest of the block could go with it."

"That's what the New York City Fire Department's for, isn't it—to prevent that from happening."

"Yeah, but fire's funny. You never know what it's going to do. The wind changes and—" He saw her expression and realized he was getting nowhere. "Maybe one of those demolition experts"—he was inventing this, right off the top of his head—"you know, the guys who can set charges just right so a building collapses in on itself? I can look around for you, see if one of them might—"

Alicia stood there, her face an alabaster mask, slowly, deliberately shaking her head.

"No. Fire. And if I'm willing to pay you, why won't you do it?"

Jack stared at her. This was not at all what he'd expected from Alicia. She seemed to care so deeply about so many things, why was she so blind about this? Almost as if her rational processes ducked for cover whenever that house was mentioned.

But whatever the reason, Jack wasn't about to get into a debate about doing the arson. It wasn't something he put up for discussion.

"Because who I work for and what I do for them is entirely up to me. And I choose not to do this."

After a moment of utter silence, during which Alicia's eyes blazed with such intensity Jack thought she might explode, she turned and walked back to the door to her apartment, opened it, and stepped back.

"Then, there is nothing left for us to discuss. Good-bye, Jack."

She had that right. But as Jack passed her at the door, he said, "Just remember, there are other ways you can handle this. Take a few deep breaths and think about it before you go looking for somebody else to do the job."

"Don't worry," she said. "I won't be looking for somebody else."

And then she slammed the door.

Jack took the stairs down slowly. Maybe it was all for the best to cut loose from Alicia Clayton. That was one seriously overwound human spring back there in that apartment. He'd rather not be around when she snapped and started bouncing off the walls.

At least now he could devote himself full time to Jorge's problem. He'd already learned some interesting stuff about Ramirez.

Jack turned and glanced back at Alicia's door. Still . . . something appealing about her. Or maybe tantalizing was a better word.

What was that expression—something about a riddle inside a mystery wrapped in an enigma? That was Alicia Clayton: a riddle inside a mystery wrapped in an enigma within a thick coat of Semtex.

And a very short fuse.

3

"I don't *have* to go looking for somebody else," Alicia whispered as she locked the door and headed for the phone. "Because I already have a name and number."

She'd call him now, and set this up as soon as possible. That house was a cancer on the face of the city, the planet, her life.

And fire . . . the cleansing flame . . . was the only cure.

WEDNESDAY

1

"He spiked 103.4 last night," Sorenson said as they entered Hector's room. "But it responded nicely to a single dose of Tylenol, and it's stayed normal since."

Alicia glanced at the nurse. "One spike? Just one?"

Jeanne Sorenson flipped through the chart and checked the temperature graph. "Just one. At four-twenty."

Maybe it was nothing. One spike could be merely a fluke. She hoped that was all it was.

She pointed to the cluster of Mylar balloons floating at the corner of the bed.

"Where'd they come from?"

"Came yesterday. Addressed to 'Hector with the mad buzz cut on Pediatrics.' The teddy bear too. But the card only said it was from a friend."

Alicia seated herself on the bed next to where Hector lay clutching a new teddy bear dressed as a doctor.

Jack, she thought, smiling. You didn't forget.

She rubbed her hand over Hector's bristly hair.

"Hey, Hector."

"Hey, Dr. Alith."

He smiled up at her, but she didn't like the look in his eyes. Something wrong here. She could sense it.

"How's it going, guy?"

"My arm thtill hurths. You thaid you were gonna take the needle out."

"Soon as I can. I promise."

Still looking at Hector, she asked Sorenson, "How was his last chest?"

"Continued improvement," the nurse said.

"Labs?"

"CBC back to normal."

X rays and numbers on the upswing, yet Alicia couldn't shake the sense that something was wrong. She'd learned to trust that sense. Despite all the years of booking, of learning how to take a good medical history, how to do a thorough physical exam, how to interpret pages of test results, sometimes you had to throw them all away and go on your instincts. Sometimes it all came down to looking at a patient and sensing an indefinable something about his health.

She listened to the child's lungs, checked his lymph nodes, his belly. All normal.

Troubled, she put on a smile for Hector and rubbed his head again.

"You hang in there, Hector. We'll get you out of here as soon as we can."

Alicia rose and turned to Sorenson. "Get another chest on him, another CBC, and urine and blood cultures too."

She noted the nurse's questioning look as they moved toward the door.

"I hope I'm wrong," Alicia said in a low voice, "but I've got a feeling Hector's going sour on us."

2

Alicia's office phone beeped and she hit the intercom key.

"There's a Detective Matthews on the line," Raymond told her. "Says he needs to speak to you."

Alicia stiffened. Just a reflex. No way Matthews could know about her meeting with that arsonist last night. Benny . . . that was the only name she had for the man. Nobody she'd been dealing with lately seemed to have a last name. He'd said he'd check out the address and get back to her. Alicia had been looking over her shoulder, literally and figuratively, ever since.

So what did Matthews want? Could he have dug up something on Floyd Stevens already?

"Put him through."

"Isn't he the cop who was here yesterday about—?"

"The same."

"Okay. Here he comes."

She lifted the handset and said, "Good morning, Detective."

"Will, remember?" he said.

"Oh, right. I forgot." A lie. She simply wasn't anxious to be on a first-name basis with him. "What can I do for you . . . Will?"

"As promised, I did a little research on an acquaintance of yours."

She squeezed the handset. Not Benny, she hoped. She cleared her throat.

"Who?"

"Someone you had an altercation with recently."

Floyd Stevens. Why wasn't he mentioning the name?

"Really. Any luck?"

"Oh, yes. I think the results might interest you."

"Really?" Suddenly glad he called, she leaned forward. "What have you got?"

"Rather not over the phone. Why don't you meet me for lunch, and I'll lay it all out for you."

Alicia closed her eyes and stifled a groan. He's interested, she thought. Definitely interested.

But she was not. She had neither the time nor the emotional resources for a relationship with Will Matthews or anyone else. Especially not now, of all times.

And even in the best of times, even with the best intentions, somehow, someway, they always managed to end up in disaster.

But how could she say no? Obviously he'd been out doing some leg-work for her. The least she could do was have lunch with him. It didn't have to progress from there. She could let on that she was involved with someone. That was good . . . she was in this serious, long-term relation-ship.

And besides, the lawyer for the hospital board had called her yester-day, saying he'd heard from Floyd Steven's lawyer who'd laid out the charges he was planning to bring against Alicia and the hospital if she didn't drop the charges against his client. The board was looking into the matter.

Her intestines had been in a knot since.

"Lunch sounds fine," she said. "As long as it's a quick one. I'm up to my lower lip in paperwork."

"Short and sweet," he said. "I promise."

They arranged to meet at El Quijote at twelve-thirty.

Alicia hung up, and stared at the FedEx envelope on her desk. A copy of the will had been delivered here from Leo Weinstein's office yesterday and she'd been planning to spend her lunch hour reading it. Frustration tugged at her as she remembered what Jack had said Monday: If Thomas and his backers were desperate enough and ruthless enough to run down her private eye and blow up her lawyer, why had she been left unharmed?

Damn good question. And the answer might lay just inches away in that overnight envelope.

She'd hoped to get a peek at it this morning, but she'd spent a lot of extra time at the hospital with Hector. She was still waiting for the results of his latest tests.

Maybe she'd be able to steal some time for the will after lunch.

3

Alicia used the walk to the restaurant to work out the details of her serious long-term relationship. She wanted them fixed firmly in her mind so she could casually drop them into the conversation with Matthews when the opportunity arose.

Let's see . . . the man in my life . . . first we need a name.

She dropped some spare change in the bucket of a sidewalk Santa and looked around at the storefronts for inspiration. English names seemed to be the exception rather than the rule in this neighborhood. She saw a sign for Jose Herrera Clothing.

All right. Let's see what we can do with that. Don't want Detective Matthews to leave the restaurant and spot the name of my beau, so let's Anglicanize that: Joseph Hermann. Great. Now, what does he do? Something that'll keep him out of town a lot. An importer. Good. But an importer of what?

As she turned onto Twenty-third Street she passed a computer-beeper-pager shop and saw the cornucopia of gadgets filling the window.

That's it: electronics. My guy Joseph Hermann imports cell phones and VCRs and computer games and all that sort of stuff from the Far East. His constant traveling is a strain on our relationship, but we're deeply committed to each other and we'll be marrying as soon as he nails down his lines of distribution and can get off the road.

And then she spotted El Quijote's canopy. She'd passed it countless times but had never thought of eating there, and that beat-up metal canopy, painted some awful shades of red and yellow, was why. The restaurant was tucked under the notorious Chelsea Hotel whose red brick front and wrought-iron balconies made it look as if it would be more at home in New Orleans. But the restaurant itself wasn't all that inviting. It looked . . . old.

She stepped inside and saw a long bar stretching toward the rear on her left. The restaurant area lay to the right. The inside pretty much matched the outside—old. And traditional-looking. High ceilings, white linen tablecloths, and faux Cervantes murals along the wall. She wondered if it had been redecorated since the forties. Even with daylight streaming in through the front window, the interior somehow managed to remain dim. She found that oddly comforting.

She saw a man step away from the bar and approach her. Detective Matthews. Wearing a trench coat, no less.

"Hi," he said, grinning. "I've got us a table."

She realized he was very good-looking when he smiled. She extended her hand.

"Detec—"

He raised his finger and waggled it. "Uh-uh-uh. Will, Remember?"

"All right. Will." She took a breath. She knew he was waiting for it, so she said, "Only if you call me Alicia."

His smile broadened. "I'd love to. Let me take your coat, Alicia."

As she shrugged out of her all-purpose raincoat, she hoped she wasn't sending him the wrong message. But he seemed like a decent guy. What could it hurt?

He checked both their coats, then signaled to the maître d' who led them through the half-full dining area to a rear corner.

Unable to think of anything else, she said, "This is nice."

"You've never been here?"

She shook her head. "I usually eat lunch at my desk, and at home it's whatever I can whip up quick and easy. I don't eat out much." *Because I don't like to sit alone at a restaurant table.*

He frowned. "I just realized I should have checked first if you like garlic. If you don't, we'd better find another place."

"I *love* garlic. But Mexican food isn't very—"

"This isn't Mexican. It's Spanish."

Alicia winced. "Of course. El Quijote. I should have known. It's just that after all those years in Southern California, any restaurant with an 'El' is automatically Mexican."

" 'All those years?' I thought you were a New Yorker."

"I was. And am again. Born and raised. But at eighteen I left for USC and stayed away for a dozen years."

She didn't tell him that she'd looked into the University of Hawaii because it was the farthest she could get from New York and that house on Thirty-eighth Street and still be in the United States. But USC had offered her a better financial package, so she'd settled for California.

The waiter arrived.

"You've got to try the shrimp in green sauce," Matthews said. "Best thing on the menu—*if* you like garlic."

She ordered that, plus a Diet Pepsi. He ordered a beer.

While they waited, he quizzed her about her West Coast years, and she found herself relaxing as she talked about herself. As long as he didn't ask her about her life before that. Premed, medical school, the residencies . . . grueling years, but good ones. She'd left New York one person and arrived in California as another. The new Alicia had no past, owed nothing to no one. As she'd stepped off the plane, she'd been reborn as a being of her own creation.

She used the arrival of their meal—a metal crock filled with plump pink shrimp nestled in a lime-green sauce—to change the subject.

"But enough about me," she said. "What about Floyd Stevens?"

"Taste first," Matthews said as he spooned a generous portion onto her plate. "You don't want to ruin a good meal with talk about scum."

Alicia bit back a sharp retort. She hadn't come for the food, she'd come for information, dammit. Instead she forked a shrimp in half and tasted it. God, it was good. Incredibly good. Quickly she ate the other half. She hadn't realized how hungry she was.

"So," he said. She looked up and found him watching her intensely. "What do you think?"

"Heavenly," she said. "So good, in fact, that nothing you can tell me can ruin it."

He sighed. "Okay. Here's what I learned: Seems this isn't the first time Pretty Boy Floyd has been caught with his hands on a child. They weren't easy to find, but I dug up three past complaints about him."

Alicia's spirits jumped. "Then, he's got a record—a history of pedophilia. How the hell did we ever allow him in?"

"Hang on here. No record. The complaints were all dropped."

"Dropped? All of them?"

He nodded, chewing slowly. "Seems he's pretty well-off financially. Made a lot of money on Wall Street in the eighties and retired as a young millionaire with lots of time on his hands and a yen for kids."

Good as the meal was, Alicia found her appetite waning. "He buys his way out."

"Or threatens his way out, like he's trying to do with you. He's got a shark for a lawyer. Nasty SOB who loves to go for the throat."

"In other words, those weren't just empty threats."

"Afraid not."

"You're really making my day."

"Sorry. Just thought you should know what you're up against."

"I guess I already knew. Fineman called yesterday."

"What he say?"

"Pretty much what you overheard. Told me I could expect to spend the next three to five years in and out of courtrooms, burning up every penny I earn in legal fees, then spending much of the rest of my working life paying off the punitive and pain-and-suffering damages he expected the court to award his client. Of course, I could avoid all that if I saw the light, realized how mistaken I was, and withdrew my complaint."

"What a sweet guy. Goes to prove lawyers get the clients they deserve."

Alicia leaned back and fought a wave of depression as a string of rationalizations raced through her brain: Kanessa hadn't been done any physical harm, and she didn't have enough self-awareness to have suffered any long-term psychological damage. And at least Floyd Stevens was out of the Center for good, so the kids there were safe from him. Maybe he'd been hurt and frightened enough by the beating to keep his hands to himself from now on.

The fact that she was allowing these thoughts to exist depressed Alicia even more.

"You okay?" Matthews asked.

"No."

"Know what you're going to do?"

Alicia stared at him. "What do you think I'm going to do?"

He met her gaze. "I haven't known you very long, but I can't see you doing anything else but hanging in there."

The sudden surge of warmth for this virtual stranger took Alicia by surprise. There'd never been a chance that she'd cave in—on something else, maybe, but *never* on anything like this—and he'd recognized that. For some unfathomable reason, she found herself smiling.

"How could you know that?"

"I don't know. I just sense it. It's part of what I find so attractive about you."

Uh-oh. There it was, out in the open, flopping around on the table. She chose to ignore it.

"You don't think I'm crazy?" she said.

"No. I think you're principled."

She wished it were principles. She wished it were that simple.

And then he reached across the table and covered her hand with his.

"And I want you to know that I admire you for it. And you should also know that you're not alone in this. There's still a few things I can do."

"Like what?

"I learned a few things in Vice. One of them was that these pedophiles don't change their spots. You can't cure them. A stretch in the joint, years of couch time with an army of shrinks, nothing changes them. The minute they think nobody's watching them—or sometimes even if they suspect they're being watched—they're out on the prowl, hunting."

"Compulsive behavior." Alicia knew all about it.

"Right. And that can work to our advantage."

Our? When had it become his problem too?

Easy, she told herself. He wants to get this guy as much as you do. Don't get your back up. He wants to help. Let him.

She wondered why she found that so hard to do. Maybe because she'd been on her own for so long, taking no help from anyone, making all her own decisions, solving all her problems by herself. Was that why an offer of help seemed almost like . . . an intrusion?

"How?"

He smiled. "Leave that to me."

Alicia straightened and found herself smiling. "You know, Will, I think I'm getting my appetite back."

Oh, no. Had she just called him "Will?" Where had that come from?

But it was true. She was hungry again. And she had to admit, it felt good to know she had someone on her side.

They finished off the shrimp and green sauce, argued over who paid, with Will winning because he had longer arms and had snagged the check. They parted at the front door with Will promising to keep in touch.

Alicia was halfway back to the Center before she realized she'd never got around to telling him about her serious long-term relationship with that up-and-coming importer, Joseph Hermann.

4

Before sifting through the pile of "While You Were Out . . ." message slips piled on her desk when she got back to the Center, Alicia checked her personal voice mail. She had one message.

"This is Benny. Call me." He left a number.

Her pulse quickened. The arsonist. She closed her office door and called the number immediately.

"Yeah?" said the same voice.

She heard traffic noises in the background. He was no doubt at a pay phone.

"Is this Benny? I'm returning your call."

"Yeah. This is about the Murray Hill place, right?"

"Right."

"Yeah. I can do that."

"Good. But I need more than that." Jack's comment about a fire leveling the whole block gnawed at her. "I don't want it to spread."

"No prob. You're dealing wit' a pro, here. The inside'll cook. It'll be done to a turn, crisped to ash before it shows outside. The water boys'll be there by then, and if they ain't, I'll call 'em myself. And that'll be it. A surgical strike. With no one the wiser."

"You're sure? Absolutely sure? And no one will get hurt?"

"Guaranteed. Piece a cake, honey. You'll be countin' your money in no time."

Benny obviously thought she was doing this for the insurance. Let him.

"Great," she said.

"But I wanna be countin' mine tonight. Like we agreed, half up front, half the morning after. In cash, know what I'm saying?"

"I know."

Benny's fee would just about clean her out. Was it worth it? Did she really want to do this?

Yes.

"Where do we meet?"

5

Alicia stood on a chair and stared out at the night through one of her skylights. She faced northwest. Toward Murray Hill.

Benny had said he'd do the job tonight.

"I'm workin' another job farther uptown," he'd said. "But why wait? Your place is empty and ready to go. Piece a cake."

Another job waiting . . . arson sounded like a booming business.

And then the police scanner she'd bought on her way home this afternoon squawked behind her. Something about shots fired near Madison Square Garden. Not what she wanted to hear.

Smoke reported from a house on East Thirty-eighth.

That was what she was waiting for.

She knew she'd never see the flames or smoke from here, but something drew her to the window anyway. She'd stay here, squinting into the darkness until the alarm came through on the scanner. Then she'd run downstairs, snag a cab to Murray Hill, and stand there on Thirty-eighth Street, watching the flames burn that house to the sidewalk.

A tremor ran through her body and she wobbled atop the chair. She steadied herself against the skylight frame and closed her eyes. Her frazzled nerves were stretched to the breaking point. She wasn't cut out for this.

God, what have I done? I actually hired someone to burn down the house. Am I out of my mind?

Sometimes she thought so.

And after finally finding time to read the will today, she wondered if madness ran in the family. Leo Weinstein had mentioned in passing that it was "rather unusual," but she hadn't realized just how unusual.

Having read it, she knew the answer to Jack's question about to why the people she hired wound up dead but she remained unharmed.

And now she was convinced more strongly than ever that the only solution was to destroy the house.

Then she'd be free of Thomas's ankle-biting lawyers. And if insurance money came of it, she'd donate it to the Center.

And her world would be free of that house and all it represented.

6

"All right," Kenny said as he came down the steps. "He's stowed in the trunk. What next?"

Sam Baker stood in a cone of light in the basement of the Clayton house and wiped the bloody blade of the filleting knife on a rag. He wanted to take a chunk out of Kenny and make him eat it for screwing up tonight. But Kenny was family, his older sister's kid, a broad-shouldered twenty-five-year-old with his mother's red hair, and you didn't scar up family, not even when they deserved it.

He'd punish Kenny and his partner another way.

"A number of things are next, Kenny. The first one is docking you and Mott five percent of your bonus."

Kenny's eyes widened. "Five percent? What the fuck for?"

"For letting that torch slip by you."

"Shit, man, we caught him, didn't we?"

"Yeah, after he was already inside and setting up his goodies. If you hadn't smelled the gasoline, this whole place'd be up in smoke, and we'd all be out of a sweet gig." Baker pointed the knife at Kenny's chest. "He shouldn't have got in in the first place."

"Guy must be a magician. We never saw him, and I swear we weren't goofing off."

"Swear all you want, but don't expect any sympathy from the rest of the crew. If this place had gone up, they'd have lost a *hundred* percent of their bonuses. You too. So maybe this'll keep you on your toes during your next shift."

"That sucks, Sam."

"Don't feel so bad. I'll see that it goes to Grandma."

Kenny made a disgusted face. "Yeah, right. Think she'll remember to send me a thank-you note?"

Suddenly furious, Sam grabbed the front of Kenny's shirt and jerked him close. Family or not, he was ready to do a tap dance on his nephew's head.

"You watch your tone when you mention your grandmother, kid. Got that?"

Kenny looked away and nodded. "Sorry. I didn't mean it."

Sam released him. "I hope not. Now, lug the rest of this accelerant upstairs and wait for the others."

As Kenny stomped up the stairs, Baker looked around the cellar and shook his head. Too close. Too damn close. He'd damn near shit his pants when Kenny had called to say they'd caught a firebug in the house. He'd run over and found this weasel-faced wimp tied to a chair in the basement. The guy had been carrying a couple of gallons of accelerant in quart bottles stashed in pockets inside his overcoat.

Hadn't taken long to break him down. Amazing how persuasive a filleting knife could be. Remove a couple of wide strips of skin and the words tended to pour out. The torch said some broad had hired him. Someone who fit the Clayton babe's description to a tee.

Shit!

Didn't that bitch know when to quit? What did it take to scare her off?

Baker had been so pissed, he'd gone a little crazy. Grabbed the nearest pistol and started bashing away. Softened the torch's skull real good. He was out cold. Maybe he'd never wake up.

Baker had considered calling Kemel, but changed his mind. Little ol' Ahab the Ay-rab was turning out to be something of a wimp. Look how bent out of shape he got over that itty-bitty car bomb. Probably work himself into a pretzel if Baker told him how he planned to take care of the torch.

Kemel just didn't get it. You don't play footsy with problems—you *eliminate* them. That way they don't come back to haunt you.

Like this firebug.

This guy had been taught his lesson—maybe permanently. But that wasn't enough. Baker wanted to send the Clayton babe another message. Her PI splattered on the street hadn't done it. Her lawyer blown to pieces right in front of her hadn't done it. Maybe the third time would be a charm.

But he wasn't doing this one alone. He was gathering all eight of his crew for this. With the body count rising, it was time to take out a little insurance. Get everybody involved. Raise the stakes all around.

Baker knew these were tough, stand-up boys. Not of the caliber of the SOG teams he'd accompanied into Laos and Cambodia in the early seventies but they knew their stuff, all veterans of mercenary ops in Central America, Africa, and the Gulf. Over the years he'd used them when he'd hired out to the various players in Medellin and Cali to do their dirty work along the drug routes in Central America.

But now the Mexicans had pretty much taken over the trade, and they preferred to use their own boys when they needed muscle.

The Mideast was the place. Saudi Arabia, especially. Plenty of money to spend, but no infrastructure. And feeling pretty paranoid after what Iraq did to Kuwait. His contacts over there kept telling him they didn't want or need mercenaries, but Baker knew different. Every Saudi he'd met thought he should be a prince. *No one* wanted to do the dirty work. That was why the country was full of Koreans and Pakistanis, imported to do all the menial work. If your Mercedes broke down, there was no one to fix it. But so what? You bought another one. And as for soldiering, why put your ass on the line when you can hire someone else's ass to take your place?

Baker wasn't getting any younger. He was tired of shopping himself around. His lion's share of the bonus when this job was done would put his finances on an even keel and pay up his mother's nursing home bills, but he wasn't about to spend the rest of his life sitting around and watching the tube. He needed a reason to get up in the morning, and Saudi Arabia looked to be a bottomless well of steady, low-risk paramilitary work, waiting to be tapped. If he showed this Iswid Nahr group Muhallal worked for that he could get things done, that he was the *man*, he'd be set for the rest of his working life.

But Baker believed in his own version of Murphy's Law: No matter how deep you've buried it, never underestimate the ability of shit to find a fan.

He wanted the whole crew in on tonight's dirty work. They could look on it as a sort of bonding ritual . . . a sort of baptism of blood.

Baker smiled. Not blood . . . a baptism of fire.

After which they'd be more than comrades in arms. They'd be accomplices.

And the Arab? Baker would tell Kemel Muhallal about it later.

7

Yoshio stood by the lamp in Kemel Muhallal's second bedroom and stared across the courtyard at his own apartment.

He had seen Muhallal leave and had sneaked over to do a quick search. Nothing. He had opened and thoroughly searched every drawer, every closet, every corner, every possible hiding place, and had found nothing unusual.

And now he stood where Muhallal and sometimes his superior, Khalid Nazer, stood and studied something almost every night. What? What could interest them so? And why did they always gaze at it here, under this lamp that was never turned off?

Was that the key? The lamp?

Yoshio reached under the shade and found the knob. He twisted it, and the lamp turned off. He twisted it again, and the bulb glowed once more.

Just a lamp.

Nazer or Muhallal must have taken the object with them. Whatever it was that fascinated them so was not here now, so that was the only answer. Was it so precious that they did not dare leave it in the apartment? Perhaps he could intercept one of them and take it from him . . . make it look like a mugging . . .

But no . . . too risky. They might get suspicious . . . might guess a third party was involved here . . .

Yoshio sighed and headed for the apartment door. A wasted trip. All he could do was keep watch, just as he had been doing for months.

So frustrating. He wished something would happen. And soon.

8

Alicia had given up peering through the skylight. She'd dropped into her reading chair and sat among her mending trees and plants, staring at the scanner.

But no word of a fire in Murray Hill.

Had Benny the arsonist scammed her? He didn't set fires, he just told people he did. Then he took the money and ran.

But then again, maybe he hadn't found the conditions right. He knew about the security guards Thomas had hired but had told her he could easily slip past them. Maybe it hadn't been as easy as he'd thought.

Maybe he'd go back tomorrow night.

Alicia shuddered.

"Do it tonight," she said to the empty room. "I don't know how much longer I can take this waiting."

THURSDAY

1

"So, did you hear about Benny the Torch?"

Abe's offhanded question stopped Jack in midbite.

He'd dropped by the shop with some bagels and Philly—the cream cheese was for Abe; Jack ate his dry. Abe supplied the coffee.

"No," Jack said as a premonition started a slow crawl up his back. "What about him?"

But Abe's attention had turned to Parabellum, perched on his left shoulder this time. The parakeet was pecking away at the piece of bagel Abe held up to him.

"Look at the little fellow! He loves bagels. A kosher parakeet."

"I think it's sesame seeds he likes," Jack said. "And that one's coated with them. But what about Benny?"

"Found him dead early this morning under a ramp to the Manhattan Bridge."

"He fell?"

"No, he burned. To a crisp, I'm told. With his own accelerant."

The piece of poppy seed bagel Jack was swallowing paused halfway down as his esophagus tightened.

"How'd he manage to do that?"

"Oh, I doubt he had much to do with it. Somebody burned the word 'firebug' in the ground next to him."

"Jeez."

"And word is he was still alive when he burned."

Jack shuddered. Benny was a lowlife . . . but burned alive . . .

"Oy, Parabellum," Abe said. "This is the way you show appreciation?"

Jack looked up and saw that the parakeet had dropped a load on Abe's shoulder. From the look of the stains up there, it wasn't the first.

"What goes in, must come out," Jack said. "And look at it this way. You only had stains on the front of your shirts before. Now you've got them on the shoulders as well."

"I know, I know," Abe said, wiping at the glob with a paper towel. "But I think this little fellow's got a condition. Colitis, maybe. Hey, you buy that stock I told you about?"

"You know I can't buy stock."

"Not can't—*won't*. You're missing out on a lot of easy money. Such a broker I've got. Puts me in these IPOs. I'm out before I know I'm in. A thousand shares, it goes up two bucks, we sell. Money for nothing. All you've got to—" He stopped and stared at Jack. "That face. You're making that 'when-will-you-drop-it-Abe' face."

"Who me?" Jack said, wishing Abe *would* drop it.

"Yes, you. And I should be making my 'when-will-Jack-wise-up' face."

"Jeez, if it isn't you, it's Gia."

"I'm not telling you to quit. You're too good a customer. I'm telling you to get your money out of those *fahkaktah* gold coins and put it to work for you."

"You need a social security number to open a brokerage account, Abe."

"So? You've got all those false identities, and I know some of them have social security numbers."

"Dead folks' numbers."

"Fine. You convert some of those ducats and Krugerands into dollars. You use a dead man's number to open an account with my broker. You let him make trades for you. He makes you twenty percent a year."

"No thanks."

"Jack! How can you say no thanks to doubling your money in less than four years?"

"Because I'd have to pay taxes on those profits."

"Yes, but—"

"No buts. I'd have to. And sitting back and letting them take their cut is saying it's okay. And saying it's okay . . ."

Jack couldn't do that. Once he crossed that line, even under another identity, he'd . . . belong. He'd have joined them. And they'd know him.

"But you wouldn't be saying okay. It'd be the fake guy with the dead man's Social Security number."

"Same thing, Abe."

Abe stared at him a moment, then sighed. "I don't understand you, Jack."

Jack smiled. "Yes, you do. And Parabellum just ejected another casing."

"Oy!"

As he watched Abe wipe the glob away, he said, "Any word on who might've done Benny?"

Abe shook his head. "Nothing. But if you should want my opinion, and I'm sure you do, I say it looks to me like Benny might've tried to set a match to the wrong building."

Jack had a sinking feeling he knew what building that might have been.

He remembered Alicia telling him how two people she'd hired to get involved in her will problems had wound up dead. Did Benny the Torch raise the tally to three?

Only one way to find out.

2

Alicia had just hung up with the hospital lab—no results yet on Hector's cultures, but the little guy was hanging in there despite more fever spikes—when Raymond's voice came over the intercom. "That fellow named Jack to see you," he said. "He doesn't have an appointment but says it's important." A faint murmur in the background, then: "Check that—he says it's 'urgent.' "

Alicia's first instinct was to send him away. He'd blown her off two days ago, so as far as she was concerned, they had nothing left to talk about.

But the word "urgent" got to her. It wasn't one she'd associate with Jack. If he said this was urgent, he probably meant it.

Oh, hell. "Send him in."

A few seconds later, Jack slipped past the door and closed it behind him.

"Did you hire Benny the Torch?"

He hadn't sat down, hadn't even said hello. But the name "Benny" made Alicia disregard all that.

He knows! But how could he?

"What are you talking about?" was the best her startled brain could come up with.

"He was found dead this morning. Someone burned him alive last night. Any connection between him and what you asked me to do?"

"Oh, no!" she gasped. "Not again!"

Jack dropped into the chair. "Okay. That answers my question."

She felt his stare as she fought a surge of guilty nausea.

That twitchy little man . . . burned alive . . .

Finally he said, "I thought you weren't going to go running off looking for somebody else. I thought you were going to think about it."

"I didn't have to look," she said. Her voice sounded dull and far away. She felt as if she were listening to herself from another room. "I already had his name. My God . . . I killed him . . ."

"You didn't kill him. But I think you may have a point about the short life span of people who get involved in this. Everyone but you. And that's what I don't understand."

"I do," she said, shaking herself and forcing herself to focus. "I read the will yesterday."

"About time. And it clears up all the mysteries?"

"No. Not by a long shot. But it does explain why I'm still alive."

Her mind flashed back to yesterday, and the crawling sensation as she read that man's words, as she tried to fathom what he'd been thinking when he'd drawn it up.

"Which is?"

"Thomas is not next in line for the house."

Jack's eyebrows lifted as he nodded slowly. "Very interesting. And who is?"

"Not who. What. Greenpeace."

"The nature folks?" He laughed. "The ones who sail around ramming whalers?"

"The same."

"No wonder your brother—"

"Half brother."

"Right. No wonder he's ticked. Your father'd rather give the house to an environmental group rather than him. The two of them must have had one hell of a falling out somewhere along the way."

Alicia remembered the date on the will—only weeks before that man had died. Was that when he'd cut Thomas out—or had he always been out?

"I wouldn't know. As I told you, I've had no contact with either of them since I left for college." *And wish it had remained that way.* "And as for that man being 'green' . . . that's almost laughable. I don't think he ever gave a single thought to the environment in his life. He had . . . other interests."

Jack frowned and leaned forward. "Then why did he—?"

"I have no idea. None of this makes any sense. The way things are worded . . . I don't know much about law, but I can't imagine this being a typical last will and testament. I mean, it's almost as if he expected this kind of violence in connection with the house."

"Why do you say that?"

Alicia leaned over and pulled the will from her shoulder bag. She had no trouble finding the passage—she'd underlined it.

"Just listen to this: 'If Alicia dies before she can take possession of said house, or if she dies after she takes possession of said house, said house shall be deeded to the international environmental activist group known as Greenpeace with this message: *This house holds the key that points the way to all you wish to achieve. Sell it and you lose everything you've worked for.*' " She slammed the document down on her desk. "Can you tell me what the hell that's supposed to mean?"

"Can I see it?" Jack said, leaning forward.

Instinctively Alicia reached for the will, to grab it and put it away. She didn't want anyone knowing about her family. But she stopped herself. She had to trust someone, and Jack was all she had right now.

She pushed the will toward him. "Knock yourself out."

She felt her jaw clench as she watched Jack scan the page. She was on edge and knew it. Ready to take a bite out of somebody. She'd thought she was free of that man, but even from the grave he was managing to make a mess of her life.

"You know," Jack said, nodding, "this really does sound like he expected trouble." He looked up at her. "Your brother ever been jailed?"

"No."

"Drug problem? Violence?"

"Not that I know of." Thomas had problems, but not those.

Jack began flipping though the rest of the will. "Then why . . . ?" He stopped and stared. "What's this? *Poetry?*"

"Yes! Can you believe it?"

Jack began reading. " *'Clay(ton) lies still, but blood's a rover.'* "

"That's from Alfred Houseman," she said. When he shot her a look, she added, "I looked it up."

"I only know John Houseman."

"The original reads *'Clay* lies still.' He added the t-o-n."

"So what's this mean? That your bro—half brother is a 'rover?' He's a wanderer? Has a wandering eye? What?"

"I couldn't say." It had baffled her too.

"Wait," Jack said. "Here's another: *'Whither away, fair rover, and what thy quest?'* "

"That's from someone named Robert Bridges. I looked up the poems to see if anything else in them helped, but found nothing."

"It's crazy."

"That's exactly what Thomas's lawyers are saying. They're using all this weirdness as evidence that he wasn't competent when he changed the will."

"And when did he do that?"

"According to the date there, shortly before he died."

"Well, whatever his state of mind, he was sure as hell determined to see you got that house."

"I'm not so sure," she said. "It seems to me he wanted to keep it away from Thomas more than anything else."

"Can you think of anything important enough about that house that your half brother would kill for it? What could your father have left behind that he wants so bad?"

"I don't know. I don't know Thomas. I can't explain him. I don't even want to try."

"All right, then," Jack said. "Your father. He seems to be at the root of all this. Who was Ronald Clayton? What did he do?"

Alicia closed her eyes and swallowed. He wanted her to talk about that man . . . who he was . . . what he did . . .

If you only knew . . .

J ack was beginning to wonder if something was wrong with Alicia— sitting so pale and silent on the other side of the desk—but then her eyes popped open and she began to talk.

"People called him brilliant," she said in a flat tone as she stared past Jack's shoulder, almost as if she were reading from a TelePrompTer somewhere behind him. "His field was physics, and at various times in his life he was attached to the departments at Princeton, Columbia, and NYU, doing basic research. Somewhere in there he worked at Bell Labs and IBM. He followed the money. I suppose he did have a brilliant mind, but he was utterly ruthless: He wanted what he wanted when he wanted it and to hell with anybody else. His son is no different."

Jack realized he'd never heard Alicia refer to Ronald Clayton as her father. "He" or "him" or "that man," but never "my father."

Had she been abused by him? Her brother? Both of them?

"Doesn't sound like you had a great relationship with him."

Her voice got colder and even flatter.

"Ronald Clayton was scum, a lower life-form without conscience or scruples. I don't care that he left me his house. I don't want it. I don't care what he left behind in his house. I don't want anything that man touched. I'd be happiest if all traces of him were wiped from this earth. That was why I wanted you to burn the house. That's why I . . . I . . ."

She seemed to have run out of words.

Jack too was speechless. Alicia's feelings for her father went beyond anger, beyond rage. She *loathed* the man. And not simply because of his character faults.

What in God's name happened in that house? Was it physical? Sexual?

Jack watched her closely, hoping she wasn't about to cry. He never knew what to do with a crying woman—or man, for that matter. Gia he could take in his arms and hug. But Alicia? Uh-uh. She was flying a Gadsden flag at full mast.

But she didn't cry. Didn't even come close. She closed her eyes, took a deep breath, then looked at him.

"Sorry."

"It's okay," Jack said, hiding his relief. "What's your next step? And please tell me it doesn't include the word 'fire.' "

The barest hint of a smile curved her lips. "Okay. No fire." She sighed. "Maybe I should think about giving in. I mean, it would sure as hell simplify my life if I simply sold the damn place to Thomas and his backers. Being a multimillionaire would solve a lot of problems."

Jack was surprised by a sudden pang of disappointment. Who killed the PI, the lawyer, and Benny the Torch? And why? What in that house was valuable enough to kill for? If Alicia gave in, all those questions would remain unanswered.

"And then again," she said after a pause, her eyes going steely. "Maybe I shouldn't. I don't like to be bullied. Especially by Thomas."

Yes! Jack resisted the impulse to pump his fist. Instead he rose to his feet.

"It's your decision," he said. "And either way, there's not much I can do for you. But I'll keep thinking on it. Maybe I can come up with someone who can help."

"Why?" she said. "Don't get me wrong. I'd welcome any help you care to offer. But I got the impression you're strictly fee for service. Why are you staying involved?"

Jack shrugged. "Curiosity."

"Considering what happened to the others who've gotten involved, curiosity could be dangerous."

"I know," he said. "You're a dangerous lady to be around."

She frowned, and suddenly he regretted the remark. She was feeling bad enough. But it was true: He'd have to watch his back if he linked up with Alicia. Have to find out who was behind all the rough stuff, then throw them off balance by feeding them a few doses of their own medicine. Get them watching *their* backs.

"Hang in there," he told her as he pulled open the door. "I'll let you know if I come up with something."

Jack walked away thinking about curiosity. One of his worst vices. Rarely did it fail to get him in trouble.

3

Jack spent most of the afternoon looking at real estate. He finally found the place he wanted: a three-story Victorian town house on West Twenty-first Street between Seventh and Eighth Avenues.

The place had a history, and Dolores, the chubby agent from Hudak Realty, told him the whole sordid story. The previous owner had been a psychiatrist who'd blown his head off near Times Square and left the place to one of his patients. The patient later had an accident in the house and didn't want to stay there. So she was offering it for lease, fully furnished.

"Perfect," Jack told her. "But I must, absolutely *must* move in *immediately*. Rehearsals begin tomorrow, and I simply *can't* have any distractions."

Dolores said she was sure that would be no problem. She seemed ga-ga over the fact that her client was the actor who would be taking over the part of Javert in *Les Misérables*. He promised her tickets for his first performance. "When I step on that stage, *you* will be in the audience."

Jack signed a one-year lease as Jack Ferris, then paid first-month and last-month rent plus a security deposit with a check from a Santa Monica bank. He'd be done with the place before it bounced.

On the way out of the Hudak office he managed to snag a few pieces of stationery, and a blank deposit receipt form.

He picked up a disposable Kodak camera and hurried back to snap a couple of photos of the town house before the light faded. Then he called Jorge and met him at the Malibu Diner on Twenty-third—decent coffee and a fabulous array of their own baked goods.

He gave him the camera and a sheet with the layout and copy for the flyers they'd planned.

"Get this printed up with the Hudak Realty letterhead on top. Then pass them out like we discussed."

Jorge looked at the camera, at the rough sketch of the flyer, then at Jack.

"This will get me the money I am owed?"

Jack shrugged. "It's bait. If Ramirez bites, we've got a shot. If he doesn't, we'll try something else."

"All right. If you say so."

Jorge left, shaking his head.

Jack couldn't blame him. This was a long shot, even if Ramirez took the bait.

He stepped out under the Malibu's bright orange canopy and watched the crowd for a while. The offices and garment factories had let out and the hordes were on the move, streaming through the dark into the subway entrances or bustling toward Penn Station. Night came so early these days. Barely past five now and already the stars were poking through the inky mantle of night.

He headed back to the Center. All the while he'd been hiking around with the real estate agent—when he should have been concentrating on Jorge's problem—he'd found himself thinking instead about Alicia and that house. He kept reminding himself that it wasn't his sort of gig, that he couldn't resolve this for her.

But it wasn't concern for Alicia. It was the questions. It was the house. What was its secret? What was it about the place that a wealthy anonymous backer would offer a fortune for it through Thomas, and kill anyone who got in the way?

Jack had to admit it: He was hooked.

He wasn't far from the Center, so he headed that way. He wanted to tell Alicia that he'd figured a way she could keep her opponents off balance: Sean O'Neill. Jack had known the feisty little Irishman for years and knew he was an expert in legal harassment. He'd make life miserable for Thomas and his lawyers. He'd drown them in paper. Jack would have to warn him about the fate of his predecessor, but he doubted that would deter Sean.

As Jack came down Seventh, he thought he saw someone who looked like Alicia step out of the Center's front door and start downtown. He broke into a trot to catch up to her, and quickened his pace when he saw her turn a corner. She looked like she was heading home.

When Jack rounded that corner, he spotted her half a block ahead. He watched her angle toward the curb to avoid some guy sweeping the sidewalk. That brought her near a dark panel truck. Jack saw the truck's side panel door slide open, and as it did, the sweeper dropped his broom and charged Alicia, knocking her into the truck. He jumped in after her. The door slammed closed, and the truck roared off.

Jack stumbled a step and blinked. Had he really seen that? One second she was there, the next she was gone.

Shit!

He kicked into a sprint, dodging people and pushcarts and hand trucks as he dashed after the truck. He saw it up ahead. The light was turning red at Eighth Avenue. It would have to stop—

But no—it ran the red with a tire-squealing turn onto Eighth. An angry chorus of horns followed it uptown.

Jack kept running. He reached Eighth and stood panting, squinting into the red river of taillights streaming uptown. He spotted the truck two blocks ahead, moving away from him.

His mind raced. What now? He wasn't even sure that had been Alicia. And even if it was . . . he should stay out of it. Chasing after them himself was dangerous. Cowboy stuff like that was a sure way to get collared, and a collar could wreck his life. He should call the cops—do the 911 thing and let them handle it.

But he hadn't caught the license plate on the truck, and hadn't seen any distinctive markings.

She's in a dark panel truck somewhere on Eighth Avenue—maybe.

Yeah, right. That would—

A horn blared to his left. A taxi wanted to pull away from the curb, and Jack was blocking him. Jack held up his hand and approached the driver.

4

Alicia felt her taching heart pound against her ribs and heard the breath whistling in and out of her nostrils as she struggled against the tape that bound her to the seat.

They're going to kill me! she thought. I'm going to end up just like the others.

It had happened so *fast!* The man had caught her in midstride, hurled her into the truck, and jumped in after her. Before she could react the door was closed, and she was taped into this chair, with a short piece slapped across her mouth. She felt tears crowding into her eyes. What did they want with her?

And then she remembered: They can't kill me. The house will go to Greenpeace if they do.

But what if this is something else? What if this has nothing to do with the house? You hear of people disappearing all the time. What if this is just some random abduction?

The inside of the truck was as dark as a tomb. She could make out the shape of the man who'd pushed her in, and sensed someone else sitting behind her. The first man had her shoulder bag and seemed to be pawing through it—she could hear the contents being pushed this way and that. What were they looking for? Who were they? What did they—?

And then the one behind her spoke. She recognized the nasal voice.

"Hello, sis."

Thomas.

Anger sliced through her. She couldn't see him, but she could imagine him—his lanky brown hair, his big-nosed, pockmarked face, his pear-shaped body. Had he gained weight since she'd last seen him a dozen years ago? Undoubtedly.

She wanted to scream at him, but knew nothing would pass her taped lips. So she stopped struggling against her bonds and forced herself to be calm. She would not give him the satisfaction of seeing her terror.

"Sorry we have to meet like this," he said in a casual, offhanded tone. Alicia could almost *hear* his smirk. "But I wanted to act out one of my bondage fantasies. And I also wanted to make it clear in no uncertain terms how disturbed we are by what you did—or tried to have done to the house last night."

We . . . he was as much as telling her that he wasn't in this alone.

"I don't want this to be a lecture, so I'm going to have my associate here remove the tape from your mouth. If you begin to scream or cause any unpleasantness, it goes back on and stays on. Is that clear?"

Alicia refused to nod.

"I said, is that clear?"

Still she wouldn't nod.

Finally she heard Thomas sigh. "All right. Take it off."

The dark figure next to her reached over and tore the tape roughly from her face. From the way her flesh stung, she was sure it had taken an upper layer of skin with it.

"You bastard," she said in a low voice without turning. She did not want to see him. "You filthy piece of—"

"Ah-ah-ah," Thomas said. "I warned you about unpleasantness."

"Just a statement of fact, Thomas."

"Really?" His voice changed to a hiss. "Then try this statement of fact: If you ever, *ever* try to do harm to that house again, you'll—"

"I'll what? Be run down by a car? Be blown up? Be burned at the stake? *What*, Thomas? I know what happens if I die. So don't try to threaten me."

"Who said anything about dying?" he said. "How about just hurting? You can be hurt. And you can be hurt again. You can be damaged temporarily or permanently. You can be scarred. You can be maimed. You can be blinded. The list goes on, Alicia. Dying is not the worst that can happen to you."

Alicia licked her lips with a cottony tongue. Was this really Thomas talking? Weak ineffectual Thomas?

"I know what you're thinking," Thomas went on. "You're thinking Thomas is just talking. Thomas is a wimp. He won't do anything of the sort. But listen well, sister: Thomas doesn't have to do any of it. He's got people who will do it for him, and enjoy it."

Her intestines coiled in fear as she realized these were not empty threats. She hid the tremor that shot through her. How had she got into this nightmare?

"Give it up," Thomas said. "I've all but won as it is. It's all just a matter of time now—a very short time. Save me the trouble of having the will set aside, and you'll walk away from the closing a very rich woman. You keep fighting me and you wind up with nothing—no house, no money. I call that a no-brainer, Alicia. Why are you being so damn stubborn?"

You of all people should know, she thought. But she said: "Why? Why do you want the place so badly?"

"I have my reasons. Nothing that concerns you." He leaned closer and lowered his voice. "I can hurt you in other ways, Alicia. I can ruin you professionally. I can make that medical degree of yours completely worthless."

Alicia froze, afraid to move, afraid to hear.

Thomas's voice sank to a whisper. "I found his stash . . . the master collection. It's mine now. And I can release parts of it to the state board, to select magazines and newspapers."

Alicia knew that if her hands were free now, she'd turn and go for his throat, try to rip it out to silence that smug voice. But the cold sick dread flowing through her stole her voice.

And then she felt his hand grab her left breast and squeeze.

"Remember the good old days?"

What Alicia remembered was the seventeen-year-old Thomas sneaking into her room at night to cop a feel while she was sleeping. Something he quit after she slashed his palm with the knife she'd begun keeping under her pillow.

Her fury broke free. She flexed her neck, then rammed the back of her head into Thomas's face.

She heard him cry out in pain, and then heard a horn blare as the truck screeched to a crashing halt.

From the other side of the front partition she faintly heard the driver say something about a "Goddam cab" as he got out.

Behind her, Thomas was whimpering. "I think you broke a tooth!"

"Shut the fuck up," said the man beside her—the first words he'd spoken since he pushed her in here. "This could be trouble."

She heard shouting outside, then something slammed against the side of the van.

"That does it," the man said. "I'm going out to see what's up. You just stay put."

Alicia didn't have a choice, so he must have been talking to Thomas. She'd thought Thomas was in charge here, but this thug showed him no respect. Who *was* in charge here?

She got a glimpse of the man's blocky build and thick features as he pulled the side door open, then it closed behind him.

5

Yoshio was amazed at the sudden, bizarre turns of events.

He had been watching Thomas Clayton and had seen him get into a dark panel truck outside his apartment house. He had recognized Sam Baker through the open door. Since this allowed him to keep track of two of his surveillance targets at once, he'd followed.

For a good half hour he had watched Baker sweep the same section of sidewalk in front of a shuttered Korean toy wholesaler's shop. Yoshio had returned to his car from a quick walk to the pushcart vendor on the corner, and was just biting into his souvlaki on a pita when he saw Alicia Clayton get pushed into the truck.

Shocked, he dropped his souvlaki—salad, sauce, and all—onto his lap, and followed.

Were they mad? What did they hope to accomplish by this?

He got caught at the red light at the next corner. He would have run through it like the truck, but the cross traffic was too thick when he reached the intersection.

While he was waiting, he noticed a dark-haired man run up to the corner and stare after the van. Apparently he had seen the abduction and wanted to do something about it. A concerned citizen. A rarity.

As soon as the cross traffic thinned, Yoshio eased through the red light and pursued the van, leaving the man behind.

He found the truck and followed it onto a cross street. Suddenly a taxi, piloted by a madman, swerved around him and cut off the truck.

After the impact, the cabdriver jumped out and Yoshio recognized him: the concerned citizen from moments before.

Yoshio watched in stunned amazement. What demon had possessed this man? What did he think he was going to accomplish alone?

6

Baker took a quick look around. He wasn't exactly sure where they were—somewhere in the West Thirties, probably. That had been the plan: take her for a ride, scare the shit out of her, then dump her in some dark deserted spot as far west as possible.

At least there weren't too many pedestrians here. He saw how the left front end of their truck had inserted itself into the rear door of a beat-up yellow cab. What kind of asshole move had this cabbie tried to pull to cause this? Was he *trying* to get hit?

Whatever. The thing was to get the truck moving again. No cops, no accident report. Chuck had the frightened-looking cabbie pinned helpless against the side of the panel truck. He was an average-size white guy, and Chuck was a monster. The cabbie wasn't going anywhere.

Good. We'll do a little tap dance on this guy's head, then we'll be out of here.

Baker stepped forward. He was going to enjoy this.

That was when the cabbie stopped cursing and looking helpless. He grabbed Chuck's right wrist with both hands and gave a sharp backward twist. Baker thought he heard a bone crack. The cabbie ducked the pile-driver left Chuck threw at him and delivered a vicious sidekick to the inside of Chuck's knee. Baker *knew* he heard a ligament pop.

Chuck grunted and dropped to the street, clutching his knee. The moves took Baker by as much surprise as Chuck. Something very wrong here. Instead of running, the cabbie was coming his way, looking anything but frightened. Baker had a big weight advantage—what was this guy thinking? But then the guy was in his face. Who was this guy? Cabbies sat on their butts all day. They weren't supposed to move this fast . . .

Baker swung a right and missed as the cabbie leaned away from it. He grabbed the guy's arm with his left hand to steady him for the next shot, but he was slippery as a greased snake. He pulled free, and Baker's face exploded in pain as the heel of the cabbie's palm rammed up into his nose. Baker swung blindly and connected with what felt like ribs, but then something—a fist or a foot, he didn't know—pounded into his solar plexus. He heard himself grunt as the air exploded from him. He grabbed for the guy as he doubled over, hoping to take him down with him, but then something that had felt like a billy club but had to be an elbow rammed into his right kidney.

That did it. Baker dropped through a haze of nausea and agony, landing on his hands and knees, with his dazed mind mumbling, *What happened? What happened?*

7

Horns were beginning to blare from traffic backed up behind the accident as Jack jumped to the panel truck's side door. He cocked his right arm as he yanked the handle with his left.

Had to be someone else inside besides Alicia, he figured, and he wanted to strike while he still had surprise on his side.

He wished he'd been prepared for this. He had the Semmerling, of course, and the knife strapped to his leg, but as comforting as they were, he'd truly have liked a twelve-ounce sap in his hand right now.

The first person he saw when he opened the door was Alicia. They'd taped her into a chair, but other than that it didn't look like they'd harmed her. Her eyes widened when she saw him.

"Jack!"

And he'd been right about someone else being with her, but the doughy guy with the bloody mouth didn't look like a problem. A quick glance inside revealed no one else.

As Jack leaped inside, Mr. Bloodymouth shrank back.

"Who are you?" His voice rose in pitch with each word. "What do you want?"

Jack pulled the knife from his ankle scabbard and pointed it at him. "Shut up and don't move."

"Jack, thank God!" Alicia said as he sliced through the duct tape. "How in the world—?"

"Tell you later."

She began peeling away the strips as soon as he cut them. In seconds she was free. But instead of jumping for the door, she turned and went at Bloodymouth, cursing and clawing at his face.

Jack pulled her away from the cowering figure.

"Come on! We've got to get away from here."

"Meet my half brother," she said through her teeth as Jack helped her down to the pavement.

Jack looked at the soft body, the lanky hair, and bulbous nose. "Must take after the other side of the family," he said.

"He does. He—"

She stopped and Jack saw she was staring at the two guys he'd flattened a minute ago. The driver had curled into a fetal position and was moaning as he clutched his left knee with his good hand. The other guy was already struggling to his feet. He had to be a tough one—a kidney punch like that usually put a guy down for the count.

He tugged on Alicia's arm again, pulling her away from the scene. Drivers backed up behind the truck would be wandering up to see what the hell was holding things up. He saw one getting out of his car now. Jack didn't want anyone giving his description.

"Let's go. Time to fade away."

8

After the collision, Yoshio had seen Baker come out and move around to the front of the truck. He did not return. The concerned citizen appeared instead and freed Alicia Clayton.

Unable to contain his curiosity, Yoshio approached the truck on foot. Peeking inside the open door, he saw a man he recognized as Thomas Clayton wiping blood from his mouth. He went around to the front and saw Baker and another man, both much larger than the concerned citizen, both looking battered.

This carnage was certainly not the work of an average citizen. It appeared that Ms. Clayton had found herself a samurai . . . a *ronin*.

And then Baker, holding a hand against his back, over his right kidney, noticed Yoshio and snarled. "Whatta you lookin' at? Get the fuck outta here!"

As Yoshio made a frightened gesture and backed away, he glanced down the street to where Alicia Clayton and her rescuer were vanishing into the shadows.

Yoshio's car was trapped behind the accident, and would be so for a long while, he feared. He would not be able to follow them.

But he wished he could. Yoshio wanted to know more about the *ronin*.

9

"I don't know how to thank you."

It must have been the twentieth time she'd said it. Jack sipped his Molson and said nothing. He'd given up on telling her not to worry about it.

They'd run a few blocks, then ducked into this sports bar to get off the street. The place traded on the Madison Square Garden crowd, and seemed to be lit solely by neon beer signs—must have been a hundred of them on the walls and over the bar. The long-haired guy in the apron on the Sam Adams sign stared at Jack over Alicia's shoulder.

At least the place was quiet. The Knicks were off tonight, so Jack and Alicia had a corner all to themselves.

And now with the adrenaline fading, his right flank began to throb where that big sandy-haired guy had connected. The man looked heavy and middle-aged but, he was in shape. Threw a mean punch.

He'd explained to her how he'd seen her pushed into the truck, how he'd commandeered a taxi and chased the truck until he could cut it off and stop it.

She was working on her second Dewar's, and when she lifted the glass to her lips he noticed that the adrenaline tremor in her hand was easing.

"If you really want to thank me," he said, "you'll forget about going to the cops."

"But this is my chance to put a stop to all this!" she said. She balled her free hand into a fist and held it over the table. "I've got them now. They abducted me! I don't have to worry about civil actions anymore. This is a felony and you were a witness. I know this detective, Will Matthews. We can go to him and—"

Jack felt his insides twist into a knot. "No, we can't."

She blinked. "Why not?"

"Because I can't be your witness."

"What do you mean? You saw the whole thing. You even cut me free."

"But I can't be a witness, Alicia. I don't exist."

Another blink. "What are you talking about?"

"I have no official existence."

She shook her head. "How can that be? You've got to have a social security number. You've got to have a bank account, a credit card, a driver license. You can't function without them."

"I do. In fact, I have a number of them. All bogus."

"Well then, be a witness under one of those identities."

"No can do. Those identities hold up with a bank looking to get my money in its vault and hoping I'll start charging everything I buy on its credit card. And they hold up with a bored DMV clerk who's transferring the license of a dead man in Toledo to a nonexistent address in Park Slope. But they won't hold up under a real background check. Especially if they check with the IRS."

"You don't file?"

"Never. And please . . . you can't ever mention me to this detective friend of yours."

"Are you wanted for anything?"

"No, and I'd like to keep it that way."

Alicia leaned back, deflated. "Damn. For a minute there I really thought . . ."

"Sorry," Jack said.

"My God, don't apologize for pulling me out of that van."

"But maybe I shouldn't have," he said.

"That's not funny."

"I'm serious. It just occurred to me that I should have done everything the same except cut you free. If maybe I clobbered your brother like the other two and left the truck's door open with you still bound to that seat,

and you started shouting for help, *someone* would have come along and
seen you and called the cops. I'd have faded away to another part of the
city, and those three would be locked up in Midtown South right now."

It annoyed the hell out of him that he hadn't thought of any of this at
the time.

Alicia was nodding slowly. "That would have been perfect. But it
didn't occur to me either. All I wanted right then was to be free of that
tape and out of that truck."

"And I was trying to figure out how many more guys I was going to
have to deal with."

"Yes," she said, leaning forward now. A small, tight smile played
about her lips. The Scotch was getting to her. "Tell me about that. Both
those men were bigger than you. And I know you didn't use your eyeball
trick. So how did you beat them? Karate? Kung fu?"

"Surprise," Jack said. "The best weapon there is. The outcome could
have been very different if they'd been ready for me. But they saw a guy
who was scared, frightened, helpless. Easy meat. The second guy even
smiled when he saw how helpless I looked. But I had my moves
planned—went for their knees and noses. Doesn't matter how big a guy
is, he's not much trouble after you pop one of his knee ligaments, or ram
his nasal bones back into his head. Those two got caught napping. That
only works once, though. Have to think of something else if I run into
them again."

"I *have* to ask you this," she said. Jack noticed her looking at her
hands. "Those thumbnails. You keep them so much longer than the
others. Can I ask you why?"

"You'd probably rather not know."

"I do. Really I do."

Jack took a breath. "Sometimes you get into spots where things don't
clean up as neatly as they did tonight. Sometimes you wind up rolling
in the dirt or on the floor and you're dodging head butts and bites and
you've got to use every trick you know and every part of your body just
to survive. And that's when it's good to have a sort of built-in weapon."
He held up his long-nailed thumbs and wiggled them. "Nothing like a
gouged eye to end a fight."

Alicia blanched and straightened in her chair. "Oh."

Warned you, Jack thought.

He tried to stare down the guy on the Sam Adams sign. That didn't
work, so he made to move the conversation away from himself and into
a more interesting area.

"This is the second time I've asked you this today," he said, "but things have changed since this morning: What's your next move?"

"I'm not sure."

"Snatching you off the street was a risky and dangerous move. It tells me they're getting desperate. And desperate people do crazy and stupid things. You might get hurt."

"I don't know if tonight had anything to do with desperation," she said slowly. "Thomas told me that they were going to win, that it's just a matter of time. I don't think he was bluffing."

"Maybe there's a clock running somewhere."

"Maybe. But I get the feeling that tonight had nothing to do with the legal battle. I heard something in Thomas's voice . . . when he said, 'If you ever, *ever* try to do harm to that house again' . . . he sounded as afraid as he was angry."

"So you think this is a direct response to your hiring Benny the Torch. Seems a little over the top."

"It does, doesn't it. But I think it *really* frightened him. The thought of that house going up in flames seems to have just about unhinged Thomas."

"And unhinged people are dangerous." Jack pounded his fist lightly on the table. "But what *is* it about that house that would unhinge him?"

Something inside him was screaming for answers.

"I didn't really care before," Alicia said, "but after tonight, I want to know. Help me find out."

Thought you'd never ask.

But he didn't want to appear too anxious. There was still the matter of his fee.

"Well . . ."

"Look." She leaned over the table, her expression intent, her voice low. "Thomas tried to frighten me off. I can't let him do that. Whatever's in that house has got to be valuable. Very valuable. I can't pay you cash, but you can have whatever we find."

"A contingency fee," he said, nodding slowly, as if he'd never considered it. "I usually operate on a cash basis, but since I'm already involved in this, I'll make an exception."

"Great!" She gave up one of her rare smiles.

"But I can't take it all. It's yours by right."

"I don't want it."

"I'll take twenty percent."

"Take it all."

How could he take it all? He wouldn't feel right. "You can toss your percentage in the river if you want, but we split or I'm out."

He finally backed her into limiting his take to a third, and they shook on it.

"When can you start?" she said.

"I've already started." He rose and threw a twenty on the table. "Let's take a ride."

10

Jack didn't have to tell the cabbie to take it slow past the house. Thirty-eighth Street was barely crawling.

"Thar she blows," he said.

The security car with the two guards was still parked out front.

He noticed that Alicia didn't even glance out the window. She sat with her arms laced tightly across her chest.

"When do you figure you'll make your first search?" she whispered.

The cabdriver's English had seemed pretty shaky, and Jack doubted he could hear much on the other side of his Plexiglas partition, but whispering wasn't a bad idea.

"For what?"

"For whatever they think is so valuable."

"Which is . . . ?"

"That's the zillion-dollar question."

"Exactly. I'm sure your brother has tossed the place but good behind those boarded-up windows. Obviously he didn't find it. So how am I supposed to find what he couldn't find when I don't even know what I'm looking for?"

She mulled that a moment. "Maybe it isn't something *in* the house— maybe it's the house itself."

"Very possible. But when it's time to search, it won't be just me, it'll be *we*."

"Oh, no. I'm not setting foot in that house ever again."

"Yes, you are. You grew up there. You know every nook and cranny of the place. Be crazy for me to stumble around in there alone when you could be my guide."

Alicia seemed to shrink inside her coat as she tightened her criss-crossed arms.

What happened to you? he wondered. What went on in that house that you won't even look at it?

He decided not to push her any further now.

"But search talk is a little premature now anyway," he said. "We need lots more information before we do anything like that."

She visibly relaxed. "Like what?"

"Like who's backing Thomas. Finding out what *they're* into may move us a long way toward figuring out what this is all about. You said this is a big expensive law firm?"

She nodded. "Hinchberger, Rainey and Guran. Leo—my dead law-yer—told me HRG is mainly into international business law. He was flabbergasted that they were handling a will dispute. Said it was like having F. Lee Bailey handle a traffic ticket. And I believe him. You should see their offices."

"You been there?"

She nodded. "Leo and I had a meeting with Thomas's lawyer in his office early on. It didn't go well."

"Where are they?"

"West Forty-fourth, just off Fifth."

Jack had an idea. "Then that's the place to start." He tapped on the cab's Plexiglas barrier. "West Forty-fourth."

"Nobody's going to be there now."

"I know. But I want to get a look at the place. And I want to start work on getting a list of their clients."

"You mean, besides Thomas?"

"I don't think your brother is a client—at least in the usual sense. It doesn't sound like you can approach—what did you call them?"

"Leo called them HRG. It's easier."

"Okay. HRG. They don't sound like the kind of firm that lets you pop in off the street with a will problem. So I'm willing to bet that one of their existing clients—an important one—told HRG to handle this 'mi-nor matter' for them. We connect Thomas to one of those clients and we may answer some questions."

She shook her head. "So obvious. But how do we connect—?"

"I follow him. But that's all later. Right now, I need you to fill me in on some details."

"Like what?"

"Like how your father died."

"He was on Flight 27."

The words jolted Jack. "Flight 27? When you said he was killed in a plane crash, I thought you meant some little Piper Cub or Cessna. But Flight 27 . . . jeez."

JAL Flight 27 from LA to Tokyo had crashed into the Pacific with no survivors, and not too many of the 247 bodies recovered either. The TV and papers had talked of nothing else for weeks. Still no clue as to why. It went down in one of the deepest parts of the Pacific. The black box was never found.

"Did they recover his body?"

Alicia shook her head. "No. They say sharks got most of them."

"I'm sorry," Jack said without thinking.

"Me too," she said matter of factly, looking straight ahead. "For the shark that ate him, that is. Probably died of food poisoning."

You *are* a cold one, Jack thought. I hope you've got a good reason.

"How about your brother? You said he quit his job. What did he do before he began devoting his life to getting that house?"

"What I know I learned from that private eye before he was killed. He said Thomas had been stuck for years in a mid-level electrical engineering job at ATT."

"Not the genius his father was, then?"

Another shrug. "Hard to say with Thomas. As a teen he always tended to take the path of least resistance. Under constant supervision and cornered like a rat in a cage, he could do work. But give him any slack . . ."

New York cabs will be signaling whenever they change lanes before Thomas gets any slack from his sister, Jack thought.

Not that he deserved any after kidnapping her tonight.

"Here we are," she said, pointing through the side window as the cab swung into the curb.

Jack stepped out, paid the driver, then checked out the building.

The Hand Building was chiseled into the stone along the apex of the high-arched entrance. Impressive carving wound around the supporting columns. And inside . . .

"Look at that ceiling," Alicia said as the revolving door deposited them in the long, bright marble-walled lobby.

High above them, gods of some sort hovered among fluffy white clouds in a pale blue sky painted on the arched ceiling.

"Do you think they're Greek or Roman?" Alicia said.

"I think some folks are taking themselves just a bit too seriously. And do you really care?"

"Come to think of it . . . no."

"What floor are they on?" Jack said as he led her to the directory that took up a large section of one of the west walls.

"Twenty-something."

He found it. Looked like they called the whole twenty-third floor home.

Out of the corner of his eye he watched the guard at the security desk watching them. It was after hours and they didn't look all that presentable, what with Jack in jeans and Alicia wrinkled from being taped up.

"We shouldn't risk trying to go upstairs tonight. Don't want to arouse any suspicions or put anyone on alert. But I wish I could get a look at their office layout."

"Not much to see," Alicia said. "You step out of the elevator and face a glass wall with a receptionist on the other side. I'm sure she's gone now, but even when she's there, you don't get past that wall until she hits a button to release the door."

Damn, Jack thought. Getting a client list was going to be tough. Maybe impossible.

"Why all the security, you think?"

Alicia shrugged. "Well, you never know what kind of riffraff will be sneaking around after hours."

"Oh-ho!" he said. "The doctor makes a funny."

"Mark the date and time," she said. "It doesn't happen very often."

"Can I help you folks?"

The security guard had walked over. He was big and black, and acting friendly, but Jack could tell he was all business. If they didn't have any business in the Hand Building, he was going to ask them to please move themselves back to the street. No monkey business on his shift.

"Fascinating architecture," Jack said. "When did this building go up?"

"I'm not sure," the guard said. "I think there's some sort of plaque in the corner behind that tree by the door. Take a look at it on your way out."

Jack gave him a nod and a smile. "Heard and understood. We're on our way."

The guard returned the smile. "Thanks."

Just to keep up appearances, Jack peeked behind the ficus tree sitting in front of the brass plaque, but he never got to read the inscription. Something else snatched his attention.

"I'll be damned!"

"What?" Alicia said. "What is it?"

"See that little mark there on the corner molding above the plaque? The black circle with the dot inside?"

"That magic marker thing?"

"That's it. I know the guy who made that. His name's Milkdud . . . Milkdud Swigart."

This was good. Better than good. This was *great*.

"And . . . ?"

"It means this building's been hacked."

"I don't get it."

"I'll explain later. But it means we may have a way to find out who's backing Thomas."

11

Kemel groaned as he hung up the phone. Surely Allah had deserted him.

First he had learned of Baker and Thomas Clayton's crazy stunt tonight. The sister would certainly file felony charges against her brother, setting back the whole operation months, perhaps years, perhaps permanently.

He had been so furious, he'd even told the swollen-nosed Baker that Nazer should have fired him last week when Kemel had told him to. Baker had not taken that well, but that was too bad. The man was jeopardizing everything.

But then Kemel's brother, Jamal, called from home, and his fury evaporated like water spilled on summer sands of the Rub al-Khali, replaced by dread for his eldest son.

"It's Ghali," Jamal said. "He's been arrested."

Kemel felt the heart dropping out of his body. Ghali? His eighteen-year-old son, the pride of his life . . . arrested? No, this could not be.

"For what? What happened?"

"He has been accused of stealing a camera from the wife of a visiting American businessman."

"Impossible! Ridiculous!"

"That is what I said," Jamal told him. "But there are witnesses. And he had the camera with him when they caught him."

"Oh, no." Kemel moaned. He closed his eyes to squeeze out the light. "Oh, no, this can't be true. Why would he do something like this?"

"I don't know, brother. Perhaps if you were home . . ."

Yes! Home! He had to go home immediately!

But he could not. Not yet.

"I will come as soon as I can. But I cannot leave right now."

"What business could be more important than this?" Jamal said with what sounded like scorn. Never in all his years had he spoken to Kemel like that. He would not use that tone if he knew the nature of Kemel's business here.

Kemel ached to tell his younger brother why he was in America but did not dare. Jamal and his whole family would be in jeopardy if it was discovered that Kemel had breathed so much as a word of it to him.

"Where is Ghali now?"

"It took me all night, but I managed to secure his release. I am keeping him at my house—I have taken responsibility for him."

Kemel calculated that the eight-hour time difference made it six a.m. in Riyadh. "Thank you, Jamal. I can never thank you enough."

"This is far from over, Kemel. I will do whatever I can, but Ghali may have to stand trial."

Kemel nodded, though there was no one to see. Yes, yes, he knew. Especially since a foreigner was involved. The Saudi authorities seldom passed up a chance to demonstrate the superiority of Islamic Law to westerners. Even if this American woman asked that no charges be brought, they might still proceed with trial and punishment.

And punishment would mean the loss of Ghali's right hand.

How could this happen? Ghali had always been wild and headstrong, yes, but never a thief. What could have possessed him? He wanted for nothing, yet he stole a camera! *A camera!* There were almost a dozen fine cameras lying about the house!

This made no sense.

He had to turn to a higher power for help. Tomorrow was Friday, the holy day. He was bound to say his noontime prayers in the mosque. Tomorrow Kemel would pray all day in the mosque for his errant son.

FRIDAY

1

After a couple of rounds of answering-machine tag, Milkdud's last message had said to meet him at Canova—not Canova's, just Canova—on West Fifty-first at ten-thirty. So that was when Jack showed up. He rode the lemming crowd of parents and kids streaming toward the red neon Radio City sign dead ahead on the far side of Sixth Avenue. With Ruth's Chris behind him and Le Bernadin across the street, Jack found Canova.

He leaned his forehead against the front window and peered past the faux pilings lined up on the other side of the glass. Looked like one of those buffet places that had been multiplying like coat hangers through most of the nineties.

He stepped inside and looked for Milkdud.

Canova was a little more elaborate than most of its buffet kin. Usually they were strictly takeout—fill your containers at the buffet counter, weigh and pay, then be on your way. Canova offered two buffet areas, and seating.

The crowd was thin—still awhile before the lunch mob hit—but Jack didn't spot Milkdud. And Milkdud was hard to miss.

He tapped the Korean guy wiping a nearby table.

"I was supposed to meet someone here—" he began.

"I don't know," the Korean said quickly, vigorously shaking his head. "I don't know."

"He's a black guy," Jack said. He pointed to his forehead. "And up here he's got—"

"Oh, yes." He pointed to the left, toward a sign with an arrow and the word SEATING. Jack wondered how he'd missed that. "Over there. He over there."

Jack stepped through the small brick arch and checked out the extra seating area. He saw the back of a tall thin black guy, short-cropped hair, facing the wall. Jack ducked back to the buffet area, bought a Pepsi, then dropped into the seat opposite Milkdud.

"Sushi for breakfast?" Jack said, checking out Milkdud's tray.

"Hey, Jack," Milkdud said, extending his hand across the postage-stamp table. "Got to preserve my slim boyish figure, man."

"For hacking, right?"

He shrugged. "A spare tire can keep me from where I want to go sometimes. Besides, this is brunch and you really can't call California rolls sushi."

They went back years. Jack kept running into this tall guy—Milkdud had worn dreadlocks then—at the revival houses around the city. They started talking, and finally got to the point of trust where they'd lend each other tapes and discs of cherished films. But if Jack had ever known the name the man's mother called him, he'd long since forgotten. He was Milkdud—or Dud—to the world. Long, lean, with milk-chocolate skin, a laid-back look, and an easy smile; but all people seemed to remember about the guy—even in the days when he had those huge dreadlocks— was the big, black Aaron Neville-class mole in the center of his forehead. Some class clown during his growing up must have compared it to a certain brand of chocolate-coated caramel, and the name had stuck.

"I stand corrected," Jack said. "So what are you up to these days?"

"Working in the Coconuts up the street."

"They're hiring MIT grads now?"

Milkdud shrugged. "I'm in the laser disc department. The hours are flexible, and the discounts help me keep up my collection."

Jack nodded. Flexible hours . . . that was something Milkdud needed for his real passion. Yeah, he was a movie freak, but old buildings were his first love.

"How many discs you got now?"

Another shrug. "Lost count. But I'm glad you called. Been meaning to get in touch with you about a recent purchase."

Jack straightened. "Something on my want list?"

Milkdud reached down and pulled a plastic Coconuts bag from under the table. He handed it across to Jack.

"Yes!" Jack said when he looked inside. He pulled out a laser disc of *An Unmarried Woman*. "How'd you find it?"

The 1978 Jill Clayburgh–Alan Bates drama was one of Gia's favorite films. Its charms eluded Jack—he'd never been particularly taken by any of Paul Mazursky's work—but he'd been trying for years to buy or tape a copy for Gia. He religiously checked the schedules of all the cable movie channels he subscribed to—TCM, AMC, TMC, Cinemax, Starz, Encore, and the rest—but they rarely listed it, or when they did, he always found out about it too late to set his recorder.

Milkdud said, "One of the used places down on MacDougal. It's a good transfer but it's Hong Kong."

"I see that. Not dubbed, I hope."

"No—just Cantonese subtitles."

"Subtitles are no problem. Can I borrow it?"

"Yeah. As long as you want. Just don't forget where you got it."

"You *like* it?" Jack knew Milkdud as a Guinea gross-out maven. Heavy into Argento, Bava, and Fulci. Hard to believe he'd even sit through *An Unmarried Woman*, let alone want it in his collection.

"Nah. But it's so damn hard to find, I feel I should have a copy. Weird, huh?"

"Just the collecting disease."

Jack understood; he suffered himself. "Your timing is perfect, Dud." Now he had at least one Christmas gift for Gia she wouldn't be expecting. "I'll do a dub and get it back to you as soon as." Jack hesitated, feeling bad about asking Milkdud for another favor after he'd found Gia's movie for him, but he had no choice. "And . . . I need your help."

"Your message mentioned a building hack."

"Right. I spotted your squiggle in the Hand Building last night."

Milkdud's eyes lit as he smiled. "The Hand Building . . . the twenty-five story ferroconcrete on Forty-fifth. Yeah, she's a beauty. A prime example of postwar urban architecture. My handle's still there? Cool. Hacked her about three years ago. Should've brought my notes, then I could give you the exact date and some details. A very cool place. That lady's full of blind spaces."

"You keep notes?" Jack said. This was great news. "Like some sort of hacking diary?"

"I like to think of it simply as 'exploring.' We were calling it 'hacking' back in the seventies, but then the computer geeks co-opted the term. I don't like the comparison. Computer hacking implies mischief, malevolence, and malfeasance."

"Not in its pure form," Jack said.

"True. The pure computer hacker is an explorer. He wants to gain entry, open all the doors, find all the hidden places, learn all the secrets, and leave everything pretty much as he found it. That's what I do. I get into a building and explore all the spaces the workaday occupants never see, don't even know exist, then I get out."

"But not without leaving your 'Killroy-was-here' squiggle."

Milkdud smiled. "Which, in a bow to CB culture, we call a 'handle.' "

"How the hell did you ever get into this?"

A shrug. "It's sort of a rite of passage at MIT."

"For everyone?"

"Hell, no. It's got its dangers. First off, you can get killed. We use roofs and elevator shafts a lot, and those shafts are dangerous. Second, it's illegal. You may not mean any harm, but try explaining that to the Man. At the very least, it's trespassing. At worst, it's attempted robbery. And you'd better not be claustrophobic, because your hallways are air shafts and ducts."

Jack nodded. "I can see how that might weed out quite a few."

"Better believe it. And add to the weeds all the ones who just don't get it."

Jack slapped the side of his head. "You're kidding. You mean there's actually some people out there who don't think crawling through air shafts is cool fun?"

Milkdud smiled. "One or two. But the ones who really understand us are the computer hackers. And there's a fair amount of crossover. A good number of keyboard geeks, at least the ones who aren't acrophobic and claustrophobic, hack buildings too. Back at MIT I used to explore with a guy named Mike MacLaglen—expert phreaker and ice in his veins when it came to building hacks. But he wasn't pure, man. There's no money in building hacking. He dropped out to hack video chips. Don't know where he is now. But he was good."

"As good as you?"

"Hell, no."

"And you're still hacking?"

"Yeah. Got a curious nature, I guess." He sighed. "But it's getting harder. Security's getting better and better. Still, when you get into the right sort of building"—his eyes unfocused here—"you know, one that's been remodeled a dozen or two times over the years—and you start finding all these blind spaces in corners, and stairways to nowhere, and maybe even a tiny sealed-off room in the middle of a floor, and you know you're the pioneer hacker here because yours is the first handle to get marked on the walls of those spaces . . . I tell you, Jack, there's nothing like it."

Jack shook his head. A brilliant guy, but definitely a few kinks in his Slinky.

"Say, I wanted to be in on a meeting in a certain office on the twenty-first floor of the Hand Building. Could you help me?"

"Sure."

Excellent, Jack thought. This is going to be easier than I thought.

"So you could place an AV pickup behind a grille where I could see and hear what's going down?"

Milkdud shook his head. "No way."

Jack opened his mouth, then closed it. That wasn't the reply he'd been expecting.

"No way? I thought you just said—"

"I said I'd help, but I'm not bugging the place for you. That's against the code."

"What code?" Jack tried to hide his annoyance, but he was sure some leaked through. "The official building hackers' code of ethics?"

"Maybe." Milkdud stayed cool. "Don't know about any official code, but I know it goes against Milkdud's."

Jack leaned back and sipped his Pepsi. "Damn, Milkdud. I was counting on you."

"You want to eavesdrop these days, you don't need anything in the room. You just bounce a laser beam off the window glass and you'll hear every word they say."

"I'm fresh out of lasers today."

"You can buy one in dozens of these 'executive security' places all over town. I think there's even one on Fifth Avenue around the corner from the Hand."

"My operation's not exactly high tech, Dud. No way I could rig up a laser on Forty-fifth Street. You see that stuff on TV all the time, but I work in the real world. And besides, I need more than just audio. I want to *see* into that office. The meeting itself isn't as important as who's present and what's said *after* the meeting."

"So," Milkdud said, "why don't you get in there and watch and listen yourself?"

"Me . . . hack my first building . . . in midtown . . . during business hours? Right."

Jack had a vision of himself wedged into a ventilation duct, mewing like a kitten up a tree, while firemen and EMS men broke through walls and acetylene torched their way through the galvanized metal to cut him free.

And then his picture on the front pages of the *Post* and the *Daily News*. He could see the headlines:

AIR SHAFT AIRHEAD
GETS CAUGHT!

He shuddered.

"No, thanks."

"I'll help you," Milkdud sad.

"What about the Milkdud Code?"

"It says I won't plant any devices for you, but it doesn't say I can't show you how to hack a building. That would make me an apostle of the building hack. I'd be . . . St. Milkdud, a missionary, spreading the word to the unenlightened, making converts—"

"Okay," Jack said, smiling and holding up his hands. "I get it."

He thought about the offer. If Milkdud could get him to a spot where he could see and hear what went on in Thomas Clayton's lawyer's office . . .

"Let me get this straight," Jack said. "You're offering to be my guide into the bowels of the Hand Building—"

"Pathfinder would be more accurate. Trailblazer even more so."

"Which means?"

"I'll check my notes and rehack the Hand this weekend. You tell me where you want to be, and I'll see if I can find a way for you to get there. If I do find one, I'll get you into the building on the morning of the meeting and point you in the right direction."

"You mean you won't be coming along?"

Milkdud shook his head. "Uh-uh. The code, you know."

"But what if I get lost or"—the Jack-as-kitten-up-a-tree vision flashed before him again—"stuck?"

"I'll diagram your route and mark the passage. If you can follow directions and road signs, you should have no problem. And if it'll make you feel better, bring along a cell phone. I'll be outside. You get in trouble, call me."

Jack drummed his fingers on the table, thinking. His instincts told him to find some other way. He wasn't claustrophobic—he'd spent long hours in cramped places before—but he preferred multiple escape routes whenever he put himself into a situation. But with Milkdud available to back him up . . . maybe it could work.

"All right," Jack said. "Let's plan it out."

"First thing I'll need to know is the location of the meeting. The *exact* location."

"I can get that." *I think.*

"Good. Next thing is, you've got to get yourself some hacking clothes."

"Such as?"

"Well, in the summer, when the AC is on, I use long johns. But in the winter, it can get hot in those ducts. Even in the returns. So I'd recommend a lightweight coverall—sans buttons, or a rugby shirt and panty hose."

"Panty hose? Jeez, Dud!"

"You're gonna be belly-crawling every which way you can, Jack. You gotta be able to *slide*, man."

"Yeah . . . but pantyhose?"

Another *Post* headline flashed before his eyes:

PANTY-HOSED PEEPER
PINCHED IN PIPES!

Jack said, "I'll go with the coveralls, I think. What else will I need?"

"A three-piece suit."

"Aw, no!"

2

"Where did we meet?" Alicia said, cradling the phone against her shoulder as she unwrapped half a turkey sub from the Blimpie's down the block. "In Gordon Haffner's office. He's Thomas's lawyer."

She'd waited all morning to hear from Jack. He'd been so excited last night after finding that magic marker squiggle in the Hand Building lobby. He'd started babbling about building hackers—whatever they were—and somebody named Milkdud. He'd taken her home, checked out her apartment to make sure it was empty and secure, then left her, saying he'd call in the morning.

Well, he hadn't called. And she'd had some very bad moments walking to the hospital this morning. She'd kept to the center of the sidewalk, eyeing every van near the curb, every passerby, tensing at every set of hurried footsteps behind her. She'd never been so relieved to see the guard at the front door.

Her relief had turned to dismay when she saw Hector's blood culture report: *Candida albicans,* the opportunistic fungus that rode into AIDS patients on the backs of other infections. She'd added IV amphotericin B to the mix of meds flowing into Hector, and crossed her fingers.

His foster mother probably hadn't been giving him his prophylactic Diflucan either. At least Alicia hoped that was the reason for the infection. If not, it meant he'd picked up a resistant strain, and that could be bad. Very bad.

She took a bite of her sandwich. She hadn't had dinner last night, hadn't been able to stomach breakfast this morning; it had taken until noon for the thought of food to occur to her. And now, just as she was starting lunch at her desk, Jack called.

"Gordon Haffner," Jack said. "Where's his office on the floor?"

She swallowed. "I'm not sure."

"It's important, Alicia."

"All right, then. Let me think."

She replayed that afternoon in her mind, walking through the glass doors on the twenty-first floor with Leo Weinstein, sitting in the reception area, then being led down a hall to Haffner's office. She remembered looking out the window and seeing the blue canopy of the Chemists' Club across the street below.

"He overlooks Forty-fifth Street."

"That's a start. But I need to know exactly. Is it a corner office?"

"No. But it's right next to a corner office—the east corner."

"You're sure?"

"Absolutely. I remember thinking that Thomas might not have the top man in the firm, but he seems to have someone close to the top."

"The office next to the east corner overlooking Forty-fifth," Jack said. "Got it."

"What's up?" she said.

"You're going to have a meeting with Mr. Haffner Monday morning. You're going to tell him you're ready to sell the place."

She almost choked on a mouthful of turkey. She coughed and swallowed.

"Like hell, I am!"

"Easy. Just listen. You're going to ask an absurd amount, say, ten million."

"They'll never go for that."

"Of course not. The offer isn't the point. It's the meeting we want. I'll explain all the details later. Right now you should be freeing up Monday morning so you can be there. A guy named Sean O'Neill will be calling you this afternoon. He'll be your lawyer on Monday."

"My lawyer? But he doesn't know a thing about—"

"He doesn't need to, and believe me, he doesn't want to. Sean's greatest pleasure in life is driving other lawyers crazy. He'll set up the meeting for you."

She checked her calendar. Monday morning . . . she'd have to excuse herself from the monthly meeting of the infectious disease department . . . but nothing else was pressing.

"Okay. Can do it. But the earlier the better."

"Good. That makes two of us."

"This is all very weird, Jack. I'd like to know what's going on."

"I'll explain everything Sunday night when we have our rehearsal."

"Rehearsal?"

"Yeah. You, me, and Sean. But the important thing for you to know right now is that setting up this meeting with the lawyers gives us a breather. No one's going to be making another grab for you or threaten you if they think an agreement might be reached on Monday. That means you can stop looking over your shoulder—at least for the weekend."

"That's a relief."

"For both of us. Gotta run. Talk to you later."

And then he was gone.

Alicia hung up and attacked her sandwich with new gusto. She felt as if a lead weight had been removed from the pit of her stomach. She wouldn't have to live like a fugitive for the next couple of days.

But what on earth was Jack planning? And how reliable was he? Sure he seemed extraordinary with the strong-arm stuff, but this was different. He'd be dealing with a big law firm, some extremely sharp minds. Could a guy from the street outwit the Harvard grads on the twenty-first floor?

She didn't know, but if she had to bet, Alicia didn't think she'd risk her money on the suits.

3

"Is that him?" Jack said as a new voice spoke from the cassette player's speaker.

Jorge shook his big head. He was dressed for business—his workday started when the offices began emptying—in a cutoff sweatshirt that exposed his thick arms to the shoulder.

The two of them sat in the cramped extra bedroom of Jorge's apartment that doubled as a business office. Down the hall his wife was clearing dinner while his two sons played the latest Mario; the apartment was redolent of spicy meat.

Jack fast-forwarded the tape, stopping and starting until he heard a new voice.

"How about this guy?"

Another head shake. "No. Not Ramirez."

"Better be soon," Jack said. "We're getting to the end of the tape."

Jorge had had one of his cousins slip the flyers under all the doors in Ramirez's building. The overkill had been necessary to keep Ramirez off guard. The flyer used the Hudak Realty letterhead but substituted a voice mail number Jack had rented, saying it was the direct line to David Johns, the Hudak agent who had an exclusive on this property. Jack had left an outgoing message saying that Mr. Johns was with a client and would get back to you as soon as possible.

He'd brought a tape of all the calls to Jorge's apartment.

"Maybe he's not interested," Jorge said.

"If what you told me about him is true," Jack said, "he'll call. He won't be able to resist. Just look at all these other—"

"There!" Jorge said as someone new spoke from the tape player. "That's him. That's the *hijo de puta!*"

Jack didn't know much Spanish, but he knew what that meant. He leaned back and listened to Ramirez's smooth, lightly accented voice. Obviously he'd been in the country longer than Jorge.

"Yes, Mr. Johns. I would like very much to meet with you about the

property you describe in your flyer. I must leave town this weekend on a business trip, and I wish to inspect the property before I depart."

Ramirez left his office and home phone numbers.

Smooth, Jack thought. He's probably been by the place and seen it from the sidewalk. He knows it's a steal and he *wants* it. So he uses a phony trip to push for a quick look-see without appearing anxious.

From what Jack had gathered from Jorge, Mr. Paco Ramirez fancied himself a wheeler-dealer, especially in real estate. Liked to pick up bargains in the current upmarket and turn them around for a quick profit. Guys like him were always on the lookout for someone in a hurry to sell. Jack's flyer had served up a deal he was sure Mr. Ramirez was salivating over.

"All right," Jack said. "He's nibbling the bait. Now we've got to set the hook and reel him in."

He used Jorge's phone to call Ramirez's office. The man was on the line only seconds after Jack told the receptionist he was David Johns. After a little polite small talk, Ramirez cut to the chase and they set up an appointment to inspect the property the following morning at nine sharp.

"What do we do now?" Jorge asked.

" 'We' don't do anything," Jack told him. "From now on it's just me. The most important thing for you to do is stay away from that town house. Ramirez gets one hint that you're involved, and he'll be gone. Just stay here tomorrow morning and answer the phone. I may have to make a call. I'll ask questions, and you answer them anyway you want—give me the weather report, I don't care. I just want a voice on the other end."

Jorge pursed his thick lips. "Esplain to me again, *por favor,* how this will get my money back,"

"Okay. Once more. I'm going to get your money by convincing Ramirez to give me a big cash deposit on the town house."

Jorge shook his head. "But he is no fool, Mr. Jack."

"I'm sure he's not. But I know his type: He gets off on screwing people. He likes to find a little guy, or someone at a disadvantage, and take them for all he can. He could have afforded all along to pay you for your work, but he chose not to. Why? Because he discovered a weak spot—your illegal relatives working for you—and he couldn't pass up the opportunity to take advantage of that. It's a power trip."

"You know others like Ramirez?"

Jack nodded. "Hell, yes. They keep me in business. I've become a sort of expert on these guys. I'm going to turn Ramirez's game back on

him. I'm going to put a sweet deal in front of him and let him think he's
screwing someone in the bargain."

"But cash? He will not give you cash."

"He will if he thinks I don't want it."

Jorge was shaking his head again. Jack had noticed him doing that a
lot lately.

"Trust me," Jack said. "Even if it doesn't work, at least we'll have
some fun with Ramirez."

Jorge's scowl said fun was the last thing on his mind.

4

The phone rang as Alicia was readying to call it a day. Raymond was
gone already so she picked up herself.

"This is Detective Will Matthews. Is that you, Alicia?"

"Yes," she said as brightly as she could. "How are you?"

Oh, hell. More bad news?

She'd had another call from the hospital attorney this morning, asking
her if she'd had any second thoughts about her child molestation charge
against Floyd Stevens. Now what?

"I'm fine," he said. "Well, the reason I called is I may have some
good news for you."

"About Stevens?"

"The one and only."

"He's pleading guilty?"

"No, but almost as good. I'd like to tell you all about it over
dinner."

Alicia felt her hackles rise. "Will . . . if this involves the charges I
brought against him, don't you think—?"

"Nothing *directly* to do with your charges. If you insist, I'll tell you
now, but if you don't have plans, I'd prefer to do it over an early dinner.
I promise, you won't be disappointed."

Alicia hesitated. First lunch, then dinner, then . . . what?

I don't have time for this.

But if he'd been checking into Stevens on his own time and had come up with something helpful, how could she refuse?

"Okay, then," she said. "Dinner it is. When and where?"

He asked if she liked Italian. When she told him she did, he gave her the address of a trattoria on Seventh Avenue about ten blocks up from the Center. He'd meet her there in half an hour.

Good news, he'd said. She hoped so. She could dearly use some.

5

"You must eat here often," Alicia said as the two of them settled into a booth built for four.

Alicia had arrived early. Normally she would have walked. But despite Jack's assurance that no one would bother her before Monday's meeting with the lawyers, she'd taken a cab.

Will showed up a few minutes later. The maître d' had greeted him with a big smile, and three people from the bar had called hello.

He shrugged. "I guess if I hang out anyplace, it's here. But we're talking once or twice a week."

Is this where you were last night? she wondered. If you'd been walking behind me instead of Jack, Thomas and his bully boys would be in jail right now and this whole mess would be settled.

"I thought cops hung out at cop bars."

"They do. I spent a couple of years funneling money into Midtown South's favorite watering hole, but you know . . . you get tired of cop talk all the time. At least I do. Here I'm just Will Matthews, who happens to be a cop."

A waiter stopped by with a basket of rolls and long anorectic Italian bread sticks. After checking with her, Will ordered a bottle of Chianti classico, then he leaned forward.

"Let's get to the latest on Floyd Stevens."

He held out the breadbasket and she took a bread stick.

"Please." She bit off the end of the bread stick with a decisive snap.

"I've been tailing him."

"They let you do that?" she said, surprised. "I mean with all the other crime going on—"

"I wish. No, I did this on my own time."

"Your own time?" If Alicia had been surprised seconds ago, she was shocked now. "But why?"

"I told you. I used to work Vice, and I know these creeps. They're out of control. You interrupted him, so I figure he might not have gotten what he wanted. And that meant he'd be on the prowl again real soon. So as soon as I got off duty, I made it to the Upper West Side and hung around outside his place, waiting for him to come in or go out."

"And?"

"Last night he went out. Walked down to the garage where he keeps his car and drove straight to the Minnesota Strip."

"What's that?"

"A place you'll probably never see. It's sort of a sex supermarket, full of prostitutes of all ages and all sexes."

"*All* sexes? I know of only two."

"Well, there are the in-betweens. Let's see . . . how do I put this . . . guys who've been changed on top—you know, breast implants and hormone treatments on the skin—but remain fully equipped below . . . they're a hot item on the Strip."

"Wonderful."

Will shrugged. "They're a pretty pathetic crew down there, but personally it doesn't bother me. Whatever gets you through the night. But when the pimps start putting kids out for the chicken hawks—"

"Chicken hawks?" This is like a new language, Alicia thought. "What's that?"

"Most times it refers to gays who cruise for very young male prostitutes, but I use it for anybody, straight or bent, looking for too-young stuff."

"Chickens," Alicia said, feeling queasy. "Young, tender, defenseless."

She looked at Will. So clean-cut, almost boyish-looking with that short blond hair; his job put him in almost daily contact with humankind at its worst, yet he seemed to have remained untainted somehow.

"That's what they like. And Floyd Stevens is one of them. I followed him. He knew exactly where he was going—in fact, I think he must have called ahead, because there was somebody waiting at a corner with a *very* young-looking girl when he pulled up. The kid got into the car and the two of them drove away."

The bread stick crumbled in Alicia's hand as her anger flared. "And you let him?"

"Of course not. But I didn't want to complicate things by nabbing him myself—didn't want that lawyer raising any questions of entrapment or harassment—so as I followed him into the dock area, I patched through to a couple of guys I know on Vice. They waited till he parked, snuck up on him, and caught him in the act."

"*Now* will someone take him off the streets?" she said, brushing the crumbs off her lap.

"He is off the street. At least for the time being. He's locked up, charged with having sex with a minor."

"And that's your good news? Another poor kid was molested by this creep?"

"Don't you see?" Will said, looking a little hurt. "He's not going to walk away from this one. Now he's got two sexual molestation charges in one week. He can't threaten or buy his way out when the witnesses are cops. He's going to be too busy defending himself to go after you. You're off the hook."

. . . Off the hook . . .

Alicia slumped back against the padded back of the booth as the truth of Will's words seeped past her anger at Floyd Stevens.

"Oh, my God," she said softly. "You're right. He can't say he never touched Kanessa. Can't say I imagined it all and overreacted."

"And best yet," Will said. "He's going down for last night. He's going to do time."

Alicia closed her eyes and took a deep breath. She felt as if a small planet had been lifted from her shoulders.

"Thank you," she said, looking at Will. She felt a sudden burst of warmth for this man, this good, good man. "What you did is above and beyond duty. I . . . I don't know what to say." Impulsively, she reached across the table and clutched his hand. "Thank you."

He shook his head. "Nailed a perv and helped a very special lady out of a jam. Trust me. The pleasure was all mine."

Alicia realized that Will had cupped her hand in both of his. She couldn't pull away now . . . and wasn't sure she wanted to.

The waiter's arrival with the wine broke the spell.

Will made a big display of aerating the tasting portion of the Chianti, checking its legs, sniffing it, swirling it in his mouth, doing everything but gargling with it, then he swallowed and puckered his face into an awful grimace.

"This is swill!" he told the waiter. "Take it out back and pour it down a storm drain!"

The waiter snorted. "Yeah," he said with a crooked smile. "Like you'd know."

He poured Alicia a glass, then casually added more to Will's.

"I'm like Rodney Dangerfield here," Will said, shaking his head. "No respect."

"With beer, you maybe got credentials," the waiter said. "But wine? Fuhgheddaboudit."

He left the bottle on the table and strolled away.

"You really *do* come here a lot."

Will laughed. "Yeah, Joey's the owner's nephew. We go way back."

Alicia sipped the wine and found the first sip a little tart, but the second wasn't so bad.

"So," she said, edging toward a question that had begun to niggle at her. "I imagine working all day and following people half the night plays havoc with your social life."

"Social life? What's that?"

"You know—friends, family, girlfriend . . . that sort of thing."

"It was no sacrifice, believe me. My friends didn't miss me, my folks retired to South Carolina, and as for the woman in my life"—he rotated his glass, staring into the swirling ruby fluid—"she up and left almost a year ago."

"I'm sorry," Alicia said, mentally kicking herself for prying. She fumbled for something to say. "I—I guess the long hours of being a cop are tough on a relationship."

Will grunted. "I wish that had been it. I could have handled that, maybe even worked something out. No . . . it was just about this time last year she went home to visit her family in Vermont—a little town called Brownsville—and ran into an old beau. They hooked up, the old sparks started burning again, and next thing I know she's on the phone telling me all about it and saying she's not coming back to New York, she's staying in Vermont and marrying this guy."

"That must have hurt," Alicia said, feeling for him. He'd delivered the story so matter of factly, but she sensed the lingering pain.

"That it did. Took about a million calls and even a trip to Vermont before it finally got through to me that she really meant it." He straightened and looked at her, as if shrugging off the memories. "But that was then. I got over it. Life goes on."

And now you think you should find someone else, Alicia thought. Please don't set your sights on me, Will Matthews. You've had enough trouble already.

"How about you?" he said. "How's your love life?"

Alicia echoed his earlier comment. "Love life? What's that?" She forced a smile. "Especially when you're married."

He blinked. "Married? I thought . . ."

For a moment she was tempted to morph her story about a traveling beau into a traveling husband, but she couldn't lie to him. Not after what he'd done for her.

"But you've already met my spouse," she said, smiling as she watched his baffled expression for a few heartbeats. Then she let him off the hook: "The Center. We're inseparable, you know."

"Oh!"

He laughed. "Married to the job," he said, nodding. "I know all about that. Got a bit of that problem myself."

It's not always a problem, she thought. Sometimes it's a solution.

She could see him relax. That was good . . . and that was bad. He probably thought he had a clear field.

They spent the meal and perhaps an hour afterward talking, Will probing for details of her life, Alicia dodging and countering with a steady stream of questions that forced him to talk about himself.

The upshot of the evening was Alicia gathering a portrait of a decent man who liked beer, bass fishing, and basketball; a dedicated detective who'd managed—at least so far—to avoid the deep cynicism that seemed to infect most big-city cops.

And Will? As they left the restaurant, Alicia doubted he knew much more about her now than he had when he'd walked in.

As Will drove her home, Alicia watched his hands where they gripped the wheel. Strong hands, and strong arms. She wondered what those arms would feel like around her. She rarely minded being alone, in fact, most of the time she was too busy to realize that she *was* alone.

But there came times, at night, mostly, when she felt an urge to cling to someone, to feel protective arms around her, when she simply wanted to be *held*.

She was feeling relaxed and safe as Will pulled to a stop in front of her apartment. And she was torn: Ask him in or not? . . . ask him in or not?

And then a beeper sounded.

Will checked his belt. "Not mine."

Alicia fished hers out of her shoulder bag, and felt the mood shatter as she recognized the number on the display.

Hector's floor. Only one reason they'd be calling her at this hour.

"Will, can you take me over to St. Vincent's? Fast? I mean, really fast."

He replied with squealing tires.

SATURDAY

1

After only three hours sleep, Alicia was back in the hospital, this time in the Pediatric ICU. Little Hector Lopez had crashed last night—grand mal seizures and respiratory arrest. She and the house staff had pulled him through—just barely.

Will had hung around for hours downstairs in the waiting area. He didn't know Hector, had never laid eyes on him, yet he'd seemed genuinely concerned. Finally Alicia convinced him to go home.

He'd hugged her and wished her luck, and she'd watched him go, thinking this was someone special.

But now she was watching Hector, unconscious, a slim ribbed endotracheal tube snaking from his mouth to a larger tube, his bony chest rising and falling in time to the hissing rhythm of the ventilator at his bedside.

She heard a knock on the glass partition to her left and turned to see Harry Wolff gesturing to her from the other side. She'd called him in on consult regarding the seizure. He'd done a spinal tap. Hector's central nervous pressure had been up, and the fluid had looked hazy. Not good, not good . . .

Alicia stepped to the door and pulled her mask down to her chin. "Harry. What have you got?"

His expression was grim. "Candida in the CSF."

Alicia sighed. *Damn.* That explained the seizure. Although not a complete surprise, she'd been hoping the pediatric neurologist would find something easier to treat.

"Any more seizure activity?" he said.

"No. But there will be if I don't get this yeast under control. Trouble is, his immune system's in free fall."

"I'll keep looking in. Good luck."

"Thanks, Harry."

She turned and looked back at Hector. She was losing him. Damn it, this was her home field, this was the only place in her life these days where she called the shots. But she seemed to be losing here as well.

There had to be a way to turn this around. Had to be . . .

2

Ramirez showed up a few minutes early, but Jack was ready and waiting at the town house, decked out in his green blazer, white shirt, striped tie, Dockers, loafers, and shit-eating grin.

He'd been here for an hour or so already, familiarizing himself with the place. The house itself didn't need any window dressing; it was in perfect shape. All the closets and dressers were filled with clothes. Whoever had inherited this from the late Dr. Gates hadn't removed a thing.

The only touch he added to the place was a photo he'd picked up in a secondhand shop—two men sitting side by side on a log. He left it in the master bedroom. Then he outfitted the sitting room off the front hall with a card table, and on that arranged manila folders, deposit receipt forms, xeroxed from the original Hudak Realty form.

Ramirez wore a full-length black leather overcoat. A single, heavy gold chain gleamed through the open collar of his golf shirt. He had broad shoulders and a thick middle. He flashed Jack a bright, wide grin, showing off his caps, but his dark eyes were on the move, taking in every detail of the front hall—the etched glass in the front door, the crystal chandelier, the brass carpet rails on the steps leading up to the second floor.

Jack handed Ramirez a card—an exact copy of Dolores's except that the name had been changed to David Johns—and gave him the tour, regurgitating much of the patter he'd heard from Dolores on Thursday. He watched Ramirez run his hands over the fine wood of the antiques as they went from room to room.

As they returned to his makeshift office in the sitting room off the front hall, Jack mentioned that a condition of the sale was that the closing had to be in thirty days.

"Thirty days," Ramirez said. "Why does this owner wish such a quick closing?"

Jack paused, as if debating how much to say, then shrugged.

"All right, I'll tell you. He's looking for a quick sale because he needs the money."

"He is in financial trouble?" Ramirez said.

"No-no." Jack lowered his voice, as if sharing a secret that should go no further. "He's in the hospital now. The poor man needs the money for medical expenses."

"Really?" Ramirez's tone was properly sympathetic; the sudden gleam in his eye was anything but. "That is too bad."

Jack could almost see the wheels turning in Ramirez's head: *in the hospital . . . medical expenses . . . the photo of two men in the bedroom . . .*

He was making a diagnosis.

"And you say the sale price includes all of the furniture?"

"Yes. All fine, fine European antiques. At the asking price, I assure you, it is *quite* a bargain."

Ramirez shrugged. "I do not know. It is very old. Have you had much interest in the property?"

"Strangely enough, no. I don't understand it," Jack said slowly, then pretended to catch himself. "Not that there's been *no* interest. There's been good interest."

Ramirez smiled. "As I said, it is an old house. But I feel sorry for this poor sick man. I will take it off his hands. But not for the asking price, I am afraid."

Jack sniffed. "It's already underpriced."

"I must disagree," Ramirez said.

And then he made a low-ball offer, a good twenty percent under the asking price.

You bastard, Jack thought. Jorge had said he'd steal from a dying man, and Ramirez had just proved him right.

Jack had begun thinking of his imaginary client as a real person, so he didn't have to fake being indignant.

"Out of the question. My client would never consider such a price."

"You will call him and ask him?"

"No. It's an insult to the property."

"Well, if you have had a better offer," Ramirez said with a shrug, "then I will go away. But if you have not, I think it is your duty to consult your client."

"I'll do just that," Jack said.

He whipped out a cell phone and called Jorge's number.

When he answered, Jack said, "Mr. Gates's room, please." While he pretended to wait for a connection, he turned to Ramirez. "Even from his hospital bed, I'm sure Mr. Gates will muster some harsh words about your offer."

Another shrug from Ramirez. "I am only offering what I can afford."

Then Jack spoke into the phone. "Yes. Hello, Mr. Gates. This is David. I'm sorry to call you so early, but I've had an offer on the house." Pause. "Yes, well, I'm not so sure you'll say that after you hear it." He gave the figure and waited, as if listening. "But—" he said, then cut himself off. "But . . ."

Jack frowned, glanced at Ramirez, then turned his back and stepped away.

"But it's an insulting offer!" he said in a stage whisper. "You can't possibly consider it!"

Out of the corner of his eye he saw Ramirez's caps appearing behind a slow grin. Oh, yes, you bastard. This is your birthday on Christmas, isn't it—getting the deal of a lifetime and screwing some poor sick bastard in the process.

Jack said, "Yes . . . yes, I see . . . very well . . ." He sighed. "I'll tell him."

Jack hit the END button on the phone, took a dramatically deep breath, then turned to face Ramirez.

"Well," he said. "Mr. Gates has expressed some interest—limited interest—in your offer. But he has two conditions if he's going to sell for that price."

"Yes?" Ramirez was keeping a calm front, but Jack could tell he was ready to Macarena down the hall.

"You must close in fifteen days."

Ramirez was polishing his diamond ring against the sleeve of his blazer. "That is possible."

"And . . ." This was the biggee. This was where Jack knew he'd either reel Ramirez in or lose him completely. "He wants a twelve-thousand-dollar deposit in cash."

Ramirez stopped polishing and looked up. "In cash? That is an un-usual request. In my many, many real estate dealings I have never left a cash deposit."

"Yes," Jack said, "you're absolutely right. Most unusual. In fact, it's absurd, and I'm sure you want no part of it."

Now it was Jack's turn to play hard to get. Risky, but the only way he could see Ramirez coming up with the cash. He took Ramirez's elbow and guided him from the sitting room toward the front hall.

"Thank you for your interest, Mr. Ramirez. I'll inform Mr. Gates that you wouldn't agree—"

Ramirez pulled his arm free. "One moment. I did not say it was un-acceptable. Just that it was unusual. Perhaps a smaller amount in cash."

"No, I'm afraid not. The twelve thousand is what Mr. Gates said, and twelve thousand is what it must be. If that's too steep—"

The doorbell rang.

What the hell . . . ?

Jack poked his head through the doorway into the front hall.

Someone was standing at the front door. Jack couldn't make out who it was through the etched glass, but he knew it had to be bad news. No one was supposed to be here but Ramirez and him.

Maybe if he ignored the bell . . .

Another ring.

Clenching his teeth and silently cursing, he stepped into the front hall and pulled open the door.

A stocky Oriental in a way expensive charcoal-gray business suit and black fedora stood on the stoop. He could have been Harold Sakata doing Oddjob from *Goldfinger*.

"I am looking for David Johns," the man said. "Is he here?"

Who's this? Jack thought. Someone from Hudak Realty?

He had a feeling his little scam was about to crash into ruin. But he couldn't be too evasive . . . not with Ramirez in earshot.

"May I ask who—?"

He saw the man stiffen as he looked over Jack's shoulder.

"Mr. Ramirez," the Oriental said.

Jack turned. Ramirez was standing in the front hall, staring at the newcomer.

"Hello . . . Sung."

The scene had a surreal déjà vu feel to it, like Jerry and Newman meeting in a Third World *Seinfeld*.

When Jack turned back to the Oriental, he saw that the man had slipped into the front hall.

"I wish to see the property," he said.

This was bad—bad because Jack had no contingency for a third player. The new guy wasn't simply a wild card, he was a wild card who knew Ramirez.

"I'm sorry, Mr. . . . Sung, is it? This is by appointment only."

"But I tried to get an appointment. I called three times but no one called back."

"Really?" Jack said slowly, knowing Ramirez was listening. "That's strange. I never got your messages. Perhaps the answering machine isn't working properly." He snapped his fingers as if he'd just had an epiphany. "*That's* why the response has been so poor! The machine's on the fritz."

"Perhaps," said Sung. "I decided to come over to see if anyone was here."

"And now you have seen," Ramirez said. "I am here, so now you can go."

No love lost between these two, Jack thought. And was that a hint of anxiety in Ramirez's cold dark eyes? Obviously they both had offices in the same building—that was the only way Sung could have seen the flyer.

And maybe they'd butted heads before in a real estate deal.

It hit Jack then that maybe he could stick this wild card in his own hand and play him against Ramirez.

"I'm glad you did, Mr. Sung. Mr. Ramirez was just leaving, so I'll be free to—"

"Wait one minute," Ramirez said. "I made an offer and it was accepted. We have a deal."

"But you said you never leave a cash deposit."

"I said that I never *have*. I did not say that I never will." He pointed back to the sitting room. "Come. We will talk."

Sung folded his arms across his chest. "I will wait."

Jack stepped back into the makeshift office with Ramirez and closed the door behind them.

"I will give you a check," Ramirez said.

Gotcha, Jack thought.

Now he could play hard to get.

He shook his head. "Sorry. Mr. Gates stated that it must be cash."

"But I do not carry that sort of money with me. No one does. Why does he want it to be cash?"

"I can't explain Mr. Gates's reasoning," Jack said with a shrug. "He's on medication, and perhaps it's affecting him. But if that's what he wants, that's what he'll get."

"But what protection do I have?"

Jack straightened and looked down his nose at Ramirez. "Sir, you have the sterling reputation of the Hudak Realty Company behind any transaction. You will get a deposit receipt. And the money will be put in escrow, of course. But I wholeheartedly agree that these are highly unorthodox terms." He reached for the doorknob. "Thank you for coming."

Ramirez flew into a rage then, stomping around the sitting room and shouting about how they had a deal, how he'd made an offer and the buyer had agreed to it and Jack was not going to get rid of him because he thought he might have a better offer waiting in the front hall.

Amazing, Jack thought, fighting to keep a smile off his face. The harder I try to keep him from giving me the cash, the more he wants to pay it.

"You will have your twelve thousand in cash," Ramirez said, finally winding down. "I will return with it in one hour."

You damn well better, otherwise I've gone to a lot of trouble for nothing.

Ramirez turned at the door. "But I warn you, Mr. Johns. If I return and find out that you have made another deal, there will be serious consequences."

"Threats are not necessary, Mr. Ramirez," Jack said softly. He glanced at his watch. "One hour it is."

Ramirez made a hasty exit, pausing only to snarl at the man waiting outside. "Might as well go home, Sung. It is sold."

Sung gave him a small bow. "Congratulations, Mr. Ramirez. But I wish to see the property anyway . . . in case you change your mind."

"That will not happen," Ramirez said, and then he was gone.

Jack turned to Sung.

"We have a deal," he told him. "No point in your waiting. And I'm afraid I don't have time to show you around."

He turned and stepped back into the sitting room. He didn't feel like playing real estate agent for anyone else. He wanted Sung gone.

But Sung followed him into the room.

"I do not need to see the rest to know that I will meet and exceed the terms you have arranged with Mr. Ramirez."

"How do you know . . . ?"

He smiled. "One could not help overhearing such an excited man."

"Yes, well—"

"You will not have to wait an hour." Sung pulled a long wallet from the breast pocket of his suit. "I can give you the cash deposit right now."

"Those terms were for Mr. Ramirez only," he said as Sung counted out twelve one-thousand-dollar bills onto the table. "The owner is not well, and I fear he agreed too hastily to Mr. Ramirez's offer. If Mr. Ramirez does not return, then new terms will have to be set."

"Does the owner know the name of the man who made the offer?"

"No, but—"

"Then, he will not know that the money comes from someone else."

"But he's sick," Jack said, wondering if he could spark some sympathy in Sung. "And it's an unreasonably low price."

"Here is more," Sung said, and laid three more thousand-dollar bills on the table . . . but apart from the rest. "If you think the seller should have more, give him this."

Jack was about to laugh at him. An extra three thousand? What was that added to Ramirez's low-ball price? Nothing.

And then Sung added, "I will require a receipt for only twelve thousand, however."

And now the meaning was clear: Sung was another screwmeister, and this was an orgy. Screw the owner, screw Ramirez, let me have the place for the fire-sale price, and the three grand is yours.

If Ramirez and Sung had a slime-off, Jack wondered who'd win.

"Mr. Sung," Jack said. "You've got a deal."

Mr. Sung bowed. Jack bowed, and gathered up the bills.

"A pleasure doing business with you."

3

After Sung left with his deposit receipt, Jack still had half an hour to kill. He wandered down to the cellar. Something not quite right down there. He'd sensed it earlier when he had shown Ramirez around.

He'd paced off the upstairs floor, but now when he paced off the cellar, he found that the visible floor space didn't match the measurements.

After poking around, he discovered a secret room, walled off from the rest of the cellar. Strange.

Here he was in a house that someone had inherited from the late Dr. Gates . . . a house with secret. Just like the house Alicia Clayton had inherited. Did all old houses hold secrets? He'd discovered this one's— one that seemed innocent enough.

But what about the Clayton house?

He pushed the thought away. One thing at a time. He was almost done here. Then he could start thinking about the Clayton house again.

4

Ramirez returned with five minutes to spare. He seemed relieved that Sung was gone. He handed over his cash and a few minutes later walked out with his official Hudak receipt for his deposit.

When he was gone, Jack laughed aloud and did a little victory dance around the foyer. Did it get any better than this? No, it most assuredly did *not*.

His only regret was that he couldn't be a fly on the wall at the Hudak Agency when both Ramirez and Sung showed up looking for Mr. David Johns.

SUNDAY

1

Kemel called home first thing in the morning and spoke to his brother Jamal. It was mid-afternoon in Riyadh. His other four sons were fine. So were his wife and daughters, but he did not speak to them. The news about Ghali was not good.

"They are going to prosecute," Jamal said.

Kemel slammed his hand down on the table. The telephone's base jumped with the force of the blow.

"No! They cannot."

"He needs you here, brother. I've done what I can, but you know people in high places that I cannot reach."

And neither can I, Kemel thought.

He'd spent most of yesterday calling everyone he knew in Riyadh who had influence in the court or the royal family's ear. No one was leaping to Ghali's aid.

If only I were *there*. I could go face-to-face with these people, make them listen, make them help.

"I will be coming home shortly."

"When?" Jamal said.

"As soon as I possibly can."

"I hope it is soon enough."

Kemel hung up and slumped back on the sofa. All his prayers on Friday had not helped.

He straightened as he realized with a start that perhaps his prayers *were* being answered. Not with the lightning strike of a miracle, but in a more roundabout fashion.

All day Friday, as he had prayed in the mosque, he had expected to hear that the Clayton woman had filed charges against Baker and her brother for attempted kidnapping. But no charges were filed.

And later in the day Kemel had learned from Iswid Nahr's law firm that Alicia Clayton's new lawyer had called for a Monday meeting, and had mentioned "settling this whole mess."

No criminal charges and an offer to settle. Surely he could see the hand of Allah in this.

Sudden elation pulled him from the sofa and dropped him to his knees in grateful prayer.

She wanted to settle. And Kemel would settle with her. Anything she wanted, just to be done with this irrational, contentious American woman. Once he had the house secured in Thomas Clayton's name, he would be within reach of protecting the future of the Arab world.

His work here would not be over, of course, but at least he would be free to travel back to Riyadh to save his family honor . . . and his son's right hand.

2

Alicia spent much of the morning with Hector in the hospital's PICU. The good news was, he hadn't had any more seizures. The bad news was that he wasn't gaining on the candida infection. They were culturing it from his blood, urine, chest, esophagus, everywhere.

She was feeling down when she got to the Center with her Sunday *Times* and coffee, but a call from Will cheered her. He'd called yesterday about Hector and asked for a progress report today. He was so easy to talk to.

He wanted to get together tonight but she couldn't. She had a meeting scheduled with Jack and that new lawyer, Sean O'Neill, tonight. Will pressed her for Monday night—an Armenian place called Zov's with a super rack of lamb—and she gave in.

She was becoming more and more comfortable with him. She didn't know if that was a good thing.

3

Jack didn't return any of Jorge's three calls this morning. The man kept wanting to thank him for returning the full six thousand Ramirez had owed him, and kept asking why Jack hadn't taken his cut. Jack had told him once that his fee had come out of the "interest" he'd charged Ramirez. He didn't want to go over it again.

One call he did return was to his father in Florida, and they went round and round again—Dad urging him to come down and cash in on all the "fantastic opportunities" waiting for him in Florida, Jack dodging this way and that, finally promising to come down for a visit "real soon."

That done, he took a moment to send five hundred dollars in cash to Dolores, care of the Hudak Agency, with an unsigned note stating simply: "For your trouble."

And then it was out to pick up some of the equipment Milkdud had told him he'd need. After that he was looking forward to some time alone with Gia while Vicky was at her art lessons.

4

"Hi, Ma," Sam Baker said as he entered his mother's room.

"Stay away from the fence!" his mother shouted, looking past him.

She was a thin, angular woman, with glistening blue eyes. The nursing home staff had secured her into her chair with a nylon mesh vest they called a "posy." Her bony fingers worked incessantly at the hem of the blanket wrapped around her legs.

"I brought you flowers, Ma," he said, showing her the half dozen short-stemmed roses he'd picked up in the city.

"And get Janey away too!" she called.

Baker sighed and sat on the bed—gingerly. His back still throbbed like some giant goddamn infected tooth from that kidney punch on Thursday night. He unscrewed the cap from the bottle of seltzer he'd brought along. He hated seltzer, but it was better than drinking straight water.

He took a sip and stared at the woman who'd raised him. She'd be sixty-eight next February. Not so old in body, but her mind had begun to slip away about ten years ago. Now it was completely shot. He'd had to move her into this nursing home two years ago, and it was sucking him dry.

He'd heard Alzheimer's ran in families, and that scared the shit out of him. Every time he forgot something he should have remembered, he wondered, *Is this the start?*

Gave him the creeps. He hoped he'd have the wherewithal to swallow the business end of a Tec-9 before he got like her.

"I'm warning you, Janey!" she shouted.

"Who the hell is Janey, Ma?" he said softly.

"It's her latest imaginary playmate," said a voice behind him.

Oh, shit, Baker thought. Karen.

He turned to see his older sister standing in the doorway. And she took up most of that doorway. Christ, his sister the eternal hippie had really let herself go to hell lately. She'd had a second chin for some time, but now it looked like she was well on her way to a third. And if she was going to dye her hair, at least keep it up. Long gray roots and long red ends—was that a look for aging hippie chicks?

Karen said, "You'd know all about Janey if you visited more often."

"Lay off," he said. "I get here when I can. I don't see you coming up with a check every month."

It was an old argument, and he was sick of it. The nursing home was in New Brunswick, New Jersey. Karen lived in the next town. Baker had to trek out from the city.

She pointed to his seltzer bottle. "You on a diet or something?"

Yeah, he thought. I bet you know all about diets.

"No. I'm just thirsty."

He wasn't about to tell her that he was treating a badly bruised kidney. He kept drinking because it kept him running to the head. And every time he took a leak, he saw red—in the water and in his mind. He hadn't checked with a doctor but he figured anything that flushed the blood out of his aching right kidney couldn't be all bad.

Karen stepped closer and stared at his face. "What happened to your nose?"

Broken—for about the fifth time. But this was a bad one.

Another thing he owed that guy, that cabbie or whatever he was. He'd done a real number on him.

Serves me right for letting myself get caught flat-footed, he thought, but it won't happen next time. And there *will* be a next time.

Baker would make sure of that.

And then his little filleting knife would come into play . . .

"Ran into a door."

"No, Sam. You got hurt." Her face showed concern, but he knew it wasn't for him. "What about Kenny? Did he get hurt too?"

"Kenny's fine."

In fact, Baker wished Kenny had been driving the van instead of Chuck. Kenny wouldn't have gotten suckered by that cabbie.

"He'd better be. I don't know what you've gotten him into this time, but if anything happens to him . . ."

I cut him in on a sweet deal, Sam thought. Because he's family. Because you look out for your own.

Same with the other guys in the crew. He'd worked with them all at one time or another. They formed a small fraternity. If something like this Clayton thing fell into their laps, they'd call him.

"He's a grown man, Karen."

"He's still my baby!" she said, her face screwing up.

Oh, no, he thought. Not another crying scene.

"He's my baby and you made a monster out of him. I'll never know why he looked up to you."

"Maybe because I was the only man who stayed in his life for more than a year or two."

"You made him join the marines!"

"I didn't make him do anything. He didn't want to be like all those creeps who kept coming and going through that revolving door in your place. He wanted a little stability. The marines made a man out of him."

"Some man! He's a goddamn mercenary! If anything happens to him, Sam, I'm holding you responsible."

"Don't worry. I'll take good care of him. Better care than you ever did when he was growing up."

She let out a loud sob and hurried from the room.

Baker sat and stared at his mother. Go ahead, Karen. Say it like it's a dirty word, but this gig is going to assure that Mom's taken good care of for the rest of her life. And even if something happens to me, my life insurance policy will do the same thing.

You look out for your own. Whatever it takes.

He rose, wincing at the pain in his kidney. He took another swig of seltzer. He'd switch to beer when he got back to his place in the city. If he hurried he could catch the Giants-Cowboys kickoff.

"Bye, Ma. See you next week."

Mom looked around. "Where's Janey?"

5

Yoshio Takita could not locate Sam Baker, so he chose Thomas Clayton as his surveillance subject for the day. He consumed a bag of Krispy Kreme donuts as he sat outside Clayton's apartment building on Eighth Avenue. They were all delightfully heavy, but the blueberry glazed were the best.

He was about to give up and call it a day when he spotted Clayton stepping from his building. He walked east. He seemed to be in no hurry.

Yoshio followed him to the West Twenties where he saw him enter a club called Prancers—"All Live! All Nude! All Day!"

Yoshio sighed. He knew this routine.

He spotted the sign for a dojo spread across a set of second-floor windows down the block. To kill some time, he climbed the steps and peeked in. After only a few minutes of watching the lazy, overweight instructor, Yoshio left in a fury. If this was a representative example of the way the martial arts were being taught in America, then . . . then . . .

Then they needed someone who really knew what he was doing. Someone like . . .

Me. Yoshio grinned at the thought. My students would be the best in the country. My dojo would kick the rice out of every other dojo.

And I would have all this delicious food at my fingertips, every day, for the rest of my life.

It was a thought worth pondering . . .

6

"You're really going to Florida?" Gia said.

Jack lay on the couch in his apartment, content and thoroughly spent after a leisurely hour of lovemaking with Gia. She lay curled against him, her head on his shoulder, her breath warm on his chest.

"Just to make him happy."

"And maybe just to shut him up?"

"Hopefully, that too."

"What happened to this firm resolve to tell him in no uncertain terms that you would never move to Florida?"

Jack shrugged, and the motion lifted Gia's head.

"I tried," he said, "but I just couldn't do it. The poor guy is so sincere. He wants so badly for me to succeed."

"Does he think you're such a failure?"

"Not so much a failure as a guy with no plan, no agenda, no rudder, so to speak. And in that sense I think he feels *he* failed *me*." Jack felt his contentment slipping away. Why had Gia brought this up? "That's what makes it so hard. It'd be easy to blow him off if he'd been a bad father. But he was a good one, always making an effort to be involved with his kids, and he can't understand where he went wrong with his youngest. So he keeps trying, figuring sooner or later he'll get it right."

"He did leave you a rudder of sorts," Gia said, staring at him with those blue wonders. "You've got a moral compass, a value system. That must have come from someone."

"Not him. He's a citizen. A white-collar, churchgoing, taxpaying veteran of Korea. He'd have a stroke if he knew the truth."

"You're sure of that?"

"Absolutely, positutely, one hundred percent sure."

"And so you're going down to Florida."

"Sure as hell looks that way."

"Can Vicky and I come along? At least as far as Orlando?"

"Hey, now there's an idea," he said, brightening. He kissed her forehead. "Disney World. We've never been there. And the Universal place. I want to see 'Terminator 3-D.' "

Maybe Florida wouldn't be so bad after all. For a week.

"Let's do it."

And then it was time to get dressed and pick up Vicky.

But "3-D" stuck in Jack's brain for some reason, and he treated Gia and Vicky to a late-afternoon IMAX 3-D movie.

Vicky loved it, but Jack came away disappointed. All that screen, those neat 3-D glasses . . . you'd think they could do something better than close-ups of bugs and fish. Why not a *real* movie—like a 3-D IMAX haunted house? *That* would be something to see.

They found a restaurant called Picholine nearby, where they had dinner and made plans for going to Florida. Vicky was ready to bounce off the walls with excitement, and Jack found himself beginning to look forward to the trip.

What better way to see Disney World than with a child? he thought, drinking in her smile and her bright eyes.

The only time Vicky stopped talking about Mickey and Donald was when the fabulous dessert tray came by. She had two.

7

Thomas Clayton had emerged from the strip joint after two hours and walked directly back to his apartment.

This, Yoshio had learned, was one of the patterns of Thomas Clayton's life. Very sad, he thought. He didn't know much about him, but felt sorry for him. This was a lonely, lonely man.

And with this Yoshio himself felt a rare pang of loneliness, a sudden yearning for home. Not for family, for he had none, and not for Tokyo, for New York had given him his fill of big cities. No, he wished he were booked into a little *ryokan* on Shikoku, overlooking the misty vistas of the Inland Sea.

He realized that he had wasted the day. All of the principals seemed to be in a holding pattern, as if waiting for something. But for what? Tomorrow, perhaps?

If so, Yoshio would wait with them.

His stomach didn't feel right. Perhaps the grease from that shish kebab meat—supposedly lamb—he had eaten while waiting for Thomas Clayton this afternoon. He decided to take a break from American food. He stopped at a restaurant in the East Fifties with a superior sushi bar. He spent a number of hours there, sipping Sapporo Draft, nibbling sashimi, and speaking Japanese.

Then he returned to his apartment and watched Kemel Muhallal and his superior hovering around that lamp in the back room of Muhallal's apartment, looking at their mystery object.

8

Jack dropped off Gia and Vicky, then hurried over to Alicia's for a meeting with her and Sean O'Neill, her new lawyer.

As he stepped through the door, Jack handed her an envelope. He liked her wide-eyed look when she opened it and pulled out Mr. Sung's fifteen one-thousand-dollar bills. He told her it was a donation to the Center. She thought it was from him, but he assured her it wasn't. He told her the donor was a very caring real estate investor who wished to remain anonymous.

"He wants you to buy some 'fun things' for the kids," Jack told her. "You decide."

Jack then spent an hour or so with Sean and Alicia working out the plan for Monday morning. Sean had called Gordon Haffner at HRG on Friday and arranged a nine-thirty meeting there with his new client, Alicia Clayton. He'd made it clear that his client did not under any circumstances want her brother present. They would confer with Mr. Haffner alone, and he would convey the substance of the meeting to Thomas Clayton afterward.

And then with everything set and in place for tomorrow, Jack had gone home, ready to end this exceptionally fine weekend with another installment of the Dwight Frye festival. *The Vampire Bat*, perhaps.

Then Milkdud called, saying he'd just returned from successfully re-hacking the Hand Building. Jack thought that was great until Milkdud explained what Jack would have to do tomorrow . . .

MONDAY

1

"You rested and ready for this?" Milkdud said as he and Jack walked down Forty-fifth Street in their suits, carrying their briefcases.

"No."

As they neared the entrance to the Hand Building, Jack said, "You're sure there's no other way to do this?"

"If there is, I don't know it."

"I must be crazy."

Milkdud laughed. "Don't worry. You'll be fine."

Jack wished he was as sure about that.

They pushed through the revolving door into the lobby, looking like they belonged there, and breezed past the security counter where a pair of uniforms were sipping coffee and raptly checking out yesterday's football scores in the morning paper.

"Kind of gives you a new appreciation of the value of organized sports, doesn't it," Jack said as they approached the elevators.

"Especially football pools." Milkdud checked his watch. "Quarter to eight. The shifts are changing. That helps too."

"As does the lack of those dreadlocks you sported when I first met you."

He smiled. "I learned the hard way that dreads and hacking don't mix. They kept getting caught on things in tight spots. Besides, a big part of hacking is going unnoticed."

"Yeah. And I imagine that's kind of hard to do when you've got what looks like a hairy octopus hanging on your head."

A bell chimed to their left, and the center elevator opened its doors. Jack stepped toward it but Milkdud held him back.

"Uh-uh. We're taking the one over there on the left."

"What's the difference?"

"That's the one that's going to put you closest to where you want to go."

"I'm all for that," Jack said.

Milkdud reached inside the center cab and pressed a button, sending it back up.

Half a minute later, the doors to the left elevator opened.

"That's ours," Milkdud said.

As they started toward it, Jack spotted a red-haired woman rounding the corner. She headed their way.

"Move it, Dud," he whispered. "Company's coming."

They'd shown up early to ensure that they'd be able to ride an empty elevator car. This redheaded early bird was going to mess up their plans.

They scrambled through the doors. As soon as he got inside, Milkdud hit "7" and then leaned on the DOOR CLOSE button.

"Hold it, please!" the woman called from outside.

"Sorreeee," Milkdud said softly as the doors slid closed and they started up. "But we need this one all to ourselves."

"Close," Jack said.

He could feel himself tensing up as the floor numbers climbed the display. He wasn't relishing the next few steps.

Milkdud squatted and opened his briefcase. He pulled out a curved piece of metal about the size of a coat hanger hook. A length of slender cord trailed from its end.

"All right. Here's your hook. You remember how to work it, right?"

"Yeah. I think so." *I hope so.*

"Just like we practiced last night." He handed Jack the hook and cord, then snapped his briefcase shut. "And you've got your change of clothes, flashlight, headlamp, and cell phone, right?"

"Right."

"Okay. Let's do it."

Jack swallowed. "Which floor?"

"Seven. A new tenant is renovating before moving in. The workmen probably don't arrive until eight, so—"

"Probably?"

Milkdud shrugged. "I did my thing here yesterday. They don't work on Sunday, so what can I say?"

"Okay. Let's assume they're not there yet."

"Right. Which is good. That way you won't be too rushed."

The car eased to a stop.

Milkdud gave him a thumbs-up. "Okay, Hacker Jack, go to it. I'll start back down—and don't let the alarm bell rattle you."

A bell is the least of my worries, he thought.

With the hook and cord in one hand and his briefcase in the other, Jack stepped through the open doors.

The seventh floor was indeed under construction, a clutter of lumber and wallboard, all coated with a fine layer of sawdust and plaster.

And no workers yet.

As soon as the elevator doors slid shut, Jack dropped his briefcase and began working the hook through the space between the metal lintel and the top of the elevator doors. He and Milkdud had practiced this a dozen times last night on the elevator in Milkdud's building. The top space here was narrower.

And then the elevator alarm bell started ringing as Milkdud hit the emergency button, stopping the cab between the sixth and seventh floors. Jack had been expecting this, but still he jumped.

He knew he had time, but the bell was a goad, pushing him to hurry. Finally the hook slipped through and dropped over on the other side of the door.

And kept dropping, taking the cord with it.

He'd forgot to wrap the damn cord around his wrist.

"Christ!"

Jack snatched at it and snagged the last foot of cord just before it disappeared into the void of the elevator shaft.

And all the while, that damn emergency bell kept up its steady, insistent ringing.

He let out a breath. The next step would be a little harder.

Jack reeled in the cord until he heard the hook clink against the other side of the door, then he worked it up and down, twisting the cord as he let it in and out.

Finally, he felt the hook catch, but just as it did, he heard another bell, a *ding!* He glanced around and saw the up arrow glowing above the far right elevator door. Someone was coming.

Jack yanked on the cord, praying it was hooked on the shaft side safety handle.

It was. The elevator doors parted a few inches. That was all Jack needed. He got his foot between them, then spread them wide with his hands.

The emergency bell was even louder now. He looked down.

Two feet below his feet the top of the elevator car waited.

Now came the hard part. The really hard part.

Jack hesitated—*I've got to be out of my goddamned mind!*—and would have loved to have hesitated longer if he'd had time, but the doors to that other elevator were sliding open. Wedging his doors open with his feet, he grabbed his briefcase and stepped down onto the roof of the elevator car. As the doors eased closed behind him, he found the switch for the light atop the elevator and flipped it, hoping the bulb hadn't burned out.

"Yes," he said as the incandescent lit within its cage.

He grabbed the hook off the safety handle and pulled the rest of the cord through. He banged the go-ahead signal to Milkdud on the roof of the car, then dropped into a crouch.

Abruptly the emergency bell stopped.

And for a few heartbeats, blessed silence.

Then the car started down with a lurch.

"Oh, shit!"

Going down wasn't the problem. The car was supposed to head down. That was in the plan. Milkdud had started it down before stopping between the floors, so it had to continue that way. Once he reached bottom, he'd start it back up . . . and take it all the way to the top.

The problem was that Jack's breakfast wanted to remain between the sixth and seventh floors. He gritted his teeth and forced the cherry cheese Danish and coffee to stay in his stomach. With his free hand, he clutched the heavy steel sling bar that ran across the top of the car. It looked like a piece of I-beam girder. Had to be strong—it anchored the hoist cables. To his left and right the roller guides rattled softly as they wheeled along in their shoes.

The car picked up speed.

"Oh, shit!"

He whispered the two words over and over in a scatological litany all the way down. He was scared. Not that he'd ever admit it to anyone, not even Gia—no way he'd even *tell* Gia about this—but he freely admitted to himself that at this moment, in this place, he was flat-out, all-but-screaming terrified.

Not the height that bothered him, because he couldn't see the bottom; and being enclosed in a sealed concrete shaft wasn't all that bad, because the light atop the car let him see where he was.

It was the whole deal: Here he was dressed in a business suit and hanging onto a briefcase while riding an elevator on the wrong side of its ceiling. Sure, there had to be a first time for everything, but Jack swore this first time would also be the last time.

Because he liked to be in control of his gigs, and at the moment he was anything but in control.

And he didn't see any quick way out of here.

Plus he couldn't help worrying about what awaited him at his ultimate destination: the top of the shaft.

Finally, a faint *ding!* and the car slowed to a stop. He heard the doors open onto the main floor, then overheard Milkdud explaining to someone how the emergency stop was his fault, how the car had started to go down when he'd wanted to go up so he'd pressed the stop button by accident. Sorry. No harm done, right? Don't worry, he wouldn't make that mistake again.

Jack used the stop time to pocket the hook and cord, then unbuckle and rebuckle his pants belt around the handle of his briefcase. He heard bodies piling into the cab, heard the doors close, and then the car started up.

If the descent had been an oh-shit moment, the ascent was ten, twenty, a hundred times worse.

Sure, Milkdud had explained it all and drawn diagrams about how much space was around and above the main support beam up at the top of the shaft, but Jack kept seeing himself squashed like a bug against the inside of the roof up there.

The middle elevator zoomed past on its way down, and his own car's counterweight flashed past the rear of the car between one of the seven stops on the way up. If he'd had his hand out, he might have lost it. Taking the local usually drove Jack crazy when he was inside; but here on the outside, he didn't mind.

"Take your time," he whispered. "Take all the time you want."

But after the sixteenth floor—Jack had seen the number stenciled above the door—the car resumed its ascent and kept going.

As he shot toward the roof of the shaft, Jack crouched and peered into the shadows above, trying to make out the details. And then he spotted the main support beam running across the top of the shaft. It was aligned with the sling beam atop the car. As he got closer, Jack saw the multi-track wheel fixed in the center of the support beam, spinning wildly as it guided the racing hoist cables.

And then the car stopped. Twenty-sixth floor. End of the line.

Jack let out the breath he'd been holding. Milkdud hadn't been exaggerating about the extra space at the top. The car had stopped well short of the support beam and the roof. In fact, the shaft continued up a good twenty feet above him.

Jack knew Dud was leaning on the DOOR OPEN button to give him some extra time, but he couldn't hold it forever. Jack looked around and spotted a metal ladder embedded in the left wall of the shaft, running up to a door—just where Dud had said it would be.

He grabbed a rung, stepped off the top of the car, and climbed to the door. Dud had said it was unalarmed and that he'd left it unlocked, so Jack pushed through.

He shut the door behind him and stood a moment in the rumbling darkness, reveling in the feel of solid floor beneath his feet as his pounding heart slowed.

What a hell ride. Only a few minutes in real time, but a good aeon or two subjectively.

But he'd survived. The worst was over. He'd be more in control from here on in.

Until he had to get out.

He'd worry about that later.

He fumbled his hand along the wall and found the light switch. A row of naked fluorescents flickered to life overhead.

He was in what Milkdud called the HVAC area—heating, ventilation, and air-conditioning. Straight ahead sat the system's air filters, each the size of a panel truck. Eight-foot ducts ran to and from them.

Jack stepped over to the nearest and freed the briefcase from his belt. He opened it and removed a one-piece coverall—let Dud wear pantyhose; Jack preferred coveralls. He stripped off his suit jacket, pants, and tie, then stepped into the coverall and zipped it to his neck. He traded his wing tips for sneakers. He slipped the slim little cell phone into the inside breast pocket. He strapped the headlamp around his head and slipped its battery pack into his right hip pocket. He adjusted the headphones to his ears, then turned on the Walkman and dropped it into the left hip pocket.

Milkdud's voice spoke softly in his ears.

"Okay, Jack. If you're listening to this, I guess it means you're not lying in a broken heap at the bottom of the shaft." And then he chuckled.

"Ha ha," Jack said.

"Go to the big return that feeds into the left air filter and open the service door. We're using the return system because it'll have cooler air. Look close and you'll see I've marked it with my handle."

Jack stepped to the door and found the lever marked with Dud's little black spot within a circle. He pulled it open and looked inside. Dark. Very dark.

"Dark, isn't it. But not for long. To the right of the door is a light switch. Flip it."

Jack did, and an incandescent bulb lit the inside of the duct—a square galvanized metal shaft, eight foot on a side. A dozen feet to his left it made a right-angle downward turn.

"Don't stand there gawking, Jack. Get inside, close the door behind you, and start moving."

Jack did and inched to the edge of the down shaft. Just below the lip, a metal ladder trailed down the inner surface of the shaft; its rungs were swallowed by the darkness beyond the cone of light cast by the single bulb.

"Use the ladder to get to the twenty-first floor. Don't worry about the dark. We'll take care of that as we go."

"If you say so," Jack muttered.

He swung over the edge and started down. As he neared the darkness below . . .

"The engineers who renovated this system were unusually considerate. Not only are there no motion detectors or grates in the ducts—something I'd recommend if I was trying to keep out people like us—but they placed a light on every floor, same as in the elevator shaft. But these have to be turned on. Keep an eye out to the right of the ladder as you pass each major seam. You'll see a pair of light switches: One operates the bulb above you, and the other the bulb below."

"Love those considerate engineers," Jack said as he found the switches and hit the one that illuminated the section below.

"Conserve energy, Jack. Turn off the light in each section as you leave it."

"You do it your way, Dud. I'll do it mine. I like to see where I've been."

"Turn me off until you see my handle on the twenty-first floor."

Jack found the OFF switch and continued his descent without a running narrative. The only sounds were his soft, echoing footsteps and his breathing. Farther down he found a big "21" in red marker facing him through the rungs of the ladder. Dud's handle hovered under the curve of the "2" like a floating eye.

Jack turned on the Walkman.

"Okay, Jack. If you're at the twenty-first floor, it's time to leave the big vertical and enter the laterals via that opening on your left. These get

smaller as we go, and unfortunately they're not lit for us, so you'll have to turn on the headlamp."

Jack swung off the ladder and into the smaller duct. It was perhaps half the width of the vertical. He adjusted the headlamp lens to the widest beam and began to crawl.

"At the first intersection you turn left. I've cleared the dust and left a little directional arrow. I've done that at each intersection—the black arrows for the way in, red arrows for the way out—just in case something goes wrong with the Walkman."

"What a comforting thought," Jack said. But he appreciated Milkdud's thoroughness.

He found the first pair of arrows—bracketing Dud's handle—and made the turn.

"And that's basically it, Jack. The arrows will lead you to the return that services Haffner's office. If you need any help, you've got the cell phone. The thing is to move slowly and carefully, easing yourself along. Sudden moves that bang against the sides will send the noise far and wide. Most people ignore an occasional rattle or such from a register. But give them a series of noises moving along above their hung ceilings and they start making calls, asking what's going on. So take it easy, Jack. We've given you plenty of time. Good hacking, man. This is Milkdud, signing off."

Must think he's Walter Cronkite or something, Jack thought as he turned off the Walkman and continued his crawl.

As he slid through the dark ducts, following the wavering beam of light stretching before him, he came to appreciate the coveralls. Its button-free front surface allowed him to glide along smoothly and silently.

The ducts, as Dud had warned, did indeed get smaller. But Jack kept following the arrows. He was, he freely admitted, utterly lost. He knew he was on the twenty-first floor of the Hand Building, and that his body was horizontal, but any orientation beyond that was a guess. Was he facing east or west, uptown or downtown? He had no idea.

That Dud had managed to hack this place—doing the elevator thing, and finding his way through this labyrinth of ductwork—on his own was astonishing.

That anyone could call it *fun* was simply beyond Jack.

And then Jack came to a left-pointing arrow and saw—literally—a light at the end of the tunnel.

Slim bands of fluorescent glow angled up through the louvers of a register at the end of a small duct. Jack heard voices filtering through from the room beyond, but couldn't catch the words. And even if he could, hearing was not enough. He wanted to see who was in that room, wanted to know who was saying what.

And he couldn't do that from here.

He had to get closer, and that meant moving into this last duct. This *small* last duct.

Jack stared into the narrow confines of the six-foot length of steel . . . just the length of a coffin. But coffins probably were a lot roomier. What if he got stuck in there?

Milkdud had given him a few hints on how to maneuver in a tight spot. This might be the time to try them out.

Jack turned off the headlamp. Then, with his right arm extended ahead and his left arm close against his side, he squeezed himself diagonally into the duct.

Tight. Very tight.

Now he truly appreciated what Dud had meant about claustrophobia being a deterrent to hacking.

Slowly, silently, he inched forward until he had about eighty percent of the office in view.

A plump, red-haired man in a white shirt—Gordon Haffner, Jack hoped—sat behind the desk, talking on the phone. Jack could hear him perfectly. As he watched, two other men entered. Jack recognized one from the van on Thursday night: Thomas Clayton. The other was new— dark-skinned, dark-haired, bearded, very intense-looking, with an accent from somewhere in the Middle East.

Jack smiled. He figured he was looking at Thomas Clayton's backer— the guy who was killing anyone who stood between him and the Clayton House. Excellent. Now, if they'd all just be so good as to discuss exactly why they wanted the house so badly, Jack could get the hell out of here.

But they didn't. They talked about Alicia and how they hoped she'd come up with a sale price this morning so they could settle the matter of ownership, but the reason was never mentioned.

And what was Thomas doing here? Sean had told Haffner that Alicia didn't want her brother present at the meeting. But here he was, and the clock was ticking, getting close to nine-thirty. He was sure Alicia would pop her cork if she saw him here. This was no way to get her to cooperate. What were they thinking?

And then Haffner's intercom buzzed, announcing "Mr. O'Neill and Ms. Clayton." Haffner got up, slipped on his suit jacket, and said he'd be back as soon as he finished speaking to her.

Jack's head jerked up and almost struck the ceiling of the duct. *What?*

The meeting was supposed to be in Haffner's office, just the other side of the register. Where the hell was he going?

Not that the meeting itself mattered. Alicia could fill him in later on anything important. Jack had crawled through these ducts to hear the postmortem. If he had any chance of picking up some choice tidbits of unguarded conversation about the Clayton house, that would be the time.

But if the meeting was being held somewhere else, so might the post-mortem.

He listened awhile to hear if Thomas and his Middle Eastern wallet man would drop anything worthwhile, but they didn't seem to be buddies: Thomas read the paper while the stranger stood at the window and stared at the street below.

Jack eased back into the larger duct and checked out his options.

2

"What are we doing here?" Alicia said as Gordon Haffner ushered them into a mahogany-paneled conference room.

"Having a meeting," Haffner said. He looked confused as he laid a file folder on the gleaming surface of the oval mahogany table. "Isn't that why you called? To have a meeting?"

"We met in your office last time, so I thought—"

"This is much roomier."

Alicia glanced at Sean O'Neill, who replied with a barely perceptible shrug.

"Is something wrong?" Haffner said.

Yes, but Alicia couldn't tell him what. They'd set up this meeting to allow Jack to identify Thomas's backers. But what if the backers met in here instead of Haffner's office after the meeting? Jack would be eaves-dropping on an empty room.

If she demanded to meet in Haffner's office, would that make him suspicious? And what would that accomplish if the backers were set to meet here afterward?

Jack needed to know about this conference room. And she could think of only one way to do that.

"*Wrong?*" Alicia said, letting her voice rise. "You want to know if something's *wrong?* Let me *tell* you what's wrong!" She raised the volume, pushing it to a shout. "Your client, my half brother Thomas Clayton, is what's wrong! Do you have any idea what kind of a slug you're representing? Do you know what he did to me Thursday night?"

She saw O'Neill turn her way and give her a quick smile and a wink.

But as she started in on the details of her abduction, she found she no longer needed to force the volume, or act angry. Suddenly the rage was real and her pitch rose.

Gordon Haffner's face went a little pale, and Sean O'Neill's smile faded.

Alicia heard her own voice . . . screaming . . .

3

You're beautiful, Alicia.

Jack smiled as he watched her wind down from her tirade. He'd been crouched outside the return from Haffner's office, pondering his next move, when he'd heard a woman screaming. He hadn't recognized the voice—a scream was a scream—but he'd followed the sound. After all, no one should be screaming in an attorney's office, unless maybe it was a client who'd just got a bill.

A few turns this way and that, and here she was, sliced by the louvers of a register high in the wall of some sort of conference room, doing a very convincing Screaming Mimi.

Finally, she began losing steam. As she wound down, Jack eased back into the larger duct and positioned himself facing the way he'd come. He turned on his headlamp and narrowed the beam to check his watch. Barely past nine-thirty. He'd be back on the street before eleven—hopefully with the answers to some of his questions.

All he had to do was wait until the meeting was over, then see where the other side chose to hash over Alicia's proposal.

*   *   *

J ack didn't have to wait long or go far. Sean presented Alicia's asking price of ten million dollars, Haffner expressed shock—genuine, Jack was sure—then tried to bargain her down. But Alicia held firm and finally Haffner said, Thenk-yew-veddy-much, and the room emptied out.

Jack gave them a few minutes, and was about to crawl back toward Haffner's office when he heard the conference door open.

"You can have the room as long as you want," Haffner said. "I'll be in my office should you need me."

Jack wedged himself into the duct in time to see the door close, leaving Thomas and the Middle East guy together. Neither sat down.

"Ten million," Thomas said, shaking his head in what might have been admiration. "Christ, she's got balls." He glanced at his companion. "Well, Kemel, what's it going to be? Are your people going to go for it?"

"I do not see that we have a choice," the guy called Kemel said. His accent was definitely Middle East, but his English had a faintly British accent. He spoke rapidly, clipping his words.

"You've got to be kidding! You heard Haffner. He's sure he can get the will set aside. Ten million for that place? That's crazy."

Jack too was shocked. He'd hauled that asking price out of the air, never dreaming they'd even consider it.

"My people want this matter settled. It has dragged on too long. And after all, what is ten million against what we will gain by keeping it out of the wrong hands? A pittance."

The wrong hands? Jack thought, mentally rubbing his own hands together. He was hot, sweaty, and cramped, but suddenly that no longer mattered. Now we're getting to the good stuff. Keep going.

"A pittance to you, maybe. But a hell of a lot of money for something that might not be there."

"If it is not, it is of no loss to you. It is not your money."

"Yeah, but then Alicia will be a millionaire and I'll have zilch. Less than zilch. I quit my job to help you with this."

"You are being well compensated. And don't forget that you will have the house—after all, we are buying it in your name."

"Yeah . . . the house," Thomas said. "What's left of it. I mean, we've turned the insides upside down—at least as upside down as you can without making it obvious—and we've come up empty-handed. We push it much further and we risk getting arrested for trespassing and vandalism."

"There is something there," Kemel said. "Perhaps not the plans and diagrams themselves, but if not, then I believe it is reasonable to assume that your father left some clue as to their whereabouts."

"That's becoming an expensive assumption."

"The will all but says so. One cannot ignore what your father's message to that ecology group—what is it called?"

"Greenpeace."

"Yes. Greenpeace. Such a strange concept. We have no such groups in my land. But your father, he said, 'This house holds the key that points the way to all you wish to achieve. Sell it and you lose everything you've worked for.' That to me is proof enough that the house is hiding *something*."

"Fine. But we've got to find it."

"Have no fear. We will find it. As soon as the house is ours, we will begin a most thorough search, breaking down the walls if necessary. And if we still have not found it, we will dismantle the house brick by brick, beam by beam, until we succeed."

"And if we don't?"

"At least we will have prevented others from finding it and using it."

"Yeah, but then I don't get my payday."

"Well, certainly you would not expect us to buy something that you do not have. Would you?"

Thomas shrugged. "What's our next step?"

"I contact my superiors to approve the purchase price—a mere formality, I assure you—and then we let Mr. Haffner arrange the details."

"Ten million bucks," Thomas said, shaking his head as he'd done when this little tête-à-tête started. "Well, I guess I should be thankful my dear sister has no inkling what we're after. If she did, she'd be asking ten million per *brick*."

"Yes," Kemel said. "And that would still be a bargain."

He's *got* to be exaggerating, Jack thought. But somehow he doubted it.

As he lay there wondering what the hell could be worth so damn much and be small enough to hide in a house, he noticed Thomas and Kemel heading for the door.

Jack felt like singing that old Peggy Lee song, "Is That All There Is?" What had he learned here?

Well, he'd seen Kemel. That was something. And he'd learned that whatever was in the Clayton house was damn near priceless to some very rich folks from the Middle East. And he'd learned that Thomas's people weren't the only ones interested in it. They were concerned about it falling into "the wrong hands." Whose hands were the "wrong" hands?

He didn't think they meant Alicia's. Another Middle East power? Israel? Or someone else?

But he'd hoped for more, especially after risking his butt in an elevator shaft, sweating and crawling through filthy heating ducts, and wedging himself into spaces where he could barely breathe.

He cursed them for being so damn oblique. What was this mysterious *it*? Why couldn't they just come out and say what was in the house? He grinned—hell, it wasn't as if anybody was listening in on them.

But maybe the *it* they were after was so important, so valuable, that they instinctively avoided referring to it by name.

As Jack wiped some sweat from his eyes, his overall sleeve caught the lens on his headlamp and knocked it off. He snatched at it but it slipped from his fingers and landed with a *clunk* on the floor of the duct.

Jack froze as Kemel stopped at the threshold and whirled.

"What was that?"

"What was what?" Thomas said, poking his head back in from the hall.

"That noise." Kemel was moving around the conference table and heading for Jack's position. "It came from over there. From that heating vent, I think."

Jack grabbed the lens and slid back as far as he could without completely withdrawing from the duct. He didn't think he could do that without making more noise, so he lay silent and waited.

He held his breath as a bearded face popped into view beyond the louvers.

"It came from in here," Kemel said. "I am sure of it."

"So?" Thomas said from somewhere behind Kemel. "Probably a mouse or something."

"This was not a mouse." Kemel tried to force his fingers between the louvers but the spaces were too small. "Quick. Give me something to remove this grate."

Jack inched back a little farther. If that vent plate started to come loose, he'd have to take off.

"You've got to be kidding," Thomas said. "What do you think you're going to find?"

"Perhaps someone has been listening."

"From in there?" Thomas laughed. "Look, Kemel, I don't know about the level of espionage technology in Saudi Arabia, but over here if we want to eavesdrop on someone, we don't stuff a midget into a vent. We do it electronically: We plant a bug."

He's right, Kemel, Jack thought. Don't be a jerk. Listen to the man.

"I know what I heard," Kemel said. "Get me a screwdriver."

"I didn't think you Moslems drank."

"This is not a matter for joking! I want to look in here!"

"All right, all right. Here. It's my nail clipper. You can use the back end there as a screwdriver."

Jack knew this was his signal to chuck caution and vamoose. He backed into the larger duct and began his return trip.

Behind him, Kemel's voice rose in pitch and volume.

"There! Do you hear that? Someone is in there, I tell you! Call Mr. Haffner. Tell him to call security. Someone has been spying on us!"

Jack paused to turn on his headlamp and replace the lens, then he resumed his crawl. He followed Milkdud's red return arrows and didn't stop until he reached the big vertical shaft.

Sweating and panting, he clung to the ladder to catch his breath and cool off. He unzipped the front of his overall to let in some air—damn thing must be insulated.

This was not good. Depending on the size of the building's security force and whether or not they called in the city cops, this little jaunt might well end with Jack's arrest. The charge would be piddly—what could they hold him for besides trespassing?

But the charge would be irrelevant. The arrest itself would do all the damage. Arrest meant photos and fingerprints and giving an address. Suddenly he'd be Citizen Jack. Officialdom would have a record of his existence. They'd want to fill in all the blanks on their forms, and so they'd start prying at his doors and chipping away at his walls, bringing down all the barriers he'd spent his whole adult life erecting between his world and theirs.

He needed out of here. Now.

Jack pulled out the cell phone and speed-dialed Milkdud.

"Yeah," Dud's voice said after the second ring.

"It's me," Jack said in a low voice. "They know I'm in here. What's the quickest way out?"

"The quickest? Jump out a window."

"That's not a big help right now, Dud."

"Sorry. The quickest way out is to go through the door from the HVAC area into the building proper, then take the stairs down. But the door's alarmed, and that'll let them know where you are and give them a chance to cut you off. Best way out is exactly the way you came in. Climb up to the HVAC area ASAP, get back into that business suit, and wait by the door to the elevator shaft. I'm on my way now, moving as we speak. When I have the left elevator all to myself on the top floor, I'll call you. Got it?"

"Got it."

Jack hit END and left the cell phone's power on, but he switched off the ringer and activated the vibration option. When Milkdud called back, Jack would feel it rather than hear it.

He climbed up the ladder and exited the duct system into the HVAC area. At last—someplace cool. He stripped off the sneakers and dusty coverall, stuffed them back into the briefcase, then wriggled back into his suit and wing tips.

At least he didn't have to retie the tie.

When he looked like a lawyer again, he buckled the briefcase into his belt, turned off the room lights, stepped over to the door to the elevator shaft, and waited for Milkdud's call.

But a couple of maintenance guys arrived first.

Jack heard their voices on the far side of the other HVAC door, the alarmed one that led into the building proper. He opened his door, swung out into the elevator shaft, and closed the door behind him.

"Here I am, Dud," he whispered. "Now where the hell are you?"

He looked down. All three elevators seemed to be at the lower end of the shaft at the moment, and it looked like one godawful long way down. Jack pressed his ear to the door to see if he could hear what the maintenance men were saying.

"Y'ever hear anyt'ing so fuckin' stupid?" said a faint voice. "A guy crawling t'rough d'heating ducts? I mean, what's dat all about?"

"Yeah. I think maybe someone's been hittin' the nose candy a little hard, if y'know what I'm sayin' and I think you do."

"Right. 'Tis the season to be jolly an' all 'at shit. But let's go t'rough d'motions an' make 'em happy."

Jack thought he heard footsteps coming his way on the far side of the door, so he hurried down the ladder and hung at about the spot where he'd stepped off the top of the elevator.

He looked down and saw that same old elevator pulling to a stop at the twenty-sixth. Too early for Milkdud to be inside. He looked down at the top of the car, where he'd crouched, clutching the sling bar.

Above him, the door handle rattled. Christ, were they going to check the elevator shaft?

Check the ventilation ducts first, you idiots!

They'd see the lights he'd left on in the shaft and think he was still in there.

But the door was opening. The elevator had stopped just below him, and Jack didn't see that he had much choice. He didn't want another ride, really he didn't, but—

He stepped off the ladder onto the car's sling bar.

As the door above swung open, Jack flicked off the cab roof bulb just in time and crouched behind the hoist cables, doing his best to conceal himself. He glanced up and saw someone silhouetted in the light from the HVAC area, shining a flashlight into the shaft.

Then the car started down. Jack closed his eyes and hung on. The ride was worse in the dark.

He groaned. "Hope you've got your running shoes on, Dud."

Jack had made three round trips and was starting the fourth when the cell phone vibrated against his leg. He whipped it out.

"Dud?"

"I've got the leftest car to myself, and I'm comin' to getcha, Jack."

"I'm already here."

"What do you mean?"

"I mean, here. As in"—Jack rapped on the roof of the car—"*here.*"

"All *right!* We'll make a hacker out of you yet."

"Don't hold your breath, my man. Just get me off this thing."

"Okay. Here's what we'll do. I'll stop her at six, then E-stop her halfway to seven. You won't need your hook, just pull the safety lever and the outer doors will open. You just step off and wait for me to join you."

Jack followed the directions to the letter and less than a minute later, accompanied by the jarring strains of the emergency stop bell, he was stepping through the doors onto the seventh floor. His relief was tempered by the two carpenters on coffee break from the renovation work.

"Hey, Mac," said the heavier of the two, staring at him. "Where the hell did you just come from?"

"Why, the elevator," Jack said.

"No, you didn't." He stepped closer, his gaze flicking between Jack and the elevator doors. "I was standin' right there watching those doors, and I'm telling you there was no elevator there when you came out. You walkin' on fucking air or somethin'?"

Jack wanted to say, *What's it to you?* But he smiled and kept his tone light.

"Don't be silly. That elevator's acting very strange. The lights went off and the bell started ringing, so I got out."

The elevator dinged behind him and the doors opened. Milkdud stepped out.

"There," Jack said. "Does he look like he's walking on air?"

"No, he don't," the carpenter said. "But I can see the elevator in there."

"Well, the lights must have come back on." He turned to Milkdud. "Did the lights come back on?"

Dud didn't miss a beat. "Yeah, just after you got off. That thing's acting weird." He pressed the DOWN button on the wall panel. "I'm going to take another one down."

"Good idea."

The center car arrived soon after, and they stepped into the empty cab.

"They saw me stepping out of an empty shaft," Jack said when the doors had closed behind them.

"That's always a risk." Dud handed him a tissue. "Here. Wipe off your hands. They're dusty."

"What's waiting for us below?" Jack said, wiping.

"They've got security guys at both doors, trying to look inconspicuous but giving everyone the once-over. But they're looking for a dusty guy, not the man in the gray flannel suit. We'll be okay."

And they were. They sailed past the guards and onto Forty-fifth Street.

"Thanks, Dud," Jack said when they reached Sixth Avenue. "I owe you, man. Big time. You ever need a favor . . ."

"Forget it," Dud said, smiling. "See one, do one, teach one: all part of the code. I just want to know if I made a convert."

"I don't think so."

"You sure? You mean to tell me after what you did this morning that you're not hooked?"

"I can honestly say I'm not."

"I don't believe that. Tell you what, I'm hacking some of the upper levels of the Chrysler building next week. It's just *crammed* with secrets."

"Tell *you* what," Jack said. "You find a giant roc egg up there, you let me know. I'll come running."

Dud grinned and gave him a thumbs-up. "Yeah, *Q*, man. If I get caught, I'll say Larry Cohen made me do it."

"Just be careful, Dud."

They shook hands and parted, Milkdud heading for his job at Coconuts and Jack heading home for a shower. Definitely a shower.

And then a call to Alicia. *See one, do one, teach one*, Dud had said. Well, Jack had seen one, and now he was going to do one. With Alicia. On her father's house.

4

Kemel hung up on the incredulous Gordon Haffner, who still was having difficulty accepting the fact that his clients were going to pay Alicia Clayton ten million dollars for her father's house.

But it was true. Kemel had held his breath as he'd contacted Khalid Nazer, but Iswid Nahr had agreed to the price.

Kemel should have been elated—so close to success, so close to being able to run home to Riyadh and his son—but suspicion soured his mood.

Someone had been listening to his conversation with Thomas Clayton.

Oh, yes, they had alerted security and called the police, and maintenance men had been sent to check the ventilation system, but no one really believed him. Even after the grate had been removed and he had pointed out the disturbed dust within, they had only shrugged and said maybe there was some sort of animal in the ducts. No one would believe that here in Manhattan, with such an extensive array of sophisticated electronic bugging devices to the public, that someone would crawl through a ventilating system to eavesdrop on a conversation.

Kemel sighed. Perhaps they were right. It did seem farfetched.

But he could not shake the feeling that someone had been listening. When he had pressed his face to that grate, straining to see through the slits, he thought he had sensed someone in the darkness on the other side, looking back, watching him.

He racked his brain to remember what he and Thomas Clayton had said in that room, reconstructing the conversation word by word.

Nothing, he was sure. Almost sure.

One thing an eavesdropper would have come away with was that the house was worth more than ten million dollars to the buyers. If Alicia Clayton suddenly raised her asking price, Kemel's suspicions would be confirmed.

If she did not . . . if the deal went through, then he did not care if a whole army had been listening.

5

Jack found a spot on Thirty-eighth where he could stand and watch the Clayton house unseen. He timed the "security force's" inspection rounds and noticed that they always operated as a pair, leaving the car twice an hour to make a perimeter inspection. No uniforms, just windbreakers and slacks.

Every so often one would walk off and return with a paper sack—coffee and donuts, most likely. And occasionally one would enter the house through the front door and return a few minutes later. They didn't need a Porta Potti; they had the house.

At ten to three, another car showed up. The first pulled out, letting the second into the precious parking space, and the next shift took over.

Satisfied that he had the security boys' schedule down, Jack called Abe for a consultation.

"So you want them down for the count, but they shouldn't be candidates for a nursing home."

"Right. A nice long nap is all."

"T-72 is what you want," Abe told him. "Colorless, odorless, no serious side effects, and best of all, it's made in America for the U.S. Army."

"Sounds great," Jack said. "I'll take some."

"And I would gladly sell you some if I had any. But I do not. It's not exactly a sporting good."

"I can't tell you how disappointed I am, Abe."

"Nu, I should stock everything in the world you will possibly need so that when you ask for it I can give it to you?"

"Yeah. Because you're the best."

"Feh! I'll find you some."

"By tonight?"

"Such a kidder he is. If I'm lucky, perhaps maybe I can have a canister for you tomorrow afternoon."

"Good enough, I suppose."

Jack had wanted to search the house tonight, but he'd have to put it off.

"Good enough? Such a feat should be acclaimed as nothing short of heroic."

"See you tomorrow, my hero."

After he hung up with Abe, Jack called Alicia.

6

"Shall I open another?" the waiter said, holding up the empty merlot bottle.

Will looked at her and raised his eyebrows.

Alicia shrugged. "I could go for a little more. It's delicious."

So was everything else she'd tried tonight. Zov's was this noisy little place off Union Square, more of a bistro than a restaurant. But the rack of lamb on the platter between them had been marinated in something indescribable and was by far the most delicious meat she had ever eaten.

And as for the wine: she could go for a *lot* more.

Jack's call this afternoon had unsettled her. That Thomas had an Arab backer willing to pay the ten million she'd asked for the house had shocked her; that they were convinced the house held a secret many times more valuable had floored her; but Jack's plan to sneak into the house and search it had stopped her dead in her tracks.

And he wasn't talking about some unspecified time in the future. He wanted to go in tomorrow. *Tomorrow!*

She'd said no. No, no, no. She'd have to prepare herself for something like that. If he wanted to search the place tomorrow, he'd have to go by himself.

But Jack had insisted, saying she'd grown up there, she knew all the hidey holes. She had to be along.

Telling herself it was only a damn house, she'd agreed.

Jack would be picking her up tomorrow night at seven.

Alicia shuddered and looked up from her meal. Will and the waiter were watching her . . . expectantly.

"I'm sorry," she said. Obviously she'd missed something.

"Do you want to do the honors?" Will said, pointing to the fresh bottle of wine in the waiter's hands.

"No," she said. "If it's the same as the first bottle, I'm sure it will be fine." She could never get into that wine-tasting rigmarole. Her palate wasn't that discerning anyway. Either you liked the wine or you didn't.

"So," Will said after the waiter had refilled their glasses, "what are your plans for the week?"

I was an accessory to an illegal trespass in midtown today, and I'm planning a breaking and entering tomorrow night.

"The usual, I guess. You know, stamping out disease. How about you?"

"Like you, the usual: seeking out the weed of crime and tearing it out by its roots."

They laughed. Maybe it was the wine, but she found she liked Will's offhanded manner, the way he didn't take himself too seriously. She liked his slightly crooked smile and the way he held his wineglass by the rim, letting it dangle from his fingertips as he talked, and the way he looked into her eyes when she talked. All things she'd never noticed about him before.

They just about killed that second bottle of merlot, and so by the time they left the restaurant, Alicia was feeling warm and happy. She heard herself ask Will to come in when he dropped her off at her place.

She felt a spasm of alarm—*Why did I do that?*—but told herself to be calm. It would be all right. Tonight, in this place, with this man . . . it would be all right. She wanted this . . . she *needed* this.

"Want some coffee?" she said as she hung up his coat.

"No," he said. "That coffee we had at Zov's will probably keep me up half the night as it is. But I would like something else."

As Alicia turned to face him, he took her in his arms—gently—and pulled her close.

She fought a stab of anxiety and moved closer. She sensed his tentativeness, and knew if she resisted, he'd back off. That was good. But she didn't want to resist. She wanted to be held, to feel protected, to relax and let go, and for once, just once, feel that she didn't have to be alone all the time, didn't have to be so completely self-contained and able to handle everything on her own, *do* everything on her own. Just once to feel that she could have someone to share with. Just once.

Her anxiety level surged as he bent his head to hers, but she didn't pull away.

It's all right . . . it's going to be all right . . .

Their lips met and his were soft and warm, and the wine was warm within her, and yes, it was going to be all right . . .

But then his arms encircled her and suddenly she couldn't breathe. She felt trapped, and she had to get away, get free, get some *air*.

She tore her lips from him, got her hands between them, and *pushed*. "Let me *go!*"

Will released her and backed away, his expression stunned. "Alicia— what's—?"

"Get away!"

He held up his hands and backed up another step. "I *am* away. Look."

Panic—wild, formless, constricting, suffocating, unyielding to reason—choked her, and she wanted to run, but she couldn't, she lived here, so he had to get out. Part of her cried, *No, let him stay!* but a larger, fiercer, stronger part was in control.

"I'm sorry, Will," she said, forcing her voice to stay calm. Still, the words seemed to rattle in her throat. "I just can't . . . I can't do this right now. Okay?"

He looked so confused. "Okay. Sure. I just thought . . . is it me?"

"No . . . yes . . ." *I'm babbling.* "I just can't explain it now." *Not now, not ever.* "Would you mind if we just call it a night? Please?"

She was so embarrassed she wanted to cry.

"Yeah. Sure." He reached out to touch her arm but withdrew it before contact. "I'll call you," he said, retreating into the hall. "To see if you're all right."

Alicia nodded. "I'm sorry. I'm really sorry."

And then she closed the door. Finally, the panic faded. She leaned against the door and sobbed.

I'm out of control, she thought.

She'd almost lost it in Haffner's conference room this morning, and now she'd done the same with Will.

She'd never done too well with men, but this was over the top.

What's happening to me?

The house . . . it had to be the house. Nothing had been right since that man and his house had forced their way back into her life. She'd tried to burn it, and tomorrow night she was going to have to go back there . . . inside . . .

That was the problem: Going back . . .

The house was the whole problem. She had to conquer that house, because by doing so, she'd conquer *him*. And then she'd be free of both of them.

Or would she? Would she ever be free?

TUESDAY

1

"It's going to be okay," Jack said as they drove east on Twenty-third in his rented white Chevy. He glanced over at Alicia sitting straight and silent in the passenger seat. "Don't worry. We won't get caught."

"What makes you think I'm worried about getting caught?" she said.

"Because you look like you're ready to jump out the window."

She'd been like an overwound spring since he'd picked her up.

She's afraid of that house, he thought. That empty house.

As he reached Broadway, the traffic light went amber. Good. He'd been waiting for this opportunity. Instead of speeding up, he held back until the light turned red, then he gunned it and yanked the wheel to the right, turning downtown.

"Maybe it's your driving," Alicia said, and made a poor try at a smile, as if to let him know she was kidding—maybe. "And if we're going to Thirty-eighth Street, this is the wrong direction."

"I know," he said, pulling over and studying his rearview mirror.

"And how come we're not taking a cab?"

"Because I wanted to make sure we weren't followed."

He watched the street behind them, waiting to see if anyone ran the red to keep up with them. Since leaving Alicia's place, he'd had this vague feeling of being watched, usually a good indicator that somebody was following him. Or maybe someone was following Alicia.

But nobody else turned off Twenty-third.

"Well?" Alicia said. "Are we?"

"Not that I can see." Or if we are, whoever's dogging us is damn good. "I also figured the car's a good idea because we don't know what we'll find in the house. Maybe it'll be something we can't carry out and load into a taxi. And besides, I needed a place to store a few props."

"Props? For what?"

"All in good time, my dear. All in good time."

He made a couple of lefts to put them on Third Avenue, and took that uptown. In Murray Hill, they cruised past the house and saw the security car out front.

"We'll never get past them," Alicia said.

Jack got the distinct impression she didn't *want* to get past them.

He checked out the exhaust pipe on the guard car as he passed and saw it smoking. No surprise. The temperature had dropped to about 40 degrees, and they had the heater running.

He smiled. Good.

"Let me worry about that," he told her.

He pulled around the corner and found a barely legal spot near a fire hydrant on Thirty-ninth.

"There's not going to be any fighting is there?" Alicia said.

"I definitely want to avoid that. And with the right kind of help, I figure I can."

He stepped out of the car and looked around at the mix of office buildings and town houses. Not many people out on this cold night. He shrugged into a shapeless old stadium coat he pulled from the backseat; next a pair of ratty leather gloves; then he yanked a knitted cap over his head, fitting it over his ears and down to his eyebrows. The final touch was a bucket containing two inches of soapy water and some other goodies.

Alicia leaned forward, staring at him through the open door. "What on earth . . . ?"

"Meet the scourge of the streets: the sight of him can cause even the toughest New York City driver to quail. Meet . . . Squeegeeman!"

"I don't believe this."

"Wait five minutes, then walk around the block and meet me in front of the house."

"But what—?"

"Be there. See you."

He closed the door and trotted around to Thirty-eighth. He stopped twice along the way to scan the passersby and the streets for a tail, but could spot no one suspicious.

Damn. Why did he feel he was being watched?

2

That was close, Yoshio thought as he turned onto Thirty-ninth Street.

For a moment there he had been sure the *ronin* helping Alicia Clayton had spotted him, but he'd managed to drive past without arousing suspicion. The man seemed to have a sixth sense, almost a counterpoint talent to the one that allowed Yoshio to tail without being seen. Yoshio would have to be very careful with this one.

He had chosen to watch Alicia Clayton for the early part of the evening, then move on to Kemel. Yoshio had been glad to see the arrival of her *ronin*. This man seemed to be popping up everywhere. Yoshio had followed Kemel and Thomas Clayton to their attorney's office yesterday; while waiting outside, wishing he had a bug in the meeting room, Yoshio had seen this man emerge from the building in the company of a tall black man, both in suits. It could not be a coincidence.

So tonight, when they had driven off in a rented car, Yoshio had followed. Along the way, the *ronin* had lost Yoshio with a sudden, last-second turn off Twenty-third Street. Yoshio had been stuck, two cars behind. But he had suspected that they might show up at the Clayton house, so he headed in that direction. He had taken his time, munching on a bucket of extra crispy Kentucky Fried Chicken along the way, and had been pleasantly surprised to see their car pass him on Third Avenue.

And now the *ronin*, shabbily dressed and with a bucket in his hand, was walking toward the Clayton house.

Very curious.

Yoshio wondered what he had in mind. He decided to follow him on foot and find out. He'd been so bored with the recent lull in events, but things had become interesting since this man arrived on the scene. Yoshio had a feeling something *very* interesting might happen tonight.

But even if it didn't, this was still more to his liking than sitting and watching Kemel's apartment.

3

When Jack reached the corner he untied his sneakers and pulled them open, leaving the tongues sticking up. He buttoned his coat wrong, and then started up the sidewalk opposite the security car.

About halfway there, he shambled across the street, approaching the car from the front. He didn't want to startle these two by appearing out of nowhere—somebody might do something stupid.

Jack stopped about ten feet from the front bumper and pointed at the car, grinning. He pulled his window-cleaning squeegee from the bucket and held it high as he approached.

Squeegeeman had spotted a customer.

Through the windshield he could see the two beef jerkies inside waving him off, but Squeegeeman is never deterred by a reluctant driver. Drivers so rarely seem to appreciate how much more efficiently and safely they will be able to perform the task at hand, namely driving, after their windshield has been smeared with soapy water and then wiped clean.

The driver's window slid down and a head leaned out. The few features Jack could make out in the dim light suggested that evolution sometimes worked in reverse.

"Keep moving, asshole," said the head.

Jack leaned over the fender and quickly lathered up the windshield.

The front door started to open. "Fuck!" said the voice. "Didn't you hear me—?"

"I heard you, man," Jack said, launching into his patter, "but Squeegeeman's offering a Try-Before-You-Buy special tonight. Here's how it works: I do your window, just like I'm doin' now, and when I'm through, if you don't think it's the cleanest window you ever seen, then you don't pay. I mean, you can't beat that, can you? I mean, I'm out here in the cold doin' all the work while you're in there nice and warm and cozy. You tell me what could be better than that. Go ahead—you tell me."

The beef jerky hesitated and stared at him, both of his brain cells obviously working overtime as he considered Squeegeeman's offer. Then the guy in the passenger seat said something, and the driver door pulled closed.

Jack smiled. He'd been counting on their reluctance to cause a scene and risk someone calling the police. But if worse came to worst, he had a Tokarev 9mm automatic in his shoulder holster.

"That's right," he said. "Roll up your window, sit back, and watch how beautiful the world looks when I'm finished with your glass."

The window slid closed. Jack added a little more lather to the windshield. When he had it satisfactorily opaque, he pulled a small vial of T-72 from the bucket and poured its contents into the heater's air intake at the base of the windshield wipers.

Then he began wiping the glass dry. He took his time on the windshield, moving slowly, dabbing at the corners, playing the roll to the hilt. And doing a damn fine job, by the way.

When he was done, he stepped up to the driver window, grinned, and held out his hand.

The driver returned the grin—and gave him the finger.

Jack looked hurt and pressed his hands together as if praying.

The driver's grin broadened as he brought up his other hand to add a second bird to the window display.

"Keep smiling," Jack said softly.

And then the guy in the passenger seat slumped against the driver's back. The driver jerked around, pushed him off, and shook him, but the guy was limp as overcooked linguine. Then the driver turned back to the window and Jack could all but see the light go on in his head.

"That's right, guy," Jack said. "You got trouble."

The driver fumbled for the inner handle and started to open the door, but Jack slammed against it and held it closed. The driver struggled and might have got out—he was bigger than Jack—if the T-72 hadn't been working on him. He made a couple of weak shoulder butts against the door, then slumped against the steering wheel and joined his friend in slumber land.

Jack waited to make sure he was out, then he opened the door and quickly ran through the driver's pockets. He found two sets of keys and took both. He closed the door and left the motor running.

He glanced around—no one in sight. Good.

After pocketing the T-72 vial, he placed his bucket and squeegee by the curb and settled back to wait for Alicia.

4

Alicia forced her feet to keep moving, placing one shoe in front of the other as she turned the corner and trod the sidewalk toward that house.

She tried to think about anything *but* the house, pushing her thoughts toward Hector in PICU. The little guy was fading away. No question about it now—a resistant strain of *C. albicans*. His white blood cells, one of the body's main defenses against infection, were disappearing from his bloodstream. The WBC count had been down to 3,200 this morning and had dropped to 2,600 this afternoon. The infection was running rampant, overwhelming his bone marrow's ability to crank out the white cells.

And there was nothing more she could do for him.

Which allowed her thoughts to escape Hector and return to the house. The house . . .

Why am I making such an ordeal of this? she wondered. It's only a building, a collection of bricks and lumber. What's the big deal?

But cold reason wasn't working. The closer she got to the house, the faster her heart raced. She wouldn't look at it. She kept her eyes straight ahead on the figure in the baggy coat leaning against the security car.

She tried to think of something else, to focus on the events of the day, but all that came to mind was the series of phone calls from Will, asking if she was all right, calls she'd been too embarrassed to return.

The hurt and confusion in his recorded voice still echoed in her brain, making her want to hide. How could she explain last night to him? It was all her fault. She shouldn't have let him get that close. When would she learn? She had to resign herself to the reality that she couldn't have a completely honest relationship with any man. Really . . . once the truth was out, what man wouldn't head for the door? And frankly, Alicia wasn't sure she'd want to have much to do with any man who didn't.

Alone was better. Alone was easier. Alone was less painful—for everyone concerned.

She was closer now, still keeping her eyes on Jack. She heard him

248

whistling and recognized the tune as the theme from "The Bridge Over the River Kwai."

"Ready?" he said as she reached him.

She bent and peered into the car, then stepped back when she saw the two bulky forms slumped in the front seat. Her already racing heart kicked its tempo up another notch.

"They're not . . . you didn't . . . are they . . . ?"

"Dead?" He smiled. "Nah. Just napping." He looked around. "Okay. Let's get moving. I don't know how much longer they'll be out."

Here it was—the moment she'd been dreading. Alicia didn't move. Couldn't move.

"Alicia?" Jack said. "You okay?"

But she had to move. She wasn't going to let this get the best of her.

Just a house . . . just bricks and lumber . . .

And she was going to conquer it.

She took a breath and turned to face it.

The wrought-iron gate, the tiny front yard, the trellised alley to the back . . . just as they'd always been. But the rest of the front had been altered enough to make it look like a different house . . . somebody else's house.

And with its windows boarded up like patched eyes, it looked like a *blind* house. It couldn't see her.

Not so bad, she thought. I can handle this.

"I'm fine," she said. "Let's go."

"Let's try the back door," Jack said, leading her toward the trellis. "I've got a bunch of keys here and don't want to spend too much time out front looking for the right one. Someone might remember us."

She followed him into the dark and held his penlight for him as he tried a succession of keys. The fifth one fit. The solid *clack* of the re-tracting dead bolt hit her like a punch.

Alicia began to shake. She felt the tremor begin in the pit of her stomach and spread outward to her limbs. She wanted to turn and bolt for the street.

No! she told herself. You will *not* run.

Bricks and lumber . . . bricks and lumber . . .

Jack pulled out a larger flashlight and stepped through the door. Bathed in a cold sweat, Alicia clenched her jaw and followed him. She had a bad moment—a trapped, clawing, let-me-out moment—when the door clicked closed behind her, but she fought it off.

Then Jack's flashlight beam found a wall switch, and he flicked it. Light flooded the room.

"Well, isn't that considerate," he said. "They left the power on."

Alicia stood blinking in the unexpected light. The carnage came into focus as her eyes adjusted.

"Oh, my God. Look what they've done."

When she'd lived here, the rear door had led into a narrow utility room that housed the washer and dryer, and a pantry. The washer and dryer were still here, but in pieces—they'd been thoroughly dismantled, and their components lay in piles on the floor. The pantry shelves had been emptied, and their contents scattered among the appliance parts.

"Now this," Jack said, "is what I call tossing a room. And they didn't have to hurry. With the power on, they had plenty of light. And with the windows boarded up, no one would know they were here."

He stepped through the debris and headed for the adjoining room.

"Let's see what's in here."

"Should be the kitchen," Alicia said as Jack turned on the light.

It was . . . in a way.

The kitchen had been as thoroughly "tossed"—to use Jack's term—as the utility room. Not only had the cabinets been emptied, they'd been ripped off the walls and broken apart. The dishwasher had suffered the same fate as the washer and dryer. The sink had been removed, leaving its pipes jutting from the wall like copper carotids. All the pieces had been piled in the center of the floor.

In shock, Alicia stumbled after Jack, who was still on the move, skirting the debris and moving into the dining room. Same story there, except that the rug had been torn up and the strips of its remains were in the pile with the remnants of the furniture and china.

In a way she was glad. All this destruction made it easier for her to be here. It turned the house into a different place, nothing like she remembered. But still, the degree of devastation was astonishing.

"I knew Thomas didn't want me to have the place," Alicia said softly, "but I never realized he was this angry."

"This isn't anger," Jack said, nudging the pile with the toe of his sneaker. "This is methodical as hell. They started in the center of the room, then worked outward, dumping everything in the center after they'd checked it. These guys know what they're doing."

"But how could they expect to get away with it?"

Jack shrugged. "I guess they figured you didn't have a chance of ever taking possession of the place. So what did it matter what they did to it? And I suspect that once they find what they're looking for, they'll just disappear."

"But what—*what* could they be looking for?"

"Something metal, I'd say."

Jack had moved to a corner where a contraption that looked like a vacuum cleaner handle attached to a frying pan leaned against the wall.

"How do you know?"

He lifted the contraption. "Metal detector."

"A key," Alicia said, remembering the Greenpeace line from the will: " 'This house holds the key that points the way to all you wish to achieve.' They're looking for a key."

Jack nodded. "Got to be. Your half brother's Arab friend quoted the same line yesterday. Obviously they haven't found it yet." He looked around. "Did your father have a workshop?"

It was cold in here—Alicia could see her breath misting in the air—but now she felt a deeper chill. "Workshop?"

"Yeah. You know, where he puttered around with his hobbies or whatever."

Jagged shards of ice needled the lining of her arteries. She forced the words past her teeth. "The basement . . . if anywhere."

"How do we find it?"

"Through the kitchen."

"All right," he said, moving past her. "Let's go."

"No. You go. I can't."

"Come on, Alicia. This is no time to—"

"No," she said, and once again heard her voice climbing the scale. *"Didn't you hear me?* I CAN'T!"

He stared at her a moment, then turned away. "Okay. You can't. I'll check it out alone. Don't go away."

"I'm sorry," she said softly after he was gone. "But I just can't go there."

5

As Jack reached the bottom of the steps, he wondered if whatever abuse Alicia had suffered had been committed in the basement. Good chance, judging from her reaction.

He found the light switch and checked out the place.

Maybe Ronald Clayton once had a basement workshop. Sure as hell couldn't tell from the look of the place now. The Arab's wrecking crew had done their thing down here too—maybe they'd started here. They'd torn out the dropped ceiling, ripped the paneling from the walls, dismantled the furniture, and sliced up the cushions. He saw what looked like a disemboweled mattress and box spring, so he guessed there must have been a bed down here too.

Jack kicked through the debris and found miscellaneous electronic equipment—circuit boards, memory chips, and the like—but if they'd found a working computer, he was sure they'd carried it off to where they could inspect its hard drive down to the last byte.

He also came across some old, rusted-looking track lighting fixtures and noticed the oversize bulb holders. Doc Clayton must have liked it bright down here.

Jack poked around a little longer, then went back upstairs. He found Alicia in the dining room where he'd left her, standing by the pile of debris, her hands clenched into fists at her sides, looking ready to jump out of her skin.

"Find anything?" she said.

"Just another pile like this."

"I . . . I'm sorry I couldn't go down with you," she said, not looking at him. "It's just . . ."

"You don't have to explain."

"I wasn't going to. I'm just telling you that this is the way I am right now, and there's not a lot I can do about it."

"Okay." Just as well, he thought. This wasn't the time or place for an explanation. "Then we'll have to work around it."

She spread her hands toward the carnage. "Are we wasting our time?"

"Maybe," Jack said. "But I know some things about hiding stuff, maybe a thing or two they don't. One thing I do know is that you tend to hide your most valuable stuff close to you, where you can keep an eye on the hiding place, and get to it quick if you need it." He looked at her. "Where was your father's bedroom?"

"Upstairs."

"Any problem with going upstairs?"

"No. My room used to be up there."

Jack led the way, with Alicia directing him. A left at the top of the stairs took them to the master bedroom.

Maybe it had been masculine-looking, maybe it had still retained feminine touches from the days when Alicia's mother had lived here. All guesswork now. The room had been stripped to the walls; whatever once might have lent it character or personality now lay in a heap in the center of the floor.

He spotted a sledgehammer and a couple of crowbars leaning near a particularly damaged area of the wall in the far corner. He crossed the room for a closer look.

"Look at this," he said as he fingered the shattered edges of the wallboard. "They opened up the wall here."

Beyond the ragged opening was a tiny room—a converted closet, really—lined with shelves—empty shelves.

"Looks like some sort of secret library. Did you know about this?"

Alicia, stiff and pale, was standing at the other end of the room, near the door, just over the threshold.

She shook her head. "No."

What had Clayton kept here? Jack wondered. Research journals and papers? His notes on whatever it is the others are after?

He turned and kicked through the pile of debris. No paper.

"Well, whatever was stored here is gone—either gone when they got here, or they took it with them." He moved toward Alicia. "Let's try your room."

"My room? Why?"

"Well, he left the whole place to you, didn't he? Maybe he left you something else. Which way?"

Alicia pointed down the hall to a dark doorway. Jack stepped through and found another example of methodical destruction. He pointed to the central pile of debris.

"Recognize anything?"

"No." Alicia had entered behind him and was stepping gingerly

through the room. "Why should I? I left when I was eighteen and haven't
been back."

"Not once?"

"Not once."

Something round and shiny black caught Jack's eye, and he bent to
pick it up. A tiny rubber tire.

"Were you into toy cars?" he said, holding it out to Alicia.

She took it from him and stared at it.

"No. Never."

"Maybe your brother, then."

"No . . . Thomas was a couch potato . . . books, movies, video games.
I doubt his interest in cars went beyond the fact that they allowed him
to ride instead of walk." She held the tire up to the light, rolling it over
in her fingers. "Where's the rest of it?"

"Somewhere in there, I'd guess," he said, indicating the pile. "I'm
going to check out the bathrooms."

"Why?"

"Because they've got pipes." At her quizzical look, he added, "I'll
explain as I go."

"That's okay," she said. "I'll stay here."

He left Alicia on her knees, picking through the rubble pile.

Jack returned to Clayton's bedroom, grabbed one of the crowbars, and
headed for the master bathroom. One thing you could pretty much count
on in these older buildings—unless someone had done a wall-to-wall
renovation—was copper plumbing. He'd noticed copper pipes in the
kitchen, and metal pipes offered unique opportunities if you wanted to
hide something metallic.

A peek into the bathroom showed that the sink and toilet had been
ripped out, but the searchers hadn't chipped off the tile to expose the
pipes. Not yet, at least.

Jack next went to the bedroom closet, which shared a wall with the
bathroom. A knock on the wall brought a hollow sound. This wasn't part
of the original house. The bathroom probably had been enlarged. He
knelt and ran his fingers along the top of the wide strip of molding at
the base of the wall until he found a tiny gap. He inserted the flanged
tip of the crowbar. A gentle twist was all it needed—a screwdriver would
have done the job—and the molding popped free, revealing a three-inch
gap between the floor and the wallboard.

Just like home, Jack thought.

Over the years he'd put a lot of his money into gold coins—bad in-
vestment, yeah, but how else could he store his savings without getting

a bank involved? He hid them in his apartment by taping them to the
water pipes. That way the coins were safe from anybody who boosted his
place, even if they brought a metal detector: The detector was expected
to beep when it passed over the water pipes.

Jack slipped his hand inside and found the pipes running to and from
the bathroom. It took less than a minute for his searching fingers to locate
the object taped to one of them.

"Hello."

Jack stripped off the tape and pulled it out.

He couldn't see the thing here in the darkness, but it felt hard and
flat, encased in vinyl. He crawled from the closet to get a look at it in
better light.

A wedge-shaped red vinyl case. He lifted the flap and pulled out a
key with "#137" stamped on the bow.

Jack smiled. "Am I good, or am I good?"

The Arab and his wrecking crew would have found it eventually, especially if they were planning to take the place apart brick by brick. But
now they wouldn't find squat. Served 'em right.

A safety deposit box key, from the look of it. Or maybe to a storage
locker. But where?

Worry about that later, when they didn't have to watch the clock.

He went to find Alicia.

6

Curiosity was devouring Yoshio.

He'd seen the Clayton woman's *ronin* wash the guards' windshield,
then lean inside the driver door. After that, no one had interfered when
he and the Clayton woman entered the house.

What had he done?

Yoshio couldn't resist a quick walk by the car. As he passed he saw
two still forms in the front seat . . . so still that he thought they were
dead. But then one of them stirred, lifting his head briefly, then slumped
back into unconsciousness.

How had the *ronin* done this? A gas, or something in their coffee, perhaps?

Very clever, Yoshio thought. Very "smooth," as the Americans said.

But it appeared that whatever he'd used was beginning to wear off.

Yoshio kept moving, glancing at the house as he passed. He wished the Clayton woman and her *ronin* well in their search. Yoshio wanted whatever was in that house found and brought into the light.

For then he could move from mere observer to player. True, he would much prefer to contend with someone as predictable as the Arab's Sam Baker than this quick, tough, innovative stranger, but Yoshio had not the slightest doubt that he could handle either. He had many years of experience in these matters. And he would take whatever steps necessary to succeed. Kaze Group would expect that and would not accept anything less.

But you and your *ronin* had better hurry, Miss Clayton. Or I fear you will soon have some unwelcome company in your house.

7

" 'This house holds the key that points the way to all you wish to achieve,' " Jack said, holding the key out to Alicia. "This could be that key. Ever seen it before?"

She was still kneeling on the floor, not far from where he'd left her. She looked at the key but didn't take it.

"No. Where'd you find it?"

"Hidden in your father's closet. You wouldn't happen to know what bank he used."

She shook her head. "Not a clue." She held up the undercarriage of a toy car. "Look what I found. I replaced the wheel."

Was she cracking up? What was she doing fooling around with a toy car?

"Swell. Look, we've got to get—"

"And it still runs," she said. "Watch this."

She flicked a tiny switch and the wheels began spinning. She set the

toy down on the floor. It zoomed across the boards and ran into the wall.
It stayed there with its nose against the wall and its wheels spinning.

"We'll take it with us," Jack said. He was worried about the two beef
jerkies snoozing outside in their car. They could be waking up now. "You
can play with it the rest of the night."

"Don't patronize me, Jack. I may be a little jumpy and twitchy, but I
haven't lost my mind. I can still think." She crawled across the floor and
retrieved the car, then returned to her original spot. "This toy does *not*
belong here. That man never played with toys, and this one is completely
out of place in my room. That's why I searched for the rest of it. And I
think I'm glad I did. Watch."

She put the car down again, this time facing away from the wall. As
soon as its wheels hit the floor, it turned a one-hundred-eighty-degree
arc and headed toward the wall, butting its nose three inches or so to
the left of where it had ended up a minute ago.

Jack was about to tell her they didn't have time to play with toys,
whether they belonged in her room or not, but something about the little
car's persistence in running up against that wall made him hesitate.

"That's the seventh—no, *eighth* time it's ended against that wall," she
said. "No matter which way it's pointing when I set it down, eight out of
eight times that's where it ends up."

"No kidding?"

Jack bent and picked it up, turning it over in his hands. Nothing
special: a remote control toy car stripped down to its a metal undercarriage, with four wheels, a motor, steering mechanism, battery
compartment, and an aerial.

The wheels were still spinning, so he put it down and pointed it toward
Alicia. It zipped around and once again wound up against the wall.

"That's nine out of nine," she said.

Jack was interested now.

"Where's the rest of it?"

"Here." She handed him the black plastic body.

"No," he said. "Where's the remote, the little box that controls the
steering?"

"Never saw anything like that."

He checked out the plastic body. Apparently someone had torn it off
the chassis, probably looking to see if anything was hidden inside. He
snapped the two pieces back together.

"Looks more like some sort of Jeep than a car," Alicia said.

Jack checked out the tiny logo across the rear hatch.

"A 'Sports Utility Vehicle,' as they're known. But this is a real upscale Jeep. This here's a Land Rover."

"A *what?*"

Jack looked up and saw Alicia on her feet, staring wide-eyed at the toy.

"A Land Rover. They're British and—"

"The will," she said. "It mentions a rover—twice . . . in those crazy poetry quotes." She snapped her fingers and looked at the ceiling. "What were they? 'Clay(ton) lies still, but blood's a rover' was one. And the other . . . the other went, 'Whither away, fair rover, and what thy quest?' "

Jack felt a tingle of excitement as he sensed pieces of the puzzle clicking into place. Maybe "the key that points the way" wasn't a key at all. Maybe it was something that simply *pointed* the way.

He placed the toy on the floor again and watched it do its thing, winding up nose-on against the wall in that same spot.

This little "rover" was sure as hell pointing the way to something.

"What thy quest indeed," he said. "Wait here."

He trotted back to the bedroom, grabbed the sledgehammer and one of the crowbars. For a moment he considered hammering a hole in one of the pieces of plywood blocking the windows to allow him a peek at the guard car out front, but thought better of it. The racket might attract too much attention.

"What are you going to do?" Alicia said as he returned to her room.

"Something in this wall is attracting our little friend there. Hang onto him while I find out what."

He lifted the sledge and swung it sidearm at the wall.

8

The phone rang just as Kemel was finishing his evening prayers.

"Someone's in the house," Baker's voice said. "We think it's that guy the broad hired. I'm goin' over there now."

Alarm shot through Kemel like a jolt of electricity. How could this be? Just yesterday she had offered to sell and he had agreed to her price. Why would she send someone to invade it tonight? Unless . . .

Unless she knows something . . . unless she has guessed why the house is so valuable and has sent her man to find it.

Kemel closed his eyes and clenched his teeth. The air duct! Someone had been in there after all—Alicia Clayton's man. And he must have heard something.

"How did this happen?"

"He used some kind of knockout gas on my guys. They just woke up and called me. They think he's still in there."

"I'm glad you called."

"Not like I have much choice."

Kemel could hear the hurt pride in Baker's voice, but that was too bad. After last week's abduction fiasco, Kemel had put the mercenary on a short leash. He was to keep Kemel apprised of every development as it happened and was to take no action—do absolutely *nothing*— without first clearing it with Kemel. The operation was too close to successful completion to risk a setback from Baker's heavy-handed tactics. In fact, if Kemel had not needed ongoing security for the house, he would have fired Baker last week.

"But time's a-wasting," Baker said. "I'm headin' over now. If it's the same guy from the van, I want to be there."

"I want no action taken until I arrive."

"I may not have a choice."

"*Nothing* until I am present. Is that clear?"

"Clear," Baker said in a tight voice. "But I won't take responsibility for anything this guy does before you get there."

"I don't think that will be an issue since you are going to pick me up and we will arrive together."

"You're up in the Seventies. That'll take too long."

"I will be waiting out front," Kemel said, and hung up.

9

Jack used the sledge gently at first, for fear that he might damage whatever was hidden inside. But he quickly discovered that this was an old, solid, wet plaster wall, and he was going to have to put some muscle into ·it. It took a lot longer than he'd planned, but finally he had a good-size hole clear through to the other side.

Alicia peered over his shoulder. "Find anything?"

"Nothing inside this wall but . . . wall." He turned and looked at the toy in her hand. "But then, why . . . ?"

And then it hit him.

"Oh, hell."

Jack took the little Rover from Alicia and placed it in the hall on the other side of the wall. It wheeled across the floor and ended up against the wall on the far side of the hall.

"What's on the other side of that wall?" Jack said.

"Thomas's room."

Jack carried the truck into Thomas's room—in no better shape than Alicia's—and set the truck on the floor there. It ran across the room and butted against the far wall.

Jack watched it in dismay. "Damn thing wasn't attracted to the wall back there. It just wants to go uptown. So much for enigmatic clues in wills." And then a thought struck. "Or maybe it only wants to go as far as the front yard."

Swell. Even if that were the case, they couldn't exactly haul out picks and shovels and start digging up the front yard.

They'd already wasted too much time on that little piece of junk. But at least they had the key.

"Let's get out of here."

The truck kept running, spinning its wheels as it nosed against the wall. Jack resisted the impulse to drop-kick it down the hall, and picked it up instead.

"You're taking that with you?"

He turned off the motor and tucked it inside his coat.

"Yeah."

"Why?"

"I'm not sure."

And he wasn't. But sensed he shouldn't toss it away. Too many aspects of this crazy situation converged on the little truck—"Rover" in the will and on its hatch, and the way it always ran in the same direction, "pointing" uptown. Jack wasn't through with it yet.

10

At last! Alicia thought as they headed downstairs. We're finally getting out of this place.

And they'd found nothing.

She began turning off the lights as they went.

"Don't bother," Jack said. "No use trying to hide the fact that we've been here—Thomas and his Arab buddy'll know as soon as they see that smashed wall."

They stepped out the back door, and Alicia jumped and yelped as a voice barked to their left.

"Hold it right there!"

She turned and saw two hulking figures standing at the corner of the house. Enough light filtered in from the street to reveal the guns their hands. Then the beam from their flashlight found her face, nearly blinding her.

"Hands up—both of you!"

The guards from the car?

"Jeez, what a jerk I am," Jack muttered as he clasped his hands on top of his head. "Damn gas wore off."

"This is *my* house!" Alicia said, squinting into the light.

"Back inside," the voice said, waggling the flashlight as he spoke. "Both of you. We've got some people coming who'll want to talk to you two."

What are they going to do to us? she wondered as fear coiled through her intestines. Torture us? What will they put us through before they believe we didn't find anything?

"Quit stall—"

The voice was cut off by a *phut!* sound—two of them. And then the light beam left her eyes, and she saw the two figures crumpling to the ground. The flashlight rolled, and the beam washed over the bulging, staring eyes and blood-leaking nose of one of the fallen faces.

Alicia screamed and felt Jack ducking into a crouch, pulling her down with him. She saw his pistol in his hand, aimed at the corner of the house.

"Are . . . are they dead?" Alicia whispered.

"Sure as hell looks like it." His gun never stopped moving, ranging this way and that.

"You shot them dead, just like that?"

He stopped moving his gun and held it up in front of her for an instant. "You see a silencer? This was holstered when those guys went down. Somebody else got them."

"Somebody *else*? But weren't they the guards from out front?"

"The same."

"Then who—?"

"Damned if I know. Yesterday your brother's Arab friend mentioned being afraid of whatever it was he wanted from this place falling into 'the wrong hands.' I think this means we may have a third player in this game."

A trilling sound made her jump.

"What's that?" Alicia said, her fingertips digging into Jack's upper arm where she clutched it.

The sound repeated, coming from one of the corpses.

"Sounds like a cell phone. Someone's calling one of them."

Jack looked as if he was about to go find the phone and answer the call.

"Let's get out of here," Alicia said.

"No alley on the other side, is there?" Jack said.

She shook her head—the house was flush against its neighbor on the west side.

"Then we'll have to escape through the house. It's safer than stepping into that alley."

She couldn't argue with that. And for once in her memory, it felt good to step through that door.

As she led him through to the front, she heard Jack curse himself all the way.

"I let them wake up! What a damn stupid thing to do. Careless idiot. Could have got us both killed."

He stopped when they reached the front door. He unlocked it, then slowly, gently pulled it open a crack.

Alicia peeked over his shoulder. The guard car sat at the curb, engine still running, the doors closed. Jack stuck his head out and checked the front yard.

"Looks clear," he said. "Let's go."

He pulled the door open and guided her onto the front stoop.

"Get moving and keep moving. Don't run but walk fast—*real* fast— to your right. We'll take the long way around to the car."

Alicia started walking, just as he'd said, but then the terror of hearing a *phut!* and ending up like those two guards took hold. Repressing a scream, she began to run.

11

"Damn!" Sam Baker said and jabbed his thumb at the END button. "Why don't they fuckin' answer?"

He dropped the phone on the seat between him and the Arab and concentrated on driving. Mott and Richards were two of his better men, but they'd got snookered by the Clayton broad's muscle. They'd been groggy when they first called in, but seemed to be coming around pretty fast. By the time they hung up they were almost a hundred percent and heading into the house to see if the guy was still there.

What Baker hoped was that they'd caught the guy and were too busy rearranging his face and innards to answer the phone.

If it's the guy from the van, he thought, save a piece for me.

His kidney still ached from that punch.

But Baker was getting uneasy. After three calls, you'd think one of them would pick up the goddamn phone.

If this operation went south it would be his ass. He'd be blamed, and that meant kissing the bonus and a regular gig in Saudi Arabia good- bye. And it wouldn't be his fault, dammit!

His unease grew as he turned onto Thirty-eighth and accelerated up the block toward the Clayton house. Something was wrong. He could feel it.

"Look!" Muhallal said, pointing through the windshield. "That is Alicia Clayton!"

Baker squinted at the figure coming down the front steps of the house and hurrying toward the sidewalk. Sure as hell looked like her. And then he saw the guy following right behind her—

"That's him!" he said. "That's the son of a bitch from last week—the one I told you about!"

Rage burst like a hollow point in Baker's brain. He gunned the engine and the car leaped forward.

"No!" Muhallal shouted. He grabbed Baker's arm. "No! Stop the car! I do not wish them to know we are here!"

"No way! I owe that motherfu—"

"Stop immediately or you are fired!" Muhallal said.

Baker knew from the Arab's tone that he meant it. Shit. He eased up on the gas pedal and watched the two figures hurry away along the sidewalk.

"But they've been in the house," he said, so pissed his hands were twitching on the steering wheel. "They probably stole something! Don't you want it back?"

Baker didn't give a furry rat's ass about what they might've taken. All he wanted was to get his hands on that rotten lousy—

"If they stole a *thing*," Muhallal said, "then yes, of course I want it back. And I will get it back. But if they are walking away with *information*—information that I do not have—then I want that even more."

"I don't get it." He wished he knew what the hell this was all about.

Muhallal pointed through the windshield at the street ahead. "Follow them. But do not let them see you. If he takes her home, we will follow him to where he lives and learn what he knows. If they drive somewhere else, then we must know where they go. We must not let them get away."

"Don't worry about that," Baker said, easing the car into motion. "Where she goes, we go."

"You are so sure?"

"Yep. Real sure." He couldn't help but grin. "That little ride we took her on last week—you know, the 'idiotic stunt' you hated so much? It wasn't completely worthless. I didn't tell you at the time, but I planted a tracer in the bottom of that shoulder bag she always carries. No place she can go that we can't find her."

The Arab didn't comment.

What's the matter? Baker thought. Camel got your tongue?

He picked up the cell phone.

"Who are you calling?" the Arab said.

"The guys who were supposed to keep them out of the house."

Still no answer. He hung up after the sixth ring.

If Mott and Richards were busy working someone over, it was the wrong guy—the right guy was walking up the street.

This could be bad. Very bad.

Baker dialed Kenny's number. He might need some backup on this. Ahab the Ay-rab sure as shit wasn't going to be any help.

But who else in his crew to call? Hell, call them all. Get every damn one of them involved. Have them bring the tracking electronics and come loaded for bear.

Some serious ass gonna get kicked tonight.

12

Yoshio waited until Kemel Muhallal and his mercenary were at the end of the block before he pulled away from the curb and followed. He had been expecting them, but had hoped the Clayton woman and her investigator would be gone by the time Muhallal arrived.

But the Arab had spotted them and now was following.

Yoshio wondered if he would be forced to intervene again.

He had seen the two guards regain consciousness and stagger from their car—the driver had leaned against a fender and vomited onto the pavement. He watched them call in and knew that Alicia Clayton had very little time left to find whatever she was looking for. As the pair drew their weapons and stalked toward the rear of the house, he'd debated what to do: Allow them to catch her and take possession of what she might have found? Or stop them and let her escape?

He chose the latter.

It had been almost too easy. The two guards had been so intent on the woman and her *ronin* that they'd ignored their rear. A quick shot to the head for each from Yoshio's silenced .22 was all it had taken. Then he had retreated to his vantage point to wait.

And calculate the death toll. Counting Alicia Clayton's first investigator, her lawyer, and that arsonist Yoshio had seen Baker and his men immolate, these two tonight brought the number of deaths connected with Ronald Clayton's secret to 252—at least that he knew of. How many more to come?

He wondered if the secret was worth it. Otherwise, Kaze Group was paying him for nothing.

He drummed his fingers on the steering wheel as he played through various scenarios in his head. If only he could be sure the Clayton woman had found some clue, then his course would be clear: Kill Muhallal and Baker, and close in on her. Clean and simple . . . but disastrous if she had nothing. He'd have revealed his presence for no gain.

Of course, he already might have done that by killing those two men back on Thirty-eighth Street, but he felt their deaths would probably be blamed on the Clayton woman's *ronin*. At least Yoshio hoped they would. His job so far had been made so much easier by the fact that no one knew of his existence.

He watched Baker hanging well back as he followed a white sedan. Yoshio followed Baker, wondering when he would have to choose.

The *ronin*'s Chevrolet headed east, then uptown to the Fifty-ninth Street Bridge, where it crossed into Queens.

Leaving town. Interesting. That might be the sign he'd been waiting for. But shortly after he followed them onto the Long Island Expressway, heading east, the decision whether or not to act was made for Yoshio: a dark van pulled in front of Baker's car. The same van used in the aborted abduction last week. The driver waved an arm out the window. Baker flashed his high beams.

Reinforcements? Yoshio wondered. It appeared that they meant business.

So now it was a four-car procession, with Yoshio bringing up the rear.

But then Baker and his men did something strange: the car and the van began dropping back . . . too far back, Yoshio thought.

Weren't they afraid of losing her?

But then, perhaps they knew where she was going.

Yes, this was turning out to be a most interesting night—perhaps a decisive night. Yoshio had a feeling the best was yet to come.

Almost a shame to take money for this, he thought as he settled behind the wheel and kept driving.

13

I don't think I like this, Alicia thought as Jack stopped his car across the street from a tiny ranch house on a gravel road in the middle of a sea of potato fields.

They had turned off the LIE awhile back, traveled through some suburban towns that had given away to farmland, and now they were . . . here.

"I want to go back, Jack," she said. She'd said that maybe a dozen times now. He probably thought she sounded like a broken record.

Broken record . . . an irrelevant question fluttered through her mind: would the next generation, raised on CDs, even know what that sounded like?

"I told you: I'll take you back as soon as I'm sure we're not being tailed."

He got out and stood with the door open, staring back along the dark country road. Alicia turned and looked through the back window.

"There's nobody there, Jack."

"But there was. Somebody picked us up as soon was we got the car moving. That's why we made this little detour."

"Little" was not the word Alicia would have chosen to describe this trek. She'd had a long day, a harrowing night. My God, when was this going to end?

First, reentering the house . . . bad enough, but then those two men had been gunned down right in front of her. That bloody face and staring eyes, glimpsed for only a second, still strobed through her brain.

Death . . . so much death connected with the house.

So now she just wanted this awful night to be over. She wished she were back in her own little place with her plants and in her own bed, getting some sleep. Or at least trying to get some sleep. She did *not* want to be skulking through this empty farming country in eastern Long Island.

Especially with an armed man who insisted he was being followed when it was obvious to anyone with eyes that he was not.

"Okay," she said. "Maybe somebody was following us for a while. But there's nobody back there *now*. There hasn't been for miles. So can we please go home?"

He looked up and scanned the sky. Alicia followed his gaze. A clear cold winter night, with half a moon and a billion stars providing the light.

"More than one way to follow somebody. And trust me, we've been followed all night. I can feel it." He leaned inside and grabbed the keys. "Maybe we'd better go inside."

She looked past him at the little house. Even in the moonlight she could tell it was run-down. The storm door hung open at an angle, and an old pickup rusted amid the knee-high, winter-brown weeds in the front yard.

"In there?"

"Yeah. It's mine." He grinned. "This 'delightful little two-bedroom ranch' is my country place."

"I don't think so."

"Come on. Just for a few minutes. I've got a feeling we're going to have company soon, and I'd rather be inside when they arrive."

Alicia looked back along the road again. "Jack . . . there's nobody coming."

"Just ten minutes. If nobody shows by then, we're outta here. Okay?"

"Okay," she said, and checked her watch. "Ten minutes, and not a second more."

She saw him pull a toothpick from his pocket, then kneel and fiddle with something inside the car door near the hinge. The courtesy lights went out.

"What are you doing?"

"Jamming the light button."

He snapped off the rest of the toothpick and closed the door without latching it.

"What in God's name for?"

"You'll see. Won't matter if we haven't been followed. Let's go."

She followed him up the walk where he unlocked the front door and flipped on the lights. Alicia stopped at the threshold and took it in.

First off—the smell: Mold and mildew had been having a ball here. Then the look: The living room rug was filthy, the furniture sagging and worn, and here and there around the room, near the ceiling, corners of wallpaper curled back like peeling skin, revealing mildewed plaster.

"Your 'country place?' " she said. "When was the last time you stayed here?"

"Never." He closed the door behind her and moved to the drawn venetian blinds. "This is my decoy place."

"For hunting?"

"No. For a situation just like this—when I'm being followed, or think I am, and can't be sure."

"You bought a house way out here just for that?"

He nodded as he lifted one of the slats on the blind and peered through. "Well, yeah. I wanted three things: isolation, low maintenance, and cheap."

She glanced around again. "I don't know what you paid for it, but you certainly got one and two."

"It was cheap enough to allow me to make some improvements."

"Improvements? Where?"

"They're not readily apparent."

"You can say that again. Looks like a crack house."

He laughed as he kept watch through the blind. "Oh, right. Like you'd know."

"Yeah, I would know," she said, resenting his sarcasm. "I've gone along when we've had to retrieve sick children from addict parents. You don't know a fraction of what I've seen."

Jack glanced at her. "You're right. I don't. Sorry. I'm sure there's lots I don't know about you."

What does he mean by that? Alicia wondered as he turned back to peeking through the blind. She was about to ask him but held back.

Ease up, she told herself. You've been acting a little weird tonight. All right, more than a little. He's got to have some questions about you. Anybody would.

She glanced at her watch: three minutes gone. In seven minutes she'd hold him to his word and make him take her home.

"Uh, oh," he said from the window. "Company."

He stepped aside and held up the slat for her. She peeked though.

Out front, beyond the derelict pickup, a car and a panel truck—her heart began to race as she recognized that truck—were pulling to a stop.

14

"Everyone get out on the street side of the truck," Baker said into the cell phone as he pulled to a stop behind the panel truck. No point in advertising how many men he'd brought.

He opened his door and jumped out to take charge. He could almost hear the blood singing through his veins, coursing through his limbs, tingling in his fingertips. This was Sam Baker's element, this was when he felt most alive.

"Remember," the Arab said, leaning over from the passenger seat. "You must not harm the woman."

"Yeah," Baker said. "I hear you."

He'd been hearing that since they'd hit the LIE. He knew all about it. Muhallal had made that a condition from Day One. Fine. They wouldn't hurt the girl.

But the guy . . . that was a different story.

Especially since Baker had got the word about Mott and Richards. When they still weren't answering their phone, he'd called Chuck and sent him to limp over to check on them. Chuck was glad for something to do. He wasn't much good for anything else, what with his right arm in a splint and his knee in a straight brace—courtesy of the guy in the house.

But Chuck had been pretty shook up when he called back. Mott and Richards were dead. Head shots. Looked like hollow points.

Baker had heard of blind rage before, but never had experienced it until tonight. He'd been so pissed, and screaming so loud, he'd almost put the car in a ditch.

Not that Mott and Richards didn't deserve to be dead. Really—how dumb were they, first to get gassed, then to get whacked out in the open? Served them fucking right.

Bad enough that guys he knew had been offed, but they'd bought it while they were working for him. That was a bitch slap to Sam Baker. He could not let this guy live to talk about it.

But he could make him squeal like a pig before he died.

His six remaining men, Kenny and the rest, were out of the van and donning their vests and checking their weapons by the time he got there. He pointed to the big black guy who was kneeling, tying his shoe.

"Briggs. Go check the car. Just to be sure. This guy's tricky, so be careful or you could end up like Mott and Richards."

As Briggs hefted his Tec-9 and trotted toward the Chevy, Baker turned to Perkowski and pointed to the utility pole. "Perk. Climb up there and cut the phones." Then he pointed to Barlowe. "Take DeMartini and cover the rear."

Briggs returned as they took off toward the backyard.

"Car's okay," Briggs said.

"Hey, look."

Baker turned and saw Kenny pointing toward the house. He followed his nephew's point and saw two silhouettes through the open venetian blinds. A second later the blinds closed again.

"They know we're here. Where's my Tec?"

Kenny pulled one of the Tec-9's from inside the van and tossed it his way. Baker caught it one-handed. He checked the clip, then worked the slide. He loved these little beauties. They emptied their thirty-two-round clips in an eye blink.

"Let's go," he said.

"Wait," said a voice behind him. "I am coming with you."

Oh, shit. What a time for Ahab the Ay-rab to get some guts.

"I don't think that's such a good idea. There may be some shooting."

"That is what I fear. The woman must not be hurt."

"Don't worry. We won't—"

"I am coming. Lead on."

Baker looked at him and thought, If you weren't paying me, you lousy twerp, I'd shove this barrel right up your nose and give you a 9mm headache.

He smiled. "Okay. Your call. But don't blame me if you get hurt."

15

"Why'd you open them?" Alicia said as Jack pulled the string to close the blind.

"Wanted to make sure they know we're here." He stepped back from the window and shook his head. "They're carrying assault pistols. Looks like they mean to do some serious harm."

Alicia's intestines writhed into a painful knot. Men with guns . . . looking for her . . . how did she ever come to this?

"You mean they're going to kill us?" Alicia said.

"That's about the only thing Tec-9's are good for," Jack said. "Close-range annihilation." He gave her a quick smile. "But not you. Killing you is the last thing they want to do."

Alicia noticed that he'd left the obvious unsaid: Killing Jack would be the first thing on their list.

Will Matthews, where are you when I need you?

"Call the police," she said, suddenly frantic. She didn't want Jack to join the other three men she'd involved in this. "Maybe if they know the police are coming—"

"That guy who climbed the pole fixed that. And even if he hadn't, the cops couldn't get here in time. And even if they could, we wouldn't call them."

He strode across the living room into the small connecting dining room. Alicia followed.

"Look, Jack. I know you have a thing about the police, but there are a dozen armed men—"

"Eight," he said as he knelt by a dusty, scratched sideboard and pulled it away from the wall. "And one of them isn't armed—or at least isn't showing it."

On the wall behind the sideboard was what appeared to be a security system keypad. Jack began punching in a code.

"All right, *eight!*" she said, her fear and frustration rising. "Whatever the number, there's a small army out there and just you and me in here.

And what are you *doing?* Setting an alarm? We don't need an alarm, we need *help!*"

"No," he said. "We need out. And that's where we're gonna get." He pushed the sideboard back against the wall and headed toward the kitchen. He motioned her to follow. "Let's go."

He led her through the kitchen without turning on a light. A quick left past the refrigerator to a dark open doorway.

"This way to the basement," he said. "The handrail is on the right. Soon as you close that door behind you, I'll turn on the light."

The basement was partially finished—half-paneled, half-bare cinder blocks. Jack crossed the littered floor to a section of paneling, poked his finger over the top, then pulled. The section swung away from the wall on hinges. Behind it, a circular opening, four feet across, gaped in the block.

"What on earth?" Alicia said.

"Not *on*," Jack said, "*in* the earth."

"A bomb shelter?" The thought of being sealed up in that dark hole, crouching and cowering while men with machine guns searched for her was too much. "Oh, no. I don't think I can."

"It's a tunnel." She sensed from his tone that his patience might be wearing a little thin. "It'll take us to the field across the street. Come on. We don't have much time."

He handed her a flashlight, and motioned her to go first. Taking a breath, she ducked inside and crawled in a few feet. She found herself in a ribbed tube of galvanized metal; cold, but surprisingly clean. Jack came in after her, pulling the wall closed behind him. She turned on the flashlight as darkness engulfed them.

"Shine that over here a sec," he said.

He set some sort of latch on the panel section, then wriggled past her. He took the flashlight and began crawling down the tunnel.

"This way."

"Do I have a choice?" she said, wondering where and when this night would end.

16

"We must accomplish this very quickly," Baker heard Muhallal say as they approached the front door.

The Arab kept looking up and down the road, as if searching for signs of life. Nothing but darkness out there.

"Worried about someone calling the cops?" Baker said.

"Yes. Of course. I am not a citizen, and I have no diplomatic immunity. My arrest would cause great embarrassment to . . . to my organization."

And just what *is* your organization? Baker wondered. He'd been trying to figure that one out since this whole thing started.

"Not to worry," Baker said. "This won't take long at all."

"And don't forget—"

"I know, I know. Don't hurt the girl."

"That is correct. Do anything you wish to the man, but she must not be harmed."

If he tells me once more . . . , Baker thought.

"You come over here with me," he whispered to Muhallal as he directed his men to spread out on either side of the front door.

Always a good idea to keep the guy paying the bills out of the line of fire.

He gave Briggs the go-ahead. The big guy pushed open the door and leaped inside with his weapon ranging back and forth before him. The others rushed in behind him.

Baker waited half a minute or so with Muhallal, watching the lights go on all through the house, then motioned him to follow him inside.

Was this where the Clayton broad's muscle lived? Place looked like a dump.

"Front bedroom clear," said Briggs, emerging from a hallway.

"Rear bedroom clear," said Toro, following him.

Seconds later Kenny pounded up the stairs from the basement and came through the kitchen. "Cellar's deserted," he said.

"What the fuck?" Baker said, scratching his head. He stepped to the far end of the dining area and pulled up a window. He had a bad moment when he didn't see Barlowe and DeMartini—had they ended up like Mott and Richards?—but then he spotted them.

"Anybody come out the back?" he called.

"Negative," Barlowe said.

Baker turned and looked around. "Shit. We know they were in here. We saw them."

He saw the Arab fucker watching him, judging him. If he blew this and let them get away . . .

"Hey, looky here," said Perkowski from the hall. He was pointing the barrel of his weapon at a string hanging from the ceiling.

"Well, well, well," Baker said as he brushed past Muhallal for a closer look. "What have we here? Looks like we got us a pull-down staircase."

"Looks like we got us a wall safe too," said Briggs as he pulled a black velvet painting of a tiger off the living room wall.

"We'll check it later," Baker said. "Right now, I think we've got a certain rat cornered real good."

He wanted this guy . . . wanted him *sooo* bad.

He raised his Tec and gave Perkowski the go-ahead to pull the string. "Do it."

Perkowski pulled and the ceiling door swung down.

Baker crouched, ready to fire at the first sound, the first sight of anything threatening. But nothing moved in that rectangle of darkness.

Perkowski unfolded the attached ladder. As it hit the floor, something black started sliding down a track fixed to the upper rungs.

Baker took a second or two to recognize the thing as a little cannon.

"Back!" he shouted.

. . . And felt foolish when the little cannon reached the end of its track and stopped with a jolt, popping a red flag from its muzzle.

Yellow letters spelled out, "BANG!"

Wait till I get you, fucker, Baker thought, glaring up the ladder as Perkowski and Toro laughed. Put the hurt on you . . . big time.

"Got ourselves a comedian, we do," Perkowski said.

"A real clown," Toro said.

Perkowski started up the ladder, holding his Tec ahead of him. "I *hate* clowns."

"Be careful, Perk," Toro said. "Remember Mott and Richards."

"Oh, don't worry," Perkowski said. "Richards was a friend of mine. I remember just fine."

Perkowski's head and his Tec were swallowed by the dark opening, then he barked a harsh, humorless laugh.

"Oh. Yeah. This guy's a real clown."

"What is it?" Baker said, climbing up behind Perkowski.

Standing on a lower rung, he had to stretch against Perk's back to get his eyes to floor level. A quick look-see showed him half a dozen toy cannons, identical to the one on the ladder, arrayed on either side of the opening. A string ran up to a naked bulb directly overhead.

Baker ducked and dropped back to the floor.

"I don't like the looks of this," he said. "Get down from there."

"Aw, just some more of the clown's funny business," Perkowski said, reaching for the light string. "Let's shed some light on the subject."

"I wouldn't—," Baker started to say, but was drowned out by the deafening roar of half a dozen shotgun shells firing at once.

Perkowski's body—his head and arms a bloody ruin—hurtled from the ladder and landed on Toro.

Fury overtook Baker then. Another of his men down! The son of a bitch!

He raised his Tec-9 and began firing. He stitched all thirty-two rounds into the ceiling that ran along the hall, and was flipping the clip to spray another thirty-two when a hand grabbed his arm.

"The woman!" It was Muhallal, his expression a mixture of anger and fright. "You'll kill the woman!"

Baker was about to tell him to fuck off when howls of pain started from the living room. He wheeled around the corner to find Briggs writhing in agony with his hand in the wall.

"What the fuck?" Baker said.

"The wall safe!" Briggs gasped. "It wasn't locked. I saw some cash inside, but when I reached in, it spiked me!"

Baker saw blood oozing out of the circular opening and dripping down the wall.

"You jerk!"

"You gotta get me outta this thing, man!" Briggs wailed. "I think I'm spiked through. It's killin' me!"

Shit! Baker thought. What else could go wrong?

That was when the beeping started.

Everybody froze. Even Briggs stopped his yelping.

The beeping . . . it was coming from the beat-up stereo cabinet across the room. Kenny stepped over to it and pulled open the doors.

An LED display was doing a countdown in big red digits, beeping as each new number appeared.

. . . 58 . . . 57 . . . 56 . . .

Kenny knelt for a closer look, then jumped back.

"Christ, Sam, it's a bomb!"

Baker froze for an instant, then stepped closer. Kenny didn't know bombs; that was his domain.

Baker felt his scalp crawl when he recognized a brick of C-4. He knew the stuff. He'd used it when he wired that lawyer's car. And this brick had *lot* of wires running in and out of it.

. . . 45 . . . 44 . . . 43 . . .

"Well, don't just stand there, Sam!" Kenny shouted. "Defuse it!"

"In twenty seconds? Afraid not."

. . . 40 . . . 39 . . .

Behind Baker, Briggs started wailing, calling on God and his mother for help.

"I'm outta here!" Toro said, and headed for the door.

"Hey!" Briggs cried. "Where y'goin'? Hey, guys—don't leave me here with a bomb! Please, guys! *Please!*" The last was a drawn-out wail.

. . . 36 . . . 35 . . .

Baker noticed the Arab heading for the door and wasn't surprised. He wanted to follow, wanted very much to be far from that bomb, but . . .

"Sam?" Kenny said, looking spooked. "Shouldn't we be—?"

"You got your knife?" Baker said, pulling his big Special Forces blade from its sheath.

. . . 32 . . . 31 . . .

"Sure," Kenny said.

"Then get it out and come over here. Move!"

"Hey, Baker!" Briggs said, wide-eyed as he saw them rushing at him with drawn knives. "What you gonna do?"

"I oughta cut your arm off for sticking your hand where it doesn't belong," Baker said, stopping on Briggs's right. "And I may have to yet, but let's try something else first. Lean back." He slapped the wall on the other side of Briggs, above and to the left of the level of the safe, and told Kenny, "Cut a hole there. Do it!"

. . . 28 . . . 27 . . .

"We'll *never* get this safe out of the wall!" Kenny said, his voice a couple of notches higher than usual.

"I know," Baker said.

He went to work on the wall directly above the safe, punching a hole in the plasterboard with the butt of his knife. Once he had the hole, he reversed the blade and used the saw-toothed edge to cut over to a stud, then angle down.

...24...23...

He tried to keep looking cool, couldn't let Kenny think he was scared, but his heart was going like a jackhammer and he could feel sweat breaking out all over his body.

As soon as Baker's blade reached the top of the safe, he hauled back and punched the plasterboard, popping the cut piece into the wall space.

Baker glanced over and saw his nephew hacking furiously at his spot on the wall. His face was waxy-white, making his red hair look like fire, but he was getting the job done. "Do it, Kenny!"

...20...19...

"I don't want to die because Briggs is stupid, Sam," Kenny said as Baker went to work on the section above and to the right of the top of the safe.

"Neither do I, kid. But you don't leave one of your guys behind if you can help it. Even if he's an asshole."

That had been one of the rules in SOG. A man went down behind the lines, you risked almost everything to extract him.

...16...15...

He heard Kenny punch through, and then he was through with his second opening. He stood on tiptoe and peered into the hole. He needed more light.

"Kenny, get that lamp over here."

"Sam..."

Damn, his nephew was practically whining.

I know how you feel kid, but you gotta hang in here with me. Don't let me down.

"Do it!"

...12...11...

Kenny picked up the lamp and held it high with shaky hands.

Now Baker could see, and he spotted the powerful spring that had powered the spike into Briggs's arm.

"There's the sucker," he said.

...08...07...

He reached in and inserted the point of his blade under the bottom of the spring. His own hand was beginning to shake, and the point slipped off the spring.

"Come on! Come on!"

He positioned the point again, then grunted as he threw all his strength into levering that spike out of the safe. It moved, and he heard air hiss through Briggs's teeth as the spike slowly withdrew from his flesh.

...04...03...

With a piercing cry, Briggs yanked his bloody arm from the safe and began a headlong dash toward the front door.

Kenny was right behind him. Baker brought up the rear, leaping off the front steps and pushing Kenny to the ground.

"Hit the deck!" he shouted.

17

"Where are we?" Alicia said as Jack helped her up the ladder from the tunnel.

"Take a look."

Alicia turned in a slow circle to get her bearings. They'd emerged in the center of a clump of bushes bordering a potato field. Fifty feet to her right, she saw the white rented car, parked where they had left it. Beyond the car lay Jack's ranch house, with every window lit.

"We're across the street," she said.

"Right."

"Are we going to—?"

Alicia jumped as a booming retort echoed from the house, followed by a burst of machine-gun fire.

"My God, what happened?"

"Somebody just became cannon fodder, I imagine," Jack said.

"You mean *dead?*"

He nodded. "Most likely. I told you, it's my decoy place. Booby-trapped to within an inch of its life."

She looked at Jack. She'd grown to like him, even trust him during the short time she'd known him—unusual for her, because her list of trusted people was a short one—but there was so much she didn't know about him. And here was something she hadn't realized—maybe she'd guessed it, but hadn't wanted to confront it: beneath that unprepossessing, low-key, regular-guy surface was someone willing and able to kill when necessary.

And he was standing only a foot away. Her mouth went dry. She took a step back.

"You . . . killed one of them?" She tried to make out his expression in the dark.

"I like to think he killed himself—by being someplace he had no right being, doing something he had no right doing."

Alicia felt weak and shaky inside. She took another step back. "This is—very scary."

"You worried about them?" he said.

"I'm not a killer."

"But they are," he said softly, his eyes on the house, not her. "They killed your PI, they burned Benny the Torch alive, and they blew up your lawyer. What was his name again?"

"Weinstein . . . Leo Weinstein."

God, she'd almost forgotten about poor Leo.

"Okay. They blew him to pieces. And for what? For doing his job. You think Mrs. Weinstein would object to her husband's killers getting a dose of what Leo got? I don't think so."

"I wouldn't know about Mrs.—"

But Jack wasn't listening. He kept talking, his voice getting lower and colder.

"But I'm not doing this for Mrs. Weinstein, or your PI, or even for Benny the Torch, who I knew in a small way. I'm doing this for me and, whether you like it or not, you."

"Not for me," Alicia said. "I never wanted—"

"Because they're killers. And once you get on the wrong side of killers—and trust me, we're both on their wrong side—the only way to deal with them is to get them before they get you. If you don't, I guarantee you'll regret it. Because someday they'll find you—maybe by accident, maybe on purpose, but someday your paths could cross and then they'll snuff you out without hesitation. Or at least they'll try to."

Jack's casual, matter-of-fact tone chilled her.

What have I got myself into?

"Here they come," he said.

Alicia looked and saw two figures charging out the front door. She recoiled when he grabbed her arm, but he held her firmly.

"This way," Jack said. "And stay low."

In a crouch, he guided her to the car and carefully opened the driver side door. The courtesy lights stayed off—now she understood why he'd jammed the button with a toothpick. He motioned her in ahead of him.

"Crawl across and keep your head down," he whispered.

He got in beside her and eased the door shut. He inserted the key in the ignition but didn't turn it. Instead he leaned close to her and stared at the house.

"Now . . . watch. Won't be long."

18

Fighting panic, Kemel crouched by the flat rear tire of the rusting truck in the front yard and watched the house. The mercenary he'd followed here huddled beside him.

How could so many things go wrong in one evening? How was it possible?

Earlier he had been upset, especially after learning that two of the guards had been killed. Two corpses could lead the police directly to Kemel, and thus to Iswid Nahr. He would be humiliated before Khalid Nazer. Baker had said he would make the corpses "disappear," but how much of that was bravado?

Perhaps none. Kemel had to admit that he had been quite impressed with the way Baker handled his men. They seemed well trained and responded with military precision to his commands. And he'd had the foresight to plant a tracer on the Clayton woman.

Baker was rising in his estimation. If only he weren't so headstrong . . .

But then the situation had rapidly deteriorated. One dead, another pinned in the house like an animal in a trap, and the house ready to explode in a few seconds.

And where was Baker now? Why was he still in the house? Was he trying to defuse the bomb?

Suddenly the mercenary who had been trapped, the one they called Briggs, burst through the front doorway closely followed by Baker and a redheaded mercenary.

Briggs ran toward the pickup while Baker and the other flattened themselves in the grass. Kemel ducked and held his ears.

A second later he faintly heard a retort—sharp, quick, like a shot.

After waiting a few more heartbeats and hearing no explosion, Kemel cautiously raised his head enough to see over the pickup's rear cargo bed. He saw Briggs standing on the far side, holding his bloody arm.

"You sons of bitches!" Briggs shouted. "You lousy fucking bastards! You left me in there to be blown to hell and the only thing that exploded was a firecracker!"

"What?" said the mercenary beside Kemel as he rose to his feet.

"That's right, Toro!" Briggs screamed as he staggered toward them. "A fucking M-80! And look at you assholes hiding behind that truck like the yellow-bellied rats you are!"

One of the mercenaries who had been guarding the rear of the house ran up to the truck.

"What the hell's going on?" He stared at Briggs's bloody arm. "What happened to you?"

"You want to know?" Briggs said. "Toro, tell DeMartini how you—"

"*Run!*"

Kemel glanced toward the house and saw Baker on his feet, back-pedaling and pulling the redheaded mercenary around to the side of the house.

"Get away from the truck!"

The other three mercenaries weren't paying attention, but Kemel decided if Baker was running, so would he—as fast as he could.

"Yeah!" Briggs shouted behind him as Kemel turned and sprinted away. "Run! You yellow-bellied Arab rat! Run before I—"

The explosion caught Kemel by surprise. One moment he was running, the next he was flying, as if a giant hand had slammed against his back and hurled him through the air. The night was full of sound and light and flying metal.

Kemel landed and rolled and stayed down, lying flat with his arms over his head, pressing himself into the cold hard earth.

And then it was over.

Kemel shook his head as he rolled over and rose to his knees. He could barely hear through the high-pitched hum that filled his head. He looked around and saw burning bits of wreckage strewn about the yard. The mercenary who had been behind the truck with him was a still dark form on the lawn. He was sure the wounded Briggs and the one called DeMartini were in a similar state on the other side of the smoking hulk.

But someone was moving. Baker . . . returning from the side of the house, shaking his fists at the night. Kemel could see the rage in his face, and knew from his wide-open mouth and the bulging cords in his neck that he was screaming into the night.

But Kemel could not hear him. And he was glad of it.

He looked back to the road and noticed that the white car they'd followed here was gone.

Kemel lowered his head and prayed. It was that or burst into tears.

19

Yoshio found himself laughing aloud as he watched from his car.

Tonight had been a thing of beauty. When he had heard shots from within the house, he had assumed the worst: That Muhallal and his hirelings had killed the Clayton woman's *ronin*. But when Yoshio had seen figures hurrying from the house and taking up position behind the wrecked truck in the front yard, he had expected a firefight to follow.

But how could there be a firefight when Alicia Clayton and the *ronin* were slipping into their car across the street?

The explosion had made everything clear. A small explosion—or the impending threat of a larger one—had driven everyone from the house to the supposed safety of the outdoors. And what better place to shield one's self from flying debris than behind the oh-so-conveniently located truck rusting in the front yard?

But the house was not rigged to explode. Why destroy a perfectly good house when you can drive out invaders with a fake bomb and induce them to cluster around the real bomb?

And as the debris from the derelict truck was still flying though the air, the *ronin*'s white car had begun moving, rolling down the street with its lights out. Slipping away into the night.

Yoshio clapped his hands. So simple. So elegant. Bravo, *ronin-san*!

Fortunately, Muhallal had survived. Yoshio wanted the Arab alive. He was the only one besides the Clayton brother who knew why the Clayton house was so valuable.

He watched Baker rage at the night as the remaining man he had sent to guard the rear raced back to the front yard. Yoshio rolled down his window to hear what Baker was screaming.

"Who *is* this guy? I want him! I *want* him! Who are you, you fucker?

Show yourself! Let's do it! You and me! That's all! No tricks! Just you and me!" Baker's voice rose to a screech. "Who the fuck *are* you?"

Good question, Yoshio thought. Who is this *ronin*?

Obviously, he was more than mere hired muscle. He was a man who was comfortable with violence but used it judiciously, and with style. He was a man experienced in his line of work and intended to stay in it for the long run—as witness this skillfully booby-trapped house. The house told Yoshio that the *ronin* planned far ahead and might well be prepared for almost any eventuality.

Which meant Yoshio would have to be especially cautious in his next move.

For Yoshio was determined to meet the *ronin* before Muhallal and Baker, by some blind luck, blundered into him and killed him. Yoshio was sure the *ronin* knew something, had learned something in that house.

He resisted the urge to gun his engine and follow him. He calculated the risks and decided it unwise to drive past the house right now. Baker or one of his thugs might empty a clip or two from their assault pistols at him. He had little faith in their accuracy, but a lucky slug might pierce his gas tank or—worse yet—pierce him.

No, he would catch up to them back in Manhattan.

Then *he* would learn what those two had discovered in the Clayton house.

20

"Really, Jack," Alicia said. "I want to go home."

Or at least get out of the car. She felt queasy.

Instead of heading back to the city, Jack had continued east, racing toward the tip of Long Island. He'd taken them into the Hamptons, and then turned north until they'd come to the quaint houses and deserted marinas of Sag Harbor. Now they were pulling into the parking lot of something called the Surfside Inn. Alicia knew there was no surf in Sag Harbor; in fact, this crummy-looking motel wasn't even near the water.

"We can't risk heading back to the city," Jack said. "They're hurting, but I don't know what kind of reserves that Arab's got. He could have spotters waiting out on the highways, looking to follow us back home. So I say, let's take the long way home."

"All right, let's." She just wanted tonight to be over. "So why are we stopping here?"

"To spend the night." He held up his hand before she could speak. "Trust me. We head back in the morning, no one will find us. We try it tonight, there could be more rough stuff."

Damn him, she thought. He knows exactly what to say. The last thing she wanted was more violence.

"All right," she said, surrendering. "But can't we find a better place than this?"

"We're not exactly in season," Jack said. "This place is open, it's got its 'Vacancy' sign lit, and we'll only be here half a dozen hours or so. And best of all, its parking lot isn't visible from the road. Wait here."

Before she could object, he was out of the car and heading toward the office.

Alicia closed her eyes, trying to blank her mind. This was all a nightmare. None of this had happened. Soon she'd wake up and find it all had been an ugly dream.

She jumped at the sound of a tap on the window: Jack—holding up a key and motioning her toward a row of doors to the left of the car. With a groan, she got out and followed him. Her limbs dragged . . . her marrow had turned to lead.

Jack opened a door marked "17" and held it open for her. As she stepped inside, he followed and closed the door behind him.

Slightly better decorated than Jack's "country place," but just as mildewy. Flowered drapes matched the spreads on the two king beds, but not the rug.

"Which do you want?" Jack said.

"Which what?"

"Which bed."

"You've got to be kidding," she said. "We're sharing a room? Look, things maybe be tight, but I can spring for—"

"Money's got nothing to do with it. It's the safest way." He pointed to the beds again. "So, which one?"

Alicia pointed to the one nearer the bathroom. God, she wanted a shower—she *craved* a shower—but she had no clean clothes to change into, so what was the use?

"That one."

"All right," he said, sitting and bouncing on the other. "Then this one's mine." He lowered his voice to a Charlton Heston baritone. "But let's get something straight, young lady: I know you're mad crazy about me, but I don't want you getting any ideas."

He's trying to reassure me, she thought, and had to smile. "Somehow I'll manage to restrain myself."

"Good," he said. "Because I'm taken."

Alicia sensed he wasn't kidding about that last part. She watched Jack a moment, trying to sort out her feelings for this man. So much about him terrified her . . . he was a deadly, murderous creature—how many men had he killed tonight? Yet here she was sharing a motel room with him and not only believing him when he said he was taken, but almost envying the woman who had won his heart.

I can't deal with this right now, she thought as she headed for her bed. I need sleep, a break, time out.

Too much had happened tonight. Returning to that house, seeing her old room, that man's room, then the murders in the backyard . . . that had been more than enough. But then that small army chasing them, the shots, the screams, that truck exploding, lighting up the night . . .

Alicia felt as if she were enveloped in a gelatinous fog, moving in slow motion toward that bed, that glorious bed.

Too much . . . too much . . . circuit overload . . . need downtime . . .

Finally she reached the bed. She pulled back the spread and crawled between the sheets.

"Good night," she said, and pulled the covers over her head.

Silence . . . and darkness . . . blessed darkness . . .

21

"Good night," Jack said, watching Alicia curl into a lump under the covers.

A weird one, all right. But then, everything named Clayton seemed to be weird in some way.

Now what? he wondered. He should take a cue from Alicia and sack out, but he was too wired to sleep. The key . . . where did it fit? And that damn little Land Rover . . . something about its persistence in trying to get to the front yard of the Clayton house nagged at him.

Jack got up and headed for the door. He unlocked the Chevy, plucked the little truck from the backseat, and carried it to the middle of the parking lot.

"All right, Mr. Rover," he said, pushing the ON switch, "let's see where you want to go now."

He placed it on the pavement, facing in the direction he assumed to be east, and let her go. The little truck raced away and almost immediately veered to the left. Jack expected it to wheel into a U-turn and head back toward him, but it came only three quarters of the way around, then angled away across the lot.

Jack raced after it and grabbed it before it ran under a parked Accord.

The truck should have headed due west, back toward the Clayton house—or rather, toward its front yard. Did he have his directions screwed up?

He scanned the stars. Good thing it was a cold, clear winter night. He traced the Big Dipper, ran a line up from the leading edge of its cup, and found Polaris. Okay. That was north.

He backed up to his original spot, pointed the truck east . . . and damn if it didn't make a beeline for that same Accord.

He found Polaris again. Back in Murray Hill, the truck had insisted on heading uptown—due north . . . toward the front yard, he'd assumed. But now it wanted to travel northwest . . . away from the front yard.

What had changed?

The Rover's position, for one.

Or had someone adjusted its controller, wherever that was?

This was going to take more investigation, and under better conditions than these.

Tomorrow . . . he'd spend all tomorrow figuring this out. And looking for the box that belonged to that key.

Jack returned to the room, taking the truck with him. He didn't want to leave it in the car overnight. Who knew? Someone wandering through the lot might spot it and rip it off.

He slipped back into the room as quietly as he could. He could make out Alicia's form under the covers, curled into the fetal position.

What are you hiding from? he wondered.

He felt a mixture of admiration and pity for her—and he knew she'd resent the pity like all hell, but still, that was what he felt. Somewhere, somehow, she'd been terribly damaged, and he pitied anyone who'd been scarred so deeply. But she'd waged—was still waging, apparently—a valiant battle against the effects of whatever had been done to her.

Maybe tonight had been too much for her. Maybe he shouldn't have insisted she come along.

But what other options had he had? She'd lived in that house, and he'd needed her help.

Still, he got a cold knot in his stomach when he looked at that fetal lump, curled and cocooned so defensively against the world.

How would she be when she awoke tomorrow morning?

Jack flopped back on the other bed and stared at the stained ceiling, wondering about that until sleep claimed him.

22

Kemel Muhallal sat with shaking hands and trembling inside. He felt as if he were on a jet racing through an endless storm.

He slumped on the couch in his apartment, too disheartened for prayer, too exhausted to drag himself to the bedroom.

For the first time since his arrival in this thrice-cursed land, he harbored doubts about the outcome of his mission. He had expected some difficulty, certainly, in securing the Clayton technology, but never this much. The Clayton woman had enlisted the devil himself as her ally.

When he had noticed her car gone, he had wanted to use the tracer to chase after her, but could not. The bodies . . . all the bodies had to be removed before the police arrived. He, Baker, and the two surviving members of Baker's team had had to carry them to the van. Then they had had to flee, running like jackals in the night.

A harrowing, humiliating experience.

But it all would have been worth it had he learned if Alicia Clayton and her devil had discovered anything in the house.

And what of the sale of that house? Haffner had sent word to her attorney that her price would be met. No response yet. Would she respond at all after tonight?

If not, the whole process would be set back weeks. And what would that mean for Ghali? Kemel had to get home to help his son.

Kemel pulled at his beard. He was being pulled in so many directions. What was he to *do?*

Should he fail to secure the Clayton technology, he then must make sure no one else got it.

Be calm, he told himself for the ten thousandth time since he had stepped through the door.

But how could he be calm when tomorrow morning he might pick up a newspaper and see a headline announcing the Clayton technology to the world?

He shuddered at the repercussions to his homeland, at the thought of the entire Middle East returning to the Saudi Arabia of his father, who had made his own shoes and lived with his fellow bedouin in goat-hair tents or in mud huts clustered around oases, with no electricity, no medication, no medical care. That was Arab life before the 1960s. That is what his own life—and his sons'—would be if he failed in his quest.

He wished he could pass this burden to someone more used to dealing with these matters, but secrecy was so tantamount to success—they could lose everything if even a whisper of the nature of the technology leaked out—that the leaders of Iswid Nahr had forbidden anyone else, even another member of Iswid Nahr, from being told.

Kemel Muhallal had been present when Thomas Clayton brought Iswid Nahr proof of his father's technology. Why had he felt blessed by Allah that day? It had been a curse. Because he was among the very few who knew the secret, the burden of resolving the matter had fallen upon his shoulders.

Kemel squared those shoulders. He must not despair. He was not yet defeated. He must trust in Allah and believe that Alicia Clayton and her devil had learned nothing.

And on the subject of devils, what was he going to do with his own devil . . . Baker? Kemel had lost all faith in the man, but the day might be approaching when he would have to make use of his brute nature and crude tactics.

For Kemel knew that if he and Iswid Nahr could not secure the Clayton technology, then he must destroy that technology, and eliminate everyone who knew about it.

WEDNESDAY

1

"No," Alicia said. "Out of the question. I've got to go to the hospital."

Are all women so headstrong? Jack wondered as he watched the ferry dock recede through the condensation-fogged glass. Or just all the ones I happen to know?

He and Alicia sat with their coffees in the passenger area of the first morning ferry out of Orient Point. The Chevy rested with the other cars below.

"Alicia—"

"Look, I've got patients and—oh, hell."

She yanked open her shoulder bag and fished inside until she came up with a cell phone.

"What's wrong?" Jack said.

"I want to call in."

He looked out the window as she dialed. The sky was a crisp blue and winter clear, but the Long Island Sound lay gray and choppy around them. He turned back to her when she mentioned "Hector," and watched her expression grow grim. She ended the call and squeezed her eyes shut.

"Bad news?" he said.

She kept her eyes closed. "Hector got shocky last night, then he crashed again. We're losing him."

"Aw, jeez." His chest tightened as he remembered that big smile, and so proud of his "buth cut." So full of life, and now . . .

"I should have been there."

"I can appreciate how you feel," he said.

She opened her eyes and stared at him, saying nothing.

He said, "All right. Maybe not completely. But no matter what, at this point I don't think those places are safe for you. I mean, if I were you and these people knew where I lived and worked, I wouldn't be going back there right now."

"I'll have to risk it. I've got to be there this morning, Jack. I've got to. And let's face it, you didn't leave many of them standing."

Jack didn't like it, but he could see he wasn't going to change her mind. And even if Baker and whoever he had left were planning a move, he doubted they'd pull it in front of the staff at the Center. But as soon as she stepped outside alone . . .

"All right," he said. "Go to the hospital, then have a guard walk you to the Center. Then *stay* there. Have lunch sent in. Do not set foot outside that building until I pick you up and take you to your hotel."

"Hotel?"

"Yes, hotel. You don't think you can stay at your apartment, do you? That's where they'll be waiting for you."

"Who's 'they?' " she said. "After you got through with them last night, I don't think there's any 'they' left."

Jack shook his head. He'd seen Kemel and his boss mercenary get away. How many more did the Arab have in reserve? And even if the answer was none, he could always hire more.

"The one who shoved you into the van is still up and about," Jack said.

That seemed to have the desired effect: Alicia stiffened and looked away.

"Okay, okay," she said. "Which hotel?"

"Haven't decided yet. But I'll pick you up at five and we'll use the rush-hour mob to our advantage."

"Fine," she said sullenly, and wrapped her coat more tightly around her.

"Do I have your promise?"

"Yes." Now she looked at him. "Why do you care what happens to me?"

The question startled Jack. "What do you mean?"

"You've got that 'key' you found. You don't need me anymore. In fact, it would probably be to your advantage if they got hold of me."

Jack stared at her, holding back his anger.

"No answer?" she said.

He spoke slowly. "No . . . just wondering if I should dignify that with an answer."

"Oh? I've offended you?"

"Damn right. You . . . you're a customer. We have a deal. A contract."

"I didn't sign—"

"We shook hands," he said. "That's a contract."

She flushed and looked away again. Her words came in a rush. "I'm sorry. Maybe I'm wrong but I just don't know what to think or who to trust anymore. Last night was very scary—*you* are very scary—and I've never been in this kind of situation. I mean, people are chasing me and the man I'm supposed to be partnered with killed God-knows-how-many of them last night. And maybe they had it coming but . . . do you know what I'm saying? You just flipped a few switches last night and *boom!*— people died. You wanted them gone, and they were gone. So is it so strange for me to wonder what happens if you decide you want me gone?"

He debated saying something about only killing customers who talk too fast, but decided this wasn't a good time to crack wise.

And maybe she had a point. Usually he had minimal contact with his customers. He made a deal, then went off and got it done—like with Jorge. They never saw the work, only the results. Last night had been an exception. He'd wound up playing bodyguard—something he'd never volunteer to do—and Alicia had witnessed some rough stuff.

Too bad, but he didn't think much of the alternative.

"I do what's necessary," he said. "But in your wonderings have you considered where we'd be right now if they'd caught us?"

She went on as if he hadn't spoken. "And the worst thing is that it didn't settle anything. We're still looking over our shoulders. I can't even go home."

"I'm sorry about that. But we're making progress. We know more than we did two days ago, and I've got a feeling we'll know a lot more when I find the lock to this key."

And get some more playtime with that little four-by-four, he thought. Something very strange about Clayton's "Rover."

He held the key in the direct sunlight and saw faint remnants of the words "Bern Interbank" embossed on the red vinyl case.

Hallelujah, he thought.

2

Yoshio took a deep, sharp breath when he saw the white Chevrolet, and nearly choked on his Egg McMuffin.

He had spent hours last night watching Alicia Clayton's apartment. She never appeared. Yoshio had been disappointed but not terribly surprised. He assumed the *ronin* had done what he would have done under those circumstances: rented a hotel for the night.

And so Yoshio was idling here on Seventh Avenue where he could see the entrance to the hospital and the children's center where the Clayton woman worked. His backgrounding on her had revealed how devoted she was to her small charges. He doubted she would stay away.

And now he had been proven correct.

Small satisfaction, but one took it where one found it.

He watched the *ronin* escort the Clayton woman to the hospital door. Yoshio was in gear and moving when the ronin returned to his car. No question as to what his next step would be: follow the *ronin*. If he and the Clayton woman had learned anything last night, now was the time to act upon it.

Carefully keeping his distance, Yoshio trailed the *ronin* west on Fourteenth Street and then uptown on Tenth Avenue. He did not see anyone else following. He smiled. Certainly Kemel Muhallal had other, more pressing concerns at the moment—an acute manpower shortage among them.

He saw the *ronin* stop his car before a row of dingy storefronts. Yoshio drove past, adjusting his speed to catch the red light at the next corner. He adjusted his rearview mirror and watched the *ronin* enter a doorway next to a dirty window with a sign that read:

ERNIE'S I.D.
ALL KINDS
PASSPORT
TAXI
DRIVERS LICENSE

Yoshio hurried around the block and was relieved to see the Chevrolet still double-parked on Tenth Avenue when he returned. He pulled into the curb by a bus stop on the far side of the street and waited, trusting the rush-hour traffic to hide him.

ID . . . why would the *ronin* enter such a place? Did he want to prove his own identity, or did he wish to identify himself as someone else? Ronald Clayton perhaps?

Yoshio rubbed his palms together to relieve the sudden tingle of anticipation. He sensed he was onto something here.

And then the *ronin* emerged from the store and looked around before he reentered his car. As his gaze came Yoshio's way, a bus edged between them. Yoshio took advantage of the cover to nose his way into traffic and position himself so that he was behind the bus when it moved on. His car now looked like just another of the countless thousands crawling through rush hour.

He saw the white Chevrolet pull away and continue uptown. Yoshio followed him all the way to West Seventy-sixth Street where the ronin double-parked again and walked into a building.

Yoshio saw the sign as he passed: BERN INTERBANK.

And now the tingle spread from his hands to the back of his neck. Yes. This was important. He couldn't say how he knew, he simply . . . knew.

Hurriedly he looked for a place to leave his car. He could park it illegally and hope his DPL plates would protect it, but he didn't know how much time he would need. The city had been cracking down on diplomats abusing their parking privileges. Yoshio did *not* want to return and find that his car had been towed away.

He saw a Kinney Park sign and accelerated toward it.

The success of all his efforts for the past two months might hinge on what he did in the next few minutes.

3

Powder from Alicia's latex gloves left white smudges on Hector's latest chest X ray as she held it up to the window. She didn't need a lightbox to show her how bad it was. His lung fields were almost entirely opaque. Only small dark pockets of uninfected lung remained, and those were becoming progressively smaller with each successive film. Soon even the ventilator would be unable to force oxygen to his blood cells.

She turned and faced the comatose child, who seemed to have shrunk since she'd last seen him yesterday morning. Naked, spread eagle on the bed, Hector seemed to be made more of plastic tubing than flesh—two IV lines, one in an arm and one in a leg, the ventilator tube down his throat, a catheter running into his penis to his bladder, the CVP line running under his clavicle, the cardiac monitor leads glued to his corduroy chest. His skin had a mottled, bluish cast. Sorenson was wiping the crusts from his eyes.

Tuning out the ICU Muzak of beeps and hisses, Alicia picked up Hector's chart and read his latest numbers in dismay. His O_2 saturation was dropping, his WBC count had been 900 this morning, and his blood pressure was in the basement.

He's slipping away, she thought. And there's not a damn thing—

A change in the beeps from Hector's cardiac monitor caught her attention. She checked the screen and saw the dreaded irregular sine-wave pattern of ventricular fibrillation.

Sorenson looked up, eyes wide above her surgical mask. "Oh, shit."

She reached a gloved hand toward the code button.

"Wait," Alicia said.

"But he's in V-fib."

"I know. But he's also in immunological collapse. He's got nothing left. We can't save him. The candida's in his brain, in his marrow, clogging his capillaries. We can break a few more ribs pounding on his chest, submit him to a few more indignities, and for what? Just to prove we can delay the inevitable for a couple of hours? Let the poor boy go."

"You're sure?"

Was she sure? She'd tried everything she knew. All the subspecialists she'd called in had attacked Hector's infection with every weapon at their disposal. All to no effect.

I can't seem to be sure of anything else in my life, but of this one thing I am absolutely certain: No matter what we do, Hector will not survive the morning.

"Yes, Sorenson. I'm sure."

Stepping aside from all her emotions, Alicia watched the sine waves slow, then devolve into isolated agonal beats, then flat line.

Sorenson looked at her. When Alicia nodded, the nurse checked her watch and recorded the time of death of Hector Lopez, age four. As Sorenson began removing the tubes from Hector's lifeless body, Alicia ripped off her surgical mask and turned away.

Staggering under the crushing futility of it all, she leaned against the windowsill and looked down at the street. The cheery glare of the morning sun seemed an affront. She felt tears streaming down her cheeks. She could not remember feeling this low in all her life.

What good am I? she thought. Who am I kidding? I'm useless. I might as well call it quits now and end this charade.

When she caught herself eyeing the cars below and wondering how it would feel to plummet toward them, she pushed herself away from the window.

Not yet, she thought. Some other time, maybe, but not today.

4

Jack had debated going home and changing, but Ernie had let him borrow a razor to shave and had made sure that his hair in the photo on the brand-new Ronald Clayton New York State driver license was combed a little more neatly than Jack's usually careless look.

He'd passed the ID check, the bank officer had used her key along with Jack's on the double-locked safe deposit door, and now he was alone with box 137.

He flipped up the lid and found a stack of bulging manila envelopes, maybe half a dozen of them, each sealed with fiber tape. As much as Jack wanted to rip them open, this wasn't the place. It might take some time to sift through these and find the one that answered all the questions. Besides, he was double-parked outside. Better to bring them home and take his time.

He gathered them up, made sure he wasn't missing anything, then headed for the street. The car was where he'd left it—not something one took for granted in the city—but a meter maid had stopped her scooter at the corner and was working her way down the street toward the Chevy. Jack dashed to his car, hopped in, and took off.

He was just congratulating himself on how smooth the morning was going when he sensed movement behind him. Before he could react, something cold and metallic pressed against the back of his skull.

Jack stiffened in shock and gripped the wheel. He wasn't being car-jacked—he'd been followed, damn it! He raged at himself for being so careless. First getting caught flat-footed in the Clayton backyard last night, and now being in such a big hurry that he hadn't bothered to check the backseat. He cooled as he seined his mind for options.

An accented voice said, "Please keep driving."

Please?

Jack glanced in the rearview mirror and saw a thin Oriental face, clean-shaven, late thirties maybe, eyes hidden behind fashionably round lightweight shades.

"And please do not try to accident the car or attract the police. These are hollow-point bullets filled with cyanide. Even a scratch will murder you."

Despite his weird verbs, the gunman's English was pretty good. He had the L's almost right.

"Hollow points and cyanide," Jack said. "Kind of overkill don't you think? If you were a good shot, you wouldn't need all that."

"I am a very good shot. But I do not leave anything to chance."

Jack believed him.

He forced himself to relax. At least the guy wasn't one of the Arab's men—or didn't appear to be. And then something occurred to him.

"That wouldn't happen to be a small caliber job, would it?" Jack said. "Like a twenty-two?"

"This is correct."

"And did you happen to use it on Thirty-eighth Street last night?"

"That is also correct."

"And can I assume that you're not working for Kemel?"

"Correct again . . . although I do not understand how you are so familiar to use the first name of a man you should not even know about."

I'm so familiar with him, Jack thought, I've been assuming it was his *last* name.

He settled back in his seat as he turned onto Broadway and joined the downtown crawl. He'd wondered who Kemel had meant by "the wrong hands," and had assumed he'd meant Israel. But this guy was anything but Israeli. He looked Japanese.

"I tell you these things," the gunman went on, "because I do not wish to be placed in the condition where I must kill you. Condition—that is the correct word?"

Swell, Jack thought. He's got a gun on me and he wants me to help him with his English. But then, he *does* have the gun.

" 'Position' might be better."

"Position . . . yes, that is better. Because I am very admiring of how you disposed of your attackers last night. You are very clever."

That's me . . . Mr. Clever.

"Was that you following me to the Clayton house last night?"

"You saw me?"

He sounded offended. Time to repay a compliment in kind.

"No. Not once. Sensed you but didn't see you. You're very good."

Let's form a mutual admiration society, he thought.

"Thank you. What is your name?"

"Jack."

"Jack what?"

He thought a moment. "Jack-san."

Jack saw the gunman's eyes narrow, then crinkle as he smiled. "Ah, yes. Jack-san. That is very humorful."

"I'm a bundle of laughs."

"And now you will please give me the envelopes you brought from the bank."

So polite . . . but despite how "admiring" this guy said he was, Jack had no doubt he'd end up like the two corpses outside the Clayton house if he tried anything. Might end up like them anyway.

With that pleasant thought bobbing through his brain, Jack handed the envelopes over the seat.

The pistol muzzle was removed from his neck. Jack watched the gunman glance down at his lap as he fumbled with the envelopes. This might be his chance . . . but he vetoed the thought. No sense in precipitating something right now. Take it easy and see how this played out.

More rustling as other envelopes were opened.

That's what I want to be doing, Jack thought.

He kept glancing at the rearview trying to read the gunman's expression. His narrowed eyes, his grimace, as if someone had shoved a rotten fish under his nose.

The blare of a horn jerked Jack's attention to the road and he saw that he'd been drifting toward a Volvo with a very frightened-looking woman behind the wheel.

"I warned you," said the gunman.

"Sorry," Jack said, giving the Volvo an apologetic wave. "Not on purpose. It's just that I was really looking forward to poking through those envelopes myself."

"Then, these are not yours?"

He checked out the gunman's expression as he opened more envelopes. The nearest Jack could describe it was . . . disgust.

What was going on?

"Well, they were for a few minutes. Now they're yours, I guess."

"How did you acquire them?"

Should he tell, or play dumb? He had a feeling dumb wouldn't work with this guy, and what harm in telling him what he'd probably figured out on his own?

"From old man Clayton's safe deposit box. I found the key in the house last night."

"Then, these belonged to Ronald Clayton?"

Why do I feel like I'm on trial? "Yes."

"And this was *all* you found?"

"Absolutely."

"And you do not know what is in them?"

"I was hoping to find out."

"You wish to see them?" the gunman said.

Something strange in his voice. Almost . . . fatigue.

"Uh . . . yeah." Where was this leading?

The envelopes dropped unceremoniously onto the front seat.

"Then you shall. Find a place to stop where no one will see us and you may look all you wish."

Normally that would have set off a chorus of alarm bells in Jack's head, but strangely enough, it didn't.

Something weird going down here.

He turned off Broadway in the Thirties and headed west. He found a deserted stretch of curb past the post office and stopped, but left the engine idling. He glanced into the rear of the car and saw the gunman staring out the window, but he didn't seem to be focused on anything in particular. His pistol was out of sight. Farther behind them, on the corner, an Oriental woman stood on the sidewalk with her video camera trained on the columned front of the post office building.

Lady, he thought, moving pictures were designed to record things that move. That's why they call them "movies."

Jack picked up the top envelope, reached inside the open flap, and pulled out a pile of negatives and three-by-five photos. He let the negatives drop back in and checked out the prints.

His stomach turned.

"Oh, jeez."

Children . . . naked children . . . having sex with each other.

He dropped them onto his lap, then picked them up again for a closer look at the little girl.

"Aw, no."

Alicia . . . no question about it . . . seven years old, maybe eight, the face was pudgy, but it was her. And the boy she was with looked about twelve, and he was unquestionably Thomas.

He let his head drop back and closed his eyes. He swallowed hard, afraid he'd lose his morning coffee.

When was the last time he'd cried? He couldn't remember. But he felt like crying now.

That innocent little face looking out at him as her brother . . .

The sheer monstrousness of it, the utter evil, the mind-numbing rottenness of a soul that could besmirch the innocence of any child like that . . . but your own daughter . . . someone who trusts you, looks up to you, depends on you for guidance and protection from the nastiness of the world . . . to take that trust, that responsibility and do . . . *this* . . .

Jack had run across the scum of the earth in his day, but Ronald Clayton took the prize. If he weren't already dead, Jack might consider correcting that situation.

This confirmed what he'd suspected about Alicia. Now he understood why she wanted nothing to do with her father or her brother or that house, why she'd looked ready to jump out of her skin last night.

What a thing to have trailing after you all your life.

"Are they all like this?"

"Yes," said the gunman.

"Poor Alicia."

"And these are all that you found?"

"Every last thing." He sure as hell wasn't going to tell him about the weird little Rover, even if it meant nothing.

"You would not lie to me?"

Jack fished the key out of his shirt pocket and tossed it onto the backseat.

"Go back and check yourself."

The gunman sighed. "No. That will not be necessary."

He's as frustrated as I am, Jack thought. And he knows more, damn it.

Which gave him a crazy idea.

"All right," Jack said. "Tell me what this is all about. What's so goddamn important about that house?"

What the hell? he thought. Can't shoot me for asking. Can he?

"I do not know."

"Come on. You've got to know more than me. How come it's a Japanese guy against the Arabs and not someone from Mossad? Tell me what you *do* know."

He watched the gunman's eyes as he stared back at Jack.

I'll be damned, Jack thought. I do believe he's going to tell me.

5

Yoshio considered this *ronin*, this Jack-san.

Tell me what this is all about.

He immediately had dismissed the request as ludicrous. But the more he thought about it, the more he wondered whether it might be to his advantage to give this man *some* information. Not everything, of course, but Jack-san's purposes did seem to run contrary to Muhallal's, and that made him an ally . . . of sorts. A little information might make him a more irksome nettle against Kemel Muhallal's hide than he already was.

Above all, the important thing was to keep the Clayton technology out of Muhallal's hands.

"Very well," Yoshio said. "I will tell you. From what I have been told, it all began a few months ago with a most happy message to my employer from a trade delegate working with my country's mission to the United Nations."

"You mean the Japanese government, right?"

Yoshio hesitated. The answer should be no . . . but it could be yes . . . in a way.

What should he reveal? Certainly nothing about his employer. Kaze Group was a corporate entity with a shadowy board of directors that produced nothing under that name, yet had a hand in the manufacture of every part that went into every product produced in Japan.

Officially a holding company, Kaze Group had been founded shortly after the war and began buying shares in the companies that were leading the battered nation's economic recovery. As new companies came to the fore, it invested in those. It bought only the best. Kaze Group thrived during the economic booms, but it made good use of down times as well. It vastly increased its holdings during the recent economic slump, taking advantage of the tumbling Nikkei prices to snap up bargains. Through a web of dummy corporations it now owned controlling interest in Japan's "Big Six" *keiretsus* and most of the major corporations.

Kaze, Yoshio thought. The Wind. Such a fitting name. *Keiretsus*, the giant vertical and horizontal conglomerates that ostensibly ruled Japan's economy, were often compared to icebergs—a very small portion visible, the vast bulk hidden. But what determines the path of icebergs through the sea? The currents. And what dictates the currents? The wind . . . Kaze.

No, Kaze was not the government, but when Kaze Group spoke—always a discreet whisper directly into the ear—the government listened.

"Yes," Yoshio said. "That is correct." Better to let Jack-san believe he worked for the government. "And this trade minister was most excited. He said he had been contacted by a man who was most surely a messenger from God Himself, a man whose technology would make"—he stopped himself . . . he'd almost said Kaze Group—"make Japan first among nations. He claimed that the details were so astounding, so *explosive*—yes, that was his word—that he did not dare explain the details, even by diplomatic pouch. He said he was bringing this man directly to Tokyo to explain to the board in person."

"The board?" Jack-san said.

"Yes. The . . . National Board of Trade. But the plane carrying the trade minister and this mysterious man to Japan exploded in midair, killing all aboard."

"JAL 27," Jack-san said.

"Correct."

Yoshio was not surprised he knew. Alicia Clayton must have told him about her father's death.

"But what makes you think this messenger 'from God Himself' was Ronald Clayton?"

"We know from passenger records that he was seated next to our trade minister on the flight."

Jack-san nodded. "That would do it."

"And we also know . . ." Should I tell him this? Yoshio wondered. Yes. Why not? "We also know that the crash of the flight was not an accident."

Jack-san's eyes narrowed. "A bomb? But nobody's said anything about—"

"We have proof. Traces of explosive on what little floating debris we could find. We have chosen not to reveal what we know."

"Why the hell not?"

"Because we do not wish the people who planted the bomb to be aware of our knowledge, or that we have any involvement in this . . . situation."

"You mean . . . ?" Jack-san's narrowed eyes widened now. "You're telling me the plane was blown up because of Ronald Clayton?"

"We believe that to be true, yes."

"But who? Why?"

"We have evidence that the bomber was Sam Baker, whom you have already met."

"I have?"

"I believe you broke his nose last week."

"Oh, *him*." Jack-san nodded. "Sam Baker . . . he bomb the lawyer too?"

"Yes. He is employed by Iswid Nahr."

"Who's he?"

"It is not a person—it is an organization based in Saudi Arabia."

"Ah," Jack-san said, nodding. "And I'll bet our friend Kemel is one of their top guns."

"Gun? No, he is a middle-level member."

"So what are they? Terrorists?"

"No, not at all. Iswid Nahr is an oil trade group."

"Like OPEC."

"Yes, but so very opposite. OPEC seeks to manage the flow of oil, tighten the spigot of production in order to secure price stabilization. Iswid Nahr wants to open that spigot wide. Its name translates as 'Black River.' It wishes Saudi Arabia to export oil at very maximum levels. Their thinking is that this will discourage development of foreign oil sources and keep the West—as well as my country—so very dependent on Middle East oil."

"Oil guys?" Jack-san said. "What's in this for them?"

"That is the question I was sent here to answer. Obviously Kemel Muhallal's mission here is to secure the Clayton technology at any cost."

"Obviously. But doesn't that go against your theory that this Iswid whatever blew up Clayton's plane?"

"I assure you that it is so very more than theory."

"Yeah, but think about it: If Kemel wants this 'technology,' why would he and his group blow up the guy who invented it?"

"Perhaps because the inventor was intending to sell it to us instead of to them."

Jack-san stared out the window. "Yeah, but to blow up a whole plane just to stop one man . . . two hundred forty-seven people dead . . ."

"Nearer to two hundred and sixty now," Yoshio said. When Jack-san gave him a puzzled look, he added, "You must count the arsonist, the lawyer, and Miss Clayton's first investigator. Also the pair that I removed at the Clayton house. Plus whoever you killed last night. Do you know how many?"

Jack-san shrugged. "Couldn't tell you. Didn't hang around to count. But whatever, the body count was way too high already. And all this is making less sense by the minute." He stared at Yoshio. "And you've got absolutely no idea what this Clayton technology is?"

Yoshio could answer that quite truthfully. "No."

"Kemel's big advantage is that he does. At least I hope he does. Hate to think he blew up a planeload of people on a hunch. So let's assume he does. That puts him way ahead of us."

Us . . . was Jack-san aligning himself with Yoshio—and therefore Kaze Group—or was it merely a word? This might be an avenue to explore.

"Kemel Muhallal has no right to the Clayton technology," Yoshio said. "My . . . country has a moral right to it because Mr. Clayton so obviously intended to sell it to us before he was murdered. And should we discover that it is so valuable as our trade minister said, we will buy it from his heir. Something Iswid Nahr does not seem to wish to do."

"Yeah, you've got that right," Jack-san said slowly. "They've offered to buy the *house* . . . they've never breathed a word about an invention or technology. Maybe they think the price will be too high."

Yoshio shrugged. "Something so valuable will pay for itself, I would think."

"I would think too," Jack said. He twisted farther in the front seat. "So where does that leave us? Do we work together on this?"

"No," Yoshio said quickly. He always worked alone. To have a . . .
partner—especially one not aligned with Kaze Group—was unthinkable.

Jack-san almost looked relieved. "Good. But I assume we can have a
nonaggression pact. And can I assume that should Alicia and I dig up
this Clayton technology, whatever it is, that we've got a buyer?"

"A *potential* buyer," Yoshio said. "It may be that this technology is
of no use to us."

"Fair enough," Jack-san said, "but we'll give you first refusal." He
extended his hand over the top of the front seat. "Deal?"

Yoshio hesitated. Something was wrong here. He had the weapon, but
somehow this Jack-san had taken charge. And somehow this meeting
had been all to the American's advantage. He had learned much while
Yoshio had learned only that Ronald Clayton was a pedophile who had
defiled his own children.

But still, an ally would not be a bad thing . . . if this was a man who
could be trusted to keep his word.

Yoshio had a sense for these things, and he felt Jack-san was such a
man.

They shook hands.

"It is a deal," he said.

Yes . . . a deal. But as Jack-san drove him back uptown, Yoshio decided it would be a good thing to keep a close watch on this man. If he
could find him.

"What do you do now?" he said as he stepped out near the garage
where he had parked his own car.

"Going home to play with a toy," Jack-san said, and sped off.

6

Jack watched the little Rover race across his living room carpet and butt
against the wall. The uptown wall. He was already farther uptown than
Murray Hill, but apparently that wasn't enough for the Rover. It wanted
to go farther. Always uptown, always north.

Except out on Long Island. Then the little bugger had run off toward the northwest.

But where was the directional control?

Jack grabbed the truck, turned off the motor, and popped off the body. He checked that out but it was nothing more than molded black plastic.

The chassis was more complicated—wheels, undercarriage, electric motor, steering control, battery compartment, and antenna. Jack knew his knowledge of remote-control toys was rivaled only by his understanding of quantum mechanics, but he pulled out a magnifying glass and made like Sherlock Holmes.

No help. Just a bunch of wires.

As long as he was here, he should check the battery compartment to see what kind it took, just in case it ran out of juice. He popped the lid and saw that it took two AAs. But the battery slots were empty. Instead he found a silvery cylinder about half the length of his pinkie wired to the contacts.

"What the hell?"

He trained the magnifying glass on it, but all that did was make a little mystery bigger. No markings on the cylinder. The whole rig had a definite homemade look to it.

Jack felt a strange prickle along the back of his neck. Not fear . . . something else . . . a sense that he was looking at something enormously important. But what?

He knew he'd taken this about as far as he could. The next step was to take it to a guy who could dismantle and reassemble just about anything put in front of him.

7

"It doesn't look like a battery, maybe," Abe said, "but it's a battery."

The little Rover lay partially disassembled on Abe's counter. The body was off, the battery compartment lay open in the exposed chassis.

Abe had a thing about the weapons he sold. He dismantled and reassembled everything that passed through his doors. He could break down and reassemble a Glock 9 in a couple of eye blinks. Jack had asked him why, and Abe's reply had been something like, "I shouldn't know all about what I'm selling?"

"That's not like any battery I've ever seen," Jack said.

"So? You've seen every battery ever made? Look, it's where a battery should go; it's hooked up to the contacts that power the motor, and the car runs. It's a battery. Even Parabellum would tell you that if he weren't asleep."

"Okay, okay." Sometimes Abe's help was no help. "It runs, but only in one direction. Explain me that."

"Easy," Abe said, and twanged the metal antenna. "This is where it gets its instructions. Somewhere, someone or something is sending its steering mechanism—via this antenna—the message to head in a certain direction. Without this little wire, the steering mechanism would be deaf, and the car would head in whatever direction you point it. Here, I'll show you."

"That's okay," Jack said, reaching for the truck.

But Abe pulled it back out of reach. "You don't want I should prove it?"

What he didn't want was Abe messing too much with the toy.

"I just don't want you should break it. I've got a gut feeling that thing will lead me to the mysterious 'Clayton technology.' But if its directional mechanism gets screwed up—"

"Nothing will get screwed up. What's to screw up? It's an antenna— just a piece of wire. Only take me a second."

Jack watched helplessly as Abe adjusted his reading glasses and picked up a pair of needle-nose pliers. After some fiddling, some twisting, and a few muttered curses, he managed to remove the aerial.

"There," he said. He handed the chassis to Jack. "Nothing to it. Go ahead. Now you'll see. Point it wherever. It's uptown-running days are over."

Jack turned it over and flipped the power switch.

Nothing.

He flipped it back and forth from ON to OFF and back again.

Still nothing. Oh, hell.

"Swell, Abe. Now it doesn't run at all. You broke it."

"What? Impossible."

"No, you did." Jack flipped the switch back and forth again. "Look."

"Quit kvetching and give it here."

Jack handed it back and leaned on the bench. He stared at the scarred surface, asking himself how he could have let this happen, wondering what the hell he was going to do now. That little car was his only lead.

And then he heard the soft whine of the little motor. He looked up and saw the Rover's wheels spinning.

"Thank God. What did you do?"

Abe was staring at the chassis, frowning. "Reinserted the aerial, that's all."

"Well, whatever it was—"

The motor died as Abe removed the aerial again. Then started up when he reinserted it. Off . . . on . . . off . . . on . . . all in time with the aerial.

"You must be breaking a circuit," Jack said.

But Abe didn't reply. His frown was deeper as he pulled out a magnifying glass of his own and focused it on the aerial socket.

"Look here," he said, pointing with a pencil. "See this fine little wire? It runs from the aerial socket to the battery compartment. And you can tell from the way it's soldered that it's not original wiring. This has been added. And I didn't notice before, but the new wire is attached to this strange little battery that doesn't look like a battery."

He straightened and began fiddling with the aerial again, in and out of its socket, starting and stopping the motor.

And then he left the aerial out and left the truck chassis in the center of the bench.

"I think I have to sit down."

Jack shot Abe a look. Something in his voice. And his face—so pale.

"Abe, you all right?"

"Yes," he said hoarsely, staring at the chassis. "I'm okay."

"Well, you sure as hell don't look it. I've seen better color on a casaba."

Abe continued to stare at the toy. His color was still rotten. Jack was worried about him, but then Abe said the magic words.

"That's because I've just figured out what we've got here."

"Swell. Gonna tell me?"

"I . . . I think this little toy runs on broadcast power."

"Is that good?"

Finally Abe looked at him. "Is that good? You ask me if that's *good*? What kind of meshuggeneh question is that?"

At least the color was returning to his face.

"Broadcast power. I never heard of it. Pardon me."

Abe reached for the truck, and Jack noticed his hand hesitate, like he was afraid to touch it, like it was some sort of holy object. But finally he grabbed it and lifted it.

"See this aerial?" he said, holding up the wire. "The motor can't run without it. No aerial . . . no power. But stick the aerial into its slot . . ."

As he did just that, the motor whirred and spun the wheels.

". . . and suddenly we've got power. Power from the air."

From the air? Had Abe just had a mini-stroke?

"You're losing me," Jack said.

"You were right about the thing in the battery compartment, Jack. It's not a battery. It's a transceiver. It's taking the signal the aerial is receiving and transforming it into electrical energy."

Jack felt a kernel of excitement begin to burn in his gut.

"Okay, but what's the aerial receiving?"

"Power. Whoever modified this toy must have some sort of a transmitter somewhere that can broadcast a beam, a wave, an I-don't-know-what—let's just call it energy, because that's what it is—that can be downloaded through the aerial and turned into electrical power."

Jack stared at the spinning wheels, feeling that excitement swell and burn hotter. He was beginning to see how big this was.

"But how?"

"If I knew how such a thing could be, would I be standing here talking to you? No, I wouldn't. I would be sitting in my palatial home on Martha's Vineyard—*my* Martha's Vineyard, because I would have bought the entire island. Jack, I'd be much too rich to even *know* you, let alone talk to you. I'd be the kind of rich that'd make Bill Gates look like he's on welfare."

"All right. I get the message."

"Do you?" Abe said. "You've heard the phrase, 'The end of life as we know it?' That about approximates it."

Jack nodded. "No power lines. No electric cords. No—"

"You're thinking small, Jack. How about saying bye-bye to the internal combustion engine?"

"Hey, you're right," Jack said. "Finally we'll be able to breathe the air around here and maybe . . ."

He heard his voice trail off as the full import of Abe's words hit ground zero. Now Jack had to sit down.

"Holy shit."

Because suddenly it was all clear . . . or most of it, at least.

"Oil," he said after a moment. His saliva had gone south. "Oil will be worthless."

"Not completely," Abe said. "As a lubricant it'll still be good. But as a fuel? Feh!"

"No wonder Kemel's been ready to do anything to get hold of this."

"Kemel? This is the Arab you told me about? Yes, of course he'd do anything. This little toy car portends the complete economic collapse of the Middle East. Not to mention Texas and the U.S. Gulf Coast."

"My God," Jack said. "The economic holocaust you've been talking about all these years . . . it's finally—"

"That was supposed to be from runaway inflation. But this isn't it. Don't worry so much. Wailing and gnashing of teeth there'll be, huge upheavals in finance and in every industry that gobbles power, but no holocaust. Unless of course, you're heavily invested in oil stocks."

"Yeah. Then it'll be time to take that long first step off a window ledge."

"But if you should have lots of your money invested in countries that rely heavily on foreign oil—"

"Like Japan?" Jack said, thinking of Yoshio.

"Japan, yes. Big time, Japan. They're virtual slaves to foreign oil. Broadcast power puts the Japanese and Middle East economies on a seesaw: one drops into the abyss, the other goes into orbit."

The pieces were falling into place. Jack could almost hear the clicks as they came together.

"That's it, then," he said. "No wonder that Japanese trade delegate was so ecstatic: Ronald Clayton was on his way to Japan to sell them his broadcast power technology. Kemel and his Iswid Nahr buddies got wind of it, and made sure he never reached Japan. That's why they're so desperate and so secretive now—they don't want anyone to even guess broadcast power exists."

Even the will's cryptic message for Greenpeace made sense now: broadcast power meant no more oil spills . . . a brand-new day for air quality, the ozone layer, the whole environment: World-changing technology . . .

Abe cleared his throat. "One thing I don't understand—I should say, one of the *many* things I don't understand—is why Ronald Clayton was taking his technology to Japan. He didn't need Japan. He didn't need anybody. All he had to do was patent it and quietly announce it. He wouldn't have to go to anybody. The world would stampede to his door. Not only would he be rich beyond King Midas's wildest dreams, he'd be worshiped as well. He wouldn't be *Time*'s Man of the Year, he'd be the world's Man of the Millennium. Why was he going to Japan?"

"Haven't the faintest," Jack said, taking the chassis from Abe and switching off the motor. "But I know someone who might."

8

". . . And so it's my guess," Jack was saying, "that this little truck is going to flip the world on its ear."

Alicia had been relieved to see Jack. Not glad, just relieved that the man at the reception desk asking to see her without an appointment hadn't been Will. He'd already called twice this morning. Alicia knew she couldn't face him, but maybe she could dredge up the courage to talk to him. At the very least she owed him a return call.

But Jack had come in with that toy truck from the house and pulled it apart on her desk, talking a blue streak. Alicia had had a hard time following him at first. She was still dazed from watching Hector die. And then she'd been a little frightened. Jack was positively *wired*. For a bad moment she'd thought he might be on speed, or maybe peaking in the manic phase of a bipolar disorder. And when she'd heard what he was talking about, she pretty much settled on the latter.

But then he wasn't simply telling her, he was *showing* her how the Rover didn't have a battery and would only run when the aerial was attached. He called it broadcast power.

"Broadcast power," she said, catching the chassis as it rolled across her desktop. "But that's science fiction."

"So was rocketing to the moon and a computer on your lap—once. Now they're history. But what's got to blow you away even more is the fact that it's all *yours*."

Was it hers? she wondered. Really? And how much was it worth? A tingle crept over her skin as she realized that a day might come when every lamp, every microwave, every TV, every car in the world would have one of those little transceivers in its works. Worth? Alicia doubted she or anybody else could count that high.

"Not all," she said, remembering something. "A third of it is yours."

Jack cocked his head and gave her a puzzled look. "Mine? But—"

"Our deal, remember? We split the proceeds—you've got a thirty-three percent share."

"Jeez," Jack said, dropping into a chair. "I forgot all about that."

"I'm sure you would have remembered eventually." She refused to let herself get excited. "But right now you've got a third of nothing. We've only got half of the equation. The receiver's not worth anything without the transmitter."

Jack nodded. "Like taking a TV set back to the 1920s, I guess. Without somebody broadcasting, it's just an expensive night-light."

"Right. So where is it?"

"Uptown," Jack said. "Or maybe farther north of here."

"Because that's the way it keeps running?"

"Got to be," he said, taking the chassis from her. " 'Whither away, fair rover, and what thy quest?' Remember?"

Jack put it on the floor and let it arc across the carpet to end bumping its front end on the uptown wall.

"I think—no, I'm sure its quest is the transmitter."

"So what are you going to do? Put it down on Fifth Avenue and follow it uptown?"

"No . . . I've got a better idea." He retrieved the chassis and turned off the motor. "Is there a back way out of here?"

"Yes. Ask Raymond. He'll show you."

"Swell. See you later." He stopped at the door and turned. "Hey, I almost forgot. How's the little guy—the one with the haircut?"

"Hector Lopez?" Alicia said, looking away, not wanting to see his face. "He died this morning."

"Aw," Jack said, more of a sigh than a word. "I'm sorry."

"Yeah," Alicia said through her constricting throat. "He was a good little guy."

And then, as precipitously as he'd arrived, Jack was gone, leaving the toy Rover's black plastic body on her desk.

Alicia swallowed to loosen her throat, then let Hector fade from her mind as she remembered the key they'd found along with the truck last night—last night? Had it only been last night? She wondered if Jack had learned what lock it fit.

And then the possibility of broadcast power took over. How many billions might something like that be worth? She thought of what she could do with all that money. She could start a foundation, find homes for kids like those at the Center, fund research to find ways to save future Hectors.

Broadcast power . . . the power to change the world . . . hers . . .

Hers because that man . . . that monster . . . had left it to her.

Alicia closed her eyes. She didn't want anything that man had touched. *Anything*. He had to have known that. So why had he left her this? Was he laughing now from his spot in the darkest, coldest, nastiest corner of hell?

She picked up the Rover body and hurled it against the wall.

9

Jack bought a good compass and started in his own apartment. He marked the truck's starting point at the downtown end of his living room and ran a string to where it ended up against the uptown wall. He checked that and found that the string ran a few degrees west of due north. He unfolded his brand-new map of New York State and drew a line from mid Manhattan up along the Hudson through Albany and Troy, through a little town called Elysium in the Adirondacks, then onto Lake Placid and into Quebec. Theoretically, the line could be heading all the way to the Arctic Circle and beyond. Jack hoped it stayed in New York State.

He didn't feature trekking all the way out to Sag Harbor again, so he took his next reading in the little park on the Flushing side of the Whitestone Bridge. This time the line traveled a more westerly path, crossing the first line in Ulster County.

Could be good news or could be a fluke. The next reading would tell.

The lower left corner of Jack's New York map showed a portion of North Jersey. He took the Lincoln Tunnel into the lovely paved vistas of the Garden State and followed Route 3 to where it crossed the Parkway. Since that particular intersection was on his map, he stopped in a nearby strip mall parking lot and let the chassis take another run.

Jack smiled when he checked the path with his compass: this time it

headed *east* of due north. Good. At least they wouldn't have to go to the
north pole to find the transmitter.

The third line met the others in Ulster County, a little west of New
Paltz.

If he was right, if the receiver was designed to point the way to its
power source, then the transmitter was somewhere in the vicinity of
intersection of those three lines.

Looked like he and Alicia would be on their way to the Catskills
tomorrow—if Sam Baker and his boys didn't interfere. Jack had told
Sean to call Thomas's lawyer and start the paperwork to sell the house.
Hopefully that would keep Kemel off balance enough to allow Jack and
Alicia to sneak out of town.

Alicia . . . he'd been so wound up about this broadcast power thing
that he'd almost forgotten about the filth in those envelopes. A big part
of him was pushing to build a fire and reduce them to ash, but another
part said that it might make Alicia's world a brighter place if she could
watch those negatives curling and blackening and smoking in the flames.

But giving her the envelopes meant he'd have to be there when she
realized what was in them. He didn't want to see her face, didn't want
to imagine what she'd be feeling at that moment. Because he could never
imagine.

Still undecided, he headed back to New York.

10

Yoshio stood in a doorway where he could see both the front entrance
to the AIDS Center and the length of the alley that ran along its uptown
flank. Earlier this afternoon he had been parked in his usual spot when
he had seen Jack-san enter the Center. He had not seen him come out,
and had assumed that he was spending the afternoon there.

But just moments ago Yoshio had been startled to see Jack-san—
carrying a large Staples shopping bag—*re*enter the Center. Yoshio knew
he had not missed his exit. This could only mean that there was another
way out.

He discovered the alleyway after a minute or two of hurried searching. How careless of him. But he wasted no time berating himself. He had missed the earlier opportunity to follow Jack-san, but he would not sneak away so easily again.

Yoshio rushed back to his car when he saw Jack-san and Alicia Clayton leave by the front entrance and walk along Seventh Avenue. Jack-san still carried the Staples bag. He followed them around the corner as they headed east. He kept waiting for them to hail a taxi or get into a car, but instead they ducked into a subway entrance on Sixth Avenue.

Yoshio groaned and pounded the steering wheel in frustration. Yes, he could park the car—legally or otherwise—and follow them on foot, but that would be futile. Even if he caught up to him, Jack-san would have no trouble spotting him.

The *ronin* was taking no chances.

Yoshio sighed. Another missed opportunity. He was not likely to see Jack-san or Alicia Clayton again tonight, so who else should he watch? Samuel Baker, Kemel Muhallal, or the other Clayton?

He would choose later. Right now he wanted to make preparations for the next time Jack-san tried one of his tricks. Yoshio would be ready for him.

He hoped.

11

"Don't tell me this is another one of your decoy homes," Alicia said, "because I won't believe it."

What am I doing here? she wondered as she wandered among the antiques and wall hangings on the second floor. They'd taken the F train down to West Fourth, then grabbed the A back up to Twenty-third, and now here she was in this elegant Victorian town house in Chelsea.

"No, afraid not," Jack said, watching the street from a front window. "I just happen to have a key to it."

"You seem to know your way around the place. Where's the owner?"

"He's dead."

"Hiding in a dead man's house . . ." Alicia shivered. She didn't like this place. "I feel like a fugitive."

"In a way, you are." Jack turned from the window.

Something about the way he was looking at her now. The same something she'd sensed during their subway ride. Something wasn't right.

"But hopefully it's just for tonight," he said. "If we can find that transmitter tomorrow, and go public with it, you should be home free."

"Why should that stop them?"

"All right, it may not stop Thomas—he'll still think he deserves a share, and every shyster in the world will be banging on his door saying they can get him a piece of the broadcast power pie. But as for Kemel . . . it's game over. His whole mission here was to suppress this invention, to keep the world from even guessing it exists. But once the word is out, he's done for. My guess is he'll wind up swinging by his neck from a Saudi oil rig. And that's probably all those rigs'll be good for by then."

He picked up the Staples bag and put it on the low ornately carved table between them.

"Are you finally going to tell me what's in there?" Alicia said.

He'd been so secretive about it on the way here, saying, "Later . . . I'll show you later," every time she'd asked him.

"I found the safety deposit box that key fits," he said, looking down into the bag as if he'd suddenly found something very interesting inside.

"And?"

"All it contained were these."

Still not looking at her, he reached into the bag and began pulling out manila envelopes—half a dozen or so—and laying them on the table.

"Anything in them?"

Finally he looked at her. The words came out just above a whisper. "Photos."

All color and texture drained from the room, and Alicia found herself in a chair, feeling weak, feeling sick.

"You okay?" Jack said, coming around the table and moving toward her.

Alicia held up a shaky hand—she didn't say yes or no, didn't nod or shake her head. Couldn't. Just wanted him to stop where he was, didn't want him closer, not near her, nobody near her.

He stopped, staring.

And then she was breathing again, deep gasps to help keep down the bile that threatened to spew all over the room, telling herself to keep calm, keep calm . . .

But how could she keep calm with those . . . those . . . *pictures* in the same room and knowing that Jack must have seen them, *had* to have seen them, else why the skittering eyes and that stricken look on his face? He knew, oh, God, he *knew!*

And worse, now *she* could see them. If she wanted to . . . if she dared to . . .

She'd never seen them, never dared try to imagine what they could be like because that would mean resurrecting the memories of those hours and days and months on the bed or the couch in the cellar with Daddy making her do things to Thomas and making her let Thomas do things to her, things that hurt her sometimes, just so Daddy could take pictures, so many pictures . . .

She took one last deep breath, held it, then forced herself to meet his gaze.

"Did you look at them?"

He nodded.

Had he stared at them? Ogled them? My God, how long had he had them? What must he think of her?

"*All* of them?"

"No. Enough to realize what and . . . who they were, and to make sure the envelopes didn't contain anything else. Alicia I'm sorry. I—"

"Why?"

"Why what?"

"Why did you bring them here? Why would you do this to me? What are you going to do with them?"

"Not what *I'm* going to do with them." He upended the Staples bag, and a wide box slipped out. "What *you* are."

He lifted the box so she could read the illustrated label on its front.

She squinted her blurry eyes. "A paper shredder?"

"Right." He pointed to the envelopes. "These aren't just photos. The negatives are in here. I could have burned them—for a while I seriously considered it. But I figured you might want to turn them into confetti yourself."

He pulled the shredder from the box, placed it on the floor in front of her, and plugged it in.

"Why are you doing this for me?" she said.

"Why wouldn't I? I've guessed you've been carrying around something heavy. I never realized how heavy."

She looked away. "I'm so ashamed."

"Of what?"

"How can you say that?" she said, hearing her voice rising. She didn't want to lose control—not here, not now. "You've seen. God, what you must think of me."

"I don't think you're to blame, if that's what you're getting at. No more than a battered child is to blame for his bruises. They call this kiddie porn—such a goddamn cutsey name. Call it what it is: pictures of children being sexually abused."

He picked up one of the envelopes and offered it to her.

"Go ahead," he said. "Time to put this behind you."

She forced her hand forward. About halfway to the envelope it stopped, as if it had run into an invisible wall. She pushed through that wall and willed her fingers to grip the envelope and take it from Jack.

He turned on the shredder and stepped back. She heard the blades begin to whir below the slot in its top.

She'd managed to touch the envelope, but when it came to reaching inside . . .

"You can do it," he said.

"This won't solve anything," she said. "There must be hundreds of prints in collections around the country. That man traded them for pictures of other kids."

"But these will be gone. No one will see them. And with the negatives gone, no one will be able make fresh copies from them. Maybe it's more symbolic than practical, Alicia, but it's a start."

Alicia looked at Jack and wanted to cry. How could she have so underestimated this man?

Yes, she thought, it is a start.

She realized that for the first time in her life she had control—power—over a set of these prints. And power over the negatives too. How could she do anything *but* destroy them?

She reached into the envelope and pulled out three or four prints, eight-by-ten sheets with glossy color surfaces—no, she would *not* look at them—and fed them into the top of the shredder. Whirring, grinding, then thin little strips cascading from the bottom, twisting into a tangle of paper spaghetti.

Yes! It worked. The images were destroyed, all coherency lost in the hundreds of divisions. No one but a madman would try to put them back together, and the more strips she added to the tangle, the harder it would be. A hundred, no, a thousand years to reconstruct even one image.

Sensing that this might be some sort of watershed for her, Alicia dug into the envelope and pulled out more to feed into the whirring maw. She felt tears running down her cheeks and heard herself laughing.

This felt so good . . . so *good!*

12

BZZZZZZT!

A woman in tears was bad enough. Never failed to bum Jack out.
What do you do? What do you say? But a woman laughing *and* crying
while she was feeding a paper shredder . . .

Very scary.

But the tears and the laughter soon slacked off, and then she started
talking about it, and that was worse, because it made him wish that
Ronald Clayton were still alive . . . so that Jack could kill him . . . very
slowly.

"I did it for my daddy," she said. "That's how it was. A part of me
sensed it was wrong, or bad, especially when it hurt, but my daddy
wanted me to do it, and I didn't have much choice. And after all, he was
my daddy . . . the man who took care of me. He wouldn't really make me
do something really bad. Not my daddy."

Her tone was remote, as if she'd cut all emotional ties with the child
she was talking about.

BZZZZZZT . . . more prints into the shredder.

"And that was the really sick part of it. Beyond his perversion. That
he would take his own child, someone who depended on him, who looked
up to him and trusted him, and use that bond of trust and dependency
to make her do exactly what he wanted in front of his camera. But that's
part of the pedophile's nature: he gets off on the power over the young
and weak and small, the power to corrupt innocence through unspeakable acts."

BZZZZZZT!

"Of course, I didn't know they were unspeakable then, but there had
to be something wrong because I was never allowed to mention them.
And some time before I reached ten, the picture taking stopped. I guess
I was too old then. I guess the people he was trading pictures with liked
their little girls under ten. Whatever the reason, it stopped and . . . would
you believe? . . . I felt sad. How sick is that? Not because of what I'd

actually been doing, but because my father no longer seemed interested in me. He'd never been warm or even vaguely nurturing—the words 'remote,' 'uninterested,' 'disengaged' don't even come close—but at least . . . at those times . . . when I was doing those things by myself or with Thomas, I'd had his . . . attention. Now I didn't even have that. Can you imagine?"

No. Jack couldn't even begin to imagine. He felt his gorge rise as he thought of someone making Vicky do what he'd seen in the few prints he'd glanced at, and fought the urge to grab the phone and call her to make sure she was safe at home with Gia.

BZZZZZZT!

"But as I grew older, I learned, and I realized what I had been a part of. I tried to tell myself that it had never happened, that I'd imagined it all, dreamed it, but I knew no imaginings like that could have originated in me. How could I make up those perversions? No . . . I must have been there. And so I worked on blocking them out, making myself believe they'd never happened, and I was doing pretty well at it . . . until my early teens when I started developing. That was when I woke up one night and found Thomas with his hand on my breast wanting to 'do it, just like we used to.' I managed to fight him off, but that was confirmation, and it brought it all back. I began sleeping with a knife under my pillow."

Jack didn't want to know this much about her, but didn't see how he could stop her. And it wasn't as if she was talking to *him*. She was talking to the air. He could have been a mannequin.

BZZZZZZT!

"I knew then and there that I had to get out. But how? I was too young to support myself and I didn't want anything—*anything*—from that man. And I know you're probably thinking, 'Why didn't you go to the authorities and—'" She stopped and looked at Jack. A wry ghost of a smile twisted her mouth for an instant. "Okay, anybody but you would say that. But how could I? Exposing Ronald Clayton meant exposing myself. It meant making those pictures public. Even now the thought of it makes me want to crawl into a hole, but can you imagine how that prospect looks to a teenage girl? I mean, a pimple on the chin is a reason to hide when you're a teenager. Making my 'sins' public—because I *knew* that everyone would think I'd been a willing participant—was unthinkable."

BZZZZZZT!

"So I worked on getting out. And I mean, I *worked*. I was pretty much asexual then. I was repulsed by the notion of anyone, boy or girl, touching me, so I became a bookworm. I all but lived in the public library, studying, studying, studying. I got straight A's. I found a book on how to 'package' your child for a scholarship. Well, no one was interested enough to package me for anything, so I packaged myself. And it worked. I got a full academic scholarship to college at USC. That allowed me to move out of that house. I left in August before my freshman year and never looked back. Last night was the first time I've crossed that threshold since."

BZZZZZZT!

"In college I worked a job while I booked my butt off. I found summer work at resorts that offered room and board as part of the job. I got into med school. A full ride to med school is all but impossible, but people will loan money to doctors-to-be. So I borrowed up to my lower lip to cover the expenses, and I'll be paying those loans off for another ten years, at least. But I did it. I got through it. And the thing that kept me going was the determination not to allow myself to become a victim. There's that expression about living well being the best revenge? Well, I may not be living well, but I'm getting there. And on my own. This is *my* revenge. I refuse to be his victim. He had power over me once, but he'll never have it again."

BZZZZZZT!

"But it wasn't going to be my complete revenge. As the years passed I began to wonder about my mother's death . . . wondered if it was really an accident. I mean, I don't know if he inherited money from her or carried a large insurance policy on her, or anything about his finances, but I know he never could have indulged his perversion with Mom around. But with her gone, he was free to do what he wanted with Thomas and me. So that was my revenge fantasy: discover some evidence of foul play and send him to jail, where he'd have no power, and everyone would have power over him. But of course, that's impossible now."

BZZZZZZT!

Jack didn't want to know the answer, and yet he had to ask.

"Did he ever . . . touch you?"

She shook her head. "No, thank God—as if God has anything to do with this. No . . . he just liked to look, and our pictures were currency he could use to get more pictures to look at."

BZZZZZZT!

She looked up. "Got some more?"

Jack shook his head. "Nope." He pointed to the huge tangle of shredded paper mounded around her feet and the shredder. "You got them all."

"No," she said. "Not them all. Nowhere near them all."

"It's a start," Jack said.

All the steam seemed to be seeping out of her. She was deflating before his eyes.

"Thomas has a set," she said softly. "He has what he calls the master collection."

"What's that?"

"That's what he calls that man's personal collection of—what did you call it?"

"Pictures of children being sexually abused. Why would he want that?"

"To blackmail me, I think. But I think he's bluffing. He's in so many of those pictures . . . exposing me means exposing himself. He's sunk pretty low, but not that low."

"Yet," Jack said. He had an idea. "You know where he lives?"

She nodded. "Not far from here. Why?"

"I've got a few questions I want to ask your half brother. Want to come along? Can you face him?"

She hesitated, then, "Yes. I can face him. I *want* to face him. Are we bringing the shredder?"

"Nah. Too bulky. But I'm sure we can think of other ways to get the same results."

Alicia stood and reached for her coat. She seemed really into this.

"Let's go."

13

They were waiting in the darkened, stuffy, slightly rotten-smelling front room of Thomas's apartment when he got home.

Alicia had watched with amazement as Jack, using just a few little wirelike tools, got them through one door after another in Thomas's apartment building. They'd been waiting only twenty minutes or so before they heard the sound of a key in the lock. Jack sprang up and disappeared, leaving Alicia sitting alone.

Thomas stepped in and turned on the light. He froze like a deer in headlights when he saw her.

"Alicia? What are you—?"

Jack moved from behind the door then and slammed it closed. Thomas jumped to his left and stared at Jack.

Alicia saw the color leach from his pocked face.

"Who?"

"A friend of your sister's," Jack said, grabbing him by his collar and shoving his pear-shaped body across the room. "Sit!"

Alicia was startled by the snarl on Jack's face. He looked so . . . feral. Not at all like the man she'd opened up to less than an hour ago. Which was the real Jack?

Thomas stumbled and came up against a chair. He folded his ungainly body into it.

"What do you want?"

"Answers," Jack said. "And maybe to look at some pictures."

"You can't do this," Thomas cried. "I'll call the police!"

Suddenly Jack had a little pistol in his hand and was pointing at Thomas's left knee. Then he shifted his aim to the right.

"Which knee first, Alicia? You choose."

Me? she thought, panic rising. Is he serious? What's he doing? And then she remembered what Jack had told her when they'd entered the apartment: *I may have to get rough with him, but whatever I do, play along.*

Jack aimed the pistol at Thomas's crotch. "Or how about here?"

Okay, she thought. I'll play along.

"I'm thinking," she said.

"Alicia!" Thomas wailed. "Don't let him! They told me about him! Please don't let him shoot me!"

She noticed a dark wet stain spreading across the crotch of Thomas's slacks. He must have heard some real horror stories about Jack.

"Then bring out 'the master collection' you told me about," Alicia said.

"Okay! Okay! I'll do it. It's in the bedroom. I'll get it."

He got up and hurried past Alicia with Jack trailing him.

" 'I'm thinking,' " Jack whispered with a wink as he passed. "Beautiful."

And now that she was alone, she took a look around. This was the first chance she'd had to see the apartment in the light. The place was a mess, littered with dirty clothes and dirty dishes and food containers. And that smell . . . her best bet was that it came from a pizza box sitting on the windowsill near the radiator.

The two men returned moments later, Thomas carrying two cardboard boxes, and Jack carrying a third . . . and another gun.

"Look what Thomas has," Jack said. "A cute little .32."

But Alicia had eyes for only the boxes.

He has the collection, she thought with dismay. He really has it. Part of her had been hoping he'd been bluffing.

"That's all of it?" Jack said.

Thomas nodded vigorously. "Yes." Still standing, he turned to Alicia. "Yes, I swear."

"Why, Thomas? Besides its blackmail value, why would you want to keep that filth? It's a catalog of degradation."

"It wasn't so bad. I mean, what's the big deal. No one got hurt."

Jack raised a fist and Alicia thought he was going to hit Thomas, but he glanced at her and she shook her head. All her life she'd wanted never to talk about this part of their childhoods—now she couldn't stop.

"No one got *hurt?* What about you? What's your life been like? Have you had even *one* intimate relationship?"

I know *I* haven't, she thought.

"You think I don't know what a loser I am?" he said, narrowing his eyes as he looked at her. "I know. Believe me, I goddamn well know. And it's Dad's fault. That's why *I* deserve the house. I *need* it. You don't. You've done fine for yourself. You're a doctor."

"You don't know a thing about me," Alicia said softly.

That overcoming line she'd fed Jack was just that—a line. A mantra. Maybe if she kept repeating it, she'd come to believe it. Maybe it might even become the truth. But she had a long way to go.

I may look okay on the outside, she thought, but inside I . . . I look like this apartment.

"You '*deserve*,' " Jack said, his voice acid. "You '*need*.' You make me sick. You wouldn't know what to *do* with the windfall you'd get from broadcast power."

Alicia caught her breath, wishing Jack hadn't let that slip, but then she saw Thomas's legs buckle. He dropped into the chair behind him. If his face had been white before at his first sight of Jack, it was even paler now. And when Thomas started babbling, she realized Jack's "slip" had been calculated.

"You *know?* Oh, dear Christ! How'd you find out? It was last night, wasn't it." The words tumbled out. "Goddamm it! We turned that house upside down and couldn't find shit! You two waltz in and—wait—do you know where the transmitter is?"

"Come on," Jack said, grabbing his arm and pulling him out of the chair. "We're going for a walk."

"What?" Thomas's knees looked rubbery as he got to his feet. "Where?"

"Outside."

"Wh-why?"

Alicia was asking herself that same question.

"Because you don't have a fireplace here." He held up Thomas's .32. "I'll leave your training pistol here. But bring those boxes with you."

14

"Give us about an hour with the fire, guys, and I promise you it'll be nice and hot when you get back."

Alicia had followed Jack farther west, down the slope toward the Hudson River, as much in the dark as Thomas as to where he was going. He'd stopped at a trash can fire in the mouth of an alley and handed a twenty to each of the three men warming themselves by the flames.

Now they laughed and grinned and low-fived each other as they hurried off.

"All right," Jack said, pointing to Thomas. "Get to work."

Alicia looked around at the dark, empty, forbidding streets. But she didn't feel afraid. Jack seemed to be in his element, and in complete control.

"You're not listening to me," Thomas said. He'd been talking nonstop since they'd left his apartment.

"Start feeding the fire," Jack said. "And not too fast. We don't want to smother it."

Thomas finally got the idea. He reached into one of the boxes he'd carried here and pulled out a fistful of photos. Alicia watched them flutter into the can, curling and blackening as the hungry flames consumed them, destroying forever the hideous images they bore. She was in there, with Thomas, but other children were there as well . . . forced or duped like her into performing an obscene dance . . .

She closed her eyes for a moment, feeling almost giddy. She reminded herself that it was only a token, but still . . . now there would be one less set of prints in existence.

But Thomas didn't seem to care about the photos, seemed only half aware of what he was doing. All he cared about was the transmitter.

"The transmitter's the key, you know," he said, starting in again. "If you know its location, I can make us all wealthy beyond your wildest dreams."

Jack appeared uninterested. "If we have the transmitter, why do we need you?"

"Because your ownership of the technology will be challenged the instant you try to sell it."

"And yours won't?"

"*Anybody* trying to patent it will run into a wall. That's because . . ." He paused. "Let me back up and explain this. Then you'll know why you need me."

"This oughta be good," Jack said, glancing at her.

Alicia shrugged. "Just as long as you keep feeding the fire."

Broadcast power was all fine and good. But first she wanted to see those photos reduced to ash.

"I found out about Dad's invention when I stopped by to visit him one day."

"You stayed in touch?" she said. She found that hard to believe.

"Not really." He shrugged. "I was a little short, and he wasn't returning my calls. So I stopped by. Anyway, he left me cooling my heels while he talked on the phone, so I wandered around and noticed he'd left a couple of lamps burning here and there around the house. It being noon and all, and me being a good, ecologically minded son"—he grinned here, but Alicia wouldn't respond and Jack only stared at him—"I, uh, went to turn them off. But as I did, I noticed these little wires sticking up from the bases of their bulb sockets. I looked closer and realized that the damn lamps weren't plugged in. What was powering the bulbs? Had Dad developed some sort of battery-powered lamp? Out of curiosity, I began to tinker with one. By the time he finished his conference call, I'd figured it out."

"I'll bet he was thrilled," Alicia said.

"Hardly the word for it. Royally pissed was more like it. He started kicking me out, but then changed his mind. That mystified me then, but I understood why later. Dad wouldn't tell me anything about the technology itself, but he did explain why he didn't want word to get out about it just yet. You see, his invention isn't completely his. It utilizes a number of discoveries he made and technologies he developed while working for various universities and corporations over the years. Those organizations hold the patents on those technologies. They'd claim the lion's share— or possibly all—of the profits from his invention. So what he was doing was searching for a way to maintain ownership once he revealed it. He leant me the money I needed on the condition I kept mum."

I wouldn't be surprised if it was the other way around, Alicia thought. You promising to keep mum in exchange for cash.

"But I thought Dad's thinking was backward. If patent disputes were going to get in the way, he should come up with a way to make all those patents irrelevant. If going public with it meant losing all your profits, then find a way to profit from *not* bringing it to market. So I started asking myself: who stands to lose the most from broadcast power? And that gave me my answer: Sell the technology to OPEC."

His head swiveled back and forth, looking for approval. Alicia wasn't going to give him any, and Jack's face might as well have been cast in bronze.

"It's as brilliant as it is obvious, don't you think? I figured the Arabs'd be willing to pay *billions* to keep broadcast power off the market. So, without telling Dad, I 'borrowed' one of his lamps and booked a flight to Saudi Arabia. But I never got there. During the layover in Frankfurt, I discovered that the lamp didn't work. Panicked, I hurried back to the US—where I found it *did* work. So there's a limit to how far the power can be broadcast."

Idly, Alicia wondered about the range, about what waveform was used . . . but what she remembered from her one undergraduate physics course was woefully inadequate.

"So I took the lamp to OPEC's UN mission but they refused to see me. Would you believe it? Here I was offering them a way to save their collective asses, and those idiots didn't want to listen. Fortunately I found another group, almost as wealthy—"

"Iswid Nahr," Jack said.

Thomas jerked as if he'd been slapped.

"Who *are* you?" Thomas said, staring at him. "How do you *know* that?"

"Keep talking," Jack said, pointing to the fire. "And keep feeding."

"All right, all right. Anyway, Iswid Nahr must have taken that lamp apart and put it back together again about a hundred times, but finally they were convinced. They contacted Dad and made him a fabulous offer. But instead of being grateful, he pitched a fit, going on and on about how he wasn't going to let anybody bury his invention. Billions of dollars on the table and he's in a screaming rage. I couldn't believe it. I still can't."

"I can," Alicia said. "I haven't spoken to the man since I was a teenager, and it couldn't be clearer."

"Well, then, dear sister," Thomas said acidly. "Pray enlighten me."

"*Half* sister," Alicia said. "And don't forget it. As for your father, he wanted more than money—he wanted glory. He wanted to go down in history as one of the great men of all time, someone whose genius had transformed the world. And more than that, he wanted to control his technology. What a power trip that would be: control the power that powers the world."

"You could be right," Thomas said. Was that a note of grudging acquiescence in his voice?

"But once his secret had been leaked, especially to people who wanted to suppress it, he had to move fast. The only way he could see to keep the credit and the riches was to take it to a country that had no oil, that would agree to almost anything to cut its oil imports. I'll bet Israel was his first choice, until he realized Japan had more money. And with a technology in hand that would not only reduce their dependence on oil, but give them something more valuable than oil to sell to the world, the Japanese government would dispute any patent claims that would arise. Ronald Clayton would be unimaginably rich, and guaranteed his precious place in history."

"Except he never made it to Japan."

"No," Jack said. "Your Iswid Nahr buddies saw to that."

Alicia thought she saw Thomas flinch. Didn't he know? Or had he merely suspected.

"That was an accident," he told Jack.

Jack shook his head. "The Japanese found explosive residues in the wreckage."

"How do you know?"

"Same way I know about Iswid Nahr."

Alicia guessed Jack didn't want Thomas to know about the Japanese agent. She watched Thomas mull this new information a moment.

Then he shrugged. "Oh, well. He never cared about me anyway."

"Only about himself," Alicia said.

"How can *you* say that? Look what he left you. Before he left for Japan he hid all his records and cut me out of the will. He left everything to you, dammit! Why?"

"I couldn't tell you," Alicia said. "I wish he hadn't."

"Then tell me what you know," Thomas said, leaning over the flames.

The shadow of his large nose flickered back and forth across his forehead. "I'll cut you in with the Arabs."

"No thought of releasing it and making the world a better place?"

He looked at her as if she were speaking in tongues. "Trust me, when I have so much money that it'll take me a year to spend a day's worth of interest, the world *will* be a better place."

"I recall an old saying about the distance an apple falls from a tree . . ."

"You'll be *rich*, Alicia. You've always hated him, always wanted to get even—"

"That's not true." But of course it was. She'd known times when it had been all she'd thought of.

"Who're you kidding? The only person in this world you hate more than me is him. Now's your chance to settle the score. We sell the technology to the Arabs . . . and they bury it. Isn't it delicious? We get his money, and he gets no credit. His only claim to fame is that he was just another unfortunate passenger on JAL 27. You've got to love it, Alicia."

She had to admit she found a certain sour appeal in Thomas's scheme . . . but the thought of conspiring with Thomas on anything . . .

"Forget it."

He leaned back, obviously frustrated. "Suit yourself. But it's only a matter of time before we find the transmitter, and then it'll be too late. You won't have anything to bargain with."

"Are you as bored as I am?" Jack said looking at Alicia.

She nodded.

"Then, let's speed this up."

He grabbed a box of photos and started tossing them into the flames.

Alicia watched them blaze and turn to ash. And then there were no more.

"All right," Jack said. "That does it for this box. Any more?"

Thomas shook his head. "No."

"There'd better not be," Jack said, jabbing a finger at his face. "Because if I ever find out you held something back—"

"That's all. I swear."

Alicia jumped as she felt Jack take hold of her upper arm, but she let him guide her away from the fire.

"Good. Then, we're done with you."

"That's it?" she heard Thomas saying as they walked up the slope away from the river. "You drag me out here and squeeze me for information, and that's it? What do *I* get?"

"You get to warm your hands," Jack said without looking back.

"Doesn't matter that they're burned," he called. "You can burn all the paper you want, but it means nothing." His voice rose to a shout as they moved farther away. "Ever hear of the Internet, Alicia? We're on it. In lots of private places. And you know what? We're stars, Alicia. How do you like that? We're *stars!*"

Alicia pressed her hand to her mouth to keep from crying out.

Beside her she heard Jack say, "Excuse me. I think I forgot something. Be right back."

Fighting the nausea bubbling just below her sternum, Alicia kept walking, breathing deeply. She didn't turn around to see what he'd forgotten. She hoped it was nothing tangible . . .

15.

Yoshio watched Jack-san and the Clayton woman walk up to Eighth Avenue and turn downtown. He would have given much to have been able to overhear their conversation with the brother.

He followed them, slipping from shadow to shadow.

Perhaps I'm being overcautious, he thought.

Dressed as he was, he doubted Jack-san would recognize him even in full daylight. He had considered disguising himself as a sidewalk Santa. That might have worked in the more crowded streets, but would have made him more noticeable elsewhere. Reluctantly, he had settled on this alternative.

Still, he would take no chances. Watching the brother's house had been a long shot, but had paid off handsomely, and he wasn't going to squander this opportunity.

Now . . . if he could just keep up with them until they reached the place where one or both were staying. He was prepared to follow them anywhere, and with this disguise, even a subway trip would not deter him.

Only walking posed a problem . . .

Because these high heels were killing him.

16

"Jack!" Gia said as he opened her front door. "What are you doing here?"

"Can I come in?"

"Sure."

She wore a quilted robe over a long flannel nightgown. As soon as the door closed behind him, Jack wrapped his arms around her and held her close. Gia returned the embrace and they stood entwined in her foyer for a long time.

"I needed this tonight, Gia," he said, absorbing her warmth. "*Really* needed it."

"What's the matter? What happened?"

"Stuff," he said. "Please don't ask me to talk about it."

After their nice little chat with her sweetheart of a brother, Jack had taken Alicia back to the town house, then he'd headed straight for home. But after a few subway stops, he'd changed his mind. He made a couple of unnecessary transfers to make sure he wasn't being tailed, then walked down Fifty-eighth to Gia's place on Sutton Square. She'd finally given up her apartment and moved into the elegant town house Vicky had inherited from her aunts.

He'd found that session with Alicia on the other side of town far more harrowing than some of the tight spots he'd got himself into over the years. Jack saw a lot of the underside of city life here, but he'd only heard about what Alicia had been through. And all the while as he'd sat there watching her shred those pictures and negatives and talking ninety miles an hour, he'd kept wondering if she might go *blooey* and start jamming her fingers into the shredder. But she'd held it together.

The whole thing had exhausted Jack, though.

Seeing those pictures, being in the same room with Thomas Clayton . . . the whole thing had left him feeling dirty. Pounding on the bastard's face a few times had helped him feel a little better, but Jack felt he couldn't end the day without seeing Gia.

He heard running footsteps and a little voice crying, "Jack-Jack-Jack!"

Vicky.

"What're you doing up?" he said, breaking free of Gia to catch Vicky as she leaped into his arms.

"Christmas vacation started today," she said. She threw her arms around his neck. "No school tomorrow! Isn't that neat?"

"As neat as can be," he said, hugging her.

He couldn't help but think of how Alicia had been about Vicky's age when her father . . . If anyone ever even *thought* of trying—

"Jack, you're holding me too tight," Vicky said.

"Sorry." He loosened his grip and stared at her innocent face. A sob nestled in his throat. His voice sounded thick as he pushed his words past it. "I just missed you, is all, and I can't tell you how glad I am you're up."

"She's got *A Charlie Brown Christmas* on for the umpteenth time," Gia said, watching at him closely.

Still holding Vicky, Jack put an arm around Gia and pulled her close. Her sky-blue eyes asked if he was all right.

Jack shrugged and nodded. He was fine. His ladies, the two most important people in the world, were here with him, where he could watch over them and keep them safe. Everything was fine.

"Can I watch *A Charlie Brown Christmas* with you guys?" he said.

Vicky clapped her hands. "Yay!"

"Not again," Gia said, rolling her eyes.

"If nothing else, you've gotta love the music."

They followed the scampering Vicky down the walnut-paneled halls to the library. Gia hadn't changed the place much yet, except maybe for removing the antimacassars from the velvet chairs. It took a whole twenty minutes of sitting snuggled between Gia and Vicky on an overstuffed settee before Jack felt clean enough to doze off.

17

"So," Kemel said. "You've had all day to find out who this man is, and you have no idea."

Sam Baker looked flustered as Kemel watched him pace back and forth in the living room of his apartment. And well he should. He deserved to be more than flustered; he should look dejected and suicidally ashamed. Not only had he been made to look foolish by this nameless stranger, his bloated bonus was in serious jeopardy.

"It's like the guy doesn't fucking exist."

"Oh, he exists, Mr. Baker. The few remaining survivors of your team can attest to that."

"Yeah, but a guy with those kind of finely honed chops should have a rep, a name, a signature. People like me, or people I know, should have heard of him. He's obviously a merc, and if he's a merc, I should know him. Guys like that don't appear out of nowhere. They don't pop onto the street full grown. They gotta come up through the ranks. But not this guy. He's like some kinda ghost, coming out of the woodwork, fucking things up, then disappearing."

"I do not care about his name," Kemel said, controlling his anger. This man was such a fool. Why hadn't Nazer assigned him someone more competent? "I merely want you to deal with him."

"Can't deal with him if I can't find him."

"Perhaps he will find you."

He caught a flash of uncertainty before Baker's expression hardened. "I'm ready for him. I see him, he's dead."

"Let us hope so," Kemel said, and turned away.

He had spent an anxiety-ridden day, monitoring the news—a radio or television on in every room—waiting to hear the dreaded announcement of a revolutionary new power source that would change the world. But he had heard nothing. What was the American expression? No news is good news. Yes, in this case, that was most certainly so.

And the longer the span of no news, the better.

336

Dare I hope? he'd wondered.

If Alicia Clayton had proof of something so awe-inspiring as her father's technology, surely she would be acting on it. Surely she would be trumpeting it to the world.

The longer the silence, the more likely that she and her hireling—her "merc," as Baker called him—had found nothing in the house.

Kemel had spent the day fasting, praying that it was so. And then, wonderful news. A call from Gordon Haffner saying he had heard from the Clayton woman's attorney and the sale of the house was proceeding.

Kemel had been jubilant. Now he could return to Riyadh and help extricate Ghali from the criminal charges against him.

But then suspicion had reared its head like a desert rat. What if her desire to proceed with the sale was a ruse, a ploy to dupe him into dropping his guard? Kemel had checked with Baker, who had been busy disposing of the bodies of his men, and instructed him to use the transponder in the Clayton woman's handbag to track her movements. So far she had not left her workplace.

Perhaps she truly meant to sell the house after all. Ten million dollars was, after all, ten mill—

The phone rang. Kemel answered it and recognized Thomas Clayton's voice, although it sounded more nasal than usual.

"They were here!" he said. "They know!"

Fear sank its cold talons into Kemel's shoulders. "Who? Who knows?"

"Alicia and her bully boy. He broke my goddamn nose!"

"You said, 'they know.' What do they know?"

"Everything! More than we do!"

The room spun. *Everything!* Oh, no. This could not be. Allah, *please*—

"The transmitter?"

"No. I don't think they have that. At least not yet. But I've got a bad feeling they may know a way to find it. What do we do?"

Kemel closed his eyes and reached for calmness, found the hem of its *thobe*, and clutched it.

"I will tell you soon."

He hung up and gave Baker a quick summary, omitting, as usual, the nature of what they sought.

"Simple enough," the mercenary said. "We go get the girl and make her tell us. And believe me—let me at her, and she'll *talk*."

Kemel closed his eyes again. This man was such an idiot.

"What if she *doesn't* know how to find what we seek?" he said softly. "That will surely change her mind about selling the house. And what if her hireling is there and disables what few men you have left? What if,

in your infinite clumsiness, you kill her before you learn what we need
to know?"

"Hey, listen. I—"

"No. You will not touch her. But you will use the transponder to track
her. If she makes any move to leave the city, you will inform me and
together we will follow her. *Together.* Is that clear?"

"Yeah, but—"

"IS . . . THAT . . . CLEAR?" Kemel shouted the words.

"Clear," Baker said.

"Good. Start tracking her immediately. And keep me informed."

He turned back to the window and stared unseeing at the night. He
asked Allah to forgive him for the instant of doubt when he thought his
God had deserted him. Now he saw Allah's plan. Alicia Clayton was His
instrument, and would guide Kemel to her father's secret.

Praise Allah.

THURSDAY

1

Yoshio shrank back and hurriedly swallowed the last of his sausage-and-egg Croissan'wich as he recognized Jack-san in the blue Taurus pulling into the curb across the street.

After following him and Alicia Clayton back to this elegant town house last night, Yoshio had assumed that this was where Jack-san lived. But then he had seen the *ronin* leave moments later. He had tried to follow but, hampered by the woman's clothing, he had been unable to keep up with him. He had lost him in the confusion of Fourteenth Street.

So he had quickly returned to his own car near Thomas Clayton's apartment building and moved it to a position across the street from the town house. He had changed back to his usual attire and had spent the night here.

And now Jack-san was quite obviously taking Alicia Clayton someplace. Yoshio was guessing that no romance existed between them, otherwise Jack-san would have stayed here last night. Therefore they were not meeting merely to share each other's company. They must have a purpose in mind, and that purpose most surely involved the Clayton technology.

And just as surely, that purpose was taking them out of the city. Else, why the car?

How could Yoshio follow them into the suburbs or the countryside without being seen? Jack-san knew him and would be looking for him.

And yet he had to risk it. He sensed that after months of waiting and watching, his mission here finally was coming to a head.

He wished he had thought to call and arrange for backup, but he dared not get more people involved at this juncture. The situation was too delicate.

He watched Jack enter the house. Yoshio was desperate. And desperate situations sometimes called for desperate measures . . .

2

"I figure we head up the West Side, catch the Saw Mill, cross the Tappan Zee, and we'll hit the thruway," Jack said as he put the Taurus in gear. The dashboard clock read 10:33. The morning rush hour would be petering out about now. "Unless you know a better way."

Alicia shrugged. "Whatever gets us there."

Jack looked at her. He'd never figured her for a barrel of laughs, but this morning she seemed more down, more subdued than usual.

"You okay with this?" he said.

"Yeah," she said with a too-vigorous nod. "I'm fine. I'm just . . ." She let the word hang.

"Just what?"

She sighed. "Just sorry you had to get stuck listening to me yesterday. That wasn't in the job description."

Tell me about it, he thought, but said, "It's okay. Don't give it another thought."

"That's just it—I can't *stop* thinking about it. I've spent too many years *not* thinking about those pictures, or at least trying my damnedest not to. I sealed up that little girl and the reality of what happened to her behind an inner wall, but try as I might I couldn't forget. Knowing those pictures existed, knowing that I was still being passed from one pervert's grubby hands to another's sickened me. I was damned if I was going to let that define me, but it sure as hell has haunted me. It's been a dissonant, ominous background music to my everyday life. But after all these years, last night was the first time I was able to talk about it. And I know it made you uncomfortable."

"Well . . . yeah."

Sexual abuse of a child . . . hearing about it from the victim . . . uncomfortable barely touched how something so awful and so wrenchingly intimate made him feel.

"But you've got to understand, Jack, that I've never been able to share this with another soul. I've never had close friends because I never felt I could be honest with them. To tell the truth, I couldn't bear to hear them talk about their families, especially about the fathers who were so special to them. Every time I heard somebody talk lovingly about their 'daddy,' I wanted to scream. Even now, when I think of how this flesh is half his, I want to rip it off my bones. I kept asking myself, why couldn't I have had a father like theirs, one who cherished me, who would have willingly died protecting me? But you'd seen the pictures, Jack—"

"Some of them," he said quickly. "Just a few."

"Even one was enough. It meant you knew. And everything I've been holding back broke free. As I said, I'm sorry."

"And as I said, it's okay. I hope it helped."

"It did. For a while. For a few moments last night as the negatives were going through the shredder, and later as the collection was dropping into the fire, I felt free. It was a . . . wonderful sensation. But Thomas's Parthian shot about the Internet brought me back to reality. I see now I'll never be free."

"Never is a long time," Jack said, cringing at his triteness, but not knowing what else to say. He wasn't a therapist, and he didn't know how to stop Alicia from going where she was headed.

"Well, as long as copies of those pictures are being traded back and forth along the pedophile networks, either through the mails or zapped through the Internet as GIFs and JPEGs, as long as I know that a single picture of me is circulating, it will never be over. Sure, easy to say 'get over it' or 'get past it' or 'let it go' . . . but how can I do that when I know that even as we speak some slimy pervert could be ogling images of me doing . . . those things? How can I leave the events in the past when the pictures remain in the present?"

Jack could only nod. She was right. Those images were an ongoing violation that would continue even after she was dead.

"He still has power over me, damn him!" she said, her voice rising. "How do I break that? *How?*"

That was a problem Jack had no idea how to fix.

"Speaking of him," Jack said, hoping to steer the subject back to the purpose of their trip, "why do you think he left the technology to you? Could he have been trying to" . . . how did he say this? . . . "make it up to you in some way?"

A soft bark of a laugh, then: "Not a chance. That would require remorse. Ronald Clayton didn't know the meaning of the word. No, leaving me the house and the clue to the technology was as self-serving as everything else he did in his life. He knew that Thomas would bury it, and he didn't want that. So he put it in my hands, absolutely certain that I wouldn't go along with Thomas." She slammed her fist on the dashboard. "You see? He's still doing it. Still using me, damn him! *Damn him!*"

3

"What's wrong?" Alicia said. "Why are we stopping?"

They'd cruised north on the thruway with no problems, and no sign— at least so far as she could tell—of anyone following them. Most of the trip since they'd left the city had passed in silence.

My doing, she thought. She'd awakened this morning feeling tired and drained, and didn't feel much better now. She didn't feel like talking anymore, and she was pretty sure that was okay by Jack.

So now they'd just paid the toll at the New Paltz exit, and Jack was pulling over to one of the phones in the plaza past the toll booths.

"Want to get my bearings," he said. "And I want to make sure no one's on our tail."

Alicia sat in the car while Jack faked a phone call and scratched hurried notes on a small spiral pad as he watched the cars pulling away from the toll booths. Not much traffic this time of day on a Thursday in December.

Finally, after a good fifteen minutes, Jack hung up and returned to the car. He nodded with satisfaction as he stuck his head in the door.

"All right. Didn't see anyone I know. How about you?"

"No one. What are you writing?"

"Makes, models, color, license plates. I see one of those cars again,

I'm going to want to know why. Now . . . one more thing and we'll get rolling again."

He reached into the backseat and came up with the Land Rover—fully reassembled now with its black plastic body snapped into place. He took it out to the shoulder and watched it run along the pavement. His dark eyes were bright with excitement when he returned to the car.

"You know, the thing's running almost due west now. I think we're close."

Low gray clouds slid across the sky, obscuring the timid winter sun as Jack drove on into the hills of Ulster County. From a distance the denuded trees lent the surrounding hills a hazy look, a light brown fuzz broken here and there by dark green patches of pines.

At every major fork in the road, Jack would stop and watch the traffic for a while, then he'd take out the truck, see which way it ran, and choose their path accordingly.

The Rover led them farther and farther into the hills. As the pavement gave way to a hard-packed dirt road, Alicia felt a growing sense of anticipation seeping through her. She fought it for a while—she didn't want to look forward to anything connected to that man—but finally she gave in. Up ahead, perhaps over the next rise or around the next bend in the road, on one of these leafless wooded slopes, something momentous waited.

But as her anticipation grew, she noticed an increased edginess in Jack.

"Is something bothering you?" she said.

He shrugged. "All this wide-open space." He gestured to an expanse of hills and valleys visible through a break in the trees. "Not my kind of place. I like my roads paved, preferably with the option of traveling *under* them, and I like my trees growing in evenly spaced holes in the sidewalk."

Just then the tires began to spin and slip on the steep upgrade.

"Should have rented a Jeep," Jack said. He seemed annoyed with himself. "Should have thought of that."

But the tires finally caught and propelled the car up to where the rutted dirt road leveled out a little.

"It can't be too much farther," she said. "There's not much more of this mountain left."

"Yeah, but what if the Rover is pointing at the *next* mountain?"

Alicia hadn't thought of that.

A moment later they came to the end of the road.

"Swell," Jack said.

Alicia leaned forward, scanning the wall of tree trunks and thick underbrush ahead of them. She didn't want to believe they'd have to go all the way back down that road. And then she saw what looked like a break in the brush.

"Hang on. Is that a path?"

Rover in hand, Jack stepped out of the car. This time Alicia followed.

"Good eye, Alicia," he said, pointing to a thin footpath trailing off into the brush. "Lucky the leaves are gone. No way you'd see that if the brush was greened up. And that's a good thing."

"Why?"

"Could mean someone doesn't want it found too easily. Let's go."

Alicia pulled her coat collar more tightly around her neck. They'd traveled north, they were on a hilltop, the sun was hiding, and a wind was rising. She wished she'd dressed warmer.

The path threaded left and right around trees and boulders for a good fifty yards before it opened into a wide clearing. Alicia gasped when she saw the old log cabin that stood at its center. Those logs were the only thing old about the scene. The rest was all high-tech. The cabin's roof and much of the yard around it were decked with photoelectric solar panels. Also on the roof, jutting twenty-five or thirty-feet above the solar panels there, stood a strange-looking antenna.

"I'm going to be very surprised if this isn't the place," Jack said.

He put the Rover down and let it run. It rocked this way and that as it plowed through the weeds, but it moved inexorably toward the cabin's front door.

"One more check," Jack said.

As he carried the Rover around toward the north side, Alicia moved closer to the cabin. She noticed that the windows were sealed . . . bricked over. Someone did not want visitors.

"Look at this," Jack called from her right. "I moved it ninety degrees to the north, and now it's running south . . . right at this cabin. No doubt about it, Alicia. We've found it. This is the place."

Alicia rubbed her upper arms through her coat. Now she was *really* cold.

Suddenly Jack was at her side. "Here," he said, handing her the Rover. "Hold this while I get us inside."

"Going to pick the lock?" she said.

"Unfortunately, I forgot to bring my pick set." He bent and looked closer at the lock. "Too bad. It's a Yale. I'm not good with Yales. Nope . . . looks like I'm going to have to do it the old-fashioned way."

So saying, he leaped forward and slammed his foot against the door just inches from the lock face. The sound of the impact echoed away down the hill.

But the door hadn't budged.

"I'll be damned," Jack said, checking out the hinges. "This door opens outward. Weird. And that's going to make it even tougher."

He took another flying leap at the heavy oak panels, with about as much success as before.

Three more times in rapid succession, with the noise echoing around them, and still the door stood firm.

Alicia froze as an accented voice behind them said, "Perhaps I might be of assistance?"

4

Startled, Jack whirled and reached for his Semmerling, but held his hands wide when he saw that the newcomer already had a pistol pointing at him.

Yoshio.

Jack knew he had to look stupid standing here and gaping at him, but he couldn't figure it out . . .

"Where the hell did you come from?"

"From the trunk of your car."

"The trunk?" Jack couldn't believe it. "When did you—?" Then he got it. "Oh, hell. Back in Chelsea, right?"

He wanted to kick himself. He hadn't had the car long enough to notice the extra weight in the rear, but still, he shouldn't have left anything to chance.

Yoshio nodded with a strained smile. "A most uncomfortable ride."

"I'll bet," Jack said, remembering all the bumps they'd bounced over and holes their tires had dropped into on the way up here. "Jeez, you must've wanted to get here bad."

"Yes, Jack-san. Very bad. And what of your promise to share information? What had happened to that?"

"Our deal was right of first refusal," Jack said, gently as he could.

Not a good idea to rile the man with the gun. "And we don't even know what we've got yet." He turned to Alicia. "By the way, this is Yoshio, the Japanese gentleman I told you about."

Alicia looked about ready to shed her skin. She stood stiff and still, her eyes never wavering from the muzzle pointed their way.

"Say, 'Pleased to meet you,' " Jack whispered out of the corner of his mouth.

"Pleased to—does he have to point that at us?"

"Very sorry," Yoshio said. "If Jack-san will please to give me his weapon, I will put this away. It is only to protect myself, I assure you."

So damn polite, Jack thought as he pulled out the Semmerling and handed it over.

But true to his word, Yoshio pocketed the little .45 and then holstered his own 9mm. It occurred to Jack that this was a guy who had to be pretty sure of his physical abilities.

"Now," Yoshio said, "shall we see what is inside?"

Jack nodded. "All right. On my count . . ."

The door cracked around the latch plate on their first simultaneous kick; the plate buckled on their second, and they were able to pull the door open.

The first thing Jack noticed was that the lights were on inside.

But then, considering what this place supposedly housed, why not?

"Please," Yoshio said. "After you."

Polite, Jack thought. And not letting me get behind him.

The single room inside was like Ted Kaczynski meets Radio Shack. A table, a chair, a cot, a couple of throw rugs, and a pair of filing cabinets completed the list of furnishings. The rest, taking up a good three quarters of the space, was an electronic nightmare of wires and metal boxes and blinking lights. And in the center of it all was this glass tube with a beam of brilliant white light shooting through it. The beam looked almost . . . solid.

Now Yoshio moved ahead of them, inspecting the humming equipment, staring at the beam.

"I don't understand," he said. "Is this the Ronald Clayton technology? What does it do?"

He wasn't putting me on, Jack thought. He really doesn't know.

He glanced at Alicia. "Should I tell him? He's a buyer."

She nodded. "Go ahead."

Jack went to the lamp sitting on the table and checked to see if it had a cord. It did . . . but it wasn't plugged in. A small aerial jutted up from the base.

"Here," he said, motioning Yoshio over. "This says it all."

He handed him the lamp. Yoshio took it and stared at it.

"I have seen a lamp like this before."

"Then you should know."

The Japanese looked at him questioningly. "Know what?"

"Figure it out," Jack said, then moved toward the filing cabinets.

He wasn't in an explaining mood. Better to let Yoshio figure it out on his own. An epiphany beat out a lecture any day.

Alicia had one of the file drawers open and was staring at something that looked like a blueprint.

"Circuit diagrams," she said. "Do these . . . mean anything to you?"

"I can program my VCR and turn on my computer," Jack told her. "Beyond that . . . I don't do wires. I am the Sergeant Schultz of electronics: 'I know nussing.' "

Suddenly Yoshio let out an *"Ayiiiieeee!"* followed by a Sten gun barrage of Japanese.

Jack said, "The light, so to speak, has dawned."

He watched Yoshio carry the lamp over to the electronic jumble, where he stood wide-eyed and red-cheeked, his head jerking back and forth between the lamp and the Clayton gizmo as he mumbled in Japanese.

"This is real?" he said, returning to English as he approached Jack and Alicia. "This is true?"

"Near as we can tell," Jack said.

"No wonder Iswid Nahr killed a plane full of people," he said, his voice filled with awe. "They would kill thousands, *millions* to stop this." He stared at the lamp in his hands. "And to think I was this close to an identical lamp and did not realize. I thought they were staring at something by the light of the lamp . . . not at the lamp itself."

"Yeah, whatever," Jack said. He hadn't the faintest what Yoshio was talking about. He pointed to the file cabinets. "Looks like all the specs are right here. Think your people would be interested?"

"Interested? Oh, yes, I am—"

"Hands up! Everyone! NOW!"

Jack jumped at the shouted commands, delivered with a military bark, but his hands acted on their own, the left rising as ordered, but the right snaking toward the Semmerling—and then he remembered . . . Yoshio had it.

And Yoshio's hands were loaded down with that damn lamp. He was no help.

So Jack raised both hands and slowly turned, knowing who he'd see.

Yeah . . . he'd figured it would have to be Kemel and Baker and the remainder of his crew. Thomas Clayton—with his swollen nose and blackened eyes—was a surprise, but not a big one.

Jack felt his gut tighten. This was bad. Worse than bad.

Of the five newcomers pushing through the doorway, Kemel was the only one without a personal grudge against Jack. And he wasn't all that sure about Kemel.

But how the hell had they got here? He damn well knew they hadn't shared the trunk with Yoshio.

What'd I do—leave a trail of fluorescent paint along the way?

5

It is here! Kemel thought, holding back tears of joy. Allah be praised, I have succeeded. I have found it.

He stiffened his knees as he stepped farther into the cabin. He was weak with relief but wanted no one to know.

He looked at the three occupants. He knew Alicia Clayton, and recognized her investigator, but the other man . . . the Oriental holding the lamp . . .

"Who are you?" he asked, pointing to him.

The man shook his head. His quick dark eyes showed no fear.

"I can find out for you real quick," Baker said, aiming his pistol at one of the man's knees.

"No," Kemel said. "No shooting in this place."

He had to be very firm here. He could not let this situation get out of control. Not with success now in his grasp.

It did not matter if the Oriental spoke. Kemel was certain he was Japanese. Who else could he represent? Ronald Clayton had been on his way to that country with a promise of a wondrous technology. They had to suspect foul play in the crash.

"All right," Baker said. "Then we'll take them outside." He bared his teeth as he approached Alicia Clayton's man. "Especially this one. He's gonna die *real* slow."

The man clasped his hands above his head and dropped to his knees. He hung his head and sobbed. "Please . . . *please* don't hurt me!"

One of Baker's men stepped forward and pulled his leg back to kick the man. "Why you sniveling pussy—!"

"Barlowe, no!" Baker said, grabbing him by the collar and pulling him back. "That's just what he wants you to do, asshole! He'd have you down and your weapon on us before you knew what happened."

With a half smile twisting his mouth, Alicia Clayton's man abruptly ceased his pleading and returned to his feet. He gave a little nod of acknowledgment, which seemed to please Baker very much. Baker took a single step closer to the man.

"We start off long distance on you, then move in close for the fun stuff."

"Not yet, Baker," Kemel said. "He may have information I need."

"Like what? What is this place, anyway?"

Kemel ignored the question. The less Baker knew, the better. "Disarm them and guard them. You may do whatever you wish when I am through with him."

He had to hold that out to Baker. During the trip into these hills, Baker and his two remaining men had talked of little else than what they would do to the man who had killed their fellows. But Kemel also had to make sure that what he saw before him now was all of it, that there was no other transmitter. He would learn from the Clayton woman and her hireling how they located this one, and if they knew of any others.

And then . . .

And then they would all have to die.

Kemel did not relish that. In fact, he had been dreading this moment. He had known about the bomb on JAL 27, but that hadn't been his idea. It had disturbed him that so many innocent lives had to be sacrificed in order to take one, yet he had also understood the absolute necessity of preventing Ronald Clayton from reaching Japan. And what were 247 lives compared to the well-being of the entire Arab world? A relative few had been sacrificed for a far greater good. Was it not so throughout all history?

But at least those faceless deaths had occurred far away, and by the impersonal agency of an explosive device. Today would be different. The dead would have names and faces, and their killers would look into those faces, watch them die. By his order.

But he had his orders, and agreed with their wisdom, their implacable necessity: No one outside of Iswid Nahr must know about this technology.

He watched Barlowe hold his assault weapon to the Oriental's head while Baker's other man, the one he called Kenny, took the lamp from him and removed two pistols. They followed the same procedure with Alicia Clayton's man who, surprisingly, was unarmed. Baker moved them and the Clayton woman to the side, allowing Thomas Clayton access to the file cabinets.

Baker had finally proved useful. In fact, despite all the setbacks, he finally had accomplished what he had been hired to do. The little transponder he'd placed in the bottom of the woman's handbag had allowed them to stay miles behind as they'd followed her here. But he would not be rewarded with the huge bonus and lifetime of easy employment he anticipated.

Baker and his men would dispose of these three and bury their bodies far from here. And not long after today—as soon as tomorrow, perhaps—Kemel was sure that Iswid Nahr would pay Baker in his own currency.

Thomas Clayton would have to go as well, Kemel suspected.

No loose ends.

"It's all here," Thomas Clayton said, looking up from an open filing cabinet drawer. "Everything you need to know to broadcast power. And it uses *solar* energy. You owe me big time. I think I underpriced our deal."

"You should feel lucky you're getting a dime," his sister said.

Thomas looked at her with raised eyebrows. "Oh, really?" he replied, drawing out the words.

"The minute you walked through that door," she said, "you went from asset to liability. They don't need you anymore. You've become as disposable as the rest of us."

"No," he said, turning Kemel's way. "We've got a deal, right, Kemel?"

Kemel held his gaze and tried his best to give nothing away. He found Thomas Clayton a reprehensible human being, but did not want to deal with him now. Let Iswid Nahr handle him.

"Of course. And we will honor our word."

But some hint of what the future held must have seeped into his eyes, for Thomas's expression hardened.

"I was afraid of that," he said, reaching into his pocket.

He withdrew a pistol and pointed it at Kemel.

6

Tommy-boy, Jack thought as he saw the little .32 appear, you're a class-A jerk, but I love you.

All eyes—Alicia's, Kemel's, Baker's, and his men's—were on Thomas now.

Almost all . . .

Jack glanced at Yoshio and found him looking his way. A quick lift of one of his eyebrows told Jack that he knew it too: This just might be their chance . . . the only one they'd get.

"That is not necessary, Thomas," Kemel said.

"Yeah," Baker told him. "Put that away before you hurt yourself . . . or someone hurts you."

Jack had gathered from talk between their captors that Baker's two men were Kenny—the redhead—and Barlowe—the dark-haired guy with the big nose.

"No," Thomas said. His voice wavered as much as the muzzle of the .32, but the little weapon remained trained on Kemel, who was only half a dozen feet away. Jack doubted even Thomas could miss at that range. "I think it's *very* necessary. I half suspected that I might get the short end of the stick once we found this. But that's not going to happen."

Jack slid his left foot a few inches toward the door. Then, making it look as if he was merely shifting his weight, he leaned left and brought his right foot over to it. Before leaving this morning, he'd stashed a Tokarev 9mm under the front seat of the Taurus. If he could get out the door alive, he had a chance to make it to the car. And then it would be a whole new ball game.

"Do not be silly, Thomas," Kemel said, holding his hands palms-out like a supplicant. "That is not what anyone was thinking. You will be paid just as we promised."

Another slide left . . . another weight shift . . .

"Damn right I will. This is mine, not yours. *Mine*. And I deserve it. So I'll be dictating the terms."

"We have terms," Kemel said.

"New deal," Thomas said. "It's my deck, and I call the game. But first . . ." He licked his lips. "First I want all the guns on the floor."

Another slide . . . Jack was closer to the door . . . a few more feet and he could risk a break. He saw Yoshio give him a barely perceptible nod, as if to say, *Tell me when, so I can time my move with yours.*

"Forget it," Baker said as if the words tasted bad. He was coiled and ready to spring, his pistol pointed at Thomas.

Thomas took a step closer to Kemel. "If you don't, I'll shoot your paycheck here."

"And when he's down, what do you think'll happen to you?"

Jack had a sudden feeling that Baker might be thinking of becoming management. He might not know what this was all about, but he must have figured out that the contraption taking up most of the space here was pretty damn valuable to someone.

"Tell them," Thomas said to Kemel. "You're paying them. Tell them to put their guns on the floor and lie on the floor."

Kemel turned to Baker. "Perhaps you should—"

"Fuck that," Baker said, and shot Thomas.

The loud report was a starter pistol for Jack—he was off to the races. As he ran he saw a spray of red from the exit wound in Thomas's back and heard Alicia scream. Then another shot, half as loud as Baker's, as Thomas's pistol went off. Kemel grunted and clutched his abdomen. Thomas and the Arab hit the floor about the same time.

Jack ducked past the one called Kenny and grabbed his Tec-9 before he could bring it to bear. The assault pistol fired a line of slugs through the ceiling as Jack tried to wrench it away, but the merc had the strap wrapped around his forearm like a good soldier and it wouldn't come free. Jack had to settle for putting him down with an elbow to the face.

And then Jack was through the door, cutting hard to the left and heading down the slope for the trees. The path to the Taurus was off to his right across the clearing, but all that open space would make him an easy target. The trees were closer down the slope. They'd provide cover as he worked his way around to the car.

The clouds had thickened overhead, darkening the afternoon sky. He remembered that this was one of the shortest days of the year. The light would be fading fast. And that could only help him.

More gunfire behind him, and another scream from Alicia. He risked a glance over his shoulder and saw Yoshio pop through the door going full tilt, his arms and legs pumping wildly as he veered toward Jack.

And his empty hands showed he'd had as much luck as Jack in capturing a weapon.

Jack reached the trees then and had to slow because of the underbrush and the branches. He put the six-inch trunk of an oak between the cabin and himself and stopped. Crouching in the brush, he looked back. Yoshio was almost down the slope to the trees—the guy was fast—when the merc called Barlowe leaped through the door and started firing.

"Come on," Jack whispered as Yoshio began weaving left and right. "Come *on!*"

And then Yoshio let out a short, sharp cry and went down, clutching his thigh. But still he kept crawling toward the trees. Baker and Kenny joined Barlowe as he caught up to Yoshio and planted a boot in his back, pinning him to the ground.

Jack watched Baker give some orders. Barlowe and Kenny split, one to the right, the other left.

Good move, Jack thought. These guys were experienced. Kenny's heading would cut Jack off from the car while Barlowe circled around to get behind him.

Jack held his ground, watching Baker who remained behind with Yoshio. He saw him say something to the prone man, then bend and position his pistol about an inch from the back of Yoshio's head.

Jack pounded back the urge to shout, to charge—he was too far away to do any good. He heard a 9mm *crack*! and saw Yoshio's body jerk, spasm, then lie still.

Jack closed his eyes and swallowed, then took a deep breath and opened them. Yoshio's body lay facedown where he'd fallen, and Baker was walking back toward the cabin like a gardener who'd just pulled an annoying weed and left it lying on the lawn.

Jack had kind of liked Yoshio, even though he'd only spoken to him that one time in the car. Some sort of kinship there; he thought they'd both sensed it. But Yoshio was no innocent bystander. He was a killer by his own admission. And he'd known the risks.

But still . . . the way Baker had seemed to relish that head shot . . .

Okay, Jack thought. Now we know the rules of the game.

And from what he'd gathered from Baker's comments back in the cabin, a bullet through the brain might be a blessing compared to what the mercenaries wanted to do to him if they caught him.

The prospect of capture was like a clump of these cold wet leaves slapped between his shoulder blades. Bad enough to have two well-armed goons after him anywhere, but out here, in the woods . . . this was about as far from his home turf as he could get. What did he know about the great outdoors? He'd never even been a Cub Scout.

One thing Jack knew: He had to move.

To his right he heard Barlowe crashing through the underbrush. Jack sensed the contempt behind all that racket: I've got a cool assault pistol with thirty-two rounds in its clip, and the jerk I'm after ain't got dick. So why bother with sneaking around? I'll make as much noise as I can and flush him out like a pheasant. Then I cut him down and drag his carcass back home.

Keeping low, Jack took advantage of all the noise and began making his own way through the brush, moving away but on an angle he figured would eventually intersect Barlowe's path. He wished it were summer, or spring at least—with all this growth in bloom, it would be a cinch to hide until nightfall evened the odds a little. At least his sweater was mostly brown, but the light blue of his jeans wasn't exactly an earth tone. With everything bare like this, sooner or later—probably sooner—they'd spot him.

His foot caught on a vine, and he fell, landing on a slim path through the brush. He had a close-up view of its packed soil, pocked with ho-ofprints. Jack knew next to nothing about hunting, but he'd lay odds this was some sort of deer trail. He disengaged his foot from the tough, flaky-barked vine strands—the underbrush was laced with the wiry stuff— and got to his feet. The path seemed to head in the same general direction he was going, so he followed it.

The trail allowed him to move faster. He stopped every so often to get a fix on Barlowe's racket, and figured the merc ought to be crossing the deer trail soon himself. Would Barlowe be able to resist the path of least resistance? Jack doubted it.

Which meant he should set up somewhere along here.

7

"Broadcast power, huh?"

Alicia watched Baker from her spot in the corner by the filing cabinets as he paced up and down before the banks of electronic equipment.

He'd wanted to know what it did—"What is all this shit, anyway?" as he put it—and she'd told him. Why not? She didn't care who knew. She just wanted to keep him distracted from her and herself distracted from the bodies on the blood-spattered floor.

Thomas was gone. So quickly. One moment he'd been standing there talking, the next he was dead. She tried to dredge up some grief, but could find none. Compassion . . . where was her compassion for someone who shared half her genes, even if it was the wrong half?

Gone. Like Thomas. And what did genes mean anyway? Why should you care for a poor excuse for a human being just because you share some genetic material?

But even Thomas deserved better than to be shot down like a dog.

"Wireless electricity," Baker said, rubbing his jaw. "Christ, that's got to be worth—"

A moan snapped Alicia's attention to the floor. The Arab, the one Thomas had called Kemel, was moving, curling into a fetal position as he clutched his bloody abdomen.

"Please," Kemel moaned, his voice barely above a whisper. "I must have a doctor."

Baker waggled his pistol at Alicia and then the Arab. "You're a doctor, right? Fix him."

"With what? He needs a hospital."

"Check him, dammit!"

"All right."

Alicia stepped over to Kemel and knelt beside him. From this angle, she could see Thomas's gun on the floor next to his body. Baker couldn't see it from where he stood. But it was far beyond Alicia's reach. Still, it was good to know it was there.

She stiffened as she saw one of Thomas's hands open and close. She glanced at his face and saw his eyes open, stare unseeingly for a moment, then close again.

Still alive, she thought, but not for much longer.

The Arab cried out when Alicia tried to roll him onto his back, so she was forced to examine him on his side. Gingerly—all her experience with infectious diseases screamed warning at the very possibility of contacting blood—she pulled his hands away from his wound. She saw the hole in the crimson wetness of his shirtfront, saw the blood oozing from it, caught the fecal odor.

Her mind ran the probabilities: perforated intestine, internal bleeding but aortic and renal arteries probably intact or he'd be dead by now. And there was absolutely nothing she could do to help him.

Kemel let out another agonized moan.

"He's critical," she said.

"I could've told you that," Baker said. "I've seen gut shots before. Ugly way to go. What can you do for him?"

"Nothing here," she said, rising. "He needs emergency surgery."

"Well, then," Baker said with a shark's smile as he pointed the pistol at her. "I guess that makes you pretty damn useless, doesn't it?"

Alicia fought panic. How much did he know? She swallowed, searching for moisture.

"Not if you want to sell the broadcast power technology," she said.

"What's that supposed to mean?"

"Because I'm the only one who can make it work."

She saw Baker's eyes narrow as he stared at her. Her insides were heaving with grand mal shakes. She prayed they didn't show.

"Yeah? Why should I believe that?"

How much does he *know*? Had he seen the will? No . . . odds were against that. But considering the Greenpeace clause in the will, he'd probably been told from the start not to hurt her. At least she hoped so. If she was wrong, her next words could buy her Thomas's fate.

"You mean you weren't told to treat me with kid gloves?"

She watched him consider that, then saw him lower the pistol.

"All right," he said. "We'll find out what's what after we finish off your boyfriend."

"He's not my boyfriend."

"I guess not. Not the way he took off without you."

Alicia wondered about that. She'd been shocked to see him run rather than attack, but when she considered his chances of defeating three armed men, she couldn't blame him. She just hoped he planned on coming back for her.

She realized with a start that she didn't have to hope. She *knew* he'd be back.

She had to start believing in *someone*.

Suddenly she heard the rattle of gunfire from somewhere in the woods.

"Sounds like my guys have found your boy," Baker said with that grin. "I wouldn't want to be in his shoes. Not even for all the money this stuff's worth."

Another burst of gunfire.

"Listen," Baker said, his grin broadening. "It's like music."

8

Jack hid behind a big oak. At least he thought it was an oak. All he knew for sure was that its trunk was about two feet across—barely enough to hide him—and bordered the deer trail. Jack held one of the lateral branches of a smaller tree growing between the big oak and the trail. He'd used his Swiss Army knife to trim most of the branch's twigs, leaving only one-inch stubs jutting out like nails.

And now he waited, listening to Barlowe's noisy approach along the trail.

He had a length of the ubiquitous vine coiled loosely about his left wrist, and the tree branch that had once stretched face-high across the trail bent back as far as he dared without snapping it off the trunk.

His knuckles looked blue from the cold, but his palms were sweating. Timing was everything here. A second too early or late and Jack would be following Yoshio into the Great Whatever.

And so he waited, letting the sounds get louder and closer, waited until he sensed that Barlowe was just about to hover into view, then he let go and ducked back, loosening the loops of vine as he slid around the other side of the trunk.

Barlowe's cry of pain and his sudden wild shooting were Jack's signals to go. He leaped from the back side of the tree, landing directly behind Barlowe. The merc was stumbling back toward Jack, his left hand to his face, firing blindly with the Tec-9 in his right. Jack waited a heartbeat until Barlowe lowered his left hand, then looped a coil of the vine around the merc's throat and yanked the startled man backward.

As he slammed Barlowe's back against the big tree, he noticed blood running from his left eye. One of the twiglets Jack had left had found its mark. In hyperdrive now, Jack dropped one end of the vine, put the trunk between them, then reached around the other side and reclaimed the loose end.

He hauled back on the two ends of the vine, putting all his weight into the job. He couldn't see Barlowe on the far side of the trunk, but Jack could hear his choking grunt as the vine garrote cut off his air. His legs thrashed frantically and he tried to fire his Tec backward, angling the muzzle around the trunk, but Jack simply moved to his left without loosening up on the vine. The two bursts Barlowe got off did little more than kick up wet leaves.

And then the shooting stopped, though the thrashing continued. That could mean only one thing: Barlowe had realized that his Tec-9 was not going to save his life. And Jack figured what he'd try next.

Quickly he twisted the two ends of the vine together so he could keep it taut with one hand. Then he stretched around to his right.

Just as he'd suspected, Barlowe was pulling his Special Forces knife from its scabbard. The wicked-looking saw-toothed Rambo blade gleamed in the light as Barlowe brought it up behind his head to saw at the vines.

"No you don't," Jack said, and grabbed his wrist.

The struggle was a short one. Weakened by lack of air, Barlowe didn't have the strength to pull free of Jack's grip.

Finally, he sagged.

But Jack wasn't about to release the vine. Barlowe could be playing possum.

Just then the bark on the trunk above Jack's head exploded into stinging fragments to the rattling tune of assault weapon fire.

He ducked and turned. He spotted the other merc, Kenny, about fifty yards away, crashing toward him.

Kenny whooped and yelled. "Hey, Barlowe! What're you shooting at? I found him! He's over here! Yo, Barlowe! Over here!"

Jack released the vine and crawled around to Barlowe's side of the tree. The merc's face was blue-tinged, his eyes closed as his body sagged to its knees.

On the far side he could hear Kenny's noisy progress, yelling and firing short bursts as he approached.

"Gotcha now, fucker! Say your prayers, 'cause you got about a minute to live. Hope you're shittin' your pants, fucker. Hey, yo, Barlowe! Where are you, man? You're gonna miss the fun!"

"Barlowe's right here," Jack whispered. "Waiting for you."

Jack grabbed Barlowe's Tec-9 but its strap was wrapped and twisted around his arm. He yanked first, then tried to untangle it, and all the while he could hear Kenny crashing closer.

"Dammit!" he hissed as he fumbled for the strap release.

And then pain blazed through the front of Jack's left thigh. For an instant he thought he'd been shot, then he looked down and saw Barlowe's knife dropping out of a bloody slit in his jeans, and Barlowe staring up at him with the reddest whites Jack had ever seen.

And Kenny just on the other side of the tree.

Ignoring the pain in his leg as best he could, Jack hauled Barlowe to his feet—had to hand it to the guy, he was one tough, determined son of a bitch—and faced him toward Kenny's sounds. As he held him up he wriggled his hand under the merc's right arm, searching for the Tec-9's grip.

Kenny arrived with his own Tec blazing, and Jack felt the jolting impact of the slugs tearing into Barlowe.

"Oh, Christ!" Kenny wailed as the shooting stopped. "Barlowe, what—?"

Jack couldn't see Kenny, but he could imagine his expression. Jack's questing finger found the trigger of Barlowe's Tec then, and he pulled it. He had no idea where he was aiming, he simply started firing blind and wild, and hoped the clip wouldn't run out.

He chanced a peek over Barlowe's shoulder and saw Kenny stumbling backward, arms and eyes wide, his chest a bloody ruin.

Jack released Barlowe and his Tec, letting him fall forward. Both mercs hit the ground about the same time.

And then Jack sagged against the big tree, clutching his bloody thigh. It hurt like hell every time he moved his leg.

Just what I need, he thought.

But at least he was no longer the only unarmed man on the hill.

9

The gunfire had stopped.

"Well," Baker said, "that's it for your boyfriend."

He leaned against the desk, his pistol still in his hand.

"You don't know that," Alicia said.

She could not imagine Jack dead. He seemed too resourceful to be dead. But then, she'd only seen him playing his tricks. She'd never seen him in a gunfight. And no matter how good he was, how could he overcome two men armed with automatic weapons?

"I do know that," Baker said. "All that shooting can mean only one thing: They cornered him and had some fun with him. Probably shot up his legs first, then started moving around the rest of his body. By the time they were through, he was probably begging them to kill him."

Fearing she might vomit, Alicia turned away. Jack—Just Jack—dead. Add one more to the list of men dead because of her. She'd involved him in this. He'd come willingly, but still, if she'd just let it go, let Thomas have the damn house, they'd all be alive, and she wouldn't be trapped in the woods with these human monsters.

She heard a loud, celebratory whoop from somewhere outside the cabin.

Baker straightened and crossed the room, grinning.

"That's Kenny. He's a noisy son of a bitch."

Another whoop.

Baker stepped outside and stood with hands on hips, staring toward the tree line.

10

Jack trained Barlowe's Tec-9 on the cabin door and let out a whoop, hoping he sounded enough like Kenny to draw Baker out.

He leaned against a tree trunk to take the weight off his left leg. The trees were smaller here and didn't provide much cover. Hopefully he wouldn't need it.

Off to his right, Yoshio's body was a pale blotch among the weeds.

His leg throbbed and burned. He'd cinched the shoulder strap from the Tec above the wound, and that had slowed the bleeding, but it did nothing for the pain.

He whooped again.

Come on, Baker. Show your ugly face.

If he'd had a pistol, he'd have been sneaking up on the cabin now. But with only this Tec, no way he could risk charging inside and shooting. Not with Alicia in there. These damn things were too inaccurate. No telling who he'd hit once he pulled the trigger.

And if he'd taken the time to go limp to the car for the 9mm he'd stashed there, Baker would have figured something was wrong and be ready for him.

So it had to be this way. He only wished he was closer. Marksmanship had never been his strong point, and with a Tec-9 at this distance he'd have to rely far more on luck than skill.

Just then Baker stepped out into the open, looking around for Kenny. Jack pulled the Tec's trigger and emptied the magazine at him.

The corner of the door above and to the right of Baker's head dissolved into a cloud of splinters, and Baker dove headfirst back into the cabin.

Furious, Jack smashed the empty Tec against the tree and hurled it into the woods.

Now what? He had a feeling things were going to get really ugly now.

11

The explosion of gunfire had staggered Alicia. As Baker regained his feet after a flying leap into the cabin, Alicia stared at the ruined door, still shuddering and vibrating from the barrage it had absorbed, and wanted to cry with joy.

Somehow, some way, Jack was still alive. He'd not only survived, he'd come back.

"Kenny!" Baker was shouting. "Oh, Christ, he must've killed Kenny!"

She looked back at where Thomas lay. His pistol was just on the other side of him. If she could—

Baker grabbed her arm and yanked her close. His breath was sour.

"Who *is* he, goddammit? Where'd you find this guy?"

"His name's Jack," she said. What could it matter if Baker knew that? "That's all I know."

"Don't give me that. There's gotta be something going on between you two, otherwise he wouldn't have come back."

"No. He gets a percentage of whatever this is worth."

Another truth, but Alicia had a feeling Jack would have come back no matter what the arrangement. Baker would never understand that, but a percentage was something he could buy.

He nodded. "Yeah, I guess I'd come back for that too."

He spun her around, grabbed a fistful of hair at the back of her head, and propelled her toward the door. Her scalp stung and burned from the rough treatment.

"You're hurting me."

"You better hope that's the worst of it, honey. Because we're gonna see if you're really as valuable as you say you are."

He positioned her in the doorway and half crouched behind her, peeking over her shoulder. She felt the cool metal of the muzzle of Baker's pistol press against her temple. Down the slope, almost to the trees, lay a body. Alicia knew from its white shirt that it had to be Yoshio. She closed her eyes. Still another death.

Back inside the cabin, she heard Kemel moaning for a doctor.

"Hey, Jack!" Baker shouted. "Or whatever your name is. Come out where I can see you or your girlfriend gets it!"

"I'm not his—"

"Shut up!" he hissed, jamming the muzzle harder against her scalp. "Not a fucking word from you!"

And then she saw Jack, moving between the trees. He stopped and stared at them, but said nothing. Then slowly, deliberately, he raised his middle finger.

"You son of a—!" Baker said.

Suddenly the muzzle was gone from her temple, and the pistol was extended before her, firing at Jack. The reports were deafening.

Jack ducked to his left and popped up next to another tree. Baker pumped more rounds at him. But Jack was gone again, only to pop up somewhere else. Baker fired again.

"Your boyfriend thinks he's smart," Baker whispered. "Know what he's doing? He's counting my shots. He knows I've got fifteen in the clip. He knows I used one on your brother, one on the gook, and now I've knocked off another nine potshotting at him. So he's thinking, four more shots and—"

Jack popped up again, and Baker fired off a pair of shots.

"There's two more. Now he's thinking, two more shots and he'll charge me while I'm changing the clip. Must think I'm a real jerk. Well, I got news for Mr. Jack. Sam Baker's changing his clip *now*. And won't Jack-o be surprised when he charges up that rise. Can't wait to see his face when that slug goes into his chest."

Baker withdrew the pistol behind her. As he let go of her hair, Alicia heard a metallic click, then something hitting the ground. Her mind raced. Was Baker right? Was that Jack's plan? She had to do something.

Alicia whirled and saw Baker with his pistol in his left hand while his right was reaching into a pocket. The old clip lay at his feet.

Shouting, "Jack! Jack! Now, Jack!" she grabbed the pistol and tried to wrestle it away from him.

Baker's right hand got caught in his pocket, and it took him a second or two to free it, but even using both her hands, and wrenching with all her strength, Alicia could not break his grip on the pistol.

"Fucking bitch!" he cried.

She put her body into it, twisting so that her back was to him. And this gave her a view of the slope where she saw Jack—

Oh, no! He was running toward her, but with a *limp!* She saw the red splotch on the denim on his left leg.

He'll never make it!

Just then Baker must have freed his right hand because she felt a rock-hard fist slam against the back of her head. But she held on. And then the edge of his hand cut down on her shoulder. Her left arm went numb, and her grip failed. The gun came free of her grasp as a third blow knocked her to her knees.

And Jack wasn't anywhere near close enough. He had a wicked-looking knife in his hand, but he wasn't going to get close enough to use it.

Alicia twisted and saw the fresh clip in Baker's hand as he fumbled it into the opening in the bottom of the pistol's grip.

"No!" she cried, and grabbed his arm.

He almost dropped the clip but maintained his grasp by his fingertips. He snarled as he kicked her away.

Alicia landed on her back. Jack was almost here, but through a haze of pain she saw Baker slam the clip home and raise the pistol with both hands. Jack wasn't going to make it. Baker was going to get a point-blank shot at him. She thought of Thomas's gun, but it was back inside the cabin, too far away . . .

Alicia closed her eyes and screamed as she heard three shots in rapid succession . . .

. . . from directly behind her.

She opened her eyes and saw Baker falling away as Jack slammed into the place where he'd been standing. She turned and saw someone crouched in the cabin doorway, leaning on the door frame.

Thomas.

He looked ghastly. The doughy white of his face made the blood trickling from both corners of his mouth seem so much redder. The pistol hung loosely at the end of his limp arm.

As she watched, he seemed to deflate, seemed to shrink within his clothes as he slumped to the floor.

Baffled, Alicia crawled over to him.

"Oh, Thomas. Thank you, Thomas. But . . ." She had to ask. She'd never known him to do anything for anyone. "Thomas, why?"

"Don't you know?" he said in a voice bubbling wet with blood. "You're supposed to be so smart. Don't you know?"

"Know what?" She was almost afraid that she did.

"Those were the worst years of your life. But they were the best of mine."

He coughed up a dark red clot, and then his body stiffened as the light went out of his eyes.

Alicia reached a hand toward him. She'd never thought she could touch him, but now she had to.

She smoothed his hair and began to cry.

12

Jack bounced off the door and dropped to Baker's side. He held Barlowe's Special Forces knife to his throat as he pulled the pistol from his limp fingers. He saw Baker's glazed, staring eyes, checked his throat for a pulse. Dead. Three .32's to the side of his chest had done it.

Jack knelt there and sucked air deep into his blazing lungs, then he stood and leaned against the door. His left thigh flamed and throbbed with pain, more so when he bent it.

He watched Alicia crouch over her brother in the doorway, and heard her sobs. He wasn't crazy about the idea, but he probably owed Thomas his life. And it didn't look like a debt he was going to get a chance to repay.

That had been close . . .

He heard a groan from inside. He stepped past Alicia and found Kemel writhing on the floor.

"A doctor," he moaned. "Please . . . get me to a hospital."

"The only place you're going is outside," Jack said.

He grabbed the back of Kemel's collar and dragged him toward the door. The Arab howled as he passed Alicia.

"Really, Jack," she said, straightening up and wiping her eyes. "Is that necessary? Can't you just leave him there?"

The adrenaline was still shooting through his arteries, his heart still pounding, his lungs still afire. He looked down at his free hand and saw the fine tremor. The fight was over but his body hadn't got the message yet. He'd come *this* close to buying it and was still shaking from the sight of Baker's pistol zeroing in on his chest a few moments ago.

He wasn't feeling too polite.

"The answers are, in order: Yes . . . and No. He's stinking up the place."

Jack dragged him outside, past Baker's body, and released him in the weeds.

"Please . . . a doctor . . ."

Jack wanted to kick him but held back.

"Get me to a hospital."

Jack squatted next to Kemel and leaned close, speaking through his teeth. "Guess what, pal? I just polled the passengers on JAL 27. I said, 'Anyone who thinks Kemel should have a doctor raise your hand.' You know what? Nobody moved. So no doctor for you."

As he rose, he noticed that it was starting to snow. He returned to the cabin. Alicia was leaning against the wall next to the door, her head back, her eyes closed. She looked pale and weak, as if the wall was the only thing keeping her upright. Snowflakes brushed her face.

"Thanks for the help," he said.

She opened her eyes. "Thanks for coming back."

"I didn't have much choice."

"You could have kept going."

"No, I couldn't."

"No, I guess you couldn't." She gave him half of a very tired smile. "And you know, somehow I knew that." She glanced down at his bloody thigh. "Let me check that—"

"I'll be all right for now. I'll get it stitched up back in the city."

"It needs more than that strap. Come with me."

Jack followed her into the cabin. Maybe she needed something to do. She pulled the sheet off the cot and began tearing it into long strips.

"Sit and pull your jeans down."

"I told you the other night not to get any ideas."

She didn't smile. "Just do it."

Jack loosened the strap, then slid his jeans down to his knees.

Alicia inspected the two-inch vertical slit. "That's a deep one. Did you feel it hit the bone?"

"No. The guy who did it didn't have much oomph left."

"Luckily it runs in line with the muscle fibers of your quadriceps," she said as she began to wrap the thigh with strips of the sheet. She seemed to have slipped fully into her doctor mode. "The femoral artery and nerve are over here, so it missed them completely. Should heal up pretty well, but you *will* need stitches. ER's have to report stab wounds—"

"I know a guy who doesn't."

"I'm sure you do."

"What's our next step here?" he said as she continued to bind his leg.

"I was hoping you'd know."

"I can take care of the bodies. Haul them off in whatever they arrived in—a dark van, I'll bet—and leave them somewhere."

"Not Thomas," she said. "We owe him."

Jack looked over at Thomas's crumpled, bloody corpse. "Yeah, I guess we do. Okay, so I'll drop the bodies somewhere and place a call, telling the local sheriff or whatever where they can be found. And then let the crime busters have a grand old time figuring out the who, what, where, when, and how."

"Do you think they will—figure this out, I mean?"

"Not if I drop them far enough away. But the other question is . . . how are you going to handle broadcast power, now that you're the sole owner?"

"I guess I'm supposed to reveal it to the world. But if what Thomas said about the patents is true, I can plan on a long fight with the patent holders. Frankly, I've had enough of lawyers for a long time."

"There's always the Japanese. Yoshio's people will pay big bucks."

"You sound like you like that one."

"Yeah, well, take the money and run, and let them worry about the lawyers."

"You know," she said, "I don't care how much anybody wants to pay. The thought of profiting from anything that man touched makes me physically ill."

"So that leaves giving away the technology to everybody. Publishing it on the Internet—"

Her eyes flashed as she looked up at him. "Along with pictures of Thomas and me?"

"Hey, I didn't mean that. I meant the Internet would allow anybody who wanted to develop the technology to have free access to the plans."

"But what about you?" she said. "A third of nothing is nothing. I hate to see you come out on the short end of this, Jack. I mean, you've been stabbed, you almost got killed—"

"Don't worry about that. I couldn't take the money anyway."

"Why not?"

"Because I already have pretty much everything I want."

Alicia's gray eyes softened as she looked at him. "Do you? Do you really?"

"Yeah, well, sort of. And what I don't have, money can't buy me, so leave me out of the equation and do what you have to."

And the truth was, Jack couldn't see any way in the world to hide the kind of windfall that even a tiny share of broadcast power would bring. He'd have to come out from under to claim it, and he wasn't ready for that just yet. Not even for a couple three billion.

"Jack," she said as she tied the last strip of sheet. And now she sounded so weary. "I don't know what I have to do. I've got to think about it."

"Well," he said, standing and pulling up his jeans, "while you're thinking, I'm going to start gathering up the casualties."

13

It took Jack awhile to lug all six bodies, especially the two from the woods, to Baker's panel truck. A quarter inch of snow had collected by the time he arrived with the last—Kemel.

He could leave soon. He wasn't traveling with this cargo until it was fully dark. The last thing he needed was someone casually glancing into the rear window and seeing half a dozen corpses.

Jack thought Kemel was dead, but he startled Jack by letting out a moan as he was dumped on top of Baker.

"Please. A doctor . . . the pain . . ."

This wasn't good. If Kemel somehow hung on until he was found, some hero with a scalpel and thread might actually save him. And that wouldn't do. Wouldn't do at all.

"Told you," Jack said. "The folks on JAL 27 voted no doctor for Kemel."

The Arab whispered something Jack didn't catch. He leaned closer to hear.

"Plane . . . not me."

"But you knew about it, didn't you, you son of a bitch."

He saw the answer in Kemel's glazed eyes.

The adrenaline had trailed off, leaving Jack with a pounding head-ache. His thigh throbbed worse than ever from the exertion of moving the bodies. Foul didn't come close to his mood now. His mood was way far beyond foul . . . somewhere out near Mars, or maybe Saturn. And he knew from experience how dangerous that could be. He tended to be-come . . . unreasonable when he got this way.

Usually when he recognized the signs he'd step back, take a time-out, and push the darkness back into his personal basement. And he'd have been able to do that now if Kemel weren't alive. But knowing this rotten piece of camel dung was still breathing . . .

"Yeah, you knew about it, but did you call and give a warning? No. You let all those people die just to get rid of one man."

"Not me . . ."

"Yeah? Then who?"

"Please . . . the pain . . . please stop the pain."

What was he asking for? A coup de grâce?

"You tell me who ordered the bomb, and I'll let *you* stop the pain."

"No . . . you . . . please."

"Sorry. I don't owe you that. But the name?"

"Nazer . . . Khalid Nazer."

"And where do I find him?"

"Iswid Nahr . . . trade mission . . . UN."

Khalid Nazer . . . Jack made a mental note of that as he drew Baker's 9mm. He popped the clip, leaving the chambered round; cocked the hammer, then pressed the muzzle into the soft spot under Kemel's jaw. He wrapped the Arab's fingers around the grip.

"Say your prayers and pull the trigger."

Then he walked away, leaving Kemel with his dose of the ultimate analgesic.

14

Alicia started at the sound of the shot. She looked up and saw Jack limping across the clearing toward her. He looked weary. The Jack who'd driven her up here had changed into someone else, someone as cold and ruthless as the men he'd killed. As she'd bandaged his leg awhile ago, she'd sensed the original Jack coming back . . . but slowly.

"What happened?" she called. "Are you all right?"

He nodded. "Just someone giving himself some permanent pain relief."

That someone could only be the Arab. Good Lord, how had he hung on this long?

"You ready to go?" Jack said. "I'll lead you out."

Alicia shook her head. "You go ahead. I'm going to stay awhile."

"The snow's sticking. You might not be able to get out later."

"That's okay. It's warm inside. And I've got a lot of thinking to do."

"You sure?"

"Very."

"Okay," he said, shrugging. "I'll leave you one of the cell phones. Call me when you get back, and I'll return the car."

"I will."

He turned to go, then turned back to her. "You sure you'll be all right?"

"Positive," she said, putting on a confident smile. "I just need to be alone right now."

"Yeah, well, that's one thing you'll be up here. Take care, Alicia." He waved as he turned. "And hey . . . Merry Christmas."

"Merry Christmas to you, Jack."

Merry Christmas . . . she'd forgotten all about Christmas. Only three days away . . . the season to be jolly . . .

She watched Jack fade into the snowy dusk, then stepped back into the cabin and closed the door.

She'd known from the moment it was over that she'd be staying here awhile. So while Jack was moving the bodies, she did her best to clean the blood from the floor. Finally she'd moved the throw rug from under the table and laid it over the stains.

She stepped over to the humming transformer-transmitter and stared at the beam of palpably bright light.

Technology to change the world . . . and make Ronald Clayton a revered figure . . . one of history's great men . . . the man of the century . . . the man of the millennium . . .

But Ronald Clayton wasn't a great man . . . wasn't even an ordinary man . . . he was a monster who sullied every life he touched . . .

And the thought of history raising monuments to him . . .

She wanted to retch.

And yet, what right did she have to withhold such a marvel from the world?

None. She was just one person, and there were billions who could benefit.

She could feel the strings . . . tugging at her . . . manipulating her like a marionette. And she knew the name of the puppeteer.

Yes . . . she had a *lot* of thinking to do.

CHRISTMAS EVE

1

Alicia drove downhill through the darkness toward the lights of New Paltz. She felt light-headed, almost giddy.

Two days it had taken her, two full days of agonizing, but she'd finally made up her mind.

And now she felt . . . clean. Yes, *clean* . . . that was the only word for it. As if she'd shed a ratty, moth-eaten old skin and now had a new one to show the world.

Going to be a different Alicia Clayton from now on. A whole new attitude, a whole new outlook. Starting tonight. Wasn't going to be easy . . . she had no illusions about that. But she had this feeling that if she kept pretending to be the new Alicia, after a while she'd start believing it.

That was the only way to go. Because the life she'd been leading lately was no life at all. Sure, the work was important, but there had to be more than that. Alicia was determined to have a full life. A good life.

Living well is the best revenge . . . how often had she heard that expression? Now she realized that it doubly applied to her.

Alicia listened to one of the all-news AM stations from the city as she made her way through the slushy, light-festooned streets of New Paltz. She'd been out of touch for two days but learned she hadn't missed much.

The only story vaguely interesting concerned an Arab trade envoy named Nazer or something who'd been murdered execution style outside his Manhattan apartment. An assassination? the newsman wanted to know. Police were speculating whether this death was related to that of the murdered Arab who was found recently along with five other bodies in the Catskills.

Alicia wondered too.

She turned off the radio as she pulled onto the thruway. She set the cruise control, then picked up the cell phone. Tension knotted in her chest as she punched in a number. Her thumb hesitated over the SEND button, but she took a deep breath and forced it down.

When she heard a familiar voice say hello, she almost hung up, but pushed the words past her dry throat.

"Will? This is Alicia. Can we talk?"

2

"This isn't exactly the Christmas Eve I'd planned," Jack said.

Gia and Vicky had dragged him down to the Center for Children with AIDS and into the infant care area. Gia kept telling him the babies didn't have AIDS—they were simply HIV-positive. As if that was a big consolation.

"And what exactly did you have planned?" Gia asked from a rocking chair where she was feeding a blanket-wrapped three-month-old. She was wearing green-and-red plaid slacks and a red turtleneck sweater. Christmas colors.

"Well . . . me by the fire with a hot toddy, you in the kitchen preparing the Christmas goose . . ."

She grinned. "And Tiny Vicks saying, 'God bless us, everyone,' I suppose."

"Something like that."

"Dream on, Scrooge."

Vicky laughed from a neighboring rocking chair where she cuddled another baby. She wore a red velvet dress and white tights. "He's not Uncle Scrooge. He's Jack Crachit!"

Ebenezer Scrooge had been Disneyfied into Uncle Scrooge in Vicky's mind, but Jack didn't correct her. Uncle Scrooge was an old friend.

"Hearty-har-har-har, Vicks," Jack said. He had his own rocking chair, but no baby, which was just fine with him.

Gia stood and lifted the baby against her shoulder.

"He *is* Mr. Scrooge," she said, patting the baby's back. "Look at him sitting there listening to his radio, the epitome of the Christmas spirit."

He'd brought along a portable radio and had set it on a window ledge, playing low.

"It's Christmas music," he said.

The tiny speaker wasn't doing any justice to Shawn Colvin's very cool version of "Have Yourself a Merry Little Christmas," but she sounded great anyway.

"Yeah, but it's that same upstate station you've been listening to for the past two days. What's so interesting in the Catskills?"

"I've been following a story up there."

Gia stared at him. "The one about . . . ?"

She didn't finish the sentence but he knew what story she meant. The six corpses found at a rest stop along the thruway—"Shocking Mass Murder!"—had made all the media.

She obviously didn't want to mention the specifics in front of Vicky.

He nodded. "That's the one."

Jack had parked the truck in a corner of the rest stop lot and called Julio. He'd eaten a couple of cheeseburgers and hung out, watching the snow until Julio arrived, then the two of them had headed back to the city. Along the way, Jack stopped at a gas station and phoned in a tip about the abandoned panel truck.

Gia's mouth tightened and she turned away. The baby, a little black girl, peered at Jack over Gia's shoulder and burped.

"There's a good girl," Gia said. She turned and approached Jack, stopping directly in front of him. "Hold out your arms," she said.

"No, Gia, really—"

"Do it, Jack. Trust me, you need this. You really do. But she needs it more."

"Come on, Gia—"

"No, I mean it."

She turned the baby so Jack could see her face. The dark eyes stared at him for a few seconds, then she smiled.

Gas, Jack thought.

"Her name's Felicity. One of the nurses started calling her that because her mother took off without bothering to name her. Felicity had to go through crack withdrawal during her first week of life; she's HIV positive, and she's been abandoned. She's got no one to hold her, Jack. Babies need to be held. So go ahead. Give her a break. It won't kill you."

"It's not that . . ."

"Jack." She held Felicity out to him.

"Oh, okay."

Gingerly, skittishly, Jack let Gia place the baby into his arms.

"Careful, now," he said. Why was she making him do this? "Careful. Jeez, don't let me drop her."

Gia laughed softly, and the sound made him relax. "She's fragile, but not *that* fragile."

Finally he had her, with her head nestled in the crook of his right arm. She skooched and squirmed, and so Jack held her tighter, snuggling his arms around her so she'd know she was secure, with no place to fall. Gia put a pacifier into her mouth and Felicity began to suck. That seemed to work. She closed her eyes and lay quiet.

"How's it feel?" Gia said.

Jack looked up at her. "It feels . . . okay."

Gia smiled. "Coming from you, that's the equivalent of 'fabulous,' I guess."

Jack stared back down at Felicity's innocent little face, thinking about what this kid had been through already in her life. And the worst was most likely yet to come. He felt taken by a furious urge to protect her . . . from everything.

"It is fabulous, Gia."

And he meant it. That something as simple as being held by another human could be so important to an infant was almost . . . overwhelming.

"Nice little gifts your folks passed on to you, Felicity: an addiction and a killer virus. Where do you go from here?"

"A foster home eventually," Gia said.

He looked up again and saw tears in her eyes. "They need so much, Jack. I wish I could take in every one of them."

"I know you do," he said softly.

Darlene Love's "Christmas" segued into the news, and the new big local story in the Catskills was the fire raging on a mountaintop west of New Paltz.

Jack repressed a groan. "Gia, can you get that little truck from my jacket?"

"You brought that here?"

"I'll get it, Mom," Vicky said, jumping up and handing her baby to Gia.

She'd been playing with the truck all afternoon, laughing at the way it always ran into the same wall. She pulled it from Jack's jacket pocket and clicked the power button.

"Hey, Jack," she said, frowning. "It doesn't work." She clicked the button back and forth a few times. "The batteries must be dead."

"Make sure the aerial is tight," he said.

He watched her jiggle it in its socket, then try the button again.

"Nope," she said. "Dead."

"We have some batteries at home," Gia said. "What kind does it take?"

"They don't make them anymore."

As Gia returned Vicky's baby to her, and went to get another for herself, Jack sat with Felicity, rocking and thinking.

Alicia had come to her decision. Maybe it was for the best. Maybe the world wasn't ready for broadcast power. But he doubted that consideration played any part in Alicia's decision. He wondered where she was tonight, and hoped she wouldn't have to be alone.

He leaned back and let the peace and warm feelings from Felicity fill him.

"Something wrong, Jack?" Gia said as she began rocking a new baby. "You look sad."

"No, I'm fine," he said. "Actually, I'm kind of glad."

Because he realized that what Ronald Clayton had discovered, others could discover as well. One way or another, broadcast power would be part of the not-too-distant future . . . but public parks with statues of Ronald Clayton would not.

"And you know," he said, "this isn't a bad way at all for the three of us to spend Christmas Eve. In fact, I think it's pretty damn good."

Gia's wonderful smile made it even better.